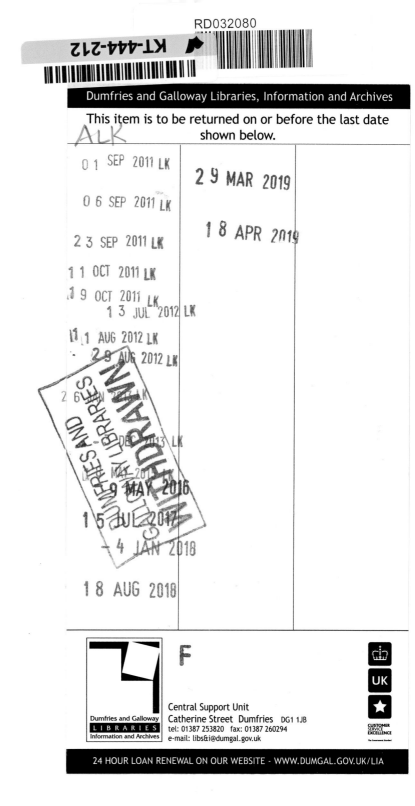

Acclaim for *The House on the Shore*

The House on the Shore is an enjoyable read. In it, Victoria Howard presents a well-crafted page turner that unfolds at just the right pace, ensuring that the reader's attention is held captive with each new mysterious development.

Howard also does a commendable job of infusing her characters with vivid, palpable personality, framing their inclinations and reactions in the three-dimensional, thus making it easy for readers to relate to them in very real, practical terms.

A quick but compelling read, *The House on the Shore* is a can't miss suspense thriller with a surprisingly potent punch, and one that fans of the genre are sure to enjoy.

Renee Washburn
Apex Reviews – *4 Stars*

The House on the Shore is a sensually suspenseful story filled with non-stop action, romance, and mystery. The facts of Scotland are told with brilliant description that bring the land to life and leave you feeling as if you have stepped out of your world and into the pages. Ms. Howard uses such passion and emotion when telling her story, making the tale flow right along until the last page is turned. With many different characters that will keep you guessing, this novel is the perfect example of how a suspenseful story should be told. ...Thrilling until the very end, this book has a who-done-it attitude with such an aching tone of sensuality and love, it will keep you up all night just so you can finish this fantastic tale.

Danielle
Reviewer for Coffee Time Romance & More – *4 Cups*

The House
on the Shore

by

Victoria Howard

Vanilla Heart Publishing
USA

The House on the Shore

Published by: Vanilla Heart Publishing
www.vanillaheartbooksandauthors.com
10121 Evergreen Way, 25-156
Everett, WA 98204 USA

ISBN: 978-1-935407-24-9
LCCN: 2008943441

10 9 8 7 6 5 4 3 2 1 First Edition

First Printing, January 2009
Printed in the United States of America

The House
on the Shore

by
Victoria Howard

Acknowledgements

I am indebted to Julian Carradice, and Richard Warren of the Wasdale Mountain Rescue Team and Andy Simpson, Press Officer for Mountain Rescue (England and Wales) for their technical assistance in the writing of this novel. This group of brave (and unpaid!) men and women save hundreds of lives each year in dangerous mountain terrain, and depend on our donations to keep doing their fine work.

I would also like to thank Chris Dalton of South Ayrshire Stalking for providing information on the types of firearms used in deerstalking.

Any mistakes are mine, not theirs.

To fellow authors, Brenda Hill and Daphne Rose, and my dear friend, Dorothy Roughley, my heartfelt thanks for their encouragement and support. To Stephen, for his continued support in allowing me the space to write and for all the hours he's spent walking the dog!

And finally, my thanks go to Kimberlee Williams and Vanilla Heart Publishing for making it possible.

Chapter One

Anna MacDonald never felt so betrayed.

Not only had Mark, the Head of the English Department, given the job he'd promised her to someone else, but he hadn't had the nerve to tell her himself. But that was just like him. He'd do anything to avoid confrontation.

What should she do? Everyone in the department knew they'd been seeing each other outside of work, and would hear on the university grapevine that she'd been passed over for promotion. How could she face the humiliation and the knowing stares? And how could she work with Mark each day knowing he'd betrayed her?

Anna leaned back in her chair and considered her options. Could she continue to work with someone she couldn't trust? The answer had to be no. But lecturing posts in Scotland where hard to come by, especially in creative writing the subject she taught. And then there was their personal relationship. By this move Mark had destroyed her trust in him, not only as a colleague, but as her lover too. Did she really want to carry on dating someone she couldn't trust? Again the answer had to be no.

The more Anna thought about her situation, the more she realised she had only one option. She crumpled the letter into a ball and tossed it into the waste paper bin.

Straightening her shoulders she marched down the university's wide corridor to Mark's office and pushed open the door. Mark sat at his desk, a pile of term papers in front of him. He must have sensed her presence because he looked up—and paled when he saw her.

"Anna—"

"A letter, Mark? After telling me the job was as good as mine, you send me a *letter* saying you've given it to someone else. Couldn't you have told me face to face? I'm not just your work colleague, I'm your girlfriend. Or have you conveniently forgotten that fact?"

Mark held out his hands as if offering an apology. "I was only following procedure." A lock of blond hair fell into his blue eyes and he brushed it away without thinking.

"I see." Anna swallowed her hurt. And rage. She didn't want to leave on a sour note. "Well, you can't complain about my letter of resignation, can you? Either you accept it, or I go over your head and give it to the vice chancellor."

"Anna, darling, I thought you enjoyed your job. Sit down and let's discuss this."

"I don't want to sit down, thank you, and I did enjoy my job."

"Then I don't understand why you want to leave. Don't you think you're being impulsive?"

"I think I'm being very reasonable under the circumstances. You expect me to carry on working in the department while...while your new blonde bimbo sits in what should have been my office, doing what should have been my job!" Anna felt her blood pressure rising. She took a deep breath.

"We only went to dinner..." Mark shuffled the papers on his desk.

"Don't lie to me, Mark."

"I'm not."

"Think again. And while you're doing that you'd better start advertising for a new lecturer because I'm leaving at the end of the term whether you like it or not!"

"But term finishes on Thursday—"

"So it does. That gives you three days and all of the summer vacation to find a replacement for me. I've marked and returned all the end of term papers to my students. I have no more classes scheduled, so this is my last working day."

"Look, can we talk about this tonight? I've a mountain of paperwork to get through. I'll stop at the supermarket on my way home pick up a bottle of that red wine you like and a take-a-way."

"Are you serious? You don't really expect us to continue our relationship, do you?"

Mark stepped out from behind his desk and rested his hands on her shoulders, his face devoid of expression. "Anna, please, this is business. Just because you were passed over for promotion, doesn't mean our relationship is over. You love me."

Anna stared at him and wondered why she had ever considered him husband material.

"No, Mark, I don't. I've realised that I don't trust you. And without trust there can be no love."

"I see. Have you found another job?"

"No, I haven't."

"Let me guess. You're going to write a book. Lecturers who give up academia usually pick that vocation because they love books but lack the talent to write them."

The arrow hit its mark, but she wasn't going to allow Mark's derisive comments dissuade her. "Look, I've made my decision. I'm handing in my notice. There's nothing more to be said on the subject."

"Then I suppose I'll have to accept your resignation. But would you mind if I dropped by your flat now and again to see how you're getting on? For old times' sake?"

"I doubt very much if the new tenant would appreciate that."

"New tenant? You're not giving up your apartment too, are you?"

Anna ignored the question. "Goodbye, Mark." Without saying another word she turned, and left his office.

It was only later that week as she boxed up the contents of her home that she began to wonder if she'd made the right decision.

Her doubt started with the picture.

It was taken at the university picnic. She and Mark knelt in the grass by a gigantic oak tree, side by side, heads slanted toward each other, arms around shoulders, clearly and disgustingly in love. When was it taken? A year ago? No, two. Had they been together that long? She swallowed the pain as she took the photograph out of the silver frame. The frame she would keep. The photo... she held it in both hands and struggled to tear it, but couldn't see it through the tears. She settled for balling it up and letting it fall to the floor.

There was no denying Mark was a complete bastard. Thank God she'd never asked him to move in with her. And it was clear that he had no intention of marrying her. He'd been adamant that he'd never stoop to such old fashioned sensibilities. For a time she'd agreed with him. What was marriage anyway, but a contract that didn't just bind two parties, but frequently strangled them?

Damn. She could have been a good wife. Would have been a good wife. But now?

Was she doing the right thing? While she could never forgive his infidelity, she would miss her job and her friends. She scrubbed a tear away with the back of her hand.

It was too late now to change her mind, she thought, folding a pair of jeans into her suitcase. She'd already surrendered the lease on her fashionable Morningside apartment. The rent, barely manageable on her salary, ate into her savings quicker than a ravenous hyena.

"It's all for the best," she told her two border collies. Their tails wagged as if they understood. "Besides, I've been breaking the lease with you here anyway. No pets allowed, remember?" The younger collie, bright eyed with dappled paws, edged over and gave her hand a quick lick. Anna ruffled the black and white head. "You're a good dog, and I'm doing all of us a favour anyway. We're off to the country, my girls. Peace, quiet, and who the hell knows what else."

Anna locked the suitcase and placed it next to the door with the others ready to carry down to the old beat-up Land Rover. She took one last look around the room. The place looked huge now, emptied of its contents. She couldn't take her furniture with her, and had arranged to put it into storage. All that remained of her life—seven years of it—was a carpet that needed shampooing and places on the wall where lighter paint called attention to where her paintings had hung.

She picked up her handbag. This phase of her life was over now. She had a book to write. Apart from her clothes, laptop, printer, and the few books she intended to take with her, the things she most wanted to leave behind were the raw sores of an aching heart.

She knew she'd be taking them too.

Five hours later she coaxed the elderly Land Rover the last few yards down the potholed track toward Tigh na Cladach, her late grandmother's remote croft on the shore of Loch Hourn, in the rugged northwest Highlands. She couldn't afford to breakdown now, not when she was so close to reaching her destination. There had been times during the drive from Edinburgh when she thought she would get no further than the city limits, but despite the vehicle's faded green paintwork and battered appearance, the engine seemed sound.

With a sigh of relief she yanked on the handbrake, climbed down out of the driver's seat, and stood for a moment savouring the silence. After the bright lights and noise of the city, it felt strange to be so far from civilisation. She glanced at her watch—ten o'clock on a summer evening—yet she could see every rock and bush clearly, for it never became truly dark this far north. Indeed, night itself became no more than deep dusk.

Ensay and Rhona, her two, black and white Border collies, relieved to be released from the confines of the rear seat, chased each other on the lawn in front of the small stone cottage.

The old squat house was small, about forty or fifty feet long, and of traditional one and a half storey height. A chimney rose at either end. The walls were at least three feet thick and built of rough, white-washed granite. The building stood some thirty yards from the water's edge, nestled in the natural curve of the hillside, as if seeking protection from some invisible force. Whoever had originally built it had chosen the location well, for it fitted into its surroundings perfectly, its stone walls standing the test of time and weather.

Either side of the bright green door were two small quartered windows, set deep into the stonework. The one on the right belonged to the kitchen, and the other to the sitting room. It wasn't much, but it had been her grandparents' home. True, it was miles from civilisation, but it was mortgage-free. And now hers.

Collecting her handbag, laptop, and a box of groceries from the passenger seat, she locked the Land Rover and made her way over the cobbled path to the croft. All she needed now was a hot drink and a good nights' sleep. The rest of her unpacking could wait until morning.

Inserting her key in the lock, she pushed open the door, flicked on the hall light, and walked into the kitchen. The scent of lavender hung in the air. Not only had her dear friend, Morag McInnes, dusted and aired the croft in time for her arrival, she'd also left a bowl of her favourite potpourri on the oak dresser.

Anna filled the electric kettle, put it on to boil, and opened the mail sitting on the table where Morag had left it. There were two letters. The first turned out to be a demand for taxes from the local council. The second envelope was made of heavy parchment, the top left hand corner of which advertised the name and address of a firm of Glasgow solicitors. Curious, as to why they would be writing to her, Anna slipped a neatly manicured fingernail under the corner of the flap, tore it open, and scanned the contents in disbelief. It contained an offer—a very generous offer—on behalf of their unnamed client, to purchase Tigh na Cladach.

"Well, of all the nerve," she said out loud. She read the letter again to make sure she hadn't misunderstood. Well, their client could go to Hell, thought Anna, as she stuffed the letter back into the envelope and propped it up against the pepper pot. Too tired to deal with it now, she'd write in the morning and tell the solicitors the croft wasn't for sale now, nor would it be at any time in the future.

Stretching to ease the stiffness in her shoulders and neck, she made herself a cup of tea, and carried it to the table. She fed and watered the dogs, then made her way up the narrow wooden staircase to the bedroom she'd slept in ever since she was a teenager.

Situated directly above the kitchen, the room nestled under the eaves of the roof. Light, airy and warmed by the heat of the range below, it was painted a delicate shade of pink. The window, which overlooked the loch, was bordered by rose-coloured chintz curtains. A large, brass four poster bed, covered by a hand-stitched patchwork quilt in shades of red, rose, pink and green, stood opposite the door. Her grandmother's music box, the key long ago lost, stood on the chest of drawers in the corner.

With a long exhausted sigh, Anna quickly undressed and climbed into bed, pulling the blankets up to her chin.

Something woke her. The digital clock on the bedside table flashed 2.00a.m. She'd only been asleep for a couple of hours. Her hands twisted nervously in the blankets, she held her breath as she listened for the slightest sound. Apart from the gentle snoring of the two dogs curled up on the rug at the foot of her bed, there was silence. She felt uneasy, but told herself it was foolish to feel afraid. Nevertheless, her hand trembled as she fumbled for the switch on the bedside lamp. A shaft of light struck her pillow, making her squint but leaving the rest of the room in eerie darkness.

She sat up, let out a long, shuddering breath, and ran a hand down her bare arm; it was cold, clammy and covered in goose-bumps. The hairs on her neck prickled, as if touched by some invisible hand. There wasn't a sound; not even the pitter-patter of the mice that inhabited the roof space of the old croft. Yet something had wakened her. She shivered, and chewed on her lower lip, as she stole a look at the dogs. Odd— they were her early warning system and reacted to the slightest noise, but neither seemed alarmed.

She sighed and rubbed her forehead wearily. Had she been dreaming? She thought not and yet the feeling something was wrong persisted.

Unable to settle, she pulled back the blankets, swung her legs over the side of the bed, and went barefoot to the window. She drew back the curtain and peered into the twilight. A ghostly silhouette moved across the lawn in the moonlight. The curtain slipped from her fingers as sheer black fright swept through her. For once she wished the croft wasn't quite so isolated and that her grandparents had installed a telephone. But they hadn't, and even if they had, it would take the police the best part of an hour to reach her.

She tried to ignore the creaking and settling of the old house, but the strange sounds only added to her nervousness. She shook her head in an attempt to clear the fog of sleep from her brain and searched for a plausible explanation.

Had she seen a figure? Or had it been a shadow simply caused by a cloud crossing the moon? Summoning all her courage she parted the curtain once more. To her relief there was no one there. Her heart still pounding, she tugged on her green candlewick dressing gown, tying the belt tightly around her slim waist, and crept downstairs.

The front door was locked and bolted.

Still fearful, she padded into the kitchen, starting when the floorboards creaked beneath her feet. Her hand shook as she made a cup of cocoa and crawled into the old oak rocking chair next to the Aga. Tucking her feet beneath her for warmth, she let the steam from the cup warm her face and thought about what she'd seen.

Was her imagination working overtime? Had living in the city made her so soft, she wondered, that she jumped at every foreign sound? Even the floor scared her, for God's sake! In town, the only noises she heard at night were ambulance sirens and traffic, while here in the glen only the occasional bark of a fox or hoot of an owl broke the silence.

Few people bothered to drive this far, even in daylight, so the chances of someone doing so in the early hours of the morning were slim. It couldn't have been a man, she reasoned. It must have been the shadow of a roe deer crossing the lawn. They often came down off the hill to drink in the loch at night.

Anna swallowed the last of her cocoa, rinsed her mug, and left it on the draining board. Stifling a yawn, she pulled the cotton blind back from the window and looked out on to the hill behind the croft. Nothing moved. Not even the leaves of the rhododendrons that surrounded the croft. She tucked a strand of her tousled, copper-coloured hair behind her ear and went back to bed, pausing to give the dogs a gentle pat. Sleep was a long time coming, and when she finally succumbed, it was into a restless and fitful slumber.

It was a little after eight when she woke the next morning, and after showering she dressed in her usual well-worn jeans, check shirt and nutmeg-coloured Aran sweater. She made her way down the narrow wooden staircase, to the kitchen.

After breakfast, she left the dogs playing on the front lawn, and retrieved the first of two suitcases from the rear of the Land Rover, and half carried, half dragged it into the croft.

On her way back for the second case, she noticed a boat had moored in the loch. Strange; it was still a little early in the season for tourists. She shaded her eyes and appraised its size. It wasn't just a boat; but a large yacht. And was that an American flag flapping in the breeze?

Only a few intrepid sailors ventured this far down the loch. The channel was narrow, twisting, and sheltered by high, steep, rugged mountains, with few places to land. Well, if the crew were looking for hot showers and breakfast, they were way off course and should have sailed west to the Isle of Skye instead.

Two hours later, hot, tired, and thirsty, she finished her unpacking and helped herself to a can of soda from the fridge. She sat down at the kitchen table and picked up the solicitor's letter from where it rested against the pepper pot. While it was common to receive offers on a property following a death, she couldn't understand why anyone would want to buy the croft when it was so far from the modern conveniences of life.

The money being offered for Tigh na Cladach far exceeded its true market value. And would certainly be sufficient for a deposit on a small house in Edinburgh, but she couldn't understand why anyone would want to pay that much for a piece of infertile land and a tumbledown cottage.

The croft had been in her family for years, and Anna had no intention of selling it. She pulled her laptop towards her, switched it on, and started to draft a suitable reply.

Her concentration was broken by the shriek of frantic barking. She tore her gaze away from the screen and looked out of the kitchen window. A tall, dark-haired man was making his way up the crescent-shaped beach, doing a weird twisting dance, holding his right arm above his head. With his left he pushed off the two boisterous, snapping collies.

"Oh hell," she groaned. She threw open the door and shouted. "Ensay! Rhona! Heel!"

The dogs instantly stopped snapping at the stranger's ankles and ran to their mistress. Anna leaned against the door frame and waited while the figure strode confidently across the grass towards her, his well-muscled body covering the rough ground with long, purposeful strides. His jet black hair was turning grey at the temples, the cut slightly longer than was considered acceptable for a man she judged to be in his forties. But somehow it suited him.

He stopped a foot from her door, close enough for her to smell the lemon spice of his cologne. Now that she could see him more clearly, she noticed the laughter lines around his eyes and mouth, hinting at a softer side to his character. His body was lean, the outline of his muscles visible through the shirt he wore. A faint white scar creased his right cheek, and she thought it gave his face a handsome rugged look. He gazed at her with dark brown eyes and smiled, slow and warm, and for some reason her breathing quickened.

She took one look and knew he was trouble.

"Hi, there. I know I'm trespassing, but do you think you could ask your dogs not to rip off my thigh?"

Anna drew herself up to her full height, which was barely up to his shoulder. "They're guard dogs and only doing their duty," she said stiffly. The dogs sat at her silent signal, but their eyes remained fixed on the stranger.

"I'm sorry to bother you, but I'm having engine trouble and I can't get a signal." He indicated his mobile phone.

"That's because there are no transmitters."

"Oh. Well, could I borrow your phone? I need to contact the nearest boatyard for some advice."

"I don't have a phone."

He rubbed a hand over the back of his neck. "Look, I haven't slept for twenty-four hours and I'm beat. Sandpiper, that's my yacht, developed a problem soon after I left Stornaway." He paused as her words registered. "Did I hear right? You don't have a phone?"

"No, I don't, so I'm afraid I can't help you. I suggest you weigh anchor, turn your boat around, and head west out of the loch."

"Perhaps I should've introduced myself. I'm Luke Tallantyre, from Cape Cod, Massachusetts." He offered his hand. She didn't take it.

"Anna, Anna MacDonald. Yachts are always straying into the loch at this time of year. Their crews seem to think this is some sort of hostel. Well, it's not, and I still don't have a phone."

"Okay, where do I catch the bus to town?" His eyes lingered on her face. "Oh, no. You're about to tell me there isn't a bus either. Aren't you?"

Anna nodded. The motion sent sunlight gliding through her auburn hair. "That's right. Welcome to Kinloch Hourn, otherwise known as the Loch of Hell."

"The name fits," Luke muttered. "What sort of place doesn't have a phone or a bus service in this day and age?"

"How about the remotest glen in the Highlands? Up here, one man and his dog constitute a crowd. And before you ask, there are no shops either, unless you count Mrs McCloud in the village, but she only opens on alternate days. The butcher's van calls every Thursday afternoon, and the library service visits once a month. I think that about covers all the local amenities. Oh yes, there's a mobile bank too, but that only comes once a fortnight. The school closed last year. But you're in luck... there's a hotel and it has a phone."

"So there's a God after all."

"However, its twelve miles down the road in that direction," she replied, pointing vaguely to some distant place.

The line of Luke's mouth tightened a fraction. "How do I get there? Walk?"

"Well, you could, but it might rain. And then again it might not. You can never tell for sure. The glen has its own eco-system because the mountains are high, and the valley floor is narrow or something like that. I don't fully understand the reasoning behind it..." Anna's words trailed off. She felt herself blush. What on earth was she rambling on about? The guy didn't need a science lesson, especially from her, but he was so good-looking that every time he gazed at her with those compelling brown eyes, she lost control of her tongue. Distractions of his type she could do without, especially when she was getting over a disastrous love affair, but the way Luke looked at her made her feel uneasy in a pleasant sort of way.

"I suppose I could offer to take you..."

"You don't have to. You've been kind enough. I'll just walk."

"You could just pull up anchor as I suggested, and sail round to Fort William. There's a boatyard there with facilities for visiting yachts and their crews."

"Which I could call if I had a phone. Thanks again," he said turning to leave.

She shifted her feet. She wasn't normally unhelpful, but there was something about his attitude which put her on the defensive.

"Wait!"

He stopped in midstride and turned. The dogs looked at him, then at their mistress, as if waiting for some clue as to what they should do with this stranger who was invading their space.

Chapter Two

"I'll give you a lift," she said, making a snap decision. "While you're making your phone call, I can visit a friend. Do you need anything off your boat? If so, can you be back here within twenty minutes?"

Luke's face split into a wide grin. "Yes ma'am, I can."

Before she could say anything more, he turned and ran across the grass towards his small inflatable dinghy. As she watched him head back across the loch, she wasn't sure she should have offered to take him, but something told her Luke was used to getting his own way. She sighed. So much for replying to the solicitor's letter, she thought, as she walked into the kitchen to switch off her laptop.

She ran a brush through her hair and plucked the keys to the Land Rover off the hall table. Once outside, she made her way round to the rear of the croft to the vehicle. It took several attempts before the elderly, asthmatic engine coughed into life, and several more for her to get it into reverse gear. By the time Anna drove round to the front of the croft Luke was leaning against the wall waiting for her, a small canvas bag at his feet. She threw open the passenger door, the rusty hinges screeching in protest.

Before Luke had chance to ease his backside onto the worn leather seat, the two collies had pushed past him and jumped into the vehicle. Anna waited while he snapped his seat belt into place, before releasing the handbrake and driving off. Neither she nor her dogs appeared to notice the almost total lack of suspension as the old Land Rover bounced over the uneven, pot-holed ground. They rounded a corner on the steep, single track road, with only inches to spare.

Luke cleared his throat. "Is the phone company about to disconnect the service? Is that why we're trying to break the land-speed record?"

Her head snapped round. "Disconnect? No, why should it? It's a public phone. Anyway why that look? I'm only doing thirty miles an hour—that's not speeding."

"Thirty, huh?" Luke replied, his eyes wide as a dry stone wall almost took the rust and paint job off the passenger door. "It feels more like fifty. Isn't that a little too fast for this kind of surface? What if we meet another car coming the other way?"

"We won't, not at this time of day. The only people who venture this far down the glen are walkers. There's a car park at the head of the loch where they must leave their cars. The track to the croft is private; it doesn't join the public road for another couple of miles."

"If you don't mind me saying, it's an odd place for someone like you to live."

Anna's foot lifted off the gas and hovered over the brake pedal, but she resisted the temptation to slam her foot down.

"Actually, I do mind. As it happens, the croft—Tigh na Cladach—is very important to me."

"A croft? Is that another word for a cottage?"

"No. A croft isn't a building, but a smallholding or a piece of land."

"I see, and Tie na..."

"*Tigh na Cladach.* It's Gaelic for the house on the shore."

"It's just that it's a pretty God forsaken place for a young woman to live by herself, that's all."

Anna briefly took her eyes off the road and glared at Luke. "I don't recall saying I live alone."

"Well, no, you didn't," he conceded. "But if I was your husband, I wouldn't leave you alone for one minute in that... what did you call it... croft? Let's see, you don't have a phone, or neighbours. I didn't notice a satellite dish for TV, so my guess is that you don't have one of those either." A smile ruffled he corner of his mouth. "I'm curious, do you have running water, or do you have to wade out into the loch for a bath?"

Anna laughed. "Now you're being stupid."

"Okay, I shouldn't have asked you where you bathe."

"Thanks for so deftly dropping the subject."

"Whoops, point taken. What if you had an accident? Or someone was prowling around? What if I was an axe murderer?"

Anna raised an eyebrow, and for a second longer than necessary, her eyes held his.

"Are you?"

"Hell no!"

"Well then, it doesn't enter the equation, does it? Now, if you've quite finished dissecting my lifestyle, would you mind hopping out and opening the gate? And please close it again after I've driven through."

"I'm sorry if I'm being too personal," Luke said, as the Land Rover rattled over another cattle grid. "I'm just curious. You look as if you belong in the city, rather than out here in cow-pie land. You're either eccentric or plain crazy. I just can't figure out which. What do you do for a job?"

Anna pulled away from the gentle pressure of Luke's arm on her shoulder as it rested on top of the bench seat, and concentrated on negotiating the narrow twisting road instead.

"My, my, you are inquisitive. I'm sorry to disappoint you Mr Tallantyre, but I have no intention of answering any more of your questions. How I choose to live my life is no concern of yours."

Luke held up a hand in self-defence. "You're right, but take a word of advice from a well-travelled and good intentioned stranger. An attractive young woman, on her own in some isolated Scottish glen is asking for trouble, and if your boyfriend, husband or whoever can't see that, he needs a whole new brain."

Anna took a deep breath and held on to her temper— just. "Look, Mr Tallan..."

"It's Luke..."

"Luke," she said, jerking on the handbrake, bringing the Land Rover to a halt in front of the hotel. "You'll find the phone in the lobby. If you don't know how to use it, I'm sure Katrina, the receptionist, will show you how. While you're making your call, I'll go and see my friend. I'll meet you back here in fifteen minutes."

"Okay, I'll be as quick as I can." Luke picked up his canvas bag, opened the door and climbed out.

Anna watched as he sprinted in the direction of the hotel entrance. What the hell was the matter with her? This wasn't the first time she'd stayed at the croft and been disturbed by lost mariners, but she'd not behaved like this. So what if he had a smile that would make the most committed spinster run for the preacher? Her brain said she wasn't interested. Her hormones had other ideas.

A knock on the partly open driver's window brought her back to reality.

Luke looked at her sheepishly. "I can't believe I'm going to say what I'm going to say. Here goes; the phone doesn't take credit cards, and the smallest thing I have is a £50 bill. The hotel people won't break it, so...I don't suppose you've got any...spare change, do you?"

Anna bit her lip. She laughed as she stepped down from behind the steering wheel. God save her from tourists and this one in particular. It was only the beginning of June. She had another three months before the summer trade died down. She fished in the pockets of her jeans and brought out a crumpled £5 note.

"Here. I'm sure they'll change this for some coins. There's ample to make a call to Fort William."

"Thanks, I appreciate it," he smiled. Only this time his smile reached his eyes, softening his features, and despite her attempts not to, Anna found herself responding. She shook her head. She sensed that few women resisted Luke's charming, easy smile, and his deep seductive voice.

While Luke made his phone call, Anna sought out Morag. She found her friend in the hotel kitchen, busy preparing lunch.

"Hi, Morag. Have you got a minute for a chat, or is this a bad time?"

"Well, well, if it isn't yourself," Morag replied, her face breaking into a welcoming smile. She hugged Anna. "I wondered when you'd find time to pay me a visit. The ghillie said he'd seen a Land Rover parked outside the croft, so I knew you'd arrived safely. Now lass, you know I've always got time for you, and so long as you don't mind me carrying on with this," she said, adding a potato to the vegetables in the pot, "we can talk."

Anna smiled, and shook her head. Morag never changed; she always knew the latest village gossip.

"I came to thank you for airing the house and making up the bed."

"You're welcome. I didn't light the old range, though. I wasn't sure you'd need it in this warm weather."

"You mean the Aga? That's fine. I used the immersion heater this morning, but the Aga is more economical. The weather is set to change in a day or so, I'll light it then. I assume when you mentioned the ghillie, you meant Sandy? How is he?"

Morag's smile faded. "There have been a lot of changes on the estate since your last visit, and not just your grandma's passing. We were all sorry to hear of your loss, by the way. Such a nice old lady; she will be sorely missed. But it's good to have you back. Are you staying long? And your intended, is he with you?"

"It's good to be back. I'm here for the summer, at least, and if you mean Mark, then no, he isn't with me. We're no longer together. It's just me and the dogs."

Morag's potato peeler paused in mid air. "Oh, I'm sorry to hear that, lass, you looked so well together. But I daresay you know your own mind best. Now pass me those carrots will you? I'm all behind this morning. There was a mix-up with the bookings. We've six new guests arrived, and I haven't even got lunch on yet."

"Look, I can see you're busy. I can come back another time."

"No, no, lass. You're always welcome, you know that. It's just that we're short-handed, and there's only me to cook and serve lunch, not to mention prepare the vegetables for dinner as well. Tell you what, Lachlan is away on the rig, so it's just me and the television for company this evening. Why don't you come round after tea, and we can have a real good blether?"

Anna smiled. "I'd like that. I'll bring a bottle of wine."

"But I've got a few minutes now. What was it you wanted to talk about?"

"I wondered if there was any work going here at the hotel, now that the tourist season has started."

Morag brushed a stray lock of brown curly hair back under her cook's hat and looked solemnly at her friend. "But what about your teaching job in Edinburgh? I thought you were due a big promotion."

"I was," Anna replied, straining to keep the bitterness out of her voice. "But a long-legged blonde called Stella started work in our department. Mark was smitten. He gave her my promotion, so I gave him back my job."

"Mark didn't know what he had in you, my girl. You're smart and gorgeous. Just look at you—you've got hair halfway down your back the colour of a new penny and a lovely figure." Anna blushed. "By contrast," Morag continued, "I'm as tall as any man in the village, skinny as this wooden spoon, with hair so kinky I've no hope of running a brush through it. I'm still amazed that my Lachlan even noticed me."

"Lachlan loves you, Morag, that's all that matters. Mark, well, I don't think he's capable of loving anyone except himself."

Morag chuckled. "Perhaps you're right. That man is just too good looking, and he knows it. I daresay this Stella woman won't be the first, or last, to tempt him to wander. He's a right patter merchant; he'd talk the knickers off you, and sell them back at twice the price! Besides, you should never trust a Sassenach."

Anna laughed. "Sassenach. I haven't heard that word used in years."

"Sassenach—English—we'd all be better off without all of them, Anna, yours in particular, or so it would seem."

"He isn't mine, Morag. Not anymore. And to be honest, I was getting fed up with him, always sprawling on my sofa expecting to be waited on hand and foot, and discovering his dirty underwear in my laundry basket. And his snoring. Do you know the man roared all night like wart-hog?"

"Is that so?"

"And that's not all. His idea of going out for dinner always included staying for breakfast too."

"It sounds to me as if you're well rid of him. You'll get over him soon enough. Besides, what you need is a true Highlander. Scots men know how to treat women right."

Anna raised an eyebrow. "Really? Is that why most women in the glen spend part of their time chained to the kitchen sink and the rest balancing a baby on their hip as they Hoover and dust? Oh, and did I mention they're expected to help with lambing, and hay-making too?"

"Sarcasm does not become you young lady, even if you are right," Morag chided gently. "What I meant to say is that a good man would never treat you the way Mark did. If he promised you the job, then he should have kept his word, especially if you were better qualified than this 'cat-walk model' you describe."

Despite feeling a little embarrassed, Anna smiled. "I didn't mean to be rude, Morag. I guess the wound is still a little raw, especially as I've given up my flat in Edinburgh too. You said Lachlan is away."

"Aye, that's right." Morag chuckled, not hiding the fact that she loathed her husband working away on the oil rigs. "He's only been gone a few days, and it feels more like a year. I've another three weeks and two days on my own before he comes home. But the money is good, and if he keeps the job for another couple of years, we'll be able to buy the farm he's hankering after. I just hate him going, that's all."

"You'll get used to him being away given time."

Morag managed a tremulous smile. "There must be plenty more jobs out there for someone with your qualifications, surely? And if you're planning to stay at the croft all summer, how will you manage for money?"

"I've some savings, and the small legacy grandmother left me. I thought if I could get a part-time job, I'd have enough money to see me through the summer."

Morag looked thoughtful. "Well, lass, there's no denying we're short-handed. The hotel is full to capacity. The mornings are so busy, what with cleaning, preparing lunch, not to mention answering the phone. There's a fancy chef who comes in to prepare dinner, but Ewan likes to keep lunch a simple affair. He's away to Inverness just now, otherwise I'd ask him for you. I'm sure he'll take you on to help out with the tourist season. The pay won't be much, mind, just minimum wages, certainly nothing like you're used to."

"So long as it supplements my savings, that's all that matters. I've an idea for a book. I'm giving myself the summer to write it. If I haven't been offered a contract by September, I'll find another teaching job. And if I can't, then I suppose I could sell shoes in *Jenners'* Edinburgh store until something more appropriate comes along."

"A book, you say? What sort of book?"

"A novel. It's a love story set in Scotland at the time of the Clearances."

"That sounds interesting. I just hope you're not planning on using me as a model for one of your characters."

Two dimples appeared in Anna's cheeks. "That's not a bad idea. I must make a note of it. You mentioned there have been some changes on the estate."

"Aye, there have been, the tenants are none too happy about them, I can tell you. But as I'm about ready to serve lunch, why don't I tell you about them this evening over that bottle of wine you're going to buy me."

"Okay. It's about time I was going anyway. I'll see you about seven thirty, is that all right?" Anna said, and turned to leave.

"That's fine. I'll see you then, and I'll let you know what Ewan says about the job. He should be back before I go home. Bye just now."

Just as Anna reached the lobby, the hotel doors swung open and she faced a large thick set man as he entered reception. His ice-coloured eyes were set close together in a pox marked face under a jutting brow. His coarse overgrown crew cut had the texture of horse hair. His colourless eyes narrowed as they met hers, his square jaw tensed, and he tightened his grip on his rifle case and small holdall.

"Excuse me," she said, and stepped aside.

He said nothing in response, and stormed up to the desk. In gruff, halting English he asked Katrina, the receptionist, for tea and sandwiches to be sent up to his room. Then his cell phone rang and he barked into it in a heavy language Anna couldn't understand. Polish? Estonian? Certainly eastern European. Involuntarily, she put a hand to her throat. *If ever there was a man who would strangle me in my sleep, this is the one.*

She sped out of the hotel to the car park, wondering why he disturbed her so much, and hoping his stay would be a short one.

ন্তন্তন্ত

After making his call, Luke contemplated having a drink in the bar; he sure as hell needed one. But something told him not to keep the lady—no, strike that—crazy woman, waiting any longer than necessary.

As a successful artist, he was rarely without a companion, but lately he'd become tired and bored with the dating game. The women he escorted were smiling and all too eager to get in his pants. And his wallet. His work too, had become stale, and although his paintings sold well, he felt that each canvas was a mirror image of the last.

His solution came to him over a prolonged lunch in the *Impudent Oyster* with a beautiful bored Boston housewife. She didn't hide the fact she wanted something other than fancy artwork to show off to her friends. He realised he needed to get away. He'd returned home and spent the week stocking the yacht with sufficient provisions for a month.

It was his own driving need for the unexpected that made him set sail with no firm destination in mind. Well, my boy, Luke muttered to himself as he strode across the car park towards the waiting Land Rover, you certainly found the unexpected—and she has long legs and emerald-green eyes!

He found Anna leaning against the driver's door. Casually, he rested his hand against the door frame above her shoulder.

"The boatyard is ordering the part. It should be here later in the week, or the beginning of next. They also said something I didn't understand, something about putting it on the mail van."

"That's correct. Provided it's not too large, your package will be delivered with the mail. It's the same throughout the Highlands. It's more convenient, and the easiest option for people who live in remote areas."

"Well that's fine, except how on earth is the mailman going to deliver it? Sandpiper is moored in the middle of the loch, for Christ's sake."

"Simple. He'll leave any parcels here at reception along with my mail."

"Oh yeah? And then what? I walk the twelve miles down the glen every day to see if he has?"

"No, you knock on my door and ask me nicely to collect it for you."

"Great," Luke replied, shooting her a twisted smile. The prospect of having to rely on this prickly female didn't inspire him with overwhelming confidence. "And what do you suggest I do in the meantime?"

"Look around you, sailor-boy. This land may appear barren and inhospitable, but it is breathtakingly beautiful, not to mention a walker's and naturalist's paradise. Go for a hike, or take a swim in the loch, although I should warn you, the water's pretty cold, even in summer. If you'd sailed west, you could have moored somewhere more civilised, like Portree Harbour on Skye. Instead, you chose to drop anchor in one of the remotest and most inaccessible lochs in Scotland. Oh, and did I mention, it's one of the deepest?"

"Okay. I'll admit it; I should have paid more attention to the chart. Now, the sooner you get back in that heap of junk you laughingly call a vehicle, the sooner I..."

Luke took at step closer, until his face was only inches from hers. Two black and white heads snarled through the driver's window.

Anna side-stepped him. "Before you what? Get bitten?"

Luke yanked open the driver's door. Anna took the hint, but the look she gave him as she climbed aboard would have made most animals curl up and die.

"Good dogs," she said, patting the two collies' heads, and then nudging them aside. "Go on, in the back." She turned to Luke. "Are you getting in or planning on walking?"

Luke closed the door and strode round to the passenger side.

The air in the confined space positively crackled with tension as they headed back to the croft. Luke wondered just what he'd got himself into. Anna might be beautiful, but she was as unpredictable as a summer storm blowing in off the ocean. He shifted in his seat, felt the warm breath from one of the dogs on the back of his neck, and froze.

Anna looked in the rear-view mirror. "Ensay, no!"

The dog backed up, and lay down on the seat next to its companion. Luke glanced over his shoulder and slowly let the air out of his lungs.

"Thanks for calling him off."

"Her. They're bitches."

"That figures...."

"The dogs aren't normally aggressive to people who appear friendly. But let that be a warning to you. They're trained to protect, and will attack if they think I'm in danger."

"Yeah, that's pretty evident. Hey, I'm sorry. I just met you and you're doing me this huge favour. I should be appreciative. But we seem to be at each other's throats. Why?"

When she didn't answer, he turned and studied her. Wild Titian curls framed her delicate, slightly tanned oval face. Her green eyes were peppered with tiny flecks of gold. Her fingers, he noted, where long and slender, and devoid of polish and rings.

The check work-shirt she wore casually tucked into her black denim jeans was open at the neck, and when she shifted in her seat, he caught a glimpse of creamy skin and black lace. And despite her antagonism, Luke found himself attracted to her.

He turned away, and stared out of the window. A bank of clouds covered the mountain tops. In the distance, the dark waters of the loch were still and glistening.

Anna couldn't stand the silence any more. "Are you staying on the boat or will you move into the hotel?"

"I'll stay on Sandpiper. Until I get the pump on the auto-pilot fixed, I can't think about going back to Cape Cod. I've got lots of food on board. The generator's running fine. I have power for heat and hot water, so I'll get by. If I get bored, I can always take your advice and go for a hike."

"Well, if you do, make sure you wear sensible shoes, and take a waterproof jacket with you." Anna briefly transferred her gaze from the road to Luke, only to find him watching her. He had the most intense brown eyes and every time his gaze met hers, her heart turned over in response. Not for the first time since meeting him, did she feel herself blushing. "The weather can change suddenly," she continued, "and people have been known to get lost or disorientated, even in summer. The nearest mountain rescue team is fifty miles away. If you're planning on exploring, let me know, I'll lend you a map."

Luke turned his smile up a notch. "Thanks, I'd appreciate that. After being cooped up onboard for the last three weeks, it'll be good to get my land legs back." The old Land Rover jerked to a halt at the rear of the croft. "I know I've been an idiot. I'm sorry. And thanks for the lift. Maybe you'll let me buy you a drink sometime to make up for me being so stupid?"

Anna shook her head. "There's no need. Besides, I don't drink with men I don't know."

"Well, we could get to know each other first..."

She rubbed her forehead. "If you need anything from the village or want a lift that far, just come and ask."

He got out of the Land Rover and waited for Anna and the dogs.

ତ୍ରତ୍ରତ୍ର

From his vantage point high on the hill behind the croft, a man lifted a pair of binoculars to his eyes, and studied the scene below. Two people, not one, as he'd anticipated, emerged from the Land Rover. He focused on the figures, and wondered what they were talking about. He didn't need the binoculars to see that the smaller of the two was the MacDonald woman. Even from this distance, the hair was a dead giveaway. The other faced away from him, and although he couldn't be sure, he thought it was a man.

The woman remained at the croft, while the second figure strode across the grass towards the beach, climbed into a small inflatable dinghy, inserted the oars in the rowlocks, and pushed off. He inhaled sharply as he caught a glimpse of the face. It was unmistakably male. Damn it! Well, whoever he was, he wasn't from the glen, that much was for sure. None of the inhabitants were rich enough to own a boat like that.

He threw the binoculars to the ground in disgust, hastily snatching them up again as the man rowed steadily across the loch towards the sleek yacht. Hopefully it would be gone by the morning, but the way his luck was going, he somehow doubted it.

The woman should have been alone. He'd been watching her ever since she'd arrived at the croft, and her routine hardly ever varied. He swore heartily. Another afternoon spent lying in the heather and what had he got to show for it? Nothing, absolutely nothing!

He pulled off his deerstalker and scratched his bald head. He wasn't happy about the sudden appearance of the man with the yacht. He picked up his shotgun, slung the binoculars round his neck and slithered backwards over the heather. Once out of sight of the croft, and using some gorse bushes for cover, he stood, turned, and began walking slowly downhill to where he'd parked his pickup.

Chapter Three

Morag's cottage was the last in a row of twenty, single-storey, brightly painted, stone cottages which bordered the only road through the village. It was small and comfortable, and Anna couldn't envisage Morag living anywhere else; yet she knew that if Lachlan got his way, Morag would move to Perthshire, many miles away. The very idea her friend would one day be gone from this wild and magical place saddened her. Consciously tucking the thought away, she swirled a glass of red wine and watched the flames lick around the logs in the grate.

"Have you made a start on your book yet?" Morag asked, breaking the silence with her soft Highland burr.

"Yes. I did all the research before I left Edinburgh. I had planned to write the opening paragraph this afternoon, but I got distracted. I've decided to be disciplined and set time aside each day to work on it. But tell me, what's been happening in the glen while I've been away?"

"The Laird has moved to London. You know he owns a house there too? He's now a full-time absentee landlord. And I don't need to tell you how the Scots feel about them!"

"But I thought he came for the fishing and shooting seasons and then again for Christmas and New Year."

A frown settled on Morag's brow. "Well, it would seem that the poor man has Alzheimer's. Can't even remember his name or how to tie his boot laces, or so we've been told. Rumour has it he's living in a nursing home. Don't get me wrong, I'm sorry for the Laird, it must be a terrible affliction, but the changes have us all worried. The big house has been closed up since the ghillies' ball last autumn. His daughter has no involvement in the estate, not since her marriage to some big hot-shot banker. She's living in Hong Kong now, and has no intention of returning. And as for Mr Alistair, the son and heir... well, he's just a playboy with his fancy cars and expensive boats. He spends all his time in the South of France squandering the profits from the estate. He wants nothing to do with its daily running. You mark my words, when the old Laird dies it will be sold off to fund the son's expensive habits."

"So who's managing the estate now the Laird is in London? What will become of the tenants if it's sold?"

"There's a new ghillie, or should I say *factor*. Ugly little weasel of a man who struts about as if he owns the place. He'd have us all doffing our caps to him, given half a chance. I can't stand the man. He's always sneaking around, turning up in places you least expect. I wouldn't trust him to cook a kipper, let alone manage 90,000 acres. I have a feeling on me that he's up to no good."

Anna wanted to chuckle but fought the urge. Something in her friend's expression warned that the situation was anything but amusing. Besides, Morag's feelings were famous throughout the glen, and were taken seriously by the locals. Like many Highlanders, Morag believed in the gift of *Dha Shealladh*, the second sight, which passed from generation to generation. Her great-grandmother had been known as a *taibhsear*, or seer, and Morag had inherited the gift, if it could be called that, from her.

Anna remained sceptical, but was forced to admit that Morag's uncanny premonitions often forewarned of some unpleasant event.

"What happened to Sandy? I drove past his cottage, but it looked empty. I was so looking forward to seeing him again."

Morag's expression grew hard and resentful. "Oh, it was such a terrible thing. Within a fortnight of the factor's arrival, Sandy had handed in his notice. One day he was here, the next he'd disappeared. He's worked on the estate for nigh on thirty-five years, ever since he left school. He's given good service to the Laird and his family. No one knows the hill and the estate better than he does. He not only deserves to be head ghillie, he's earned the right."

Anna reached for the bottle of wine and poured Morag another glass.

"So where is he now? Does anyone know?"

"Well, Anna, there's the mystery. Everyone assumed he'd gone to his daughter's farm in the Borders. Lachlan telephoned Katrina, but she hadn't heard from him. In fact, she didn't even know her father had left his job. That really upset me. She obviously doesn't speak to him very often. I don't know what the world's coming to when a man's own daughter can't be bothered to keep in touch. It's all wrong, I tell you. Anyhow, before he left for the rig, Lachlan went to the cattle market in Fort William, just in case Sandy had been seen there. He asked around, but no one had set eyes on him. I'm worried for the man. He has so many friends here in the glen, it's unlike him to go off and not say a word to anyone."

Anna stared into the fire. The old man had been like an uncle to her. She hated to think of him being treated badly. When she spoke her voice was tinged with sadness.

"But surely someone must have seen him leave? I don't remember; did he own a car? And what of his dogs? Do you think he took them with him?"

"No, Sandy didn't have a car of his own. He drove one of the estate vehicles, and on the day he vanished, it was found outside the factor's house with the keys in the ignition. As for the dogs, who knows, lass? They're a fine pair of working collies, and valuable too. It saddens me to think anything untoward has befallen them or their master. But if Sandy hasn't gone to his daughter's, I can't see what use he'd have for two sheepdogs. Can you?"

Anna shivered. "Sandy is a sensible man, Morag. He wouldn't do anything stupid, nor would he harm his dogs. They mean the world to him. But I agree with you, this is all very strange."

"Yes, it is, and that's only half of it. Just before Christmas the Laird increased the tenants' rents, and for the old folks like Mrs McPherson, with only her pension, it's a struggle. Three families have left the village in the last six weeks, and I daresay before the summer is out, others will follow. The only work for the men is on the estate, or in the forestry, and neither pays particularly well, but you know that. There's hardly a family in the area that doesn't rely on the big house for housing or employment, and if the estate is sold it will signal the end of the community."

"Oh, Morag. Are things really that bad?"

"Aye, lass, they are. It's one of the reasons Lachlan is determined to buy a farm."

Anna rubbed her chin. There was no doubt Morag was telling the truth. More and more small communities such as theirs were dying out. Once the young folk left to go to school and university, very few ever returned. Most preferred to take well-paid city jobs, rather than face unemployment in their isolated villages. And while city folk clamoured for the country life, few could take the isolation or lack of modern day conveniences places such as Kinloch Hourn afforded.

It was close to midnight when Anna left Morag's cottage. Driving back to the croft she found it hard to put their conversation out of her mind. The Monymusk Arms Hotel, while owned by the estate, was let on a long term lease. Ewan Abercrombie, the manager, relied heavily on the summer trade, for the winter months brought few visitors, just the odd climber looking for the thrill of an ice climb. The road from Fort William could be blocked by snow for days on end, often making passage in and out of the glen impossible. Morag's prediction that the community would die could easily become a reality. And when that happened, Anna realised, she'd no longer be able to stay at the croft, despite all the happy memories it held.

She pulled the Land Rover to a halt and climbed out into the brilliance of a starry night. Out on the loch, through the faint mist that rose off the still, dark water, she could see Luke's yacht bobbing up and down on its mooring. In the tall pines at the side of the croft, an owl hooted. A lump rose in her throat. God forbid she would ever have to part with the croft in its spectacular wilderness. Abruptly, she turned, walked up the path to the door, and inserted the heavy key in the lock.

Chapter Four

Although the promised change in the weather hadn't materialised by the time Anna finished breakfast, she decided to tackle lighting the old iron stove anyway. Using the immersion heater was not only expensive and inconvenient; it took too long to heat sufficient water for her morning shower.

The Aga, a huge cream coloured range that stood in the inglenook fireplace, had been in the croft for as long as she could remember. Her grandparents had relied on it for hot water, heating, and cooking until the electricity board brought power to this part of the glen.

She tried to light it, but smoke filled the kitchen. She sighed. She knew what that meant. A trip to the roof. She'd seen her grandfather clean the chimney before. How long ago, ten? Fifteen years? More? She could do it. After all, she owned the croft now. It couldn't be that hard, could it?

Wearing her oldest clothes and a pair of overalls she found in a chest in the spare room, she piled her hair up in a careless knot and surveyed her project. She dragged a weathered wooden ladder from the cow-shed and rested it against the gable end of the croft. Suddenly, the top of the chimney looked awfully high. She swallowed nervously. While accustomed to decorating her flat, climbing up a twenty foot ladder and peering down a chimney was a different thing altogether.

Pulling a pair of gloves from her pocket she placed a foot on the first rung of the ladder. It creaked noisily and sagged under her weight, but didn't give way, so she put her foot on to the next. It too rebelled, but didn't break. She took her time, climbed rung by rung, and eventually made it halfway up the ladder.

"Do you think it's smart to be doing that?"

She jerked. The ladder swayed precariously. She gasped in panic. Fearing she was about to fall, she closed her eyes, tightened her grip, and clung on with all her might. Leaning against the ladder for support, she swivelled her head to look at the man below.

Luke.

"I might have known it was you. What do you think you're doing scaring people half to death?"

"People? I was aiming for 'person'. And only half to death? I must be losing my touch," Luke chuckled. "Honest, I saw you from the yacht and thought you might need some help."

"That's kind of you, but unless you have a set of sweep's brushes stashed away on that boat of yours, there's nothing you can do."

"Why don't you come down and let me do whatever you were doing?"

Anna shook her head vigorously. "No, thanks I can manage. I've nearly finished."

"Then at least let me steady the ladder for you. I wouldn't want you to fall... unless that's your usual way of getting down. Forgive me, I'm still unclear on the local customs, you see."

"Ha, ha, ha. Oh, you're really funny today, aren't you? All right, laughing boy, hold away." She removed the torch from her back pocket and peered down the chimney. An old bird's nest had fallen inside; she reached down and pulled it out. Apart from that, the chimney appeared to be relatively free of soot. She started to climb back down. One of the rungs gave way, and the next thing she knew, she was flying backward through the air.

"Arrrrrrrgh!" She screwed up her eyes expecting to land on hard Scottish granite, but instead Luke's strong arms wrapped around her waist and pulled her roughly, almost violently, to safety. Without thinking, she buried her face against the corded muscles of his neck, and clung to him with trembling limbs. If Luke hadn't caught her she would have most likely broken her neck. Slowly the tremors subsided, and she became acutely aware of the warmth of his body. His nearness was overwhelming and she was filled with a strange inner excitement. She tried to rationalise her feelings by putting them down to the shock of her fall, but failed. There was no doubt that what she'd felt was the first flush of sexual desire.

Colouring fiercely, Anna backed out of his grasp. "Er... I'm sorry about that. I guess the rungs weren't as strong as I thought."

"That old twig? I can't imagine how you ever thought it'd hold you up. You're lucky I was here. Are you okay? No bones broken?"

"I'm fine. The only thing that's dented is my pride! Thanks for catching me."

His tawny brown eyes meet her green ones. "Trust me, the pleasure is all mine."

Keenly aware of his scrutiny, Anna willed herself to look away.

Luke bent down and examined the ladder. Although old, it was in reasonably good condition. He picked up the remains of the rung and ran his thumb over the wood. The break should have been jagged and splintered where the wood had given way. Instead, part of it was smooth, as if someone had taken a hacksaw and sawn part way through the rung.

"You've been lucky. You could have been seriously hurt. It's about time this old ladder was retired and turned into firewood."

Anna wrapped her arms around her body, and shivered at the image his words created in her mind.

He rested his hand on her shoulder. "Are you sure you're all right? You look a little pale to me. Want me to fetch you a glass of water?"

"No. I'm fine. Please stop fussing. I'm not about to faint."

"I'm glad to hear it. Are you planning any more gymnastics today?"

She grinned mischievously. "Later, I thought I might try a triple Lutz on the lawn. Seriously, I've had enough aerial acrobatics to last me a while. I appreciate your thoughtfulness in offering to help."

"Well, if you're sure. I'll be on my way." With that he turned and walked back across the lawn to his dinghy.

Anna watched Luke stride across the grass towards the beach. Each time she saw him the pull on her senses was stronger. And if she were honest, she'd enjoyed the feel of his arms around her. Yet, such an attraction would be perilous and would only end in more heartache coming as it did so soon after the end of her affair with Mark.

She picked up the torch from where it lay on the lawn and headed back to the kitchen. Once inside she undid the inspection plate on the flue where it entered the chimney and shone her torch around inside. Satisfied that everything looked all right, she re-filled the firebox with an old newspaper and some kindling she'd found in the cow-shed, but rather than set it alight, she decided to wait until after she'd stocked up on groceries. The last thing she wanted was for the house to burn down while she was out.

It was mid-morning when she returned to the croft. Pushing open the front door with the toe of her boot, she carried four plastic bags of groceries into the kitchen, dropping them on the table with a sigh of relief. She rubbed the circulation back in to her bloodless fingers, thankful that she wouldn't have to shop again for a while.

Anna stared at the Aga and wondered if her meagre savings would stand the strain of using the immersion heater for another day. But common sense got the better of her, and seeing how she'd risked life and limb climbing the ladder to check the chimney, she'd light it.

Squatting in front of the Aga, she opened the firebox. She gasped, and rocked back on her heels. Two shiny brass bullets lay on top of the firewood in the stove. If she hadn't bothered to check the kindling before adding the firelighter and striking the match, they would have exploded, causing God knows what sort of damage.

Someone had left them for her.

Her breath caught in her throat. The colour drained from her face. Her hands clenched until her nails dug into her palm. Someone had been in her cottage. In all her thirty-two years on the planet, she'd never felt so scared.

Her first inclination was to bolt out the door, jump into the Land Rover, and drive screaming to the nearest police station. But that was some distance away, and besides, chances were they'd laugh, and then remind her that she lived on the edge of one of largest sporting estates in Scotland. Finding cartridges was not that unusual. In all probability, a passing sportsman, without a thought to his actions, had carelessly tossed them into the cow-shed. They'd fallen into the box of kindling, and she'd not noticed them when she laid the fire.

Carefully she removed them, placing them on the table behind her. She glanced round the small kitchen; everything seemed to be in its proper place. Telling herself she was being foolish for feeling scared, she stepped into the hallway, and stood motionless, her head slightly to one side, listening for the slightest sound. There was only silence.

Her movements stiff and awkward, she rested her hand on the banister and stepped onto the bottom tread of the narrow, wooden staircase. It creaked under her weight; the sound reverberating through the small cottage. Her heart jumped in her chest, her stomach clenched, and every nerve in her body felt as if it had been electrified.

Anna swallowed the scream bubbling in her throat. One by one she climbed the stairs. The door to her bedroom was slightly ajar. Had she left it that way? She couldn't remember. She threw it open with all her strength. It crashed against the wall. The room was empty, yet she knew someone had been there.

She crossed the landing to the second bedroom. The door was shut, just she'd left it. Her hand trembled as it reached for the doorknob. It turned easily. She pushed open the door and stepped inside. It too was empty.

Back in the kitchen she sat in the wooden rocker next to the Aga, and took one, then another deep breath and tried to relax. She plucked a bullet off the table and examined it. There was an outline of an animal etched into the brass. A lion, or a tiger, perhaps? Either way, it meant nothing to her. As far as she was concerned, it was just the same as every other bullet she'd seen—deadly.

Anna rolled the bullets in her hand, before dropping them in the dresser drawer out of harm's way. She told herself she was being silly to worry. If she'd paid more attention when laying the fire instead of rushing to the village, she probably would have noticed them lying amongst the bundles of old papers and firewood.

An hour passed before she was finally able to pull herself together and drag the old table and chair she'd found in the cow-shed into the shade of a tall Scots pine. Armed with her laptop and notebook, she sat down at the table with the intention of writing. She stared at the small screen, but lingering fear blocked her inspiration.

A flash of movement on the small pebble and sand beach in front of the croft caught her attention. Sure enough, it was the otter she'd heard calling earlier that morning, out with her young cubs on a hunting trip in the still of a Highland summer's day. Anna watched them frolic in the rock pools and kelp beds, safe from human interference. When they disappeared into the gentle lapping waves she rested her chin in her hands and re-read her notes. Slowly, a scene formed in her mind.

The stranger came again last night. He wore the kilt and the plaid, but I knew from the cut of the cloth that he was no ordinary Highlander. In the dim light cast by the fire, I judged him to be tall, certainly taller than my father. As for his colouring I could not tell, but thought his hair to be dark as a raven's wing. He appeared to be of gentle birth, for he spoke no Gaelic. His manner and bearing suggested he was an educated man.

I had been sent to bed early, but could not sleep. Instead, I lay huddled under my thin blanket in the corner of the box bed I shared with my younger brothers and sisters, and listened to the hushed voice of the stranger as he told my mother and father the dreadful news. Of course we'd heard the rumours—there was hardly a glen in the Highlands that had not—of tenants being forced to leave their homes for poorer land on the coast, the roofs of their houses being torn down and burnt to prevent their return. We'd heard tales of women and children being left to starve, of the elderly dying in their beds. But we never thought it would happen to us.

Suddenly, the voices stopped and the stranger raised his head and looked directly at me. A cold shiver gripped me. I sensed something was wrong and I knew that our lives were about to change forever. Like my grandmother and her grandmother before her, I had been blessed with the gift of the Sight, the ability to see into the future, but tonight all I could feel was a sense of foreboding, so strong that it was almost palpable.

Anna had just finished typing the last word when she heard the sound of an approaching vehicle. Shading her eyes against the sun, she saw a Range Rover drive through the narrow gate to the croft.

Irritated at being disturbed, she saved her work, closed her laptop, and turned to look at the vehicle. A tall, sandy-haired man climbed out from behind the steering wheel. He wore a red and green tartan kilt and a plain lovat green tweed jacket and waistcoat. There was something about his bearing that was vaguely familiar. As he drew closer it suddenly dawned on her who he was.

"Alistair. Alistair Grant!" she said, rushing forward to greet him. "Of all the people, I certainly didn't expect to you to come and visit me. I supposed I should call you Laird now."

He laughed and kissed her cheek. Apart from a few laughter lines around his eyes and his sun-streaked hair, he'd changed little over the intervening years, whereas she had. Her hair was longer now for one thing, and she was slimmer too, yet Alistair had recognised her at once.

"No need to be formal, Anna, my dear. How lovely to see you again, and looking so radiant too. I heard you where back in the glen and felt I had to come and say hello."

"It's been a while."

"Yes it has," he said, resting his hip on the table. "It must be all of what? Ten, no, twelve years since we last saw each other?"

"Your sister's wedding, if I recall. How is she, by the way?"

"Sophie's living in matrimonial bliss in Hong Kong. She has two children now, with a third on the way. I was sorry to hear about your grandmother. I know the old lady was very dear to you."

Anna swallowed the lump which had suddenly formed in her throat. "Yes, she was, and I miss her dreadfully. Look, why don't you come up to the house, I was about to make some coffee or there's iced tea, if you prefer."

"Iced tea would be nice."

"Come on then," she said, linking her arm with his and leading the way. "This must be a difficult time for you too, with your father's illness. I hear you've been living in the South of France. It must be quite a culture shock coming back here after so many years away. Are you home for good, or is this just a flying visit?"

"I have a few business matters which require my urgent attention, so I'll be here for the foreseeable future. What about you?"

"I'm planning on staying for the summer at least."

"That's marvellous. We can renew our acquaintance. We used to be er... good friends when we were younger, didn't we?"

"That was a long time ago, Alistair. If I remember correctly, you dumped me in favour of Lord so-and-so's spotty daughter. Now what was her name?"

Alistair pulled out a chair from under the kitchen table, and sat down. "Fiona. Fiona Douglas. Her father owns an estate in Aberdeenshire."

"That's right. When I left at the end of that summer you were about to be led up the altar. What happened?"

"I saw sense, and realised I was in love with you," he replied, with an infectious grin.

For a long moment Anna stared at him, and then laughed out loud. "Oh Alistair, you always did have a good sense of humour."

"You wound me, my lady." he said, placing his hand on his heart.

"Oh, please...we were teenagers. We didn't know how to make a commitment for the next twenty-four hours, let alone a lifetime." Anna handed him a glass.

"My, my, you have become cynical in your old age. But we won't fall out over the past. Surely, you must have realised that it was my father who interfered."

"Really? I didn't know that."

"He had this idea about merging the Douglas estate with ours, so he insisted I end our relationship."

"What relationship?" Anna asked, taking a sip from her glass. "We hung round together. We were nothing more than friends, and you know it. I wouldn't even let you kiss me. I was seventeen years old! I was going up to university. I wasn't ready for a serious relationship, and what's more, you were halfway through your studies at Cambridge. It would have been a disaster for both of us."

"Perhaps the timing wasn't quite right. We're both more mature now, and you're no longer the gangly teenager you once were. You're a beautiful woman, if you don't mind my saying so. And if rumour is to be believed, you're still unattached."

Anna's green eyes sparkled with amusement. "Are you trying to chat me up, by any chance?"

"I never did like that turn of phrase—far too common. Just let's say that I'd like to renew our acquaintance. Have dinner with me? I know this delightful restaurant in Glasgow. It's chic and intimate, and the food is wonderful. We could take in a show and make a night of it."

Anna thought about his offer for a millisecond. He was attractive, intelligent, and at times, amusing. All the qualities she admired in a man, but a cynical inner voice cut through her thoughts. He was also a love-them-and-leave-them Lothario. But could his father's illness have forced him to change his ways? She doubted it. Besides, she wasn't ready for another relationship. At least not yet. And when she was, it would be with a man she could trust with her life.

"Alistair, it's very kind of you—but no thank you."

"Not even for old time's sake?"

Anna wavered. "Well... may I think about it?"

"Of course you may. You never know, you might enjoy yourself."

"We move in totally different circles and have absolutely nothing in common," Anna said looking out of the window to where the dogs lay on the lawn.

"On the contrary, I'm sure if we took the time to become re-acquainted, we'd find we have many mutual interests."

"I've only just arrived, Alistair. Let me get settled in, then ask me again."

"Very well, my dear, if that's what you want. But just think of world I could introduce you to. Who knows? You might even end up being mistress of Killilan House. Maybe I'll drop by the croft one day next week and ask you again." He tugged at his waistcoat and stood. "Now, if you'll excuse me, I really must be going. I have an appointment with my factor. Thank you for the drink," he said, giving her a hug.

Anna watched him drive off before returning to her manuscript. It was only when Ensay, bored by hours of inactivity, wandered over, and sat at her feet, that she looked up.

Leaning back, she cast a critical eye over the words on the screen. Not bad for an opening chapter. Of course the grammar would need to be tightened, and the storyline needed tweaking, and her characters needed names. But it was a start. She smiled to herself, feeling guilty. She always told her students they must plan each chapter down to the last comma, but now she realised she couldn't write like that. She much preferred the freedom to develop her characters page by page, rather than have them fully evolved before a word was typed.

Absentmindedly, she reached down and stroked the black and white head resting on her knee. When she stopped, the dog nudged her hand for more attention. Anna looked into the trusting brown eyes.

"I suppose you think I've been ignoring you."

The collie pushed at her hand once more. Anna's gentle laughter rippled through the still air. She was sure the dog understood every word she said.

"I get the message. You want to play. But if I'm going to keep you in dog biscuits all summer, you'll have to learn to amuse yourself and let me work." She saved her manuscript and then carried her laptop into the croft. The dog followed faithfully at her heels.

Chapter Five

Grant returned to Killilan House, and shut himself in the library. What was wrong with him? He'd always had success with the ladies—it took little effort. And yet that little effort hadn't made Anna MacDonald accept his offer of a date. No, nothing was wrong with him. It was her. She'd clearly become a man-hater. Still, he had to do something about her... something...

He opened the small rosewood drinks cabinet, and poured himself a large measure of Scotch. He stared into the glass, and a resentful expression settled on his aristocratic features. Until a month ago, his life on the Riviera had been perfect. A yacht, admittedly leased for the season, an Aston Martin, fabulous parties, attended by A-list celebrities. But it had all come to an end the day his father was diagnosed with Alzheimer's.

At least the old boy was safely ensconced in a nursing home where he couldn't do any more damage. But the cost, added to the estate's huge overdraft, was crippling. And Sophie, his sister, and her Hong Kong banker husband were of no help. They'd refused to assist with the fees, saying that all their spare cash was tied up in stocks and bonds and other investments, and would take some time to convert to cash. It was a poor excuse. He knew they were lying, and had told them so, and the ensuing argument was bitter and futile.

Sophie said she'd never speak to him again. He had every reason to believe her.

A grim letter from the family accountant had arrived that morning. Things were worse than he imagined. He tossed back the whisky, then picked up the decanter, and carried it back to his desk. While drinking didn't solve his problem, it sure helped, although having the servants see him drinking this early in the day would have given his mother apoplexy, Alistair thought as he refilled his glass.

Ordinarily, he would have found comfort in the library, but today its sombre decoration only added to his depression. The walls, apart from one, which held portraits of his father and grandfather, were covered in floor to ceiling bookshelves. Chinese rugs covered the polished wood floor. He paced the room, stopping in front of the Louis XV mantel clock. He wondered whether it was an original or a copy. He turned it round to examine it when someone knocked on the door. A wiry, bald headed man opened it and glared at him wordlessly.

"MacKinnon. Come in. I've been expecting you." Alistair sank into his overstuffed leather desk chair. McKenzie MacKinnon had been recommended by a friend of a friend in France as being having the skills necessary to do the job, but God alone knew which gutter he'd climbed out of, or where he'd found his clothes.

MacKinnon kicked the door closed with the heel of his right boot.

"For God's sake!" shouted Alistair. "Be careful. You nearly sent a Minton vase toppling. It's worth all of three grand."

Mac pulled off his deerstalker and scratched his bald head.

"Aye? But then I suppose that's nothing compared with the value of this place as a whole, and once you've signed yon piece of paper, you'll be able to afford even more fancy jugs."

"Well, that rather depends on you, doesn't it?" Alistair replied. "So far, we haven't discussed the finer details of our...our little business transaction, which brings me nicely to the subject. Take a seat."

Mac dropped heavily into the Chippendale chair. The delicate chair legs creaked rebelliously under his weight. He rested his shotgun on his knees, and then folded his arms across his chest. His gaze settled on the young Laird's face.

"I have four weeks in which to sign the contract. If I don't meet the deadline, the deal is off, and along with it our arrangement."

Mac's thin lips twisted into thin line. "That's what you think, your Lairdship. We have an agreement and it says nothing about payment being conditional on completion."

"Don't try veiled threats with me, MacKinnon. I know enough about your activities to put you inside for a very long time."

"I'll bear that in mind. Even so, you must be desperate to hire the likes of me."

Alistair took out his handkerchief and dabbed his palms. He felt dirty having to deal with this disreputable man, but time was running out and he had no other option. "I was told you could get the job done quickly and without any fuss."

"Aye, so you said on the phone. The taxes on this place must be crippling. Even so, it must be really tough owning all this," MacKinnon said, waving his arm about the room. "But don't worry, your Lairdship. There's plenty of time for me to deal with your little problem."

"You've made little progress to date. You told me that you'd have everything sorted within no time at all. What happened?"

"It will be sorted, so long as you stop interfering. You should have stayed in the south of France."

"I couldn't, you know that. An estate of this size doesn't run itself, you know."

"That's as may be. But these matters take time your Lairdship, if they are to be handled properly. You've only just appointed me as factor, so I can't start shouting orders or your tenants will get suspicious. That McInnes woman, for one.

She sees everything. It's positively uncanny. Anyway, you don't want the village gossip spreading rumours."

"Good Lord, man! The last thing I need."

"In that case let me do the job *my way*."

"All right. But be careful. And keep me informed. I can't afford to miss the closing date."

"You're not the only one with a vested interest in this project, remember. You've promised me a hefty bonus for a successful outcome."

"Yes, well...just as long as we're clear on what is at stake. You can go now."

"That's it? No affairs of the estate to discuss? As your factor, I'm supposed to be seen with you—quite often."

"Oh, yes," Alistair sighed, "how silly of me to forget. You'd better tell the lads to get the silage cut. You'll also need to book shearers for the sheep. The shooting season gets underway in a few months. I assume the pheasant pens are well stocked? And you will need to hire some beaters. I can't afford to turn clients away."

"Aye, I'll make sure it's all taken care of. Now, if there's nothing else, your Lairdship, I've a few things to attend to." He picked up his gun.

MacKinnon rose, scraping the antique chair against the polished wood floor. Alistair winced. "I'm counting on you, MacKinnon, for an early resolution to this problem. Don't let me down."

MacKinnon snorted. "We'll, see. It all depends on how I feel, your Lairdship. It all depends on how I feel." He scuttled out and slammed the door after himself. Alistair jumped and looked back to see if the vase was all right. It was, but his stomach wasn't.

He swivelled his chair and stared out at the ornamental garden. How had he got into this mess? And, worse still, how could he control that vicious Glasgow rat? He slammed his fist on the desk. His glass crashed to the floor, shattering into a hundred pieces, spilling its contents onto the Chinese rug. God damn it! Did everything he touched have to go wrong?

He picked up the largest shards of glass and dropped them into the wooden wastebasket, narrowly escaping cutting himself. He looked down at the ever-spreading pool of whisky. Oh, the hell with it. Let Mrs McTavish mop it up. Poor or not, no proper Laird did his own cleaning.

There had to be another way to resolve his problems, but he couldn't see any course of action other than the one he was already taking. He looked at the papers lying on the desk in the vague hope they held the answers, but what he saw there only made him more depressed. Clasping his hands behind his head, he leaned back in his chair and stared at the painting of his father on the opposite wall.

"You rotten old bastard. It's your fault. If you hadn't...if you'd only...oh, I hope you die and go to hell!" After a moment's contemplation, he snatched up the phone and dialled.

"About that matter we discussed last time I was in town," he growled before the person on the other end of the line had chance to answer. "I've decided you can go ahead."

Chapter Six

The short-wave radio crackled above Luke's head. The announcer's voice was barely audible above the static. Luke adjusted the dial hoping to catch the weather report, but it was impossible to get a decent signal. He wasn't too concerned. Until the replacement pump for the auto-pilot arrived, he couldn't sail back to Cape Cod anyway, not unless he found someone to help crew the yacht and take a turn at the helm while he slept.

The scenery and diversity of the coastline amazed him. The Hebridean islands were stunning, with their white-sand beaches and low grassy, wild flower-strewn *machair*. But they were nothing compared with the dramatic, impenetrable sea-cliffs of the mainland, interspersed with beaches and fjord-like sea lochs, which, according to his chart, stretched inland like the fingers of an arthritic hand.

In that respect, Loch Hourn was a perfect example. Its steep mountains, a mixture of bare rock, heather, gorse and bracken, tumbling streams, and waterfalls were inhospitable. But in some respects it was also a modern man-made wilderness, as along the shoreline he'd seen the ghostly, roofless remains of earlier dwellings.

While his dinner cooked on the small two-ringed stove, Luke gazed out of the cabin window to the solitary, white-washed cottage across the loch. The setting sun dipped ever closer to the horizon, its red fiery orb casting a rich ochre shadow on the walls of the cottage. The colours and panorama were spectacular, and his fingers itched to capture the scene unfolding before him. It would make a wonderful painting, with the rock and pebble beach in front, and the majestic mountains behind. About half a mile to the left, he could see a waterfall cascading over granite boulders into a stream below, which in turn, meandered into the loch and the sea beyond.

Luke lifted the pan off the stove, gathered up his sketchbook and pastels, and went up the companionway to the deck. With the cabin window against his back for support and his sketchbook resting on his knee, his pencil strokes soon captured the image of the croft, bathed in the light of the setting sun.

He remembered the time he and Nicole, his fiancée, had headed up to Lake Tahoe for the weekend. It had been what, three? No, five years ago. He'd insisted they go for a walk along the lake shore after dinner. It had been an evening similar to this. Tall, blonde, with vibrant blue eyes, and a ready laugh, Nicole had captured his heart from the moment they'd met. Despite the warnings from his superior about agents not getting involved, he'd fallen in love with her. They'd been dating for six months, when he decided to propose. He had it all planned. He'd ask her to give up her job in San Francisco and move into his house on Cape Cod. They'd be married from there. He'd even picked out a ring the week before while on a business trip to New York. A two carat solitaire diamond set in platinum. When he'd slipped the ring on her finger she'd cried and clung to him. He'd been the happiest man on the planet.

But his world fell apart three months later on the day she died in his arms. If he'd only told her true nature of his work rather than concealing it from her, he might have been able to protect her. But he hadn't. And her death was his fault.

Luke rubbed his eyes. No use pretending there weren't any tears. No one was there to see him cry. Damned memories—what would it take to finally burn them away?

He gazed over at Anna's cottage. He'd seen similar houses on the Hebridean islands, but on those, the builder had used turf as a bed for the thatched roof of bracken and heather. Tigh na Cladach's hip-ended roof was tiled in slate, its one apparent concession to modernity. Two small dormer windows were set into it. Could they be bedrooms? Surely not, for anyone over five foot would find it difficult, if not impossible, to stand upright in such a confined space. No, he reasoned, they must be for additional light and he guessed the bedrooms would be at the rear of the property, although it was difficult to imagine the internal layout without actually looking inside.

He wished he'd brought his camera on deck, but with dusk descending, he had little time left in which to sketch the scene, let alone capture it on film. For this evening, at least, he'd have to be satisfied with his drawings. There'd be other opportunities to take photographs, which he would use as an aide-memoire once back at the easel in his Cape Cod studio.

The water rippling against the hull soothed him. Even though he'd lost the light, he remained on deck thinking about Anna. This was a wild and isolated place for a woman to live, especially a young woman, and he wondered again what had brought her to this remote glen. Was she ever lonely in the croft, with only her dogs for company?

His drawing momentarily forgotten, Luke watched a shadow cross in front of one of the windows. A light snapped on, followed by that of the porch, creating an eerie dance of shadows on the lawn. Anna appeared, pulling on a jacket as she walked across the grass towards the rocky beach. The two dogs followed close behind. The breeze instantly whipped her hair into disarray.

He turned to a clean page and quickly started sketching the tall, slim figure as she paused now and again to throw sticks for the dogs. She lingered at the water's edge, bending down to investigate something. At the precise moment he lifted his eyes from his drawing, she straightened and looked across the loch to the yacht. She stood motionless, her hands by her side, staring into the twilight. At first he wasn't sure if she could see him sitting against the bulkhead, but then she gave a brief wave in acknowledgement. Before he realised it, he'd returned the gesture.

Although her features were indiscernible, he knew she would be smiling, her bright eyes sparkling, as she enjoyed the walk with her Border collies. Abruptly, she turned and walked on toward the waterfall, and was soon out of sight.

Luke felt a sudden stab of envy at her uncomplicated life. It had been years since he'd enjoyed such simple pleasures. If he'd suggested to Kate, his girlfriend in Chatham, that they go for a walk or stay in a remote mountain cabin rather than a five-star hotel, she'd have been horrified. Limousines, designer clothes, exclusive restaurants, and champagne were far more her style than loafers, a sweater, and old blue jeans. And up until now, he'd felt pretty much the same way.

Continuing to work on his sketch, he thought about his life back home. He owned a fine house, an old converted coastguard station on the seaward shore of Cape Cod. There was an SUV in the garage, and this yacht. He enjoyed great success as an artist, with his paintings exhibited in galleries all over the States. His bank balance was healthy. And there was Kate, with her too-blue eyes and beach-girl hair. Life was good, yet now he yearned for something else, such as a walk along the beach with a woman who could love him for himself, and not for his wealth and social status. As classy as she was, Kate hardly qualified.

Twenty minutes later, the dogs trotted back into view, Anna trailing behind. She paused and looked up into the sky. Luke couldn't see what she was searching for. Then he saw them. First one, then two, then four tiny black dots came wheeling out of the old barn at the side of the croft. Bats! He hadn't seen a bat since childhood, when his uncle in Austin had taken him to Congress Bridge to see them emerge at dusk. He certainly hadn't expected to see them this far north or in such an isolated place.

He looked at his watch; it was nearly eleven-thirty, yet felt much earlier. The strange half-light of a Scottish summer evening confused him, despite the fact that he'd first dropped anchor in the Outer Hebrides.

Across the loch, Anna called the dogs, her voice carrying over the water in the still evening air. When she disappeared inside the cottage, Luke rose. He checked the sails to make sure they were securely stowed for the night, and that the anchor was firmly set. He picked up his artist's materials and headed for the companionway, pausing on the top step to enjoy scent of woodsmoke drifting across the loch.

Chapter Seven

The following Monday, Anna started work at the Monymusk Arms. Originally built as a hunting lodge for Killilan estate, the two-storey granite building had been converted into a hotel by Alistair Grant's father some ten years previously, to prevent it from falling into disrepair.

Set amidst spectacular scenery, it stood on a rise overlooking the village. Bordered by rhododendrons, and extensive gardens, it retained much of its Victorian charm. An outpost of comfort and graciousness, the hotel restaurant offered good food, comfortable accommodation, and rumour had it that Queen Victoria had once stayed there.

The fifteen letting bedrooms, each named after a clan, were decorated in its clan colours. The Lindsay room, which doubled as the honeymoon suite, overlooked a small lochan at the side of the hotel, and had recently been refurbished in muted shades of green and deep rose.

Although remote, and surrounded by unspoilt countryside, it remained popular with hillwalkers, climbers, and fishermen who came to try their hand at trout and salmon fishing in the nearby rivers and lochs. An impressive array of stags heads and stuffed fish hung on the walls of the bar and entrance hall. A certificate displayed in reception proudly announced the hotel had been designated the 'Best Sporting Hotel in Scotland' for three years running.

Last winter, much to the surprise of Ewan, the manager, it had been hired by a major TV production company to double for 'the local hostelry' in a series of programmes about the life of a fictitious Scottish laird.

Employed as a chambermaid and girl Friday, Anna stripped and made beds each morning, and when necessary, helped out in the kitchen.

"I hear there's a yacht moored in the loch," Morag said, as she helped her make up the twin beds in room seven.

"Morag, how on earth do you know that?"

"Well, lass, you know how the village grapevine works. One of the shepherds saw it sail into the loch. He told his wife, who mentioned it to Ewan, who then told me. I understand it's quite large and expensive looking, has two masts for the sails and there's an American flag flying off the stern on a wee pole. Oh, and it's anchored opposite Tigh na Cladach."

Anna pulled the pillowcase on a bolster, plumped it up, and placed it on the bed, avoiding her inquisitor's gaze. "Yes, that's right, although the sight of a boat in the loch is not that unusual, even this early in the tourist season."

"And would I also be right in saying that it belongs to the gentleman you brought down to the hotel the other day?"

Anna's whipped round to stare at her friend. "Who told you about that?"

"Katrina saw a Land Rover—*your* Land Rover, in the car park. She just happened to be in the bar when a man came in wanting to change a £50 note."

"Just because there was a Land Rover in the car park, doesn't mean to say it was mine."

"No, it doesn't. But there were two border collies in it, and it was driven by a woman with ginger hair—"

"It's not ginger!" Anna declared, mildly irritated.

"You're the only woman in the glen with hair that colour. And as your house is the only one which stands on the shore of loch, he couldn't have got a lift from anyone else."

"Actually he could have walked as far as the car park and hitched a lift with one of the hillwalkers."

"He could have, but he didn't. So what's he like, this American friend of yours? And why didn't you tell me about him the other evening?" Morag smiled benignly, as if dealing with a temperamental child.

"I'd hardly call him a friend. I did him a favour, that's all. He's got a problem with the pump for the auto-pilot, and needs a part for it. Besides, I couldn't very well let him walk the twelve miles to the phone, now could I?"

"No, lass, you could not. You've been brought up to treat people better than that. So how long will he be staying?"

"I don't know. It depends on when the part arrives. That might not be until sometime next week, or possibly the week after. I think he said it's unsafe for him to return to the States until he's made the repair, and even then he might have to take the yacht into the boatyard in Fort William to be checked over."

"I see. Where exactly in America did you say he comes from?"

Anna tucked the top sheet under the mattress. "I didn't. And since when are you an expert on American geography?"

"I'm not. It's just a point of curiosity, that's all."

"My goodness Morag, you'd have made an excellent police interrogator. I only gave him a lift to the hotel. He said Massachusetts, but for all I know that's next door to Seattle or

Coney Island. If you're that curious about him, why don't you swim out to his yacht and ask him for yourself?"

Morag nodded slowly. "I could, but I doubt my Lachlan would sanction the activity. So tell me, what does your errant American look like? Is he young, or old? Is he alone, or does he have a companion, a woman friend perhaps?"

"He was very rude, and I wasn't paying attention."

"Mm. Then your eyesight must be failing."

"There's nothing wrong with my eyes."

"Are you sure you don't need to borrow my glasses? Because I can't believe you could spend an hour in a man's company and not remember what he looked like."

Anna had seen that look before and knew its meaning well. "All right. He's tall, dark-haired, greying at the temples, tanned, and if you like mature men, good-looking. His voice is deep, sensual, and positively oozes sex appeal. I'd say he's about forty, or maybe even a little older. You already know he's an American."

"That's the same thing Katrina said."

"Then why bother asking me if you've already got all the answers? Really, Morag, you know I hate gossiping as much as I hate being the subject of curiosity and chitchat."

"Aye, lass, I do. And in that respect, I should be apologising. But you can't blame an old married woman like me for being curious. I only have your best interest at heart now that your grandmother has gone. If he's as good-looking as you say, I'm surprised he hasn't asked a pretty girl like you out."

Anna blushed. "What makes you think he hasn't already done so?"

"Well if he had, you'd have told me, now wouldn't you? Anyhow, you don't want to be jumping into another relationship so soon after Mark. It will only end in tears."

"Credit me with some sense. Luke's only here for a few days. Besides, I'm not the type to leap into bed with the first man who comes along. Anyway, he could be married."

"I'm sure he's not. If he was, he wouldn't be sailing across the Atlantic searching for a past he doesn't know he has. You need to be watchful of that man."

Anna rolled her eyes. "Oh, Morag! That's ridiculous. He's just a sailor who has a problem with his yacht and nothing more. It was pure chance that made him sail into Loch Hourn."

Morag's eyes grew dark and unfathomable. "That's what you think, lass. But I'm telling you different, and you should be careful. There is danger in the glen. I see it around you."

Anna shivered. "This isn't the time or the place for one of your premonitions. And what's more, you know I don't believe in the 'Second Sight.' There's no scientific proof. At best, it's a matter of coincidence, and at worst it's a load of rubbish."

Morag blinked and focused her gaze on Anna's face. "Scottish history tells it differently, as you well know, but I'll not argue with you. You are entitled to your opinion, as I am. You may not believe what I say at the moment, lass, but you will. Something evil is going on, and I can feel it."

"Oh, please!" Anna snapped. "Your imagination is running away with you. You've been watching too many late night horror films on the television. They always give you nightmares when you're alone. Speaking of you being alone, when does Lachlan get back?"

Morag wouldn't be side-tracked. "Have it your own way, lass. You've known me long enough to know that the Sight has never let me down. I can see that my warning isn't what you want to hear just now, so I'll say no more. Shall we get on? We've still got another three bedrooms to tidy and lunch to prepare."

Anna bit down on her temper. "Yes, let's, in fact, why don't you go and start lunch? I'll finish off up here. When I'm through, I'll come to the kitchen and give you a hand."

"Of course, dear," Morag smiled. She turned, and started down the stairs, but paused halfway down.

Wondering what the problem was, Anna leaned over the banister. A family with two young children and a baby were checking in at reception. She saw the look of indescribable sadness on her face. How long had it been? Two, three years since Morag's last miscarriage? She'd shared Morag's delight at being told she was pregnant, but couldn't begin to understand the pain and disappointment she and Lachlan must have experienced each time Morag miscarried.

Anna wanted to reach out and give her friend a hug, and was about to tell her that there was plenty of time for her to have a family, when Morag broke the silence.

"And don't forget to give the tiles in the bathroom in room four a good wipe down. They look as if they're covered in snow. I swear the woman in there showers in talcum powder instead of water!" She called, as she continued down the stairs.

The more Anna thought about Morag's warning, the more concerned she became. Certainly, since arriving at the croft she'd had more than her fair share of disturbed nights, but she'd put those down to the unaccustomed silence, rather than Edinburgh's traffic noise. And this talk of her being in danger—well, that was just nonsense, wasn't it? Even so, Morag had a point. The croft was isolated. But she had the dogs, and they would attack anyone who threatened her.

No, Anna decided, Morag was just being her overdramatic self. No matter how much the warning echoed in her ears, nothing could persuade her that Luke was anything other than what he appeared, a yachtsman whose boat was in need of urgent repair. As soon as the necessary part arrived, he'd be on his way back to America.

Using her pass key, she opened the door to room thirteen, and pushed the service trolley inside. Only one of the two single beds had been slept in. As she moved the bed away from the wall the toes of her right foot hit something hard. She bent down and reached under the bed. Her fingers closed round a handle. Why guests couldn't use the stand provided for suitcases, she would never know. She dragged the case out of the way.

Only it wasn't a suitcase, but the gun case she'd seen the man carrying the day she'd visited Morag. She starred at it for a moment, then something made her undo the catch and flip open the top. A bolt action rifle with a telescopic sight lay inside. She shivered. Did the guest have no sense? He should have asked Ewan to lock it in the safe rather than leave it in his room. She closed the case and put it back under the bed. She'd mention it to Ewan and suggest he speak with the guest before she left the hotel.

Three quarters of an hour later Anna rejoined Morag in the kitchen.

"Ewan tells me the young Laird has returned from London," Morag said.

Anna raised an eyebrow. "Yes. I know. Alistair called at the croft the other day. I thought you said he'd shown no interest in the estate."

"Until now he hasn't. But that might be about to change. He's holding a meeting on Friday to inform the tenants of his grand plans."

"Actually, he mentioned something about having some business problems to sort out. I wonder what they are."

Morag looked thoughtful. "I'm not surprised he has problems. If he keeps on putting up the rents, his tenants will move away to less expensive housing. Then what will he do?

And more importantly, what will happen to the families in the village?"

"Well, he could sell or lease the estate to some oil-rich Arab or pop star."

"Now who's being silly? Why would a pop star want to live up here, when he or she could have the bright lights of London? Besides, the estate is Alistair's heritage; he'd never sell it."

"Yes, Morag, I realise that. But if what I read in the papers is true, half the estates in Scotland are now owned by overseas investors, musicians, or film stars."

"Ewan says there's to be a Ceilidh too. In fact, he's already been asked to provide the refreshments."

"Really? Alistair's hosting a dance? That doesn't surprise me. He was always the one for a party. So, when is this great event to take place?"

"Three weeks on Saturday. You will come, won't you?"

"I'm not a tenant, so I won't be invited."

"No, but you are part of the community. Besides, it will be good for you to get out and enjoy yourself."

"Oh, I don't know, Morag. I'm not thrilled by the idea. Lachlan will be home by then, and everyone else will have a partner. Perhaps if Mark and I..."

"Well, think on it, lass. You never know, something might happen between now and then to change your mind."

The antique mahogany grandfather clock in the dining room struck two. Anna stopped at the reception desk to see if any post had been left for her. For a reason she couldn't identify, she half-hoped for a letter from Mark. But there was nothing from him. She felt stupid for thinking about him. He was happy in Edinburgh with his bombshell. What need had he of her? And had he ever needed her?

For the first time since her arrival at the croft, she felt isolated and lonely. She'd lost her boyfriend and given up her job in the space of a day. And she was living in a tumbledown cottage in the middle of nowhere. Her parents would have advised her to stay in Edinburgh, swallow her pride, and ask for her job back, even if it meant working as an assistant to Mark's new blonde. In her younger days she would have done as they'd recommended. But the new Anna said no, even though it pained her to the core.

Twenty minutes later, she carefully manoeuvred the old Land Rover along the pot-holed track towards the croft. A new and unexpected warmth surged through her at the sight of Luke leaning against her door.

He walked over and opened the driver's door. "Hi there," he said, his face splitting into a wide grin.

When his gaze swept over her face and lingered on her lips, Anna felt her pulse quicken. A hot blush rushed to her cheeks. Luke intrigued her; he radiated a vitality that drew her like a moth to a flame. No matter how hard she tried not to, she found herself responding with a smile of her own.

"Don't tell me," she said, climbing out from behind the wheel. "You want a lift to the phone again."

"No. Actually, I came for the map you offered to let me borrow."

Anna stared at him.

Luke tilted his head. "I thought you said I could borrow a map. Look, if this is a bad time or something, I'll get by. Never mind."

"Come in and I'll get it for you." She pushed her key in the door and threw it open. "Just watch the dogs..." but before she could finish the sentence, the two collies rushed past, nearly knocking Luke off his feet. Anna smiled apologetically. "Sorry, but they've been shut in since early morning and get—"

"Don't worry, I'm fine," he interrupted, rubbing his left knee where it had come into contact with the wall. He limped after her into the small kitchen.

She took the map out of the dresser drawer. "How far were you thinking of going?"

"I thought I'd climb the hill behind the cottage— if it's not private property, of course."

"It is, but don't worry. There's no law of trespass in Scotland. Provided you don't cause any damage, you can roam pretty much where you want. The only exception is in the deer stalking season, when you have to be careful, but that doesn't start until July. Most of the land around here belongs to the estate. It's open to hillwalkers, except for a few weeks during the shooting season." She glanced at his feet. "Those trainers aren't suitable; you'll break your ankle if you fall."

"I don't plan to fall. Besides, I don't have anything else."

"I think Mar—a friend left a pair of boots here last time he stayed." She fished inside the cupboard under the stairs. "What size do you take?"

"Ten, but it doesn't matter. I'll just follow the shoreline instead."

"It's no bother, besides I was going to throw them away. Ah! Here they are. Mm, size eleven. They should be just right with a pair of thick socks. I'll get you some, and you can try them on."

Luke pulled off his trainers. "This...friend...won't he be pissed off when he finds out you gave away his boots?"

"I doubt he even remembers buying them, or leaving them here. Besides, hillwalking was definitely not his forte. I can assure you he has other things on his mind, and he's too busy pursuing them to think about driving all this way to collect a pair of walking boots."

"I can't just take another man's boots. I—"

"Trust me, Mark won't miss them. Do you want to go hillwalking or not?"

"Yes."

"Well quit arguing, and try the damned things on. Otherwise it'll be midnight before you get out the door!"

Luke pulled on the socks and boots, and took a few tentative steps around the kitchen. "They're actually pretty comfortable. Good ankle supports."

"Right then, you're all set." She pushed the jug of marigolds to one side, spread the map on the table and pointed to a dot. "Here's the croft. You follow this track for about a mile through the trees until it forks. Take the left-hand fork past the ruins and then follow the stalkers' path steadily up toward the top of *Buidhe Bheinn*. It's fairly easy going, just one or two steep sections that you need to take care over. You can get to the top and back in about four hours, so I wouldn't recommend you go that far this late in the day."

Luke squinted at the map. "What are all these squiggly brown lines?"

"They're contour lines. The closer together they are, the steeper the mountain. And these blue lines represent streams or waterfalls." One glance at his face told her she'd lost her audience. "You have seen an Ordnance Survey Map before, haven't you?"

"No. But I'm sure I'll figure it out."

"I'm sorry, but I can't let you go." She folded the map.

"Anna, I'm not stupid." He placed a restraining hand on her arm. "Once I understand what all the symbols mean, it'll be fine."

"Mr Tallantyre..."

His grin flashed briefly. "I've told you, call me Luke."

"Luke. This is how it is. The Scottish mountains are dangerous even in summer. I'd be irresponsible to let you go wandering the hillside when you can't understand the map. And I refuse to be answerable to the mountain rescue service when I have to call them out because you got lost."

"What if I give you my word that I'll only go half way up crag what's-its-name?"

Anna was torn. She knew he'd be a liability out on the hill on his own, but when he gave her his irresistibly devastating grin, she was all but helpless to deny him the pleasure of a walk. Oh, what the hell, she thought, putting the kettle on the hob to boil.

"Let me make you a coffee, and then give me five minutes to change. I'll come with you." Luke started to complain, but she held up a hand. "Look, this is your first time hillwalking in Scotland. It's not like going for a walk in the park or a stroll along the beach. It's essential that you go with someone who knows the terrain, and besides, the dogs need exercising. It doesn't matter to them whether they go along the shore or up the hill."

While he waited for Anna to change, Luke wandered around the room. It was clean and tidy, but lacked modern gadgets. The pale oak units blended perfectly with the beamed ceilings, and polished granite worktops. A small table with two chairs snuggled against the front kitchen window, which looked out over the rocky beach. A cooking range, the likes he'd never seen before, stood in a stone clad alcove, which on closer examination appeared at one time, to have been a huge inglenook fireplace.

Minutes later, Anna padded into the room, wearing faded denim jeans and a T-shirt. She'd braided her hair, and casually thrown a russet-coloured sweater about her shoulders. Luke's gaze was riveted on her face as she sat down at the table, took a mouthful of coffee, then proceeded to pull on her socks and well-worn walking boots.

Chapter Eight

Anna set off at a brisk pace with Luke and the dogs in tow. Every now and again she would shake her head and wave her arms about, as though arguing with some invisible entity. So much for her plans for spending the afternoon writing. The next chapter of her novel was fully mapped out in her mind—all she needed to do was get it down on paper. Instead she'd volunteered to take this handsome stranger up a mountain.

I must be insane, she thought, as she covered the steep, rough ground with the grace of a gazelle. But it wasn't insanity that had made her volunteer. It was pure, unadulterated lust. While there was no denying she found Luke attractive, it was barely a fortnight since she and Mark had split up. She was on the rebound, she reminded herself, but her hormones refused to listen. Whenever Luke was close she found his presence disturbing. But a summer romance? That wasn't her style at all. If, and when she was ready for another relationship, it wouldn't be with a man who'd only be around for a week or two.

Annoyed at the direction her thoughts were taking, she quickened her pace, crossed over a small bridge, and continued along the path as it climbed steadily higher. The two dogs raced ahead stopping now and again to check their mistress was following. They investigated every old rabbit burrow and animal track as if it were some newly discovered treasure. Halfway up the hill they disturbed a grazing ewe, which stamped a foot in anger before darting into the bracken.

"Hey, slow down," Luke gasped, as he reached out and placed a restraining hand on her arm. "We're going for a walk, not a forced march."

Anna turned and smiled. "Sorry, I wasn't thinking. I do this every day. I should have realised you might not be as fit as me."

"It's not a question of fitness. I want to get my bearings. And what's more, I can't very well hold a conversation with you if I'm talking to your back."

Something about the way Luke looked at her jolted her heart, and made her pulse pound. His fingers accidentally brushed her cheek as he tucked a strand of her hair behind her ear. She gasped in delight, as a shiver of awareness rippled through her body in response to his touch. When his eyes dropped to her lips she wondered if he might kiss her—in fact, she rather hoped he would. Confused by her conflicting emotions, she lowered her gaze.

"I didn't mean to be rude; it's just that I don't usually have company when I come up here. Besides, in case you haven't noticed, the path isn't exactly a four lane highway."

"No, but there's room enough for us to walk side-by-side," he said, matching his stride to hers. "Hey, I noticed some ruins along the shoreline as I sailed into the loch," he continued. "Was there an ancient town here or something?"

Anna moistened her dry lips. "Yes, and there were two other villages further along the coast. Sadly, the houses and crofts have long since been abandoned, and the ruins you see today are all that remain."

"What happened?" Luke took her hand, as if it were the most natural thing in the world. She wanted to pull it away. She didn't.

"It's quite an involved story. Are you sure you want to hear it?" Suddenly, her fingers laced with his.

"The sun's shining, the dogs are having fun and I like the company. So if you can spare the time, yes, I'd like to hear the story."

Ambushed by Luke's slow smile, Anna reminded herself she was no longer an eighteen-year-old experiencing the thrill of a first date, but a grown woman. She wasn't going to fall prey to this man's charms. But who was she kidding? She lifted her head and found him watching her.

"You've heard of Bonnie Prince Charlie, and the Jacobite rising of 1745?"

"Nope. Scottish history wasn't covered in school. Wait a minute—I read something about him in a magazine somewhere. Didn't he lose some big battle and then run off to France?"

"That's right. Shortly after that the clans were disarmed and wearing of tartan was banned. Even bagpipes were forbidden."

"No big loss there," Luke said, helping her negotiate a steep, rocky outcrop.

"Thanks." Anna dropped his hand and walked on. "Never let my friend, Morag, hear you say that! Her husband Lachlan plays the pipes, and although she won't let him practise in the house, she won't have a word spoken against them, or his lack of musical ability."

Luke laughed. "I'll try to remember that, when I meet her."

"Ensay! Rhona!" Anna called the dogs as they darted into the gorse after a rabbit. They came panting back into view. "Most of the clan land was given to the English aristocracy, and in the process, tens of thousands of

Highlanders were evicted from their homes to make way for sheep. It's a period in Scottish history known as 'the Clearances'."

"But that doesn't explain the ruins along the shore."

"Actually, it does. You see, after the crofters were driven out from the glens they settled on the poorer, infertile land near the coast, but they still paid rent to the estate owners. As a result, nearly all of them lived in hunger and poverty."

"I can't imagine how anyone could survive under those conditions, especially in winter. Brrrrr!"

"Yes, it must have been horrendous. But that isn't the end of the story. When the potato crop failed, the resulting famine left many families with no choice but to emigrate to the New World or Australia, or move south to the lowlands and England."

"So they just abandoned the crofts?"

"Yes. And it's something that's repeated in the Highlands today. Young folk are leaving for the cities in their hundreds, as there's no work for them here. Many homes in the Highlands are second or holiday homes, only used at weekends."

"Then how come your croft is still here while the others are deserted?"

"Hm. I don't really know the answer to that question."

"It's in a stunning setting, and would make a great painting, but you have to admit it's pretty inaccessible. So it's now just a vacation home?"

Anna smile was tinged with sadness. "Tigh na Cladach was my grandparents' home. They lived here all year round. When my grandfather died, Daddy wanted my grandmother to move to Edinburgh, but she refused and lived at the croft until she moved into a nursing home, a few months before her death. It belongs to me now."

"I see. So you're just here...temporarily."

"No."

"Well, I don't get why anyone would want to live way out here. There's nothing. What do people do at night for fun? And what kind of jobs could there possibly be?"

Anna stopped in midstride and turned to face him. "I have a job, thank you very much. I work in the hotel."

"Yeah? But what happens when the tourists leave? Does the hotel close up? Besides, whatever you do there can't pay very much."

Anna raised a fine, arched eyebrow and yanked her hand free of his. "What is this, a police interrogation?"

He held up his hands in defence. "Hey, I'm just curious, that's all. A pretty lady holed up in some shack—whoops—I mean croft—way out here in the sticks...I don't get it. Are you running away from something? Or somebody? Now that would make sense."

Anna met his accusing eyes without flinching. How dare he question her lifestyle, her character, and above all, her motive for staying in the glen? She was even more annoyed with herself for allowing him to goad her.

"Do you think I'm some sort of criminal? Because if you do, I've a good mind to leave you here and let you find your own way!" She stomped off up the path.

Luke caught up with her. "Whoa, whoa, easy there, girl. I got way out of line. I don't why, but I just got sorta...I don't know...concerned about you being out here on your own."

Anna took a steadying breath. "I don't understand why you feel the need to be concerned for my welfare. I'm quite capable of looking after myself. I've been coming here for years. I know these hills intimately. Come on. There's a stunning view of the islands a little further on."

Without waiting to see if he was following, she turned and walked on until she reached the viewpoint. She sat down with her back to a large rough granite boulder, and drank in the view she'd loved since childhood. Ensay and Rhona lay panting at her feet.

Shaking her hair free from its braid, she allowed it to tumble down her back. She closed her eyes, and wondered why she felt so short-tempered, tired and unhappy. Perhaps coming to the croft hadn't been such a good idea after all. Her break up with Mark, the continued lack of sleep, the unexpected letter from the solicitor, and now Luke's odd behaviour had just about ruined her visit. She wasn't sure how much more she could take.

Luke sat down next to her, his thigh warm and hard against hers. Every breath she drew in smelt of citrus and sandalwood, and something indefinably male. She opened her eyes to see him watching her. Sighing, she smiled with no trace of her former animosity.

"Sorry. I didn't get much sleep last night. I'm a bit touchy when strangers start asking me about my life."

"That's okay. I understand. We all have bad days. As for strangers, I thought we were past introductions." His husky voice held a faint challenge. His gaze travelled over her face, and searched her eyes.

"Well...I..."

"I'll take that as a 'yes' then. Do you have a boyfriend, a significant other?"

Heat burned her cheeks. She gave him a chilling look. "I'd prefer not to answer that right now, if you don't mind."

"I've overstepped my bounds, have I?"

"By a foot or two."

"Any way to back out of this gracefully?"

"Not in the slightest," she grinned, forgiving his faux pas. "That's the Isle of Skye—the Misty Isle, as it's sometimes called," she said pointing to the islands in the distance. "And the jagged mountains you see are the famous Cuillin."

"Wow!" His tawny brown eyes crinkled at the corners. "What a view. It must be even more spectacular at sunrise or sunset. How far are we from the top?"

"It's another thousand feet to the summit. I often come up here to watch the sunset. Under the right conditions it can be quite spectacular. But I like it best after a storm, when the sky is still dark and moody, yet the visibility can be as good as it is today."

"It's like that on the Cape. My studio faces the ocean. The light after a storm is amazing, but hard to capture on canvas. I should have brought my sketchbook. This would make a great watercolour. Do you get many days like this?"

"Yes, although you never can predict a Scottish summer. Do you paint often?"

Luke's smile deepened into laughter. "Now who's asking questions?"

Anna felt herself flush. "You don't have to answer if you don't want to."

"I'll answer your question. I'm an artist. I paint for a living."

Anna's eyes widened in surprise. "Really? When you first appeared at my door, I had you down as some sort of rich company executive playing with one of his toys. From what I understand, yachting is a very expensive hobby. Look, I didn't mean to imply...your financial status is none of my business," she said colouring fiercely. "Oh dear, that didn't come out right at all. What exactly do you paint?"

"Mainly land and seascapes. I've had some showings in New York and Boston. So, yes, I've been pretty successful—so far. But tastes change, and what's considered hot today might be considered not-so-hot tomorrow."

"Would I recognise your work?" Her mind rolled back to a Saturday afternoon when she and Mark visited art exhibitions and museums. "That didn't come out right either. Are your paintings hung in any of the galleries over here...perhaps in Edinburgh?"

"Not that I know of, although six months ago I did get commissioned by a Boston lawyer who eventually moved to London."

"I'm impressed. So why did you stop painting?"

Luke sighed, his eyes fixed on something at the far edge of the sea. "My work lost its edge. I feel like I'm churning out the same painting over and over again. I was having lunch with this client when it finally hit me that I needed to get away—that maybe that would fix things. I drove home, stocked the yacht, and sailed up the coast to Maine."

Anna's mouth twitched in amusement. "What did you do, take a wrong turn?"

He threw back his head and laughed. "No. And despite what you might think, I really can read a chart."

She tucked a lock of hair behind her ear. "What's it like to sail single-handed? It can't be easy."

"It's damned hard work. Not to mention lonely and sometimes scary. One night there was a particularly bad storm; the waves were huge, at least twenty feet high. Sandpiper was pitching and yawing so much I thought she'd capsize. I started to wonder if I was up to the task. I even thought about turning back, but I guess I was just too stubborn to give in."

"I've seen hints of stubbornness in you a couple of times. But keep talking. What is it about sailing that draws you? What started it all?"

"I crewed for a friend once. He entered his yacht in the America's Cup. There were twelve of us onboard, working the winches."

"Did you win?"

"No. We finished. Alive. That was all that mattered. You know I thought that was the hardest thing I've ever done, up until this trip. I had nightmares about running into another vessel in the dark, especially in high seas. Or worse, that I'd end up like Jonah in the belly of some God forsaken whale."

Anna chuckled. "But you didn't."

He smiled. "No, thank God."

"How do you manage to sleep?"

"I slept an hour or so at a time. The yacht has the latest navigational aids and an auto-pilot—when it works—which allows you to take cat-naps."

"An artist. A yachtsman. You're a regular Renaissance man, aren't you?"

"I wouldn't go that far, but I do a lot of different things."

"Why come to Scotland?"

"Funny story. I was originally going to sail up the up the coast to Nova Scotia."

"So why didn't you?"

"I took a break in Bar Harbor. I found this little oil painting—a landscape. This is going to sound really stupid—but something about it just plain fascinated me. I asked the owner about the artist, but all he knew was that it came from an old lady whose family came to America from Scotland sometime in the 1800s. I bought it and hung it in my cabin. I couldn't get the image out of my mind. The following morning I set sail, and the next thing I knew, I was headed east across the Atlantic. Does that sound romantic and foolish or more like a load of bullshit?"

"Definitely the latter. Morag would have great fun talking to you!"

Luke studied her face. "Is she a psychologist?"

Anna laughed so hard tears ran down her cheeks. She pulled her handkerchief from her jean's pocket and wiped her eyes.

"No, no, not at all. Morag is a...a strong believer in Highland folklore. She says she's got the Sight."

"What's that? Some kind of night vision or something?"

Anna suppressed another giggle. "No, no. Physically, she can't see any better than you or me. She thinks she's a kind of... psychic. She'd say that your actions were predestined—that your ancestors had decreed that you would find the painting at that particular moment in time, or some other such mumbo-jumbo."

"And you don't believe in that stuff?"

"No way! Very few modern Scots do."

He raised an eyebrow. "What about providence? Do you believe in that?"

"In what context?"

"Oh, I don't know. Do you think you and I were destined to meet?"

Anna thought for a moment, and shook her head. "No. There's a perfectly reasonable explanation for us meeting. You sailed into the loch because your yacht had a problem. You needed to use a phone, saw the croft and knocked at my door. It's nothing more complicated than that."

"What if I said I wasn't so sure? I don't deny the auto-pilot is pretty messed up. But that happened after I left Stornaway. I could have turned back, but I didn't do that. I sailed south until I ended up in Loch Hourn. Why? And what made me drop anchor here, when I could have limped along to another harbour?"

"I don't know. I'm not clairvoyant."

"Personally, I think it was fate."

"You don't really believe that, do you?"

He didn't answer. His tawny brown eyes held hers.

"Oh, my God, you do! Remind me never to put you and Morag in a room together, you'd spend all night telling each other that the Loch Ness Monster really does exist and that its cousin lives in Lake Erie!"

Luke stood and offered his hand. He pulled her to her feet, but his hands took on a will of their own and slipped up her arms, drawing her closer. When he cupped her chin tenderly in his right hand and his mouth covered hers, Anna found herself powerless to resist, and her instinctive response to him was unlike anything she had experienced before. His kiss was slow, thoughtful, and as tender as the breeze.

Before she realised it, she was kissing him back with a hunger she didn't know she possessed. Within the space of a second, their kiss had gone from simple contact to raw passion. Instinctively, her arms went round his neck, her fingers burying in his think black hair. Currents of desire swept through her, filling her with an inner excitement.

Then her brain kicked in. She jumped backwards, pushing him away, too stunned to speak. This was wrong, all wrong. It was too soon. She wasn't ready for another relationship, let alone one with someone who wouldn't be around for more than a week or two.

Luke cleared his throat. "I'm sorry. Wow... I don't know what made me do that. I'm sorry I let you kiss me."

Flustered, Anna's temper flared. "What? *You* kissed *me*!"

"Well, maybe I did, but you kissed me right back," he insisted. "I don't normally go around kissing girls I don't know, especially one who isn't much more than a teenager."

"Teenager? I'm thirty-two; you can hardly call me a teenager. Please don't try and tell me that it was destined because I won't believe a word of it."

He rubbed his forehead with both hands. "Somehow I'd figured you were younger. Besides, I'm far too old to be behaving like an adolescent. Look, this conversation is getting weird very fast. I'm sorry. With you, I'm always sorry. I don't know why, but maybe that means something too. Once the part gets here, I'll split. You won't be bothered with me anymore."

Her anger evaporated into embarrassment. "There's no need to explain. I made a mistake too. It was just a kiss. It meant nothing. Let's just drop it and go. The dogs are getting restless, and I have still have chores to do." With that, she straightened her shoulders, called Ensay and Rhona, and set off back down the path towards the croft.

She took a deep breath. What was wrong with her? She was a grown woman for goodness sake. She'd been kissed before, and not acted all prissy. It wasn't as if they'd made passionate love in the heather. It was just a kiss—but a kiss so intense it sent her hormones into overdrive! So, she found Luke attractive, but it was more than physical attraction; a tangible bond was forming between them. She took another steadying breath and tried to regain her equilibrium.

"Anna! Wait! I acted like a jerk and I've taken up most of your afternoon. I really don't know what made me do that and I apologise. I mean it, really."

She stopped and turned around. "I overreacted too. Anyway, as it's not likely to happen again, it's no big deal."

"You sure you're not mad at me?"

"I am. I have a strong feeling you have someone back home."

"I do—well sort of. Anna, she's just someone I see sometimes. We aren't a regular 'thing'."

"How romantic, I'm glad I'm not a regular 'thing' with you. Now, if you don't mind, I think we should go back."

The crack of a gunshot bounced off the hill side.

Anna screamed.

A brace of grouse called loudly and took to the air.

Luke pulled her into the bushes, and covered her body with his. "Keep your head down!" he hissed. "I thought you said the stag hunting season didn't start until July?"

"It doesn't." Anna whispered, all too conscious of the weight of Luke's body where it touched hers. She squirmed and wriggled against him, trying to get free, finding the contact too intimate.

"Then why in Hell's name is someone using us as target practice? And for God's sake keep still!"

"I don't know. It was probably an accident. They were most likely aiming at something else. I'm more concerned about Ensay and Rhona. They hate loud noises."

"Yeah? Well, I'm not too fond of being shot at either! Any fool knows you don't fire a rifle without checking to see if someone is in your line of fire!"

Anna studied Luke's face as he scanned the hillside. Suddenly, he seemed to know an awful lot about guns.

"Luke, I—"

He shifted his weight slightly, and held up a hand to silence her. "Shush! On a day like this, the slightest sound can carry a long way."

Anna did as she was told, but apart from the leaves rustling in the breeze, the only other sound she could hear was that of their breathing.

After five minutes of lying in the heather, Luke pulled her to her feet. "Come on. I think he left. Let's go and find those precious dogs of yours."

They rejoined the path and had only gone a little way when they found the prone body of one of the collies.

Anna screamed with all her might and dropped to her knees beside the dog, gently stroking its head and sobbing. "Oh, Ensay! What have they done to you?"

Trembling, the dog raised its head and wagged her tail in response.

Luke leant down next to her and ran his hands over the dog's sleek coat. When they came away clean, he examined the dog's legs to ensure none were broken.

"Anna," he said softly. "Look, there isn't any blood. She hasn't been shot. She's fine. She's just winded and pretty scared. Give her a few minutes to get her breath back, okay?"

Anna bit back her tears, and stared at his hands in disbelief. "Thank God. I hate to think of any animal in pain...but one of my dogs..."

"I know, honey, they mean the world to you." His hand closed over hers. "Don't think about it. Be grateful that jackass missed."

Anna nodded woodenly. She fished in her pocket for her handkerchief, and blew her nose.

"You're right, I should be grateful. Everyone, including the ghillie on Killilan estate, knows I will not tolerate hunting of any description on Tigh na Cladach land!"

"Maybe one of the village kids is out taking a pot shot at a rabbit," he said. "Maybe he just didn't account for the recoil."

Her disbelief showed in the tone of her voice. "I haven't seen one rabbit, deer, or fox, since we left the house. Have you?"

He put a hand her shoulder, and turned her round to face him. He felt her body sag in defeat. Slowly her tears began to fall.

"Anna, stop. I know you're upset, but nothing happened. Really. So, shush." He gathered into his arms, and held her snugly. "The dog is fine now, and I'm sure other one...Rhona, right? I'm sure she's waiting for you at home," he whispered against her ear. Reluctantly, he held her at arm's length. "Come on, let's take Ensay back to the croft and let her rest. I don't know how to make tea the Scottish way, but I'll try. And if you're still worried about Ensay, I'll drive you to the nearest vet to get her checked out."

She wiped away a tear and regarded him for a moment. "You—drive me? On the wrong side of the road?"

"Well, I can try. And think of it this way. If I have a fender bender in that old rust bucket you call a Land Rover, who the hell with ever be able to tell?"

Chapter Nine

Luke made sure Anna and the dogs were safely settled in the croft before he left. Once out of sight of the house, he took the path up the hill rather than returning to Sandpiper. Despite what he told her about the shooting incident being an accident, he didn't like the fact that some jerk who couldn't shoot worth a damn was roaming the hills with a loaded shotgun.

He trudged on until he reached the point where he thought he and Anna had been standing, and tried to work out the direction the shot had come from. The sun had been on his right, so he knew he'd been facing south-west. He reckoned that whoever had fired the gun had been standing more than thirty or forty yards away. The problem was, there were so many boulders and short stubby bushes littering the hillside that it was difficult to be sure which clump they'd sheltered in.

He walked up and down, examining the view from every angle, until he was certain he was in the right spot. He dropped to his knees and slowly inched forward, searching every clump of heather, every thicket of bracken with his fingertips.

For a moment, his attention shifted to Kate. He hadn't called her since he left; she probably thought he died at sea. She might not even be there. If she could find some place to surf or buy designer shoes, she could easily forget all about him for weeks at a time. Before he left, he wondered if he'd been in love with her. Then he met the redhead.

Keep checking the ground. Got to keep checking...

His fingers wrapped around a spent brass shell. Then another.

So the jerk had been using a rifle.

Sitting back on his heels, he tossed the shells up and down in his hand. He didn't need a ballistics expert to tell him the make, he recognised them instantly. *Lynx Game King.* Originally made for shooting gazelles and deer, they were mainly sold in Africa. He hadn't seen that make in years, not since...he shuddered; the shells were powerful enough to bring down a large animal. In the wrong hands it could easily maim or kill a man, or a woman. But how in God's name had someone in Scotland managed to get their hands on that particular brand?

Any good sportsman always made sure he took away the ejected shells. The moron was careless or a rank amateur, or...something darker. Luke closed his eyes and remembered the time he and his partner had cornered a guy suspected of counterfeiting. He'd been holed up in his granddaddy's shack in the wilds of Kentucky and had taken pot shots at them with a twelve bore. He'd kept Luke and his partner pinned down for the best part of an hour, before finally running out of shells, and giving himself up.

Luke shook his head. He didn't like the direction his thoughts were taking. He stood, and pocketed the shells. One thing was certain, when he caught up with the owner of the cartridges, he wouldn't be polite when he asked his questions.

While Luke scoured the hillside, Anna put a match to the fire in the sitting room, and sat on the floor next to Ensay, stroking the black and white head. Every now and again the dog whimpered, its body trembling under her hand. She swore silently. Thank God Luke had been with her, because she'd never have coped if Ensay had been injured. How could anyone hurt such a loving creature? Despite what he'd said, there was no way she was going to let the incident go. She'd find out who was responsible and see them punished. As the dog drifted off into a fitful sleep, Anna eased her hand away and tiptoed into the kitchen.

She listened to the news on the old radio, and sat down at the table with a cup of coffee. The events of the afternoon would have to find some other place to go. She banished them from her thoughts, opened her laptop and concentrated on the next chapter.

Two days after the stranger's visit, Coll, my youngest brother, came to me with a message from our mother—I was to return home immediately. When I entered the croft, mother greeted me with tears in her eyes. Fear gripped me. I felt the 'Sight,' my future suddenly vague and shadowy. I stared into her dark, unfathomable eyes, but saw nothing except emptiness and pain. She wrapped her arms around me and stroked my hair, as she had often done when I was a small child. I was told to bathe, put on the clothes she'd laid out on the box bed. I looked at mother questioningly. Where had such finery come from? She did not answer, but merely handed me a small cup of uisage beatha—the water of life, or whisky as the Sassenachs call it. It made my eyes water, burnt my throat, and put fire in my belly, but I felt stronger for it.

Then, in an instant, I knew. This was something to do with the stranger's visit and the evictions—the violence and cruelty—that was clearing folk from their homes in the glens to make way for sheep. My mother recognised my understanding and nodded. The sadness I saw in her eyes was beyond my comprehension.

I knew if I disobeyed, the fate that had befallen other families would be ours too. With a heavy heart, I bathed and washed my hair. When it was dry, mother braided and pinned it into a coil at the nape of my neck. The clothes were new, fine lawn under-garments, and a corset, the first I had worn. When tightly laced, it pulled at my waist, making it difficult for me to breathe. But when I begged to take it off, mother refused, saying it was necessary. My breasts were barely contained by the stiff fabric, and rose and fell with every breath I took. I felt myself blushing at their exposure, and wrapped my arms around my chest to cover my embarrassment.

Finally mother helped me put on the riding habit. It was similar to those I'd seen worn by the Laird's daughter. The skirt was full, the jade green velvet falling in heavy folds at my feet. The narrow waist and tight bodice, with its tiny pearl buttons, would not have fastened but for the corset. The neck was low cut and trimmed with delicate lace, the sleeves long, tapered at my wrist and fastened with pearl buttons, like those on the bodice. I felt strangely excited, yet vulnerable. My breath came in shallow, quick gasps, a shiver of panic knotting my stomach.

There came a quiet cough at the door, and then my father entered. He nodded his head in approval when he saw me, and took my hands in his, kissed them, and gave me his blessing. A tense silence enveloped us. Minutes later the door opened and the man who'd visited my parents but two days earlier entered. My small hand was placed in his, and the ferocity of the passion I observed in his eyes made me shake, as fearful images built in my mind.

Anna stretched and rolled her shoulders, trying to ease the knot that had settled there. She studied the screen. It had taken her two hours to write three pages. If this had been a student's work, she would have said it was stilted and forced. But she was no longer a student, and knew she could do better.

Her determination to make it as a writer faltered. Perhaps Mark had been right all along and she should have stuck to teaching. But the mere thought of him made her defiant. She'd finish her book and sell her novel if only to prove him wrong.

She highlighted an offending section, hit the delete button, and watched the words vanish into the ether. She tried to re-draft the paragraph, but it was no use, the words had gone.

What was the matter with her? She'd planned this chapter for days. She even had pages of notes filled with snippets of dialogue, yet the words refused to flow. She didn't have writers' block, but something was stifling her progress, and that something was six feet of dark-haired, brown-eyed American male.

Chastising herself, she saved the file and switched off the laptop. There was no point in trying to write, not when she couldn't concentrate. She glanced at her watch, seven in the evening, still early enough to drive to Morag's house, but somehow listening to her friend drone on about Lachlan or have questions asked about Luke, held no appeal. Worse still, she feared what she'd say if Morag asked how the book was going.

Anna selected a CD from the rack in the sitting room, slotted it into the player, and turned up the volume. The sound of a jazz guitar filled the air. She settled back into the cushions of the sofa, but was startled by a knock at the door. Her heart hammered in her chest as she felt her nerves tense. She wasn't expecting visitors. She went into the hall, but didn't open the door.

"Who is it?" she called.

"Luke Tallantyre. Remember me? The brilliant sailor who can't get out of the Loch?"

She drew back the bolt, opened the door, and offered him a welcoming smile.

He held out a carrier bag and grinned broadly. "Hey. Had dinner yet?"

"No, I haven't eaten since I had a salad sandwich at work. Why?"

"Do you like sea trout?"

"Do mice like cheese?"

He grinned and reached into the bag and pulled out two fish. "I guess that means yes. I caught these two beauties this morning. I thought I'd cook you dinner. What do you say?"

Anna hesitated, but his smile had a way of making her forget she didn't really want him here. "It's very kind of you, but really, there's no need."

"Look, I know I've been a general pain in the butt, but after all the excitement this afternoon, I wanted to make sure you and the dogs were all right."

"I'm fine. Ensay and Rhona are asleep on the rug in front of the fire." She paused for a moment. "Do...do you think this afternoon was just an accident?"

"Yes," he said smoothly. "Now, are we going to stand here until these fish rot, or can I come in and make the best dinner you've had in years?"

Anna stepped aside to let him pass. "The kitchen is to the left, but you already know that. Is there anything I can do to help?"

"Yeah, you can tell me where you keep the frying pan. And you could make a salad. You got any bread? Oh, and how about a lemon?"

"Coming right up. Would you like some wine to go with the fish?" she asked, as she passed him the skillet.

"Sure, why not? Wait a minute; I think I recognise this CD. Is that Chris Camozzi?"

"Mm. It's his 'Windows of the Soul' album. Do you like jazz guitar?"

"Yeah, and sax. I like classical too, and opera, but only in small doses."

"Something we have in common, then." She leaned against the dresser and watched as he squeezed the lemon and added seasoning to the fish in the pan. He looked at ease in the kitchen, and she wondered why that woman back home hadn't taken off his shoes and socks, and chained him to her stove. But then again, they weren't a 'thing,' were they? That opened up a world of possibilities.

"Ensay and Rhona, are pretty unusual names for dogs." He said, breaking into her thoughts. "How did you come up with them?"

Anna hadn't been paying attention. She blinked and tried to recall what he'd said. When she couldn't, she pulled open the cutlery drawer and started to lay the table, in an effort to hide her embarrassment at being caught daydreaming.

He winked at her. "You were a thousand miles away. What were you thinking about?"

"Nothing important. You were saying?"

"Ensay and Rhona... not the usual names people give their dogs..."

"They are out here. Sandy, the ghillie on Killilan Estate who gave them to me, named them after Hebridean Islands."

"How do you tell them apart? They look the same to me."

"That's easy. Ensay is slightly shorter, and has black spots on her white front legs. She would play fetch all day long, given the chance, whereas Rhona's legs are black. She'll herd anything that walks by—hens, goats, sheep, children, even the odd stray yachtsman. Anyway, I'm sure you didn't come here to talk about my dogs."

"No, but I'd like it better if I didn't make you nervous."

Anna lost her grip on a plate. It clattered onto the table. "I beg your pardon?"

"You see what just happened? I do something that shakes you up."

"You do not!"

"I do, and I'd like you to feel more comfortable. Just think of me as a neighbour."

Comfortable? Slippers are comfortable, thought Anna. Being around this man was anything but. As casually as she could manage, she asked, "Why?"

"Because I'll be stuck here for a while. Accept it. It can't hurt us to become friends."

She put the salad bowl on the table. "No, I suppose not."

"How about if we start over?" He took his place at the table and poured her a glass of wine.

Anna scooped up a forkful of fish and thought about her answer. Friendship? She could handle that, couldn't she? She was an adult, after all. Men and women worked together all the time; being neighbourly was no different. It wasn't as if he was asking her to leap into bed with him. Yet she felt uneasy, and found his presence in the small room disturbing. There was no denying she was attracted to him, but it went deeper. Much deeper. Every time he looked at her she felt a frisson of desire. Dropping her guard and trusting this man would be stupid, wouldn't it?

"I'll even take you sailing on the yacht." He offered, turning his smile up a notch. "Please don't say no."

"There's no need for bribery."

"No, but its working, isn't it?" He let out a peal of laughter.

In spite of her doubts, Anna chuckled and clinked her glass against his. "Here's to friendship."

"Good. Now that we've drawn a truce, what do you want to talk about?"

She pushed the food around her plate while she thought about her answer. "Let's see... is this your first visit to Scotland?"

"Yeah. And I like what I've seen of it, so far." He gave her a killer smile, leaving her in no doubt that he wasn't only referring to the scenery.

Anna finished the last of her wine.

"Can I refill your glass?"

She shook her head. "No thanks. I'd better not. I have to be up early in the morning. So what happens when the part for the auto-pilot arrives? Will you stay in the UK a while longer or sail home right away?"

"I'm not sure. I'd like to see more of your country, but I guess I should head back to Boston. I've been away for nearly two months. For a working artist, that's half a lifetime."

"And there's your lady friend. You must miss her, of course."

He narrowed his eyes. "Now, Anna. I told you it's not serious. Actually, I thought it was going to be serious, but I was wrong. I'm not good about judging those kind of things."

"Things being...?"

"Relationships."

"I see." She looked down at her plate. "I was about to tell you there's a lot more to Scotland, than Loch Hourn. You could always see about hiring a car from the garage in the village and do some exploring. Perthshire is very beautiful, then there's Edinburgh, and of course, every tourist has to see Loch Ness."

"Mm. I might do that if I have to wait any longer for the part." He rose from his chair. "Well, well, will you look at the time? If you have to get up early I'd better say goodnight."

"Are you sure? You're welcome to stay for coffee."

"Thanks, but no. There are a couple of things I need to check before I turn in for the evening." He walked into the hallway, and paused by the door. "Thanks for dinner. I enjoyed it."

"I should be thanking you. You cooked it."

"No problem. It was worth it for the company."

They stood for a long moment. Then he caught her hands, backed her against the wall, and kissed her hard. Her hands went to his shoulders, but instead of pushing him away, they locked round his neck. A moan escaped her lips.

He let her go and stepped back. "For the first time since I met you," he said, "I'm not going to apologise."

By the time she regained her breath, he was out the door, whistling into the night.

Chapter Ten

A fine mist hung in the air as Anna drove the twelve miles down the glen to the village. It was the evening of the tenant's meeting, and although she hadn't been invited, she'd decided to attend. Any plans Alistair had for the estate could easily affect her.

The car park adjacent to the village hall was packed with vehicles of all shapes and sizes, including, Anna noted, a tractor. Rather than struggle to find a space, she left her Land Rover outside Mrs McCloud's shop and walked the short distance back to the hall.

Leaving her umbrella in the porch, she eased open the huge wooden door, and slipped inside. About seventy people were crowded into the low-raftered building. Any gathering in the glen was always well attended as it was a change from routine, and every crofter and tenant made the most of it.

Just inside the door, a group of older women were busily handing out cups of tea and biscuits. Anna took the proffered cup, but declined the shortbread biscuit, and went in search of a seat. But every chair was taken, and rather than look for Morag, who she knew would be seated at the front somewhere near the stage, Anna leaned against the rear wall for support. At least she could slip away unnoticed if the meeting became too heated or protracted.

Alistair Grant sat at a table in the centre of the stage. Dressed in tweeds, chequered shirt and yellow waistcoat, he looked very much the part of Laird. A thin, bald-headed man, whom Anna did not recognise, sat on his left. Reverend Cameron, the local minister, sat on his right.

The sound of voices filled the air as people settled themselves in their seats. Anna could hear snatches of conversation, but as some of it was in Gaelic, she could only guess at what was being said.

The bald man stood, banged his fist on the table, and called the meeting to order. "Quiet! Quiet, please!" he shouted. "Let the Laird speak!"

A hush went round the room.

Alistair cleared his throat and got to his feet. "Thank you for coming here this evening, ladies and gentlemen. I shall try to be brief. As you know, my father is no longer able to perform his duties as laird, and as his only son, that task now falls to me. Sadly, as a result of his illness, the management of the estate has not been what it should be. I plan to rectify that."

"Aye, the old Laird was a good man," shouted MacIver, the estate carpenter.

"He was," added Mrs McCloud, adjusting her hat. "We'll not see his like again!"

Alistair nodded in acknowledgement. "In the past, Killilan Estate was one of, if not the finest, sporting estate on the west coast of Scotland. Under my management it will become so again. However, there will have to be changes. I've already spoken to Ewan about opening the hotel all year round. I plan to turn the dowager house into an adventure centre, offering among other things, mountaineering holidays for school children."

"Is that so?" called a sour voice from the back of the hall. "Ye'll get all the money and we'll get all the hooligans. None of us will be safe in our beds!"

"Hush your noise, Malcolm Fraser. You can talk! Weren't your twins a right pair of scallywags, always causing havoc in the village when they were young? Why, I boxed their ears more than once."

"Aye, that you did Morag McInnes. And I'm grateful to you. No doubt the experience you gained will stand you in good stead when the Laird opens his doors to these delinquents!"

The gathered throng erupted into laughter. Alistair held up his hand for silence.

"I shall also be working closely with the Highland Council to see what businesses we can attract to the area. There are grants available from both the English Government and European Union which will assist us in making this village the thriving community it once was. I assure you these changes will benefit you all." He waved a bunch of papers in the air.

"What businesses?" Mrs McCloud shouted. "I don't want some foreigner coming in and stealing my trade and profit. There's no room for another shop, I'm telling you."

Muted protestations from all around the hall rose to a small uproar.

Alistair thought quickly. "I wasn't talking about another shop, Mrs McCloud. I was thinking in terms of something more enterprising and productive."

Morag got to her feet. "Such as what, Mr Alistair?"

"Well—there's forestry. In the past, my father limited the amount of land put into forestry. That could be extended. Timber products, such as wood floors, are in great demand. I don't see why the estate couldn't produce these. The women could start a weaving enterprise, and we could develop the loch...for...for...salmon farming. Many communities such as ours have profitable salmon farms."

A ruddy young man Anna recognised by sight, but not by name, leapt up in protest. "That's as may be. But the market is awash with farmed salmon. And then there's the problem with sea lice infestation. The papers are full of articles about farms having to destroy their stock. Besides, fish farms only employ two or three men at most. What about the rest of us?"

"Hear, hear!" yelled MacIver.

Anna was about to point out that the estate didn't own the loch or the land around it when Charles Downie, one of the tenant sheep farmers, spoke.

"Get away with you, man. We don't want folk coming in and spoiling the glen. Think of all the extra traffic through the village. And who would pay to improve the road? Not the estate, that's for sure. That would be the responsibility of the local council, which would mean higher taxes for us all. It's not fair Mr Alistair, and we want none of your grand plans. Go back to France and let us be!"

Angus Murray, the owner of the garage, stood, and pointed at the man standing next to Anna. "Hold your tongue man! It will be your turn to speak once the Laird has finished telling us his plans. Have the grace to listen to what he says."

A murmur of voices went round the hall. Alistair banged his hand on the table.

"If I may be allowed to continue," he shouted above the noise. "I also plan to increase the number of shooting parties on the estate, both for stags and game birds. That will not only bring more trade for the hotel, it will also bring further employment opportunities for the rest of you, at least during the shooting season. I've only mentioned a few of the possibilities, all of which will improve your standard of living and breathe new life into the glen."

Anna felt a reluctant approval for Alistair. His voice had depth and authority. He was calm, articulate, but more importantly, was prepared to dispel his tenant's reservations. She thought about leaving, but he started speaking once more.

"However, unless the estate can be put back into profit, I'll have no choice but to make some of my employees redundant, and possibly even consider selling some of the cottages. The estate will not, and cannot afford to continue as it did under my father's control." He sat down and took a sip of water from the glass in front of him.

Old Dougal stood and took off his cap. "With respect, Mr Alistair, do I understand you to say that the estate has financial difficulties? If so, how to you propose to pay for all these changes?"

Alistair flinched. "The financial stability of the estate has nothing to do with my proposals. I am, however, proposing a rent increase of ten percent to take effect immediately."

The room erupted. Mrs McPherson looked ready to faint. Old Dougal fanned her with his cap. "But, our rents were increased only six months ago...," a grudging voice barked from the middle of the room.

"Your father would not be doing that," shouted Fraser. "He'd find another way."

"The only person, who benefits from these wild plans, is you Alistair Grant! Not us!" Morag screamed, pointing an accusing finger.

The Reverend Cameron stood. "Quiet, please. Mr Alistair, would you care to respond to the allegation?"

Alistair ran a hand through his hair. "The truth of the matter is that my father let things slip. The nature of his illness is such that, most the time he is unaware of what he is doing. I know for a fact that until six months ago, there had been no rent increase for five years. I'm assured by my factor," Alistair nodded to the little man on his right, "that the new rent proposed for the crofts and cottages are still well below the market value."

"Aye, but we only have your word for that!" they shouted as one.

Alistair held up both his hands. He shouted over the protests. "If...if you are unhappy with the increases, there is provision in your leases for arbitration. But be warned. If you decided to invoke that clause, and the rent on your property is subsequently found to be less than it should be, then the estate not only has the right to charge the correct amount, but also for any costs incurred in the arbitration hearing."

"Well, I'll no pay you anymore," a woman near the front yelled.

Alistair stared at the woman. "Mrs Stewart, isn't it?"

She nodded, grey curls bouncing in anger. "Aye. I've lived on Killilan Estate since you were in nappies, and like many other folk here tonight, I've only my pension to live on since my man died. Hamish worked for your family all his life. Your father and his father before him always looked after the folk who served him, unlike you, you...upstart...with your extravagant ways and expensive tastes!"

Alistair rested his hands on the table and glared at the woman. "That's not quite true, is it, Mrs Stewart? You're forgetting the estate provides you with all your winter fuel free of charge."

"A few loads of logs and a bag of peat! How generous you are, Alistair Grant! I'm telling you, if you put the rent up again, your tenants will not stand for it. They will move elsewhere. The village will become deserted like others in the Highlands. Then what will you do with your fancy plans?"

Exasperated, Alistair sat down. His factor shouted over the heads of the villagers in an attempt to regain control of the meeting, but it was pointless. Annoyed that the meeting had fallen into bedlam, Alistair stood. Accompanied by his factor, he climbed down off the stage, and left the hall.

Anna slipped out of the door. She'd heard enough. The villagers would stay and argue for hours. Alistair might think he could develop the estate, but without considerable aid, and the approval of the local council, his plans were likely nothing more than empty dreams.

She was about to unlock the Land Rover when someone took her arm and spun her round.

"Oh, Alistair, you surprised me."

"I thought I saw you at the meeting," he said, smiling.

Her cheeks burned. "I know I'm not a tenant, but I didn't think you would object if I attended the meeting, seeing as Tigh na Cladach shares a boundary with the estate. Any plans you have might affect my land."

"Why should I object? You're as much a part of this community as everyone else. Look, why don't you come across to the hotel and have a drink with me, and you can tell me how you thought the meeting went."

She hesitated. "I should be getting back, but...all right. Just a quick one mind, since I'm driving."

Alistair touched her elbow, urging yet protective. "Come on; if we hurry, we can get there before everyone else." They turned and walked the short distance to the hotel entrance.

"There's a table in the corner free. Go and sit down and I'll bring the drinks over. What would you like?"

"A glass of white wine, please."

While Anna waited for her drink she looked around the crowded bar. Malcolm Fraser and Charles Downie sat at a table opposite, their heads bent together, no doubt discussing Alistair's plans.

And then she saw him, the mysterious guest from room thirteen. His hooded eyes studied her with a curious intensity as he perched at the end of the bar. Anna shuddered involuntarily. Relief washed over her a second later when

Alistair returned with two glasses. He placed one on the table in front of her.

"Thank you." She struggled to focus on him. Do not look at the ugly man, she told herself. Even though he's looking at you. Don't turn around.

"Are you all right?" Alistair asked.

"Yes, of course. But the tenants don't seem very happy about your plans, Alistair."

"No. But then I expected some resistance. Things have changed since my father inherited the estate. Sheep farming and forestry no longer bring in the income they once did. The estate needs to diversify, Anna, if it's going to survive for another fifty years."

"I understand that. But do you really think turning the Dowager House into an adventure school for children is a good idea?"

"Perhaps not. But most estates have other sources of income."

"You will need specialist staff, and that means there won't be many well-paid jobs for the villagers." Anna watched a frown settle into his features.

"These were only suggestions, Anna. I'm still discussing my options with the accountants and solicitors. I just wanted the tenants to understand that they can't expect things to remain the same now that I'm in charge."

Anna rested a hand on his arm. "I see that, Alistair, but you have to admit that two rent rises in six months is a bit unfair. This isn't Mayfair, you know." She forced a smile.

"I appreciate what you're saying. Father just didn't keep up the land." He held up his hand when she tried to interrupt. "I know that isn't entirely his fault, and that I should have shown more interest, but there's no getting away from the fact that the tenant's have had an easy time of it for the last few years."

Anna picked up her glass and played with the stem. She felt irked by his cool, aloof manner in dealing with such an emotive subject, and could understand Morag's and the other tenants' hostility to his proposed changes.

"I know it's none of my business, but will you take some advice?"

"I'm always happy to listen to you, Anna dear."

"In that case, Alistair, don't rush into making changes without considering all of your options. Whatever you decide will affect everyone in the glen. You could try to involve as many people as possible before committing yourself to one scheme or another. Otherwise you could find yourself fighting the very people you need to implement them."

His patrician features stiffened. "Anna, I own the estate and what I do with it is my decision."

"You may own the land, Alistair, but without the hard work of the people of this glen, the estate would be worthless. I'm telling you, if you don't consider their needs alongside those of the estate, you might as well move back to France now." She swallowed the last of her wine. "Thanks for the drink. I'll see you around."

As she left the bar, she felt the ice-coloured eyes watching her.

She dashed into the car park, praying all the while that the stranger at the bar wasn't following her.

She allowed herself one last look. There was no one around.

At least not now.

Chapter Eleven

By the time Anna left the hotel, the early evening mist had turned into damp, patchy fog. The white sea-cloud floated through the village like a ghostly spectre. Anna shivered. In places, visibility could be measured in metres rather than miles. It wasn't far from the hotel to where she had left the Land Rover, but she tread warily for fear of walking into something. The yellow glow from the overhead street lights, barely discernable in the fog, did little to help her progress.

A walk that should only have taken five minutes took her ten, and when she finally climbed aboard the Land Rover she felt her stomach churn with anxiety. Common sense told her that she should knock on Morag's door and ask her for a bed for the night rather than attempt the drive back to the croft, but she couldn't leave the dogs on their own any longer. Gripping the steering wheel tightly, she peered through the windscreen and drove slowly down the main street toward the garage, where she stopped and filled up the Land Rover with diesel.

The fog closed in as Anna left the village. She contemplated turning around. But the narrow, unlit road, combined with the need to get home to Ensay and Rhona, forced her to carry on. Once or twice she thought she caught a glimpse of headlights in her mirrors, but visibility was so poor, she couldn't be sure.

The knotted and gnarled branches of trees, illuminated by the headlights of the Land Rover, loomed toward her out of the fog like outstretched arms. Anna bit her lip and stared at the road ahead. Keeping her speed down and her eyes on the grass verge, she slowly made her way down the twisting road to the shore of Loch Hourn. Suddenly the engine began to cough and splutter. Then it stopped.

"Please, not now. Don't let me down," she said out loud, as she turned the ignition over. Much to her relief the engine started on the fifth turn. Releasing the handbrake she set off again, but had barely gone half a mile when the engine died again. This time no amount of coaxing would make it start.

Anna flicked on the hazard warning lights, pulled a torch from the glove box, and stepped out of from behind the wheel. She walked round to the front of the Land Rover, opened the bonnet, and shone her torch into the engine compartment. She had no idea what she was looking for, but none of the cables seemed to be loose when she examined them.

She looked around, trying to see a landmark. But there was none. No bend in the road or crofter's cottage, not even the smell of woodsmoke to indicate where she was. Just the gentle sound of lapping water nearby. She had two options. Either she could stay with the vehicle and hope that someone would come along, or she could walk. Slamming the bonnet shut, she turned up the collar of her coat, put the keys in her pocket and started walking toward the village.

The thrust in the middle of her back was so powerful that she hardly had time to scream, before she was hurtling sideways into thick white space. Frantically, her outstretched arms sought something to hold onto, but there was nothing. She felt a blinding pain as her shoulder hit something, and then she was lying on the ground. The world spun.

When her eyes opened again, she felt winded and disorientated. Her limbs were tense and shaking with fear.

She lay in the heather, and listened for the slightest footfall or sound of a scrape of rock. When she didn't hear anything, she tried moving one leg, then the other. Satisfied that she hadn't any broken bones, she eased herself up onto her knees, and realised she was kneeling in water. She'd landed in the ditch that ran along the side of the road. There was no sign of the torch, but there was a steep bank to her right. Overhead, through the patchy fog, she could just make out the eerie shape of a birch tree. Reaching out with her right hand, she grabbed hold of a clump of heather, and slithered and clawed her way out of the ditch. When she reached the grass verge at the top, she sank to her knees and cried with relief.

With no torch to guide her, she had little choice but to return to the Land Rover. Keeping close to the verge, she limped along the road wondering what had hit her. Maybe she'd got in the way of a roe deer or one of many the feral goats that roamed the hills. They frequently came down off the hill at night. But something told her that it hadn't been an animal that had slammed into her, but the hand of a man.

She tried to control the spasmodic trembling of her body, but failed. Her eyes darted left and right as she searched for the slightest sign of movement. Then, appearing out of the fog, she saw the flashing hazard lights of the old Land Rover.

Cold, tired, and edgy, she fumbled in her pocket for the keys. Panic gave way to relief when her fingers closed around them. Using the steering wheel as a lever, she hoisted herself into the driver's seat and inserted the key in the ignition. To her astonishment the engine roared into life on the first turn of the key. She wept aloud as she put the Land Rover into gear and drove off. Gulping hard, she brushed the tears from her eyes, and driving as fast as she dared she headed straight for the croft.

Only when she had locked the door behind her, and called the dogs to her side, did she begin to feel safe.

Chapter Twelve

In the imposing library room of Killilan House, Alistair Grant faced an ugly choice. He could either ignore the letter from the Bank or pretend he hadn't received it. Either way the outcome was the same—disaster. He knew he couldn't stall them forever. If he could just hold them off for another few weeks until his plans came to fruition, then all his problems would be solved.

He thought about approaching his sister once more. She must be good for five thousand at least, but after their earlier acrimonious argument, he knew that her answer would be no. There was only one thing for it; he would have to sell something. But what?

He glanced at the gilt bronze Louis the XV clock on the marble mantel. The casing was very ornate. Made in the Rococo style, surmounted by the figure of a draped woman holding an oval sun face disk, it was not his taste at all. But his mother had loved it, and for that reason alone, he would be sorry to sell it. But its disappearance would be hard to explain. He needed something smaller...

He walked around the room picking up objects here and there. A tall, delicate Minton vase, decorated with a foliate and floral pattern in greens, blues, and browns drew his attention. The glazing was badly crazed and there was a crack in the rim. He replaced it on the table. Whatever he chose had to be small enough not to be missed by Mrs McTavish, his eagle-eyed housekeeper, but large enough to raise sufficient cash to make the repayment on the overdraft, pay the staff, and cover the household bills for the next month.

He pulled a book from the shelf, and blew the dust off the faded leather cover and spine. *The Works of Thomas Carlyle.* He turned to the flyleaf hoping for a first edition. Although published in 1800, it was a second edition. He put it back and picked up another. *Bleak House by Charles Dickens.* How ironic, he thought, and roared with laughter. This time luck was on his side. He set the first edition on the arm of a chair and continued searching the shelves. Then it dawned on him. He'd need to sell a large number of books to raise the sort of money he needed. And besides, Mrs McTavish would notice the gaps on the shelves and no doubt search the house for the missing volumes.

Apart from the books, the only other items of interest in the library were the oil paintings of his father and grandfather. Even if the painter had been some famous artist, they were far too large, and their disappearance would raise too many questions among the staff. He didn't want them knowing he was financially embarrassed.

So what else could he sell? Then he remembered. Six years ago the insurance company had insisted his father have the household contents valued and they'd given the old boy a copy of the appraiser's report. Had his father given it to the Bank, or was it with the other estate papers? Alistair rifled through the drawers of the ancient desk. At length he found it tucked into a folder marked 'Killilan House.'

He sat down and read the valuation. It listed the contents of the house, room by room. Halfway down on the page for the library, he found an entry for a Georgian silver snuff box valued at £3,500. That would do nicely.

He flicked over the page. Somewhere in the dining room there was a set of four, George III silver candlesticks. He had no idea what a rounded base and bead decoration meant, but decided they shouldn't be too hard to identify. The valuation listed next to the description, showed them to be worth £12,000.

Now, he needed one or two more items and then he'd have sufficient money to see him through until the contract was signed...less any commission the dealer might charge.

That just left the bedrooms in which to find something. There appeared to be nothing suitable...then, on the last page under the 'Rose bedroom' he saw an entry, for a pair of George III chambersticks valued at £4,950. Chambersticks? Where they the same as candlesticks? They had to be.

He glanced at his watch—twelve noon. Mrs McTavish would be leaving shortly. He had plenty of time to find the objects, drive to Inverness, sell them, and be back in time for dinner. And if she happened to notice the items were missing, he'd simply say that he'd sent them away to be valued. He could easily replace them once the contract was signed, if he chose too. Which, he chuckled to himself, he might well not!

The clock on the mantelpiece struck the half hour. He peered out of the window and waited until he saw Mrs McTavish, dressed in her uniform of tweed skirt, white blouse and sweater, tie a headscarf under her chin, climb on her ancient bicycle and cycle away down the drive. Picking up the inventory off his desk, he went in search of his booty.

There was only one part of his plan which needed more consideration, and that was how to sell the items. He thought about this as he climbed the stairs and walked along the gallery to the Rose bedroom.

Named after his great-great grandmother, the room overlooked the formal gardens on the south side of the house. He pushed open the bedroom door. He wrinkled his nose. The room smelt faintly of lavender, mothballs and damp. The wallpaper of roses and intertwined ivy leaves, long faded by the sun, had peeled here and there. He noticed a huge damp patch on the ceiling, no doubt caused by a leak in the roof. He shook his head—just another problem to add to the already impossibly long list. The furniture was old fashioned, and in need of a polish. There was a chestnut armoire, matching chest of drawers, and a huge four-poster bed.

To his delight, he saw the chambersticks on either the side of the bed. He gathered them up and carried them back down to the library, placing them on the table by the door next to the snuff box. All he needed now were the candlesticks from the dining room and his problem was halfway to being solved!

While there were a number of antique dealers in Inverness, he'd get a much better price if he sold everything in Glasgow, but it would take him longer to get there, and doing the rounds of the antique shops on Sauchiehall Street filled him with dread. What if he bumped into someone he knew? He'd be humiliated. There was always that Internet site—the one where people auctioned unwanted items. What was it called? E—something. E something. EBay! That was it.

Leaving the dining room he made his way to the estate office at the back of the house. Thankfully it was empty. He turned on the computer. The old modem wheezed its familiar song as it connected him, albeit slowly, to the Internet. He typed in the web address and waited. The page slowly loaded as he drummed his fingers on the desk. When it was finally complete, he clicked on the link that told him what he'd need to do to start the process.

All the fine print baffled him. There was jargon about sellers' accounts, a long table detailing the commissions he could expect to pay, and the list of reasons why he should upload photographs of the items he planned to sell. Photographs? He had to take photographs too? It was far too complicated, in his opinion, and to make matters worse he was required to provide his name, address, and details of his bank account. That was the last thing he wanted to do! There had to be some other way.

Just then, the outer door to the office jerked open and MacKinnon stepped inside. Alistair stared at him.

MacKinnon had connections.

But could he trust him?

"What do you want, MacKinnon? You know I don't like you coming to the house uninvited."

MacKinnon scowled. He took a drag on his cigarette and blew out smoke. "One of the lads said he'd seen a fox hanging round the pheasant pens. I came to get some more shells for my shotgun. I thought I'd go down to the wood and take a look around."

Alistair's eyes narrowed. "Mm. In that case, you'd better have the keys to the gun cupboard." He opened the desk drawer and tossed them to MacKinnon.

"Thanks. By the way, I hear the MacDonald woman's Land Rover broke down on her way home from the meeting last night. While she was walking back to the village, someone jumped her and knocked her out. By all accounts, she ended up in a ditch."

Alistair visibly stiffened. His blue eyes became flat and unreadable as stone. "How dreadful. I hope she wasn't badly hurt?"

"According to Ewan at the hotel, she's got a few bruises. But she got a nasty fright—a real nasty fright."

Alistair's face was devoid of expression. "Mm. Perhaps she would have been wiser to stay in Edinburgh, instead of in that isolated croft on her own."

"It might make her think twice about staying, especially after an accident like that. Anyway, it's not often you come in here, your Lairdship. What are you up to?"

"I'm just checking the bookings for the start of the grouse season," Alistair blustered. "The numbers are down on last year. I think it's time I put another advertisement in the *Horse and Hound*."

"Why bother? You'll have millions in the bank by then."

"Because Killilan Estate is renowned for its grouse moor, that's why." Alistair shot him a withering glance. "Haven't you finished yet?"

"I'm going. Keep your wig on." He said, tossing the keys on the desk and striding out.

Alistair counted to twenty before getting up and locking the door. He didn't want that nasty little man wandering around the house in his absence, poking his nose in where it wasn't needed. Besides, he' didn't trust MacKinnon not to do some pilfering of his own.

On his way back to the library, Alistair stopped by the flower room and picked up his old cricket bag. He dropped the silver inside it, and it clanked as it settled to the bottom. He started, worried that he might have dented something, so he quickly checked. It looked all right. He carried it out to his Range Rover. With any luck he could be in Glasgow in four hours, complete his business, have a good dinner, and be back at Killilan House by midday tomorrow.

On the long journey south, through the lonely mountain passes and brooding glens, he contemplated how best to go about disposing of the silver without drawing attention to himself, and decided that a small auction house might be best. But he needed the cash now, not in three or four weeks' time.

As the miles passed he became more and more uneasy. Hadn't he read somewhere that the police regularly checked antique shops for stolen goods? If so, he'd have to be very careful. It might be better to sell the items separately rather than to one dealer.

And then he remembered his old school chum, Findlay Armstrong. He'd inherited the family estate on his father's death, but had been forced to sell it in order to settle the death duties payable to the Inland Revenue.

Last time he'd spoken to him, Fin still owed the Revenue several thousand pounds and was living in a stylish apartment overlooking the river Clyde. Surely, he would be prepared to help an old school friend in his time of need. In return, Alistair was more than willing to line his pockets with a little cash.

He'd made a note of Fin's number in his diary. He pulled into a lay-by, got out his mobile phone, and started dialling. Three minutes later a disgruntled voice answered the phone.

"Fin? Fin, is that you? It's Alistair Grant. Can you hear me?"

The voice that answered was full of false joviality. "Alistair. It's so good to hear from you. Are you back in Scotland, or still living it up in the South of France? Ah, I remember the marvellous shooting parties we used to—"

"—Actually, I'm on my way to Glasgow. I was wondering if we could meet. How about that new hotel on Jamaica Street? We can have dinner—my shout."

"Sure, why not."

"About seven-thirty, would that suit you?"

"Let me check my social calendar. Unbelievably, I am free tonight. I'll see you then."

By the time Alistair drove into Glasgow city centre it was the middle of rush hour. The traffic around Central Station had ground to a halt. Frustrated, he left the Range Rover in a multi-storey car park and walked the short distance to the Royal Scot Hotel.

Once in his room, he hid the holdall on the top shelf of the wardrobe behind the spare pillows and blankets while he had a quick shower. When he entered the bar, Fin was sitting at a corner table with a large glass of malt whisky in front of him. He stood when Alistair approached the table.

Alistair motioned for the barman to bring him a drink and another for Fin, who accepted, and raised his glass to his.

"Alistair, you haven't changed one bit," Fin said.

"Neither have you, my friend." Alistair replied gazing at his friend's well cut suit. "You're doing well for yourself, I see. But didn't you have a run in with the Inland Revenue?"

"They were on my back, but that's resolved now. You know old Fin—Rubber Ball Fin. Wasn't that what you used to call me, eh? Throw things my way and I dodge them every time. Remember?"

"Ah, yes." Alistair smiled. "You were always the one to get yourself out of trouble. I wish I could say the same."

"So what's the story? Girl trouble? I can see it in your face. One's got a broken heart and she means to get you to the altar no matter who gets hurt in the process. Am I right?"

"Girl trouble, yes, although marriage doesn't quite figure into the scheme of things."

Fin grinned. The skin around his eyes folded into heavy wrinkles. Odd, thought Alistair. He never thought his charming, handsome friend would age so rapidly.

"Fin, I need your help."

"Really," Fin said, ignoring the no smoking signs and lighting a gold filtered cigarette. "I was about to ask you for a favour, old boy. You see, I'm not as well off as I seem. You see this button? I sewed it on myself."

Alistair cast his eyes on his schoolmate's sleeve. The button was different in size and shape from its fellows.

"I'm better off than I was, but if Pater had taken the accountant's advice, well, I'd be living your kind of life."

Alistair waved away Fin's invading stream of cigarette smoke. "My kind of life...isn't what you imagine."

"It's not?"

"And I was hoping you might be able to help me." Alistair looked over his shoulder at the adjacent table. It was empty. "I need to sell a few things and I was hoping you could put me in touch with someone...suitable."

"Dear boy, whatever are you talking about?"

"I'm talking about the black market."

"Why on earth do you think I'd know anyone in that despicable trade?"

Humiliated by the admission, Alistair lowered his gaze. "Look Fin, say what you will, I know you have the connections."

"Is that so?"

"It is."

Fin took a deep drag on his cigarette and released a long stream of smoke. "Sorry to disappoint, dear friend, you can tell whatever you think to whomever you like. Publish it in the papers for all I care. Who knows? Maybe it would be a good idea. Then I could sue you for slander and collect a few pounds in the process."

Alistair knotted his fingers. "Don't even think of suing me. Think about what might happen if your precious family were to find out that it was really you who disposed of some of their most valuable pieces on the black market."

"I see." Fin raised an eyebrow. "Now, that would pose a bit of a sticky wicket for me. Might have to have you killed."

"That would be doing me a favour!"

"What are friends for?" Fin smiled, revealing perfect but yellowed teeth. "Seriously, no more talk of lawsuits and violence. How's your sister?"

Alistair started to sweat. "Not helping me, that's how."

"Oh, that's sad. Family's supposed to stand by you," he said, laughing. "Just like my beloved clan has. I'll need another drink if we're to continue talking about a business arrangement."

Alistair waved over the barman, who neatly refilled Fin's glass, then disappeared into the dining room.

"Fin," Alistair hissed. "Help me. Please."

"Mm—now that I think about it—I believe I do know a couple of gentlemen with the knowledge you require. I think they prefer to call themselves fences."

Alistair stirred uneasily in his chair. "Fences?"

"Admittedly, low-class slang for those who buy and re-sell property that has been...misappropriated, if you will."

"It's not been misappropriated. It's mine and I'm disposing of it as I see fit."

"Well, then why not sell it at auction? Why involve your poor dear old school chum?"

"Like you Fin, I'm just a bit short of cash at present. And I need to move quickly. What do these—er fences charge?"

Fin took out another cigarette, and regarded it as if it were more important than the subject of the conversation. "It depends on the goods. They have to be compensated for the risk they take."

"I understand that. You may as well know I'm under pressure from the Bank. It's threatening to freeze my account."

"You don't say. And you want to sell off the family silver, so you can meet its demands? What a shame, that's true. I can help you, and that's a shame. And more's the pity, Alistair, that you and I have sunk so very low."

Alistair rubbed his jaw. His knees shook. He was sure his blood pressure was at an all time high. "Yes, yes. We're both complete losers. I admit it. But we can help each other. I'll make it worth your while."

"I should hope so. The entire affair is quite beneath my station, you understand."

Alistair swallowed hard and tried to conceal his anger. "I'll give you two percent of whatever your associates get for the items."

"That sounds like a very small sum." Fin tapped the ash from the end of his cigarette. "And what are they worth?"

"Twenty thousand, at the last valuation, but I would hope to get more than that."

"Sorry, no can do. Five percent and I might think about it."

Sweat beaded on Alistair's brow. He couldn't afford to go back to the estate empty handed. "All right. Five percent. Not a penny more."

Armstrong leaned back in his chair and studied his fingers. "I'm tired of Glasgow. I need a break. Throw in a weekend in Paris, and seven percent of what I get for your trinkets and you've got yourself a deal."

"You drive a hard bargain, Armstrong. You'd better not let me down."

"Oh, no of course not," smiled Fin. "Now, shall we have a look at what's on the menu? I feel some escargot and champagne are in order. Don't you?"

Chapter Thirteen

Anna hadn't seen Luke for two days, but every time she wrote about the dark-haired stranger in her book, he stole into her thoughts, making it impossible for her to concentrate on her work.

"Oh, botheration!" she said to the dogs as she passed them on the way to the kitchen. As a student, when she'd had trouble with an assignment, a glass of wine helped her order her thoughts into coherency. Maybe it would do the trick tonight, she thought, as she uncorked the bottle of wine left over from dinner.

She carried her glass into the sitting room, and put it down on the table next to the sofa. Balancing her laptop on her knee, she started to type.

For five days we journeyed through the long and lonely glens, leaving the hills of Knoydart far behind. At night we found shelter where we could, but more often than not we slept under the stars with only bracken and heather for our beds, and our plaids for warmth.

Twice we came across a huddle of ruins where a village had once stood. Nearly every cottage had been burnt to the ground by unscrupulous factors and henchmen of the Laird. Those inhabitants who remained were in a sorry state, being either injured, old or too infirm to travel with their families, who had already left for the coastal lands. They had little food and shelter and no means of finding more. I knew in my heart that they would not survive the winter. Where the hardship was greatest—my husband—as I shyly came to call him—gave what money he could spare, but we knew it would not be sufficient to help these poor destitute souls.

On the morning of the sixth day, we entered a town and procured lodging in a small inn, not far from the quayside. We ate a meagre supper before retiring to our bed chamber. I shook with fear at the thought of sharing the bed with my husband. But I need not have worried, for he did not touch me, other than to pull me into his arms for warmth.

As my eyes fell heavy with sleep a vision came to me. I saw my village with its cluster of cottages, the smoke no longer rising from the chimneys. Most of the houses lay in ruins, their roof timbers burnt and charred. The women stood weeping, their shawls wrapped tightly around them against the bitter wind and driving rain. The men sat in despair, for there was nothing they could do but accept their fate. What few possessions they had were either burned or destroyed, and those that could be salvaged provided little comfort. I saw the children clothed in rags, haggard and shivering from the cold. There were no fires, no cook-pots of steaming broth.

I saw a people betrayed by a master they'd served all their life.

A glass and a half later, she gave up working on her manuscript. Although more relaxed, she was no nearer getting Luke out of her mind than she had been an hour earlier. Why? Why did he have to turn up just as she was getting over Mark? Why did he have to be so attractive? And that sexy grin...well, that sent her heart rate soaring every time he looked her way. The man should come stamped with a health warning! And she wasn't completely sure that this woman back home wasn't serious. Maybe even his fiancée or wife.

A wife. She couldn't imagine him being married.

Stop—stop this nonsense! She told herself. So, he had a smile that would make the most committed spinster run for the preacher, but he was damned annoying too. She took another sip of wine. What was it about him that managed to keep her on the defensive?

She looked at the dogs. "And a fat lot of help you two are!" Their tails thumped in response, but neither moved from the rug in front of the stove. "He's your new best friend since he came and took you for a walk!" She leaned back into the sofa, and emptied her glass. "At least he's not blond like Mark. I now officially hate men with blond hair!"

Not quite sure how she would react when she saw Luke again, she gave up thinking of men and him in particular. Unsteadily, she got to her feet, realising she'd drunk way too much, and would pay for it in the morning with a ferocious hangover. She turned out the light and made her way up the steep stairs to bed.

Someone in Anna's dream was knocking at the door.

Only it wasn't a dream.

In the hallway below, the dogs barked as if the devil was pounding at the door. She sat straight up in bed and screamed. Cold, icy sweat trickled down her back as her heart began to beat erratically. Her breath caught in her throat, and no matter how hard she tried, she couldn't gulp in air. Panic like she'd never known before coursed through her veins. She threw back the quilt and traced the line of the wall until her fingers closed around the heavy walking stick her grandmother always kept propped against it. She slid one foot to the floor, then the other. Every muscle in her body shook. Tip-toeing out of the bedroom, carefully avoiding the squeaky floorboard on the landing, she made her way downstairs.

Her legs shook as she followed the dogs into the kitchen. Her trembling fingers felt for the light switch. Damn! Where was it! She ran her shaking hand up and down the wall. There it is! She flicked on the switch, but nothing happened. She clamped her lips together and choked back a cry, wondering why the emergency generator hadn't kicked in as it should. Fumbling in the darkness, she edged her way to the dresser, opened a drawer, and felt for her torch.

Its light was dim, but everything appeared to be normal. Yet her instincts told her something was wrong, very wrong. And the dogs howling in the near darkness, knew it too. She crossed the hallway and swept the torch around the small sitting room. Everything was in its place. Too scared to open the curtains to peer outside, she retraced her steps.

"What is it, girls?" she whispered. "What can you hear?"

The dogs stood on each side of her, the warmth of their bodies seeping through the thin fabric of her oversized T-shirt to her ice-cold skin beneath. Teeth bared and snarling, they stared at the door. The silence was suddenly broken by an explosive bang. Anna shrieked and dropped the torch. Ensay and Rhona barked and jumped at the door. She picked up the torch and spun around.

Another loud crash, this time from the rear of the croft. She jumped but held tightly onto the torch. Should she let the dogs out to chase off whatever was out there, or should she keep them with her for protection?

Hysteria getting the better of her, she half laughed, half cried, and collapsed on to the bottom stair, her eyes fixed on the firmly bolted door. She weighed the walking stick in her right hand, and the torch in her left. Neither offered her comfort. She needed something more substantial.

The poker—there was a poker next to the Aga.

Carefully, she edged her way into the kitchen. She put down the walking stick and grabbed the poker along with the largest of her kitchen knives. She crept back into the hallway and took up her vigil once more.

Suddenly, the front door handle turned. The door rattled, pushed back and forth by an insistent hand. She swallowed a scream, dashed into the kitchen, grabbed a chair, and wedged it under the door handle. The dogs went berserk. The sound of their barking echoed off the walls, and filled the tiny house with a cacophony.

The knob rattled.

Anna couldn't breathe.

Then it turned again. And stopped.

Anna sat immobile. She hugged her knees. Cold, too scared to move, listening for the slightest sound or movement, she rubbed her arms and legs vigorously, trying to bring some warmth into her frozen limbs. But she could only hear the rapid beat of her heart and her own ragged breathing.

Ensay and Rhona grew quiet, but still darted from room to room as if chasing some spectre. Anna leaned her head against the wall, and willed her body to relax.

She remained on the stairs until she was no longer able to bear the cold, then she staggered into the sitting room. Laying the knife and poker on the rug, she knelt before the fireplace. The embers in the grate were almost gone, but she threw on some kindling anyway, crying in relief when it began to crackle and burn. She added a little coal and the driest log from the basket and sat back on the rug.

A vague scratching sound came from the window. Her head whipped round, and she stared at it, hardly daring to breath.

Silence. Then more scratching.

Someone was trying to force the catch.

Her heart pounded. Spasmodic shivers prickled her skin. Mesmerised, she watched. *Would the old lock hold?* She wasn't sure. She wanted to run from the house, but there was no one to run to for help.

She stood in the dark and screamed.

Chapter Fourteen

Bright sunlight flooded in through the cabin's tiny porthole, carrying with it the 'gah-gah-gah' cry of the herring gull which had taken up residence on top of the Sandpiper's mast. Luke groaned and pulled the pillow over his head. Four mornings in a row the bird had wakened him. If he had a shotgun, he'd have blasted it into a million feathers, but knowing the way his luck was going, he'd just as easily have missed and punched a hole in a sail. He opened one eye, looked at his watch, and groaned again. Six-thirty! Not only was the gull consistent, but it was also as accurate as his Rolex.

He climbed out of his bunk and shuffled his way across the cold, unyielding deck to the small galley. After taking two painkillers, and drinking a cup of coffee, he felt able to face the day. He peered through the galley window—not a ripple showed on the surface of the loch; even the rigging was silent. There was no sign of movement over at the croft either, making it a perfect morning for a swim.

With a towel slung over his shoulder, he opened the hatch. Safe in the knowledge that there was no one to see him, he emerged naked, walked across the deck, and dived in. The icy water enveloped him, shooting agony through every muscle. He came to the surface gasping for breath. Anna was more than right about the temperature; it was so cold he felt as if ten thousand needles were stabbing him.

He whipped his head round to clear the hair out of his eyes and set off in a fast crawl around the yacht. Ten laps later, his breathing fast and hard, he heaved himself up on to the swim step, wrapped the towel around his waist, and headed for the shower.

By ten-thirty the thermometer had climbed into the mid-seventies. The weather forecast had predicted even higher temperatures by midday. Stripped to the waist and wearing a pair of cut-off jeans, he sat sketching on deck. His yacht had been anchored in the loch for nearly a week, but every day he saw something different in the landscape. Today it was serene, with the water so dark and still beneath a cloudless sky. The mountains, with their snow filled crevices, reflected perfectly on its glassy surface. The door of the croft, he noted, remained closed. Now that he thought about it, he hadn't heard the dogs, or Anna's cranky old Land Rover. He wondered if she'd taken the day off.

Dismissing her whereabouts as none of his business, he concentrated on his drawing. Every now and again, he gazed over to the croft. Noon came and went with no sign of Anna or the dogs. By one-thirty, he started to feel uneasy about not seeing her. It wasn't right. True, he hadn't known her long, but the absence—wasn't normal. He clambered into the dinghy and rowed across the loch towards her cottage.

Her curtains were still closed. Puzzled, he tried the door, but it was firmly locked. He circled round to the rear of the croft. The Land Rover was parked in its usual place adjacent to the cow-shed, but when he felt the hood, the engine was cold. He was about to walk away when he noticed the left front tyre was flat. He squatted down to examine it more closely.

It wasn't simply flat. It had been slashed.

This was no accident. It was deliberate. Swallowing a curse, he ran back to the front of the croft, and pounded on the door.

"Anna! Anna, if you're in there, open up."

On the far edge of her nightmare, Anna heard someone calling her name. The voice sounded familiar, but she couldn't tell whose it was. Disorientated, she fought her way through the cob-webs of sleep and opened her eyes.

"Luke? Luke, is that you? Oh, thank God!" Shaking and gasping, she staggered to the door, dragged the chair from under the handle, drew back the bolts, and opened it.

He gathered into his arms and held her while she sobbed. "Hey, sweetheart. Shush. It's okay." He waited until she cried herself out and then held her at arm's length and studied her face. Her green eyes, wide with fear, were ringed by dark shadows. Her skin was clammy, but that didn't surprise him, since the T-shirt she wore barely reached to the middle of her thighs.

"Come into the kitchen," he said, slipping an arm around her waist and gently steering her towards the old rocking chair. "I'll make you a hot drink." He added a log to the firebox of the stove and opened the vent.

"That would be nice, but I must see to the dogs." She struggled to stand, but Luke pushed her back into the chair. "The dogs are fine. They're outside. So stop worrying about them and concentrate on yourself. Now tell me what happened."

Too tired to argue, she nodded, biting her lips to control her sobs. She sat huddled in the chair, her hands twisting in her lap while he filled the kettle and placed it on the hotplate to boil. He found two mugs in a cupboard, a jar of instant coffee and a packet of teabags in another.

He turned to check on Anna. She was shaking violently. Without hesitating, he dashed up the narrow stairs, and flung open the first door he came to. He pulled the quilt off the bed and carried it back down to the kitchen. When he wrapped it around her shoulders, she flinched and shrank from his touch before snuggling into its soft, downy warmth.

Luke leaned back against the kitchen table and watched her from under hooded eyes as she nursed the mug of sweet tea. Her hands were trembling so much that some of the hot liquid spilt into her lap. He'd never seen anyone this scared. Her eyes darted to the door, as if she expected someone to appear at any moment. She looked so fragile, so vulnerable, that he wanted to hold her in his arms until her fears melted away.

Despite his need to comfort her, he was angry with her too. She was a grown woman and didn't need reminding of the risk she took living in such an isolated place. He fought his temper. There was no point lecturing her about it now, at least not until she told him what had frightened the living daylights out of her.

"Feeling better?" he asked.

Anna nodded with a taut jerk of her head.

"In that case, do you think you're up to talking now?"

"Last night...the dogs," she hesitated, her voice barely more than a whisper. "I woke up screaming because they were growling and barking, as if...as if someone was in the house. I couldn't hear anyone moving around, so I came down to investigate. When I switched on the lights nothing happened."

Luke crossed the room and flicked the switch. The overhead fitting bathed the kitchen in light.

"It seems okay now. Maybe there was a minor power outage."

"I don't think so," Anna replied, her confidence slowly returning. "The cable is buried. My grandparents insisted on it because of the bad weather in winter. It only surfaces again when it reaches the pole by the cow-shed. Even in the worst winter storm, the croft never loses electricity. Besides, if there'd been a power cut, the generator should have cut in. But it didn't."

"I'll take a look at it shortly, and we'll check with the power company next time we go to the village. Keep talking to me about what happened last night."

"Ensay and Rhona were frantic. I couldn't see anything wrong. Someone pounded on the front door, and then there was this almighty boom. It sounded like a cannon. I came in here for the poker and the carving knife, and sat on the stairs. Then I saw...I saw the door handle start to turn..."

Luke swore heartily. "What did I say about living out here on your own?"

Anna lifted her chin and boldly met his gaze, refusing to be drawn into an argument. "When I saw the door handle turn, I pushed a chair under it, and waited. Nothing happened. After that, there was just silence."

"Well, it's obvious you can't stay here. You'll have to move into the village, at least until the police check things out."

"But this is my home!"

"Anna, sweetheart, be reasonable," he said, kneeling down in front of her and taking her hands in his. "Someone tried to break in last night."

"Well, they tried, but they didn't get in, did they?"

"A mere technicality." Something in her expression made him ask, "This isn't the first time this happened, is it?"

She looked away.

"Anna? Tell me the truth."

"No...yes. I don't know. I've woken a couple of times with the feeling that something is wrong. I assumed it's because I'm not used to the peace and quiet. Edinburgh is a noisy city."

He stood up and pushed his hands in his pockets. "But surely the dogs—"

"This is the first time the dogs have reacted in any way."

"You must realise that somebody made a conscious decision to come all the way out here. So ask yourself why. And while you're at it, ask yourself if he might not just come back!"

She jumped to her feet. The quilt fell to the floor. "I'm perfectly capable at looking after myself."

"Really? Look at you. You're half naked, and you're a mess. You just got through telling me you slept on the couch because you were too darned scared to go upstairs. Ghosts have more colour than you do!"

Suddenly conscious of her state of undress, she snatched up the quilt and wrapped it around her shoulders. "The dogs protected me."

"*This time.* What happens if whoever it was comes back with a knife or a shotgun? The dogs won't be much protection then."

Anna gasped at Luke's words, and as much as she tried to deny it, he was right. "I'll...I'll ask for police protection."

Luke raised an eyebrow. "Get real, Anna. What's the local Barney Fife going to do? Camp out on your front lawn, waiting for the bad guys to show up? The police aren't going to bother about you. They've got enough on their hands dealing with crime in the cities to be concerned with a woman who's stupid enough to live in the sticks."

"I'm not stupid..." She jumped to her feet.

"Oh, yeah? Prove it. Move to the village until this mystery gets solved."

Anna hesitated. If she agreed to Luke's suggestion, she would lose her independence, yet part of her wanted to get as far away from the croft as possible. Only pride prevented her from giving in.

"I can't," she said finally.

Luke watched her collapse back into the chair. She pulled the quilt tightly around herself, and rested her head in her hands. For a few seconds he contemplated picking her up, slinging her over his shoulder, taking her to the yacht, and keeping her there until he could find out who was terrorising her. But the slam of a car door stopped him.

"Stay where you are. I'll see who it is." He ran into the hallway.

A tall, thin, brown-haired woman met him at the door.

"Oh, hello. I was wondering if herself was about, only she didn't turn up for work this morning."

"If by 'herself' you mean Anna, she's freaking out in the kitchen."

Morag's eyes widened. "I've been worried about her. Now I know why. I need to see her..."

He stepped aside. "Be my guest. And while I'm walking the dogs and checking the generator, try talking some sense into her. Anna, there's a woman here to see you."

"Morag? Is that you? I'm so pleased to see you!" Anna said, holding the quilt more tightly to avoid tripping over it.

Morag gave her a hug, clicked her tongue and shook her head. "Well, lass, it's a fine state you're in. I think you'd better tell me what's been happening and why that American is here."

"It's not what you think."

Morag frowned. "You have no idea what I'm thinking, lass. I'll put the kettle on and we'll have a wee cup of tea. Then you can explain."

Anna groaned. "Would you mind if I got dressed first?"

"No, my dear. You go and put some clothes on; you must be fair chilled."

"Thanks, Morag," Anna replied and kissed her friend's cheek. "Would you also make me a piece of toast? I haven't eaten since yesterday."

"No breakfast? Tut-tut, it's no wonder you're so pale, lass. I'm just surprised you haven't fainted clean away. Off you go and get dressed. By the time you come downstairs there'll be a bowl of porridge waiting for you. Toast indeed! That's no breakfast for a young woman."

Twenty minutes later, Anna had showered, dressed, eaten a bowl of porridge, and a slice of toast under Morag's watchful eye. She recounted the events of the previous night.

"Wasn't I only telling you the other day there was danger around you?"

"Oh, for goodness sake, Morag!" Anna snapped. "I've had just about as much as I can take. I've already had a lecture from Luke. I don't need another one from you. There's probably a perfectly reasonable explanation for what happened."

"Oh, and what might that be?"

Anna thought quickly. "A hillwalker...a hillwalker could easily have become disorientated or injured, and seeing the croft, thought it was a bothy where he could shelter."

"In the wee hours of the morning? I don't think so, lass. Besides, if he'd come from the hill, he'd have seen the Land Rover and realised the croft was occupied."

"Nor does it explain why two of your tyres got slashed," Luke added from the doorway.

"What?" Anna gasped in surprise.

"I said—"

"I heard you the first time. Slashed, as in cut with a knife? Are you sure they're not flat?"

"Trust me. I know the difference. And your generator's been tampered with too. At a guess, I'd say someone contaminated the fuel, probably with a bag of sugar. It would be easy enough to do, even in the dark. Now, will you take my advice and go and stay with a friend?"

"I've told you, I can't!"

He slammed his palm on the door frame. "Wake up, girl! You're going way overboard with this independence thing. It's a cover and you know it. You won't accept help when it's offered. You should learn to trust people more!"

"Now, lass, the man's right," Morag interrupted, "you shouldn't be staying here on your own, not when there are such dangerous people about." And smiling at Luke, she added, "Anna seems to have forgotten her manners. I'm Morag McInnes."

"Luke Tallantyre," he said, holding out his hand.

"Pleased to meet you, Luke. It's a terrible thing that's happened. I don't know what the world is coming to, when a body isn't safe in its own home, I really don't. But you're right. It's obvious Anna shouldn't be left alone."

"Stop right there! Stop discussing me as if I have no more sense than a child—"

Luke's eyes narrowed. "Haven't you been acting like one?"

"My grandmother lived in this house on her own, and so can I."

"Yes," Morag said, "but times have changed, lass. It's no longer safe to leave your house unlocked. Why even Mrs McPherson bolts her door at night. What about your parents? Could you no go and stay with them?"

"No, I can't. You know they're in Beijing and not due home for another year. Besides, Daddy went to a lot of trouble arranging for the house to be opened up temporarily so I could store my furniture in the basement. He'll be very annoyed if I said I wanted to move back into my old room."

"But it's your home, lass."

"Morag, you of all people know that's not true. My parents lost interest in me the day I started boarding school. That's why they sent me here for the holidays. We haven't seen each other in years, but all that's beside the point."

Morag glanced at Luke. "You'd be welcome to stay with me as Lachlan is away, but—my hens don't get on well with yon dogs. And ever since Mrs McPherson's Jack Russell terrier chased my cat Jasper up a tree—"

"What about the hotel?" Luke interrupted. "Doesn't it have a place where staff can stay? An apartment or something?"

"Aye, it does," replied Morag. "But Ewan let the new chef have it for the season. And what's more, he'd never agree to have the dogs. Besides, all the guest rooms are booked for the foreseeable future. Well, lass, I don't see what's to be done, unless...."

"Unless what?" Luke asked.

"No, it's a silly idea." Morag looked pointedly at Luke where he lounged casually against the door frame. When he appeared to ignore her, Morag stared at him. "Unless you move in with Anna, of course."

Anna and Luke both shouted at once. "No! No way."

"Now, you're both being silly," Morag told them.

For the space of several breaths Luke's gaze held Anna's in silent question. He tried not to think about how much he wanted her, how sharing a house with her would test his resolve to the limit. His conscience wouldn't—couldn't allow him to let stay her on her own. And since she wouldn't take his advice and move into the village, he had no option but to agree to Morag's suggestion.

"Okay," he said holding up his hands. "I give in. I'll stay here. But just for a few days, until we're sure this was just an isolated incident."

Anna was too stunned to say anything.

Morag smiled knowingly. "Good. That's settled then. I daresay yon wee boat must feel a bit cramped, especially if you've sailed all the way from America. And Anna's a great cook, so you'll have some proper home-cooked food for a change. You wouldn't get under each other's feet during the day as Anna has her work, and no doubt you have things to do, so you'd only be spending the evenings together. There's ample room as there are two bedrooms. Don't you see? It's the perfect solution for both of you."

Morag picked up her keys and handbag and headed out the door. "Now, no doubt you'll be needing a lift to the garage to get those tyres replaced."

Luke jumped in the truck bed of Morag's four-by-four, and Anna climbed into the passenger seat, her previously threatening headache now a fact. She gave her friend a sidelong glance and wondered how she could look so innocent yet be so...so devious.

"Morag, you had absolutely no right manoeuvring Luke into staying at the croft."

"I did no such thing."

"Perhaps not, but I've no doubt it was you who planted the idea in his mind."

"How could I do that? I'm not a hypnotist. As it is, he can't very well stay on the boat and turn a blind eye to what's happening under his nose, now can he?"

"If I didn't know you better, Morag McInnes, I'd say you were a witch."

Morag smiled. "Not all who have the Sight are witches. Do you see any warts?"

"No—yes—oh, I don't know!" Anna held her aching head. "No one can fight with you; you don't fight fair."

"I'll take that as a compliment. Sorry about your head, my dear, but someone has to take charge of the situation. And as fate brought the man back there sailing into the loch, it seemed logical to put his appearance to good use. It's as plain as day that you can't stay there on your own, and you know it. But you're too stubborn and proud to admit it, so there's no other option but to have him move into the croft."

"But—"

"There is no but. He's a gentleman, so he won't do anything...improper, either."

Anna's cheeks coloured. "Morag! For goodness sake, keep your voice down. Luke might hear you."

"Now, lass, don't fret. I'm well aware why you're staying at the croft, but you have to agree that having that fine figure of a man around is no bad thing!"

Chapter Fifteen

Anna was too wrapped up thinking about the events of the previous evening, to talk to Morag on the return journey. As if she didn't have enough problems, the new tyres had taken a huge chunk out of her meagre savings. If she wasn't careful, she might even have to ask Ewan if she could work extra hours to make up the loss. Then there was Luke, who'd said hardly a word to her and who now sat morosely in the back of the pickup. The only one of the trio who appeared happy was Morag.

The closer she got to home, the more agitated Anna became. Yes, she was frightened of staying in the croft on her own, but the thought of Luke staying there too disturbed her even more, but for totally different reasons. He was too attractive, too virile, and all too male for his own good—correction—for *her* own good, and it would be too easy for her to fall for his charms.

The pickup came to a halt in front of the croft. Morag yanked on the handbrake. "Here we are, lass."

"Thanks for the lift, Morag. I don't know how I would have managed without your help."

"It's not just me you ought to be thanking, but that man too. Now don't go fretting over last night. Get some rest, and I'll see you at work tomorrow, as usual."

Anna shook her head in disbelief. That was typical of Morag, always organising folk. With a wave of her hand, Morag sent the pickup hurtling back down the potholed track, and left Anna covered in dust.

Luke rolled the tyres toward the Land Rover. "I'll go and put these on for you. By the way, I bought this for you." He handed her a sturdy padlock. "I thought if we cleared out the cow-shed, you could use it as a garage."

"Thank you. But what's this 'we' business?"

Luke stopped in front of her. "Look, I know you're tired. Even if you weren't, you're not capable of moving all those boxes, not to mention the rusty ironwork on your own. If you were, you'd have done it already."

"I suppose you're right." She watched, fascinated, as Luke stripped off his T-shirt and set about manoeuvring the first of the heavy wheels back on the axle. His broad, suntanned chest was lightly covered in crisp dark hair.

Subconsciously she moistened her lips. "Er...I'll go and sort something out for dinner first." Without waiting for him to respond, she scooted off in the direction of the kitchen, his laughter ringing in her ears.

Twenty minutes later Anna recoiled in horror at the number of cobwebs hanging from the rafters in the cow-shed. They were the reason she'd avoided going inside, not that she would ever admit it.

"Are you going to stand there all day admiring my body, or are you going to give me a hand clearing out this place?"

"In a minute," Anna replied. She bent down and tucked the legs of her jeans into her socks and covered her hair with a scarf, then pulled on a pair of rubber gloves. There was no way she was going anywhere near those gossamer threads, and if she saw as much as one big, hairy spider, she'd be out of there faster than she could say 'Ben Nevis!'

Luke's mouth quirked with humour. "Is this the latest fashion?"

"I hope a tarantula crawls into your shorts," she muttered.

"What?"

She suppressed a giggle. "I said, when it comes to spiders, out here you see all sorts."

His dark eyebrows arched in confusion. "Huh?"

"Forget it. It's just my weird Scottish sense of humour."

Between the two of them, they half-carried, half-dragged an assortment of rusting farm implements out of the way and put the boxes in the wood shed. Anna decided to sort through their contents when she was less tired. When they finished they were both hot and covered in dust and grime, but the Land Rover was now safely locked inside the cow-shed.

"Okay," said Luke. "I'll go back to the yacht, get cleaned up, pack a bag, and be back in an hour. I doubt anyone will return in daylight. If they do, scream blue murder. It will carry across the loch, and I'll hear you."

Anna pulled off her scarf with a grubby hand. "Look, it's very kind of you to do all this, but you really don't have to stay. Morag was just being overanxious as usual. I'll be perfectly all right on my own."

Luke offered her a sudden, arresting smile that had all her objections floating away on the air. "Concerned that my intentions maybe less than honourable?"

She coloured fiercely. "No—no, of course not." But as soon as the words left her mouth Anna realised that she'd have no objection if they were. She stared wordlessly at her rescuer; there was no point yearning for something that was doomed before it started.

"Then let's not get into that argument again. I volunteered to stay, and that's all there is to it. Now, please go take a shower and make up the spare bed, okay? I'll be back as soon as I can." He planted a kiss on her dirty cheek and was gone.

Anna brushed ineffectively at the dust on her jeans, dumping them along with her T-shirt into the washing machine before heading upstairs to the small bathroom in her underwear.

"Oh, what the heck," she said aloud to no one, turning on the taps, and adding some of her favourite scented oil to the water in the bath. "Luke said he'd be an hour, plenty of time for a long soak."

Three minutes later, she lowered her tired body into the steaming tub, closed her eyes and allowed her mind to drift. No matter how hard she tried, she couldn't think of one reason why anyone would want to harm her. But if she was right and it had been a hillwalker seeking shelter, why did he slash the tyres and sabotage the generator? It just didn't add up. The more she thought about it, the more confused she became. And then there was Morag. If only she hadn't interfered, Anna would have convinced Luke that she would be all right on her own. As it was...oh, it was all such a mess!

A short time later, dressed in a pair of navy chinos and white V-necked top, she padded downstairs. There was still no sign of Luke, so she busied herself laying the kitchen table. She hoped he liked haggis because that was all there was for dinner.

"Serves him right if he doesn't," she said, adding a jug of iced water to the table.

"*What* serves me right?" A deep voice shattered her thoughts.

"I wish you'd stop creeping up on me like that!"

"I'm sorry, honey. I didn't mean to freak you out. The front door was open. I didn't think I needed to knock."

"You didn't...freak me out. I just didn't hear you come in, that's all."

"Yeah. It's a good thing you didn't have a knife in your hand when you spun around. You might have inadvertently gutted me."

"I would not... never mind. I've made up the spare room. It's the one on the left at the top of the stairs. Just watch your head on the ceiling, it's rather low. The middle door is the bathroom. You'll find clean towels in the cupboard. If you want to take your bag up and er...wash your hands, dinner will be ready when you come down."

"Okay. See you in a minute."

Luke dumped his holdall on the bed and looked around the room. It was miniscule, scarcely larger than his cabin. However, it was bright and welcoming, and came with a view of the loch and mountains beyond. The walls were painted a delicate shade of blue. Bordered by sapphire-coloured velvet curtains, the small dormer window, faced south out over the loch, and was ideally suited for keeping an eye on his yacht.

An antique chest of drawers stood on either side of the door. Their surfaces gleamed with a patina that only came from years of polishing. The brass bed that filled the centre of the opposite wall was so large, that Luke wondered whether the room had been built around it. Two paces either side of the bed and his head came into contact with the sloping ceiling. He opened his bag, took out his sketch book, and propped it on the chest of drawers nearest the window.

Anna's lilting voice floated up the staircase. "Dinner's ready."

He entered the kitchen just as she placed two plates steaming plates of food on the table.

"I'm sorry, there's no wine."

"That's all right." Luke sniffed cautiously at his meal. The aroma of herbs and spices and something he couldn't quite identify assuaged his senses. "What's this?"

"Tatties, neeps, and haggis."

"Could you translate that into English?"

Anna's knife and fork paused in mid-air.

"Potatoes, turnip, and haggis. Trust me, you'll enjoy it."

"Mm." Luke replied, somewhat sceptical. "And what *exactly* is haggis?"

Her eyes twinkled. "Oh, it's a wee furry animal with only three legs, and one of those is shorter than the other two so they can run round mountains. They're the very devil to catch."

"Something tells me that's the oldest joke in Scotland." He poked his knife at the brown substances on his plate. "Come on, you don't honestly expect me to eat this without knowing what I'm putting in my mouth."

Anna swallowed the mouthful she'd been chewing. "Lamb's liver, onion, oatmeal, spices, suet, all cooked in a sheep's stomach."

"Gross!"

"Hardly. Just think of it as the Scots' equivalent of a boil-in-the-bag meal!" she replied, unable to keep the laughter from her voice.

"Oh, my God, that's revolting..." Luke pushed his plate away.

"Taste it. I dare you."

"You dare me?"

"Yes, I do. In fact I double dare you."

"But not double dog dare."

"Haven't heard of that one, but yes. I double dog dare you."

"Really?"

"Yes. Times infinity. Ha!"

With a sharp intake of breath he scooped up a small amount onto his fork and tentatively took a bite. Anna watched the range of expressions on his face with glee.

He nodded. "Not bad, even if it does look like kitty-litter. But if it's all the same to you, I think I'll pass in future."

"Okay. But don't accept an invitation to a Burns' Night Supper, expecting to eat foie gras," Anna warned. "Because all you'll get is haggis and whisky."

"I'll remember that. I like your friend, Morag. She's very down to earth."

"Yes she is. She reminds me of one of the hens my grandmother used to keep, always darting here and there, making sure the younger birds are safe. Even when we were young, her maternal instinct was strong. She always wanted to nurture everyone."

"Does she have children?"

"No. Morag's had a number of miscarriages."

"That must have been tough on her and her husband."

"It's one of the reasons Lachlan is insisting they buy a farm of their own. He used to work on the estate, but gave it up in favour of working on the oil rigs. Morag hates him being away, she's terrified he'll be hurt in some unspeakable way."

"When Morag asked you about having a friend stay, you mentioned something about them being busy with classes. Are you a teacher?" He leaned back in his chair and gave her a leisurely smile.

"Sort of...I'm a lecturer in media studies and creative writing, or at least I was until recently."

"I'm impressed. So what made you quit?"

A momentary look of discomfort crossed her face. "I never said I quit. It's just...well, if you must know my situation became intolerable, partly through my own stupidity. What is it they say? Never mix romance with business? Unfortunately, I didn't take my own advice. Mark and I had been seeing each other for nearly two years when a more senior post became vacant. He promised me the job, and would have given it to me, had he not become involved with someone else in the department."

"Mark? Does he own the boots you let me use?"

"Yes. But hillwalking isn't his favourite pastime."

"Anyway, so you felt you had to leave."

"It was bad enough that he'd been two-timing me, but when he gave his new girlfriend the job...well you can imagine how I felt, especially as I'm better qualified. Her experience obviously lies in other directions."

"You mean the bedroom? Mark sounds like a genuine bastard. I think anyone in your position would have done the same thing. Would you pass the salt, please?"

Anna handed Luke the cruet. "Perhaps, but when I gave up my job, I also gave up my flat too."

"Oh? Why was that?"

"The rent was extortionate. If I'd stayed, my savings would have been gone within a few months. Fortunately, I had this place to fall back on."

"But you could have found another job."

"I could have, but I had this rather naïve idea of becoming a writer."

"And are you...writing a book?"

"My life is simpler now, so I can."

"Except for crazed intruders who wreck your house at night."

She frowned at him. "Except for recent events, things are good for me here. I only work mornings at the Monymusk Arms, which leaves me free to write all afternoon. The dogs are happier because I'm home more." She began to clear the table. "Would you like some fruit or cheese?"

"No, thanks."

"How about some coffee?"

"Yes, please. I like solitude too, especially when I'm painting. My house overlooks the Atlantic, but it's nowhere near as isolated as this place."

Anna put a cafetiere of coffee on a tray. "It sounds fantastic. Do you take milk and sugar?"

"No to both. Here, let me carry those for you." He took the tray from her hands and carried it to the lounge.

Anna poured two cups, and settled back into the sofa, tucking her legs beneath her.

Luke took a sip. "You said your parents are in China. On vacation?"

"My father is a diplomat."

"I see. Could you have gone to stay with them for a while? Why the big hurry to move out here?"

"It's complicated." Anna looked away lest he see the sadness in her eyes. "I was sent to boarding school when I was seven. Unlike other children who went home for holidays, I spent the term breaks in the dorm being looked after by the teachers. The only exception was the summer holiday when I joined my parents in whichever country they happened to be in at the time. But the airline tickets stopped arriving on my fourteenth birthday. So, I came here to the croft, instead. The last time I saw my parents was at my university graduation."

"Don't you miss your friends in Edinburgh?"

"At times, I enjoy socialising like everyone else, but I'm also comfortable with my own company. I think my childhood at boarding school prepared me for that. I also believe it's one of the reasons my grandmother left the croft to me—she knew I would use it and appreciate its surroundings."

"My childhood couldn't have been more different. My brother Jack and I grew up in a small town in Vermont. Dad taught art at the local high school, and Mom is what we used to call a housewife. I guess the new term is 'stay-at-home-mom'. Anyway, we spent our summer vacation at the beach having picnics in the dunes. We skied in Colorado almost every winter. Even now, Jack and I still go home for every Thanksgiving, Christmas and birthday. Jack's quite a guy. You'd like him."

"Is he anything like you?"

"He's darker. Taller. Meaner. No, seriously, he's the funny one in the family. Owns a garage. Builds race cars in his spare time. Every now and again he wins something."

"Any races I'd know about?"

"Doubtful. All I know is that he keeps my old MG roadworthy. Growing up with him was great, although I didn't appreciate him at the time. All I wanted to do was kill him. And with all the BB's I shot at him, I'm still surprised I didn't!"

"And he shot at you?"

"Of course. That's how I came by this." He fingered the faint scar on his right cheek. "We were both armed and dangerous with our air rifles. He was fourteen. I was eleven, and sometimes we were downright determined to take each other out."

"Which is why you know so much about firearms."

He looked at her with an expression she could not define. A long moment passed. She grew uncomfortable in the strained silence.

"All right, I've a fair picture of your childhood. Now, tell me about your home on Cape Cod."

A half smile crossed Luke's face. "It's a three-storey—four if you include the watchtower—old wooden Coastguard station. It was built back in the 1930s and stands on the dunes overlooking one of the best beaches on the Cape. My studio is in the tower and has windows on every side. The light is perfect for painting watercolours and watching the whales. I love it best in the fall and winter when the tourists are gone and the Atlantic rollers come thundering ashore. The beach is pretty deserted then. We only get a few die-hard locals out walking their dogs."

"It sounds idyllic."

"It is. But there are times when the house feels empty. It should be a family home, not a bachelor pad."

"So why isn't it a family home?"

Luke went silent again; his eyes distant. He fumbled with his Rolex.

"Nicole, my fiancée, died a week before our wedding. She went to get her wedding dress altered and was crossing the road to come home when a car ran a red light. She didn't even have a chance to see it. She died in the hospital three hours later."

"My God. How dreadful for you. I'm so sorry."

"It was a long time ago. See this watch? Nicole had just given it to me. She called it an early wedding present. Funny thing. She always said there was no reason to rush a wedding. She said we had all the time in the world. Turns out we didn't."

Anna looked at the watch. Sleek, masculine, elegant, a perfect complement to its owner. "You must have been in great pain. But you kept the house. I'm surprised."

"It was semi-derelict when I first saw it. I spent a couple of years restoring it. Then I met Nicole while on a job. She was a curator of a museum in San Francisco. I'd been hired to investigate a case of art fraud. You know the drill; boy meets girl, love blossoms, etc, etc, etc. I convinced her that San Francisco wasn't nearly as wonderful as my digs, and she moved in with me. Left her whole world behind. What a girl. After our wedding, we planned on using the house as a gallery and studio. Keeping it seemed the right thing to do."

"And you've never met anyone else you wanted to marry?"

His eyes glistened in the half-light. "Let's change the subject, okay?"

"Sure."

"I've been meaning to ask about your accent. You don't have much of what we Americans call a Scottish lilt. Is that because of boarding school?"

Surprised by his question, Anna took a moment or two to reply. "I presume so. I went to school in England. Any child who didn't speak the Queen's English was given elocution lessons, so my accent was tempered to what you hear now. However, when Morag and I get together for any length of time, it does revert somewhat."

"I like it. It's a soft round sound. Kinda sexy."

Anna smiled but didn't answer. She was thinking exactly the same thing about his voice.

"—It's not at all like Morag's or the people I met in Stornaway. I couldn't understand any of them."

"You're not alone. There are certain dialects I have difficulty comprehending, and I'm a native. You only have to drive from Edinburgh to Aberdeen to notice the difference, and of course Gaelic is still spoken in the islands."

Luke stretched out his long legs, careful not to kick the collie lying on the rug in front of the fire.

"What do you do at nights, besides work on your book?"

"I have a radio and my CD collection. Unfortunately, there's no TV reception, unless you install a satellite dish, and that's an expense I can do without. Sometimes I visit Morag or she comes here, and we share a bottle of wine. Now that the tourist season is picking up, the hotel hires a band at weekends to entertain the guests. Twice a year the estate holds a Ceilidh—a dance. In fact there's one in a couple of weeks' time, so there are things to do." Anna stifled a yawn.

Luke glanced at the clock on the mantelpiece. He stood and pulled her to her feet. "It's late. You must be exhausted.

Why don't you go to bed? I'll take the dogs out and look around before I lock up."

"Well, if you're sure…"

"I'm sure. Besides, you look worn out." The hand that took hers was strong, firm, and protective.

She lowered her gaze. "Thanks. I couldn't have made it through the day without your help." Standing on tiptoe, she dropped a kiss on his cheek and began to climb the stairs.

"Anna?"

"Yes?"

"Don't worry, everything will be all right. I'll make sure no one hurts you, sweetheart."

For a long moment she looked back at him. An emotion without a name flickered through her heart. She nodded and climbed the rest of the stairs to her bedroom.

Chapter Sixteen

"You don't look as if you slept very well," Luke said, placing a plate of bacon and eggs in front of Anna. "Why don't you take the day off?"

She poured herself a cup of coffee and took a sip. It was hot and strong, just as she liked it. "I can't. The hotel is full this week, and what's more, Morag will be expecting me."

Luke's dark brows drew together in a frown. "The hotel ran just fine before you ever started working there. Besides, Morag's not stupid. She knows you need time to recover."

"You don't understand. I need this job," she said, stifling a yawn.

"I know you do, but I'm sure when everyone hears what happened they'll be sympathetic."

"Maybe, but I can't run the risk of losing my job. I don't think you appreciate how difficult it is to find work in the countryside."

Luke took a grip on his temper. "You're right, maybe I don't. I can also see that arguing with you is pointless. So, since you seem to be determined to go, I'll drive you."

"There's no need."

"Boy, are you wrong. Don't think I didn't notice your hand shaking when you lifted the coffee pot—"

"It was not!"

Luke's expression contradicted her. "Liar. You've got black circles under your eyes, and your face has no colour at all."

"If you can't find anything positive to say about my appearance, shut up."

"Temper, temper," he said sweetly. "That's no way to talk to your knight in shining armour."

"I thought knights were always young and virile. Aren't you a bit old to be rescuing damsels in distress?" Anna smiled sweetly. She picked up her knife and fork and took another bite.

"I didn't hear you complaining yesterday. What happened this morning, Cinderella? Did you wake up and realise life isn't one long fairy tale?"

Anna ignored him.

"What you need," he continued, "is a day away from the croft, and I've got the perfect solution."

Anna sighed and shrugged her shoulders. "You're not going to drop the subject are you?"

"Nope."

"All right, let's hear this solution of yours."

He passed her the plate of toast. "I'll take you sailing. The forecast is good; it's warm and sunny, and there's just a light breeze. A day on the water will help you relax and feel better."

"Thank you. I thought it wasn't safe to take your yacht into open water."

"Sandpiper is safe. Maybe I didn't explain it well enough. The pump on the auto-pilot is what's screwed up. When you're sailing single-handed you use the auto-pilot to steer the boat so that you can eat, and sleep. I don't need it since I'm only planning on going as far as that little island at the mouth of the loch."

"You mean Sandaig Island?"

"If that's what it's called, yes. Hey, what's that dirty look? If you're that concerned about letting Morag down, I'll use my considerable American charm to placate her."

Anna raised an eyebrow. "And you really think that will work?"

"Sure. She'll be powerless to resist," he replied with a grin.

"You don't know Morag; she can be as stubborn as a goat."

Luke laughed. "Somehow I doubt that. Besides, I've charmed my fair share of goats. In the meantime, you go and get ready. I'll go through your fridge and we'll have lunch on the yacht. We'll stop in the village on our way back from the hotel, and pick up some stuff from the shop. How does that sound?"

"It sounds a lovely idea, but I still feel guilty about letting Morag down."

"Relax. I'm sure she'll understand. You had an ugly experience. Give yourself another day. Better yet, take the weekend...please?" He flashed a comic grim that showed way too many teeth.

Anna didn't have it in her to argue further. She gave his shoulder a gentle push. "You are a very naughty boy encouraging me to play hooky. You win; I'll take the day off. But I'll speak to Morag. I know how her mind works. I only hope I don't lose my job."

"That's better. You're much prettier when you smile. And if Morag and whoever owns the hotel gives you a hard time, you can blame the damned foreigner."

"Oh, don't worry, I will." Anna started clearing the breakfast table. "Ewan has been known to reduce the most fearsome of chefs to tears, and I for one, have no desire to feel the lash of his tongue."

"Ewan? Would he be the short tubby guy, with the beard and big smile, I saw the day I used the phone?"

"Yes, that sounds like him. Don't be deceived. He might look jolly, but believe me, if you get on the wrong side of him, he'll slice your face open with his tongue."

Luke started. He rubbed his cheek. "I'll bear that in mind."

A short time later, having made her apologies to the hotel staff, Anna waited in the Land Rover outside Mrs McCloud's shop while Luke made his purchases. She knew from experience the village store stocked little in the way of luxuries, so there would be no pâté or champagne. Just sliced ham, cheese, pickles, fresh rolls, and, if they were lucky, a bottle of wine. But none of that mattered.

Luke had been right. Despite his reassuring presence in the spare bedroom, she'd slept badly. Every time she started to drift off her body jerked awake at some imaginary noise. As a consequence, she felt tired and lethargic. A weekend of making beds, dusting and polishing, Morag's endless questions was more than she wanted to face. Besides, what woman could resist a day in the sun, sailing on a beautiful yacht in the company of a good-looking man?

Across the road the shop bell tinkled. Anna watched in admiration as Luke emerged carrying two bags. With a quick look left and right, he crossed the narrow street, his movements swift, full of grace and virility. His broad shoulders, she noted, filled every inch of the denim shirt he wore, and his long legs, ensconced in faded jeans, looked firm and muscular.

Anna let out a sigh, and wondered why Luke had chosen to remain single after his fiancée's death. From what she'd read, every American woman dreamed of meeting a rich, successful, attractive man, and Luke was the very embodiment of one. Everything about him screamed 'marriage material.' Yet he remained unattached. Why?

Before she could think of a suitable answer, the object of her thoughts opened the tailgate of the Land Rover. She turned around and studied Luke's face, feature by feature, as he deposited the carrier bags in the cargo space. There was an inherent strength in his face that said 'trust me, I won't let you down.'

"What? Have I got egg on my shirt from breakfast?" He examined the blue denim. When Anna didn't reply, he closed the tailgate, walked round to the driver's side, and slipped behind the wheel.

He put his hand on her shoulder. "Hellooooo. You hiding in there someplace?"

"Sorry, I was miles away," she replied, swivelling in her seat to face him.

"Is my driving so bad that you have to put yourself into a Zen-like state?"

"What? No. No, it's quite good, considering you probably own an automatic, and aren't used to driving on the left."

"I go off-road a lot when I'm looking for new landscapes to paint, so I have an SUV. Granted, these roads are much narrower than those back home, but just give me another day or so, and I'll get accustomed to them, and to driving on the wrong side. In fact, you'll start thinking I'm one of the locals."

"God forbid. There are a number of 'locals' who shouldn't be in charge of a pram, let alone a car."

"Does that include you?"

"Why you—?" Anna replied, hitting him playfully on the shoulder. "I'll have you know I passed my driving test first time round."

"Let me guess. You drove away so fast the examiner didn't get a chance to jump into the car. You passed by default." He caught her hand before it could strike him again.

Anna leaned back against the worn leather seat and laughed.

"Do you always have a ready comeback?"

"Hey, I'm an American. It's my job." He put the Land Rover into gear and drove off. "I learnt to stand up for myself early on. Jack's doing. Do you want to take the dogs with us?"

"If it's all the same to you, I'll leave them. I've taken them on a boat before, but it was a large inter-island ferry where there was room to walk them. I'm not sure how they'd react on such a small vessel."

Luke brought the Land Rover to a halt outside the croft.

He opened the passenger door, helped her out and led her toward the small dinghy on the shoreline. "Miss MacDonald, please step this way. Today's cruise will begin in a moment."

He pushed off, slipped the oars into the rowlocks, and rowed steadily across the loch to his yacht. Close up, it was stunning. There were other superlatives to describe it, but none more appropriate, Anna thought as they approached the stern. Fully sixty feet in length and painted white, with two blue lines just above the waterline, it stood tall and proud against the rugged mountains.

Luke extended his hand to her. "Watch your step. The rungs of the ladder can be slippery." He showed her to one of the padded leather seats behind the helm. "Here, take a seat. I had these done in leather. Pretty comfy. I'll just stow our lunch in the galley and then I'll give you the guided tour."

Anna leaned back and examined her surroundings while Luke busied himself below. She was amazed by what she saw. Morag's comment about the yacht being a 'wee boat' was so far wide of the mark that she laughed out loud. It was the height of luxury.

The deck was teak, and the fittings, she noted, were stainless steel. If she craned her neck she could just make out the top of the mast fully eighty feet above her. In front of that stood the rigging for the spinnakers, and furled up against the boom was the mainsail. One thing was certain—Sandpiper was no poor man's toy.

Moments later Luke reappeared. He'd swapped his shirt and jeans for a T-shirt and cut-off blue denim shorts.

"Watch your head as you come down the companion way. The steps are quite steep."

Anna stepped into the galley...and lost the ability to speak. The galley, and saloon beyond, were both sumptuously fitted out in teak and cream leather. There were two tables, a wine rack and cupboards for storage. Even a VCR, DVD and a TV.

"I was lucky. Sandpiper was a custom build. Her previous owner, a Greek business man, went bankrupt. She'd been laid up for six months when I found her in a boatyard in Turkey. She was designed for world cruising, although not for single-handed sailing. I had the boatyard install the latest navigational aids and electric winches, before a friend and I sailed her back home."

"A female friend?"

"No, a big, burly Canadian fisherman named Ike. He'd have looked damned ugly in a dress. And you sure are nosy about the women in my life."

Anna turned away. "I am not! It was a stupid question. I'm sorry I asked. I always imagined the accommodation on yachts would be a bit Spartan. I had no idea it could be like this."

"Come and have a look at the master suite. Sandpiper sleeps six comfortably in three double staterooms. There's even room for a crew."

Luke led her aft. The master suite, fitted in teak like the rest of the yacht, had a double bed, small bathroom with shower stall, and cabinets for storage. The bed was covered in a rich, red and green Thai silk throw.

A small oil painting hung over the head of the bed. Anna leaned closer to examine it. The brush work was exceptionally fine. The painting depicted a Highland loch, with the figure of a woman carrying a basket walking towards a croft on the shore. Smoke curled from the chimney into the surrounding trees. Painted in shades of greens and browns, it looked very similar to the ones Anna had seen in Edinburgh. "Is this the painting you found in Bar Harbor?"

"Yep. Do you like it?"

"It's stunning. The frame looks original, too. You know, I think it could be a Breanski or a Jamieson. Jamieson was famous for painting Highland scenes. You might want to check that out when you get home."

"Thanks for the tip. I'll be sure to do that." Luke closed the door of his cabin and they climbed back on deck. "Well, what do you think of Sandpiper? Isn't she something?"

"If she were mine, I would travel the world. I don't think I'd ever want to set foot on dry land."

"Yeah, well, you might feel different after a few weeks at sea." He took his place at the wheel. "Once I've turned her around, I'll set the sails. There should be enough wind. If not, we can use the engine."

Acutely conscious of Luke's athletic physique as he crossed the short distance to the helm, Anna felt a ripple of excitement deep in the pit of her stomach. Had her feelings for him had gone beyond simple attraction? Could she be falling in love with him? Too busy fighting emotions and the desire to feel his arms around her, she paid scant attention to the conversation.

"Right. Whatever. I'm sure you know the best way to do things."

He glanced over his shoulder. "Are you okay? I know you've been through a lot of late. You seem distracted. Can I help?"

"I'm fine. Just fine." But the look he gave her was so electrifying it took all her strength to stop her fingers from reaching out and touching him. She closed her eyes and turned her face to the sun. The gentle motion of the boat drew her thoughts away. She'd never experienced anything like it before—a hypnotic, perfect harmony between man, boat, wind, and water. Seconds later her day-dream was broken by the clank of the anchor chain as the electric windlass dragged it up into the chain locker.

Luke turned his attention back to the helm. He manoeuvred the yacht until it faced seaward, killed the engine, and then hoisted the jib. The wind immediately caught the sail and soon the yacht was gliding across the water towards the mouth of the loch.

Behind his dark glasses, his eyes were sharp and assessing. The short-sleeved green shirt she wore matched the colour of her eyes. The top three buttons were undone, exposing a creamy expanse of neck. The cropped trousers showed off her slim calves and ankles to perfection. Unlike other women of his acquaintance, Anna didn't flaunt her attributes and was completely oblivious to her own beauty, which was why he found her so attractive.

She was no longer pale and gaunt, he noted with some satisfaction as he took his time examining her face. He saw both delicacy and strength—a strength that did not lessen her femininity. Her long lashes rested on high cheekbones, which were covered with a faint sprinkling of freckles. When his eyes lingered on her full lips, his body stirred as he remembered the kiss they'd shared and how it had felt to hold her in his arms. She'd felt too damned good.

The breeze gently fluffed Anna's red-gold hair and blew tendrils into her face. His hand automatically tucked them behind her ear, just as he'd done when they were out for their walk.

"What...?" Anna gasped, as Luke's fingers brushed her cheek, disturbing her serenity.

He took off his glasses. "Sorry. I should have known better than to touch you, but your hair..."

"For a moment...I thought...I'm sorry, I overreacted," Anna replied, breathing deeply trying to relax. But it wasn't easy, especially with Luke holding her gaze.

"No, you didn't. I should have realised you still feel vulnerable."

"I don't."

The look on his face said he didn't believe her.

"Honestly, I'm fine," she said firmly, trying to convince herself as well as him.

"Well, if you're sure..."

Something intense flared between them. Anna realised her erratic heartbeat had nothing to do with her anxious state. The way Luke was watching her sent desire rippling through her. It was as if an invisible, delicate thread pulled them closer and closer together. When Luke caught her hand in his, and pulled her close, she didn't hesitate. His strong arms circled her waist, and his hands caressed the small of her back.

She tilted her face to his. What she saw in his eyes left her with no doubt of his intention. His mouth covered hers. The kiss was urgent, demanding, and left her lips burning. When he released her, she backed out of his grasp and leaned against the helm, her heart pounding in her breast, her eyes fixed on his.

"Whoops," he said softly. "Just me being stupid again."

Anna felt so confused it took her a moment to think of a suitable response. "We just shared the most passionate, nerve tingling kiss, and you say 'whoops'?"

He rubbed his thumb over her lips. "Don't be angry, sweetheart. I got as much pleasure from that as you did. And I won't deny that I want you. I want to be so far inside of you that I forget everything but you."

Anna was shocked. Even Mark hadn't said such things to her.

"However," Luke continued, "I can't let my need for you take over my common sense. In case you forgot, we're on a thirty-three ton yacht in the middle of a sea loch. We could easily run aground or hit another boat."

Anna looked over her shoulder. "I don't believe there's any danger. There are no other yachts, and the loch is deep, so there's plenty of water under the hull.

"Maybe not. But I was still reckless. Besides, the timing is all wrong. You're way too vulnerable right now. When it happens, it's not going to be on the hard deck of a yacht."

"When what happens?"

"When I finally make love to you."

"Oh," was all she could say.

Chapter Seventeen

It was late afternoon when they dropped anchor in the small bay opposite Tigh na Cladach. Anna stared over the water. The house looked so small from this distance, like a tiny white cottage on a train set.

"Cat got your tongue?" Luke asked.

"No, you did," Anna replied, laughing in sheer joy.

"Mm, and very enjoyable it was too. I might even be tempted to come back for seconds."

"Don't you mean thirds? And what's this *might* business? Perhaps you need a reminder," she suggested playfully as she reached over to put her arms around his neck.

"Anna, behave. Otherwise we'll run aground. Look, there's a pickup parked outside your door. You expecting anybody?"

She squinted at the vehicle. "It's not Morag's, it's the wrong colour. No, I don't recognise it. There's lettering on the side, but I can't make it out. Can you read it?"

"Not from this distance. Here, try these," Luke said, handing her a pair of binoculars.

"P-r-o-t-e-u-s S-u-r-v-e-y-s. What are they doing on my land? And would they be surveying here?"

"Maybe they're from the highway department or whoever is responsible for roads in this part of the world."

"That doesn't make sense. I would have received notification if they were going to send anyone."

"Or maybe someone thinks the croft's for sale."

"I don't know how they could. I don't understand this—unless it has something to do with the estate. Luke, we need to go ashore now."

"Okay. Okay. Just give me a chance drop anchor, stow everything away, and lock up."

"There's no time—"

"Anna, wait!" But she'd already climbed over the stanchion and dived into the water. By the time Luke followed her in the dinghy, she'd waded ashore.

Dripping wet and shivering with cold, Anna marched up the beach and stood in front of a middle-aged man loading a theodolite into the bed of a blue pickup.

"What the hell are you people doing?"

The tall, thin surveyor with lank hair, pushed his glasses back up nose, took one look at the soaking wet woman and laughed.

"What does it look like, love? We're carrying out a survey. Another half hour, and my mate and I'll be finished. Nice dive by the way. You'd get my vote in a wet T-shirt competition." He winked at her.

Anna folded her arms across her chest. "Surveying? Why? This is private property and it belongs to me. Let me see your authorisation."

"I don't have to do that. Besides, it's restricted information."

"Restricted from the person who owns this land? That's ridiculous!"

"How do I know you own the land? Nobody was home when I knocked at the door. You could be a tourist for all I know."

"I'd gone out for the afternoon. And those are my dogs you hear barking."

"So? Unless can prove you're the owner, get out of my way."

"See that dry stone wall?" Anna said, pointing to her left. "That marks the boundary. All the land between it and the shoreline, including the croft house, belongs to me. Everything on the other side is owned by the estate. If you're working for the estate, why are you on my land? And if you're not, I demand to know who sent you."

"I've only got your word for any of this. I don't have to tell you a thing."

"I'll give you the name of my solicitor. He'll confirm what I say is true. Now stop what you're doing and get off my land."

"Look, love, I'm just following instructions," he replied, placing a tripod in the truck.

"Yes, but whose instructions? The Highland Council? The Forestry Commission? Alistair Grant? Killilan Estate?"

"Never heard of 'em."

"Then who's paying you? And stop patronising me by calling me your *love*!"

"I need to pick up my mate; he's waiting for me further down the track. In the meantime, do yourself a favour—keep out of our way."

"You can't leave until you've answered my questions." Anna followed him round to driver's door.

"You'll have to take those up with the boss. I need to re-check a few measurements before I lose the light. Come on darlin', move or I'll run over you."

A male voice cut the silence.

"What's going on here? Are you threatening her?" Luke's eyes bored into the surveyor's.

Recognising authority, the surveyor's tone mellowed. "As I was explaining to the little lady, I'm doing a preliminary survey. I've finished for today, but I'll probably need to come back to check one or two things out."

"Like hell you will. Get off my land now! If you come anywhere near Tigh na Cladach again, I'll have you arrested."

"I don't know what the survey is for, or who authorised it," the man said, getting in behind the wheel of his pickup.

"But if you've any sense, you'll not interfere; you'll let us get on with our job."

Anna blushed with rage. "I'll find out who sent you. I want you off my land now, or I'll set my dogs on you!" She fished her keys out of her soggy pocket and thrust them into Luke's hand.

The surveyor let out a long breath and scribbled something on a piece of paper. "Look, here's the office number, but don't tell them I gave it to you. The guy you need to speak to is called George. He usually gets in around ten o'clock. I suggest you take your argument up with him."

"Oh, I will. Trust me."

Anna watched the surveyor drive off before turning and storming towards the croft, where the dogs barked furiously.

She marched into the kitchen, filled the kettle and slammed it on the hotplate. "As soon as I've showered and changed, I'm going down to the gate and I'm going to lock it. That way, no one will get in or out without my knowledge. I'll phone Proteus Surveys in the morning and get to the bottom of this."

"Do you have a lawyer? You might need one to find out what the legal deal is."

"Yes, I do and I shall speak to him in the morning as well." Grateful for its warmth, Anna leaned against the Aga.

"Good. You'll get it figured out tomorrow," Luke said as came and stood beside her.

"Do you really think so?" she asked, her voice fading.

"Yes. I have faith in you. You're one strong chick," he said, kissing her on the cheek.

"Yeah, right. I'm a real tower of power. First someone tries to break into my house, now a surveyor turns up. All I can do is shake. What's going on Luke?"

"I don't know, but I'll tell you this, honey; I'm going to find out. Go and take a hot bath. I don't want you getting sick on top of everything else."

Luke waited until he heard the water running before removing the revolver tucked in the waistband of his jeans.

He figured it was a bit too soon in his relationship with the sexy Ms MacDonald to explain why an artist needed to carry firearms. When he judged she was safely up to her neck in bubbles, he climbed the stairs to his bedroom and opened one of the drawers.

He held the gun for a moment, feeling its weight in his hand. Then he dropped it in the drawer. Firearms belonged to a part of his life he preferred to forget. This gun was usually locked away in the safe in his cabin. But until he could be sure that the events of last night, and the unexpected appearance of the surveyor, weren't connected, he wasn't taking any chances. He was prepared to shoot.

To kill.

Chapter Eighteen

Anna sank down into the tub of hot water and thought about the events of the last twenty-four hours. Morag was her only visitor, or had been until Luke showed up. Luke...now there was an enigma. A man who, by his own admission, was successful, yet he'd sailed across the Atlantic on a whim. And alone. Why? Morag had said something—what was it? Oh, yes. Something about looking for a past he didn't know he had. Well, if he was seeking his ancestors, what did they have to do with her and Tigh na Cladach?

Pondering the answers, she poured a dollop of shampoo into her hand, and massaged it into her hair.

The croft had been in her family for generations, and as far as she knew, none of her ancestors had emigrated. And if they had, surely her grandmother would have told her.

Luke. He should have been unprepared for the croft's remoteness and inaccessibility. But he hadn't seemed surprised. What if he'd been acting? That would explain why he'd made such a big deal about her staying there on her own.

He was in an ideal position to kill her. All he had to do was row across the loch and bash her head in. But, that wasn't the man she was getting to know. Hadn't he shown up the following morning full of concern? No, Anna reasoned as she towelled herself dry, Luke couldn't be responsible. Besides, when he looked at her, the air positively crackled with sexual tension, and just thinking about the way his mouth felt on hers made her lips tingle and her pulse quicken all over again.

A knock on the bathroom door interrupted her thoughts. "Dinner's ready!"

"I'll be down in a tick!" She zipped up her denim skirt, fastened the buttons of her blouse, and scurried down the stairs into the kitchen.

"I hope this is all right," Luke said placing a bowl of tomato soup in front of her. "There's cheese and ham, and salad too."

"It's perfect. Thank you, Luke. Do you mind if I ask you a question?"

"No, go ahead."

"On still nights, sound carries clear across the loch, so I was wondering...the night someone tried to break in, did you hear anything?"

"I tend to listen to the radio before I go to sleep, it helps me relax. No, I'm sorry, I didn't hear a thing."

"In that case, do you recall if there were any other boats anchored in the loch that night?"

"No. But the loch doesn't run straight to the sea, it narrows into a dog-leg about a third of the way down. But you know that. I guess it's possible that another vessel was anchored further out. Why do you ask?"

"Well, if my midnight caller arrived and left by car, the dogs would have heard its engine. And I probably would have done so, too. I didn't. So, either the prowler came on foot, in which case he's familiar with the terrain, or he came by boat."

"Mm. I see what you're getting at." His gaze caught and held hers, as his mouth spread into a thin-lipped smile. "You're not suggesting it was me, are you?"

Anna moistened her dry lips, and avoided looking at him. "No. No, of course not."

Luke studied her face for an extra beat. "You are! I can see it in your face." He pushed back his chair and carried his soup bowl and plate to the sink. "You think I'm the one who tampered with the generator, and slashed your tyres."

"No, Luke, I don't."

"You might remember that I was with you when someone took a pot shot at us."

Anna's face paled. "You said that was an accident!"

"Well, maybe I'm not so sure anymore. There's a pattern forming here. Can you see it?"

"No, I can't." She bit her lip and looked away. But what if Luke was right? "It just seems a coincidence that all these things started happening right after you turned up on my doorstep!"

"What possible motive could I have for trying to drive you out of this place? I'd never set foot on Scottish soil until a few weeks ago. My passport confirms that. I'm exactly who I say I am, an artist. Call Jack. I'll give you his number. He'll vouch for me, or if you prefer, call the police and have them check me out. Either way, I have got nothing to hide."

Anna flushed with humiliation. "I'm sorry. I didn't mean to imply that you were in any way responsible for what happened. Please let's not argue. We've spent a lovely day together. Let's not spoil it because of a simple misunderstanding."

"You mean *your* misunderstanding."

"Yes, *my* misunderstanding."

He held out his arms. "Come here."

She covered the distance to him in two quick strides.

He wrapped his arms around her waist and gazed down into her eyes. "I'm sorry too. I overreacted. The thought of you not trusting me was a kick in the guts. Anna, I think I'm—"

Standing on tiptoe, she wrapped her arms around his neck, and smiled.

"Don't think, just kiss me," she whispered huskily in his ear.

That was all the invitation Luke needed. His kiss was slow and thoughtful, and meant to be conciliatory, but when Anna's lips parted, seeking more, he found himself fighting for control. His arms tightened around her waist and pulled her closer. He reclaimed her mouth and deepened the kiss. The depth of her response broke all Luke's earlier resolve to behave like a gentleman. Suddenly kissing her wasn't enough. He wanted her naked, and under him, and now. When he finally got his ragged breathing under control his voice was thick and unsteady.

"Sweetheart, I think we should continue this somewhere more comfortable. Don't you?" He took her hand and led her towards the stairs. When she hesitated, he turned, and pulled her against him, the hardness of his arousal pressing into her thigh.

"Don't get all coy on me," he whispered. "We both know we've been moving toward this moment ever since we met." He lowered his lips to hers and kissed her with a ferocity that made her fully aware of his intentions. Without waiting for her denial, he swept her into his arms and carried her up the stairs to his bedroom, then closed the door behind him with his foot.

Once by the bed, he set Anna on her feet. With one fingertip he traced the line of her trembling lips. The passion he saw reflected in her emerald green eyes answered the fire in his own. He reclaimed her lips, his left hand slowly exploring the hollow of her back, while the right moulded her soft derrière to the contour of his hard, lean body. Hungrily he took all she gave and more, his tongue exploring the soft recesses of her mouth. When he finally lifted his mouth from hers, his breathing was ragged and fast.

Anna clung to him, responding without hesitation or thought, as her body instinctively arched towards his. She wrapped her arms around his neck, and buried her fingers in his thick jet black hair. Her senses reeled as his tongue traced the soft fullness of her lips before seeking the velvet softness of her mouth once more.

When his lips left hers to trail a path down her neck to the pulse beating at the base of her throat, sending shivers of delight through her, she inhaled sharply. She felt his hands slide under her blouse, and skim her back, caressing every contour. The gentle massage sent desire spiralling through her, filling her with an inner excitement she never believed possible.

"Luke..," she said huskily, tugging his T-shirt out of his shorts.

"Mm—" he murmured against her neck as his fingertips traced the outline of her bra.

"I haven't...I haven't done this in a while."

"That makes two of us, honey. Don't worry. I'll take it slow."

Luke pulled his T-shirt over his head. Unbuttoning Anna's blouse with trembling fingers, he slipped it off her shoulders, and down her arms. It fell to the floor. Her skirt quickly followed. His eyes dropped from her mouth to her shoulders, and then to her breasts.

"You're so beautiful," he said huskily, as he outlined their fullness through the black lace of her bra. "I've wanted to make love to you, since the moment I saw you." He watched her intently as his unsteady hands reached for the fastening. When she didn't protest, he freed her breasts from the lace, gently fondling each smooth, firm globe. Slowly and seductively he traced circles around her dusky pink nipples, the nubs hardening under his expert touch. His body quivered with desire, the ache in his groin almost unbearable. He tried desperately to slow the pace, wanting their first time to be perfect, but he couldn't resist the invitation in her eyes.

Gently, he eased her down on to the bed. His gaze lingered over her full breasts with their swollen rosy nipples, and the curve of her thighs. In one quick movement he stripped off his shorts and stepped out of his boxers, and joined her on the bed. His hands roamed intimately over her body, and when his tongue sought her taut nipples, drawing them into his mouth, she arched her back and called out his name. He stroked her legs and thighs, the silky skin of her belly, before finally pulling aside the lace of her panties and slipping a finger inside, seeking the core of her desire.

Anna's skin burned where he touched her. His lovemaking was exquisite, sending flames of passion racing through her. It was as if they had been lovers forever. He knew exactly how to arouse her, to give her pleasure. When she thought she could take no more, he slowed the pace; and showered feather-light kisses on her face and shoulders. Her body ached for fulfilment, and with a sigh of pleasure, she rested her cheek on his chest. She could feel his heart thudding, answering the beat of her own. Slowly her fingers explored the muscles of his chest under the covering of hair, and where they touched, her lips followed, sending fire coursing through his veins. She pushed Luke on to his back, and straddled him. Her fingertips softly brushed his lower lip before tracing the line of his collarbone, luxuriating in the feel of the coarse hair on his chest.

When her hand found his erection and stroked the hard, silky length, his body jerked and throbbed in response. All he could think about was sinking into her. Luke watched as her tongue slowly followed the trail left by her fingers and remembered to breathe—just. When she lowered her mouth to taste him, the pleasure was pure, and explosive, and almost drove him over the edge.

In one quick movement he rolled Anna on to her back and covered her soft warm body with his, one muscular leg resting between hers. With passion-darkened eyes he entered her, moving slowly at first, prolonging the moment, until desire and passion overwhelmed them and they sought release. Just when he thought he couldn't get any deeper, she opened herself to him, welcoming him further into her body.

Luke felt the first waves of her orgasm, and his body picked up the rhythm. Anna trembled under him, her breath coming in long surrendering moans as her body arched in final surrender to his. Unable to hold back, his powerful orgasm coursed through him, exploding in a million fiery sensations.

Chapter Nineteen

The grandfather clock stuck ten, as Luke and Anna pulled into the hotel car park. The day was warm and the heavy oak front doors, with distinctive ice axes for handles, stood open. As they entered the reception area, they met Morag who was carrying a tray of glasses through to the kitchen. They'd come to use the phone to find out who'd sent the surveyor.

Luke leaned against the door frame, watched the play of emotions on Anna's face as he listened to her side of the conversation.

"Well?"

"There's no such number," she replied, replacing the receiver. "I've checked with Directory Enquiries too, and they have no listing for Proteus Surveys. It would appear that the surveyor gave me a wrong number."

"Or Proteus Surveys is a fake company," Luke said. "I've got a bad feeling about them. Is there some kind of business registry you could check with?"

Anna let out a long, audible sigh, and sat down at the kitchen table. Morag placed a mug of coffee in front of her. She nodded her thanks, and turned to face Luke once more.

"In this country anyone can set up a business, irrespective of whether they have the know-how or experience to run it. Only limited companies have to be formally registered."

"Aye," Morag chimed in. "There are a lot of cowboys, right enough. The television is always showing programmes about how people get ripped off."

Anna took a sip from her mug and looked at Morag and Luke. They were both deep in thought.

"Have you heard any rumours, Morag? Is it possible that the estate is planning to enlarge the hillwalkers' car park? Or what about the Forestry Commission? Does it have plans for a new plantation?" Anna asked.

"No, lass, it doesn't. Sandy always knew what was going on, but since he's left..."

"In that case, I don't see what else I can do."

"You could always go and see Mr Alistair," suggested Morag.

Anna shook her head. "If I thought he would be honest with me, I would do that. Alistair's changed. He's become very business orientated, if you know what I mean. I think it's better if I try and find out what's happening for myself. Don't you? The only thing is, I don't know who to ask."

Luke dropped down beside her chair.

"Supposing I wanted to build a house. Wouldn't I have to submit the plans to the authorities for approval?"

Morag and Anna spoke as one. "The local council!"

"Luke, you're wonderful," Anna said and planted a kiss on his lips. Snatching up her bag, she grabbed his hand. "Come on."

"Where are we going?"

"Fort William. To the Council Offices. That's where all the planning applications are filed. Are you coming too, Morag?"

"What, in that old bone shaker you call a vehicle? No, I don't think so. Besides, some of us have work to do!"

"In that case, I'll see you tomorrow as usual."

Luke wrapped his arm around Anna's shoulder, and they walked towards the door.

"Wait lass," Morag said. "I'll look after the dogs for you. I'd feel much happier if you took my pickup." She handed Anna the keys. "You can drop it off at the house on your way home and collect the Land Rover then."

"I don't deserve a friend like you," Anna said, giving her a hug.

"Oh, be off with you. And mind you take care of her, Luke."

"You can count on me," he replied.

As Luke and Anna walked across the car park toward the pickup, a man stepped out of the hotel. His bushy eyebrows drew to a frown as he watched them climb into the pickup.

"Did you see that guy staring at us, Luke?" Anna said as she started the engine.

"What guy?"

"The one standing in the doorway."

Luke bristled. "What does he look like?"

"Dark hair, foreign looking, strange eyes. He's staying at the hotel."

Luke turned and looked over his shoulder. "There's no one there now. He must have gone back inside."

"I just keep seeing him, that's all..."

ৡৡৡ

The town hall clock struck the hour as Anna and Luke walked along the High Street toward the modern glass and concrete, three-storey building which housed the Council Offices.

"Three o'clock. That gives us two hours to check out all the recent planning applications, before they lock up for the night," Anna smiled.

"Well, given the number of houses in the glen, I would say that's more than ample. Who owns the land that borders yours, anyway?"

"The Grants. It's been in their family for generations, although there's a strong rumour circulating the village that they've transferred into a holding company to avoid taxes and death duties. I don't fully understand the legalities, but no doubt Morag knows the reason behind their decision."

"How did your family get the croft?"

"According to the deeds, the thirty acres which now form Tigh na Cladach, was gifted to the then-Laird's son in 1750."

"So you're related to the Grants."

"No."

"Then I don't get it."

Anna smiled. "Many estates were entailed and passed to the eldest son on the death of his father. However, if a Laird had an illegitimate son, he couldn't very well leave him the family home as that would mean acknowledging the child was his. Instead, he would transfer a small piece of land, and possibly settle a sum of money on the child too. I've always assumed that's how the croft came into the MacDonald family."

"So you *are* related."

Anna laughed. "Not in Scots terms. Ah, here we are." She pushed open the door marked Planning Department.

A spotty clerk stood behind a well-worn wooden counter.

"Hello, Jason," Anna said, reading his name badge. "I wonder if you can help me."

"It depends what you want. If you've come to file a planning application you'll have to wait until the office manager gets back. I'm only a trainee."

Anna smiled. "Actually, I'm enquiring whether any one has lodged an application for Tigh na Cladach, in Kinloch Hourn. Do you think you could have a look for me?"

Jason hesitated. "I'm not supposed to—Mr Jeffries could be back any minute. He's my boss."

"I'm sure he wouldn't mind if you took the tiniest peek on your computer. It would only take a moment."

"Well..." he looked down at his feet. "I suppose I could. But only for a moment. Mr Jeffries doesn't want me doing things without him. I'm new, you see."

"That would be really helpful. And don't worry, we won't tell...Mr Jeffries."

"I would hope not. He gets quite angry."

"We'll prevent that. You can be such a help to me, Jason. It's my property, you see. I just want to make sure my architect has filed the plans for my house...er my extension. He can be a bit forgetful."

"There's nothing listed under Tigh na Cladach."

"What about MacDonald, or Killilan Estate?" Anna asked.

Luke drummed his fingers impatiently on the desk while the Jason accessed his computer.

"No, nothing listed for them either."

Crestfallen, Anna looked at Luke. "I don't know what else to suggest."

"Try looking under the holding company," Luke replied.

Anna turned to the clerk. "Is there anything listed for Grant Holdings or Killilan Holdings?"

"No, sorry."

"Thanks for your trouble, Jason," Luke said, and slipped a £20 note across the desk.

Jason grinned. "Thanks. Sorry I couldn't help. I'd have a word with your architect if I were you. And thanks for not telling Mr Jeffries. If you see him, of course."

"It will be our secret," Luke said. "Come on, Anna." He caught her hand in his. "There's just enough time for us to go to the boatyard and see if the pump for the auto-pilot came. After that, we'll get something to eat." He held open the door for her.

"It was a long shot, but I felt sure we'd find something," Anna said as they left the building.

"I know you did. I don't think you have any other choice now except to contact the police."

"But I don't see what they can do."

"Let's put it this way," he said pulling Anna to a halt. "It'll become a matter of record, and if anything else happens, they'll have to take you seriously."

It was nearly midnight when Luke and Anna arrived back at Morag's cottage. A solitary light showed through a gap in the curtains. They found her in the kitchen drinking cocoa.

"I thought I heard a vehicle. Come in with you, you must be fair worn out. The kettle's just boiled. I'll make you some tea."

"Thanks, Morag, but if it's all the same to you, we'll get on our way. We only stopped to hand your keys over and pick up my Land Rover."

"Well, if you're sure. But you must tell me how you got on before you go."

Luke put his arm around Anna's shoulders. "It was a waste of time. Nobody's applied for planning permission in the last six months. We tried searching under different names—nothing. So Anna went to the police and reported the incident with the prowler and the bogus surveyor."

"And a good thing too. But this business with the surveyor got me thinking. About two months before your grandmother's death she received a letter from a solicitor, offering to buy Tigh na Cladach."

Anna threw up her hands. "Oh, my God. I completely forgot! I had a letter too. It was from a firm in Glasgow. I was going to write back and tell them to go to hell, but it clean went out of my mind. I wonder why Nana never told me. I don't recall seeing anything in her papers after she died."

"Perhaps she didn't want to worry you, lass. And you have to remember, her mind did wander towards the end. But more to the point, she loved the croft and would never have agreed to sell it. It was her dying wish that it should go to you."

"And you think these letters are significant? That whoever sent the letters also sent the surveyor?" Luke suggested.

"Aye, I do."

"But it doesn't make sense," said Anna. "Why would anyone want to buy Tigh na Cladach? It's barren and rocky and totally unsuitable for farming. It wouldn't sustain a cow, let alone a flock of sheep. The house is basic, to say the least. The only person to whom it has any value is me."

Luke tapped his chin with his index finger. "Obviously someone somewhere has a reason for thinking otherwise. Did you see the letter, Morag? Can you remember the name of the solicitor?"

"No. Sadly Alisha never showed it to me. But I doubt that I would have remembered, anyway."

"Not to worry. I'll write to grandmother's solicitors to see if they know anything."

"You're not angry with me for not telling you earlier, are you?"

"Of course not," Anna replied, and hugged her friend.

"That's a relief." Morag yawned. "Did you have time to enquire about the part for the yacht?"

Luke sighed. "Yeah. Seems it's not a make easy to find over here. The boatyard is having one shipped from the States."

"So you'll be staying with Anna a little longer?" Morag smiled. "That's good. My, my, will you look at the time. It's well after midnight and we've work in the morning. I think you ought to take the lass home." And with that she handed Luke the keys to Anna's Land Rover.

Chapter Twenty

Unable to sleep, Anna crawled out of bed. Her eyes were dry. Staring at the clock every twenty minutes will do that to a person, she chastised herself.

When Luke didn't wake, she pulled on her dressing gown and crept down the stairs to the kitchen, being careful not to tread on the two sleeping dogs lying in front of the Aga. Although dawn was only just beginning to creep over the horizon, there was enough light for her to see clearly. Taking a glass out of the cupboard next to the fridge, she poured herself a glass of milk.

She thought about the letter from the Glasgow Solicitors.

It had been waiting for her when she arrived at the croft. She remembered sitting down at the table and reading it, but what had she done after that?

She jerked open the centre drawer of the oak dresser, which doubled as her filing cabinet, and rooted through the disordered contents. The first thing she found was the guarantee for her iron. That's a really big help, she thought, and put it to one side. There was also the receipt from the garage for the two new tyres on the Land Rover. Had they really cost that much? She yawned and dropped it on top of the iron guarantee. Hidden underneath the tea towels were some batteries for the torch, a ball of string, and a dog lead, but no letter. She dumped it all back in the drawer and slammed it shut.

She leaned against the dresser, and took a sip from her glass. Luke had arrived the day after she'd received it. She'd been drafting a reply when she saw him walking up the beach.

She hunkered down and examined the floor. But there was no sign of the letter. If it wasn't in the drawer in the dresser or on the table, then it had to be in the sitting room. Right?

Silently, she crossed the hall and opened the door. The hinges squeaked in protest. Her heart beat speeded. Her laptop lay on the table next to the armchair. She reached to pick it up.

"And just what do you think you're doing?"

Anna spun round. The laptop slipped out of her grasp and landed on the chair with a thump. Luke was standing in the doorway in nothing but his jeans. She hadn't known him long, but she recognised the warning in his voice.

"Nnn...nothing. You scared me!"

He rubbed the sleep from his eyes with his left hand. His right hand, out of sight from Anna, tucked the gun he was holding into the waistband of his jeans. "*I* scared *you*? I thought the prowler came back. You're damned lucky I didn't run down here and smack the crap out of you—accidentally of course."

Anna swallowed. "I'm sorry. I couldn't sleep. I thought I'd come down and look for that letter."

"Anna. It's five in the morning. What were you going to do if you found it? Drive to Inverness and demand to know who their client is?"

"Glasgow! The solicitors are in Glasgow."

"Glasgow. Inverness. Edinburgh. Toronto. Whatever. What difference does it make? No one will be there. I'll help you look for it in the morning." He cupped her chin.

"I suppose you're right."

"You know I am. Now come on, let's go back to bed. I'll give you a back rub to help make you sleep."

"I'll let Ensay and Rhona out first, then I'll be right up."

Luke let out a sigh. He opened the door and stepped aside to let the dogs out.

Across the loch a light glowed in Sandpiper's main cabin.

He hadn't left any lights on.

"What the hell!" He pushed Anna out of the way.

"That hurt! What do you think you're doing?"

"Someone's on the yacht! Call the dogs. Lock yourself in the cottage. Don't open up until you see me."

"But—"

It was too late. Luke sprinted barefoot across the lawn. Crippled by renewed terror, Anna stared as he untied the rope securing the small inflatable dinghy and started rowing across the loch.

Luke pulled steadily on the oars, they hardly made a ripple on the surface of the loch. He circled the yacht. Tied up against the hull, out of sight of the croft, was an inflatable. He rested his hand on the casing of the outboard engine. It was still warm. He shipped his oars, being careful not to hit the hull, tied his dinghy to the swim step, and climbed aboard.

The hatch leading to the accommodation was open.

He hadn't left it that way.

He drew his gun and flipped off the safety. Crouching and listening, he stepped into the cockpit and crept down the companionway to the galley. Even in the twilight the interior of the yacht looked like it had been through a hurricane. Books, CDs, DVDs, and charts lay strewn all over the cabin floor.

Quietly, he eased his way passed the dining table toward the master suite. He swept the gun in an arc round the saloon.

The scraping of rough soles against the deck. The sound of a drawer squeaking open.

He smiled.

His cabin door was ajar.

The bastard was still inside.

He kicked the door open. It slammed against the bulkhead. He dove for the floor. He looked up. He was alone.

Suddenly, something hard connected with the back of his head. His heart slammed. The walls and floor spun. The bastard had been hiding in the shower stall all along. He struggled to reclaim his balance and stumbled through the cabin after his assailant.

He heard an engine sound coming from the deck. With a silent curse Luke crawled up the companionway ladder. As he reached the top, he saw the other inflatable head for the far shore, the dark figure of a man at the helm. His body sagged. There was no point in him trying to follow. His assailant had too much of a head start.

He climbed back down to the galley and pulled some ice out of the fridge. He wrapped it in a cloth, and held it to his pounding head. He poured himself two fingers of bourbon and sat down. His vision was improving. He looked around the cabin. As far as he could see nothing was missing, but the knowledge gave him little comfort. It did, however, tell him something about the prowler. He might be an experienced burglar, but he was an amateur when it came to boats.

Which meant only one thing.

Whoever had crept aboard Sandpiper was looking for information.

He put down his drink and went on deck to examine the lock on the hatch. There were scratch marks on the woodwork. It had been picked, not forced. So his uninvited guest had come tooled for the job.

While he stowed his books, CDs, charts and drawing materials away, Luke wondered what the hell he'd gotten himself into. His dark eyes narrowed. It wasn't often that he thought about his old life, but tonight was one of those rare occasions. For the first time since he'd left the service, he wished he had access to the Bureau's vast database and resources.

He'd retired five years ago. Most of the forgers and thieves he had a hand in convicting were still serving jail time, although it was possible one or two might be up for early parole. What if they'd somehow tracked him down? And if so, his very presence could be endangering Anna's life.

He'd felt uneasy ever since she had told him about the prowler. Burglars targeted towns and cities—places where they could make a quick buck. They didn't drive into the countryside unless they were planning to rob a million dollar country mansion stuffed to the rafters with antiques. If this had been Boston or New York, he could believe some asshole was stalking a woman with the intent of scaring the bejesus out of her. But out here?

By her own admission, Anna wasn't rich. Her father was a diplomat in China. If she was the target, could that be the reason?

He chewed on this for a while. If her father had upset the Chinese Government, they'd have simply expelled him. They wouldn't threaten his daughter.

Luke swallowed the last of the bourbon and poured another. Perhaps her father had been instrumental in some company or other failing to win a lucrative contract, and they were planning on using Anna as leverage. He tossed that idea out. Anna would have to be in China for that to work.

The more he tried to reason it out, the more his head ached. He picked up the small oil painting, and wrapped it in a bag. Better to keep it in the croft than here on the yacht.

He glanced at his watch—almost seven—time to get back to the croft. He'd left Anna on her own for way too long.

Clutching the collar of her coat, Anna stood on the pebble beach, as Luke dragged the dinghy ashore.

"The next time I tell you to stay put, you damn well better stay put!" He grabbed her hand and pulled her toward the croft.

"Ow! Let go! You're hurting my fingers!"

"You're lucky it's only your hand."

"Listen, you—"

He spun her around. "No, *you* listen. Here you are standing out in the dawn—a perfect target for a marksman. Am I missing something critical about your personality? Do you just *want* to die?"

Anna's face drained of colour. Her mouth opened. No words came out.

"Somebody could shoot you where you stand and you're practically inviting them! Now do you understand why I told you to stay indoors?"

Anna understood only too well.

"I'm—I'm sorry. You were gone so long I was worried you were hurt."

"There's nothing that a hot shower and some food won't cure."

"And Sandpiper? Is there any damage?"

"No. Whoever broke in picked the lock. They trashed the cabin, but as far as I can tell, they didn't take anything."

"I can't understand it. Nothing like this has ever happened before."

"Yeah, well, it's happening now. Your glen's having a regular crime wave."

Chapter Twenty-One

Fin Armstrong steered his ruby red sports coupe through the twisting glen toward Killilan House. The little car hugged the tight corners as if on rails. It was heaven to drive. It might not be brand new, but it was new to him, and there was plenty of life in the engine and hardly a mark on the paintwork. He smiled. If it hadn't been for the chance meeting with Alistair Grant, he'd still be driving that old heap of a Mini. At last things were on the up.

He turned through the tall ornate granite archway, topped by the Grant family crest, which marked the entrance to Killilan House. He pulled the car to a halt, lit a cigarette, and wound down the window.

When times began to change the Grants grew more safety conscious; Alistair's father had added white metal bars and fencing to ensure that the great unwashed stayed out of Valhalla. Fin laughed at the thought; he used to be one of the gods. Now he was pretty unwashed, and no longer great.

Before going off to Oxford University, he'd been a constant visitor to the estate. The Grants had been known throughout the county for their lavish parties. He'd rubbed shoulders with dukes, earls and princes, even kissed a few princesses in his time.

The country set from all over Scotland and Europe came to shoot grouse and deer on Killilan estate. They'd be up before dawn for a breakfast of porridge, eggs, and bacon, topped off with a glass of whisky, then venture into the hills for a day's stalking. They'd walk miles in search of their quarry. Around noon, a leisurely lunch would be served at one of the many bothies on the estate. Champagne, caviar, smoked salmon, better than a Fortnum and Mason's hamper. Then it would be off stalking again before returning to the house in time for a sumptuous dinner of pâté foie gras, grouse, pheasant, salmon, venison or beef, rounded off with numerous wines and good port.

One year, he recalled, he'd caught a fourteen pound salmon in the morning, shot three brace of grouse and a stag in the afternoon, and danced with Alistair's sister, Sophie, until dawn. It had been a capital day's sport.

He pitched the cigarette, and started the engine. The driveway seemed to have more pot-holes than he remembered, and the overgrown bushes on either side could do with a trim. The front offside wheel bounced over a particularly deep rut. He cursed. As he turned the last corner, the house came into view.

The Georgian mansion complete with grand portico, and perfectly symmetrical facade, had always impressed him. In fact he'd always been envious of Alistair living there. The formal gardens, which stretched down to the river, had been designed by Alistair's mother. Set against the mountains, and surrounded on either side by trees, it was one of the finest houses in Scotland.

Or it had been.

He got out of the car and stretched his back, and stared up at the front of the house. Most of the windows in the east wing were closed and shuttered, something never seen when Alistair's father had been in charge of the estate. Two of the four centre chimney stacks leaned at an alarming angle, and tarpaulin covered part of the roof.

He slowly climbed the leaf covered steps to the front door and rang the bell. A plump, middle-aged woman dressed in a green and blue kilt with a navy sweater, opened the door.

"Findlay Armstrong. An old friend of the Laird. Is he in?"

"Mr Alistair is in the library. If you'll wait in the hallway, I'll tell him you're here, Mr Armstrong."

Fin stepped inside, and waited while the old woman shuffled away. There was a strange smell in the air. It reminded him of the cellars in his former home near Crief. Damp. It was mildew—the arch enemy of any householder.

He ran a hand along the heavy oak furniture; it was covered in dust and grime. He looked around for something to wipe his hand on and settled for the threadbare seat of a Chippendale chair. There had been other Chippendales, he remembered sitting on them. Where had they gone?

Alistair's mother would never have allowed the house to get in such a state. But then in her day, the house was staffed by a bevy of servants.

"Fin! This is a surprise! Come in. Come in." Alistair said.

"I was in the area and thought I'd drop in. I hope you don't mind."

"Not at all. Come through to the morning room. Mrs McTavish, rustle up some coffee and sandwiches for our guest. There's a dear."

Mrs McTavish shot him a glare and shuffled away.

Fin followed Alistair down the hallway. The faces of previous generations of Grant's peered down at him from the numerous portraits.

"Ah, I remember these people," Fin said. "They looked down on me a good bit since I always seemed to be inebriated whenever I stayed here. So were you. Good times, eh, Alistair?"

"Very good," Alistair mumbled.

"What's happened here, old chum? The estate used to be quite the playground. It's all gone rather depressing, don't you think?"

"It's still got its charm."

"If you say so. But these paintings—ooh! If it were me, I'd sell the lot."

Alistair scowled. "I can't, at least not until I inherit the estate."

"You mean you haven't? I'd have thought with the old man out of commission...well, doesn't that mean this is place is all yours?"

"Not precisely. Father would have to pass on before I officially got it."

Fin went directly to the drinks cabinet. He found a collection of crystal decanters inside and sniffed at the contents of each until he found one he liked. Looking for ice and finding none, he poured himself a lavish drink. "Hope you don't mind, old thing. Long drive and all that." He sank down onto the faded chintz covered sofa, the springs groaning under his weight. "I still say the old place looks a bit different from when I was here last. Do you have only the one servant now?"

"Yes. It's hard to find good staff these days—"

"You mean it's too goddamned expensive! In your parent's day you had what, ten? Twenty?"

"Only seven, including the cook."

"The estate used to hold such grand parties. And the fancy dress balls, do you remember the time we had the same costume and that girl, what was her name?"

"Lucy. Lucy Colquhoun."

Just then there was a knock at the door. Mrs McTavish scowled as she set the tray on a wide rosewood table.

Alistair smiled extravagantly. "Ah, coffee. Just leave the tray, if you would, Mrs McTavish."

The servant nodded and left.

Fin swirled his drink. "Too bad you've no ice in here. What were we talking about? That's right, Lucy Colquhoun.

God she was a stunner; blonde hair, sapphire blue eyes, long legs, and big breasts. She couldn't tell us apart. She kissed you and thought it was me! God that was so funny!"

"Look, can we cut the social chit-chat now, Fin. I assume there's a purpose to your visit."

"My dear boy, that's no way to talk to your saviour. I've driven a long way. You could at least refill my glass instead of expecting me to drink this...this coffee. Couldn't you?" He smiled, revealing even teeth—although slightly yellowed they were the only remnant of his boyish charm.

"What do you have already? Whisky?" Alistair asked, opening the drinks cabinet.

"Very good, old man." Alistair refilled the proffered glass. Fin drank the contents down in one mouthful, then held the glass out for a second refill.

"Go easy on the booze, Armstrong. We don't want you being stopped by the police for being over the limit."

"Aren't you going to offer me a bed for the night?"

"I wish I could. But you've seen how things are. Most of the house is closed up. Mrs McTavish cooks for me or I eat in the Monymusk Arms."

"I see. You have indeed fallen on hard times, old boy. In that case, you'd better have this." He took the thick envelope from his jacket pocket and weighed it in his hands. "I've taken my seven percent as agreed, plus the cost of my little trip. There's £16,000 plus in there. Not quite as much as you expected, but at least it will keep the bank off your back for a while."

"*Only £16,000?* You should have been able to get at least £20,000!"

"What can I say except that old cliché about beggars not being able to choose? And times are hard, dear Alistair. One only needs to watch the evening news to see we're in the midst of a recession. You still have satellite TV, don't you?"

Alistair ignored the question and thumbed through the cash. He wouldn't say no to it, but his stomach seized at how little his precious antiques had garnered.

"By the way," Fin continued. "Strangest thing. I passed a caterer's van as I came down the drive. Are you planning a party?"

"No. Just a small gathering for the tenants, that's all."

Fin screwed up his nose. "Oh, how positively boring. But I suppose you must keep the plebs happy. If you ever decide to host a ball and invite the country set, do let me know. I could use some cheering up." He put down his glass. "Well, thank you for the refreshments and fine company. I'd better be going. I've a plane to catch tomorrow. The sea breeze in Monte is always welcome at this time of year. But oh, I forgot. You know that, don't you?"

Chapter Twenty-Two

Suddenly it was Friday. How could the week have slipped by so quickly? Anna wondered as she drove home after her morning's work in the hotel. Thankfully, there'd been no further sign of her midnight prowler, and neither had the surveyor returned, but despite Luke's reassuring presence in the croft, Anna still felt uneasy. If anyone asked why, she'd be hard pressed to explain and would say it was feminine intuition. She shook her head and laughed out loud. As if talking to herself wasn't bad enough, now she was beginning to think like Morag! Whatever next?

The problem was she really liked having Luke around. He was attractive, funny, intelligent, a considerate lover, and if she was honest, she was more than a little in love with him. But the part for his yacht would arrive any day. Then he'd sail off, leaving her with only memories. Anna swallowed the lump in her throat; she wasn't going to think about that until the day it happened. In the meantime, there was a Ceilidh to attend.

The croft came into view as she steered the old Land Rover round the last bend in the track, and she let out a sigh. It was home. *Her* home. The only place where she'd ever felt truly happy. With summer already half over there were major decisions to make. But she'd worry about them later, she told herself as she climbed out of the driver's seat. She greeted the two dogs and walked towards the loch.

Luke had set up his easel close to the water's edge. Anna stood and watched as he roughly sketched in the scene before him with a pencil. Once satisfied with his drawing, he opened his palette of watercolours and started mixing until he had the exact shade he needed. Selecting a broad flat brush, he applied a pale blue wash to the heavy paper. Next, he took a paper towel and carefully dabbed away the excess.

Anna shifted from foot to foot and continued to watch. When the paper had dried, Luke chose a rounded brush, and started adding detail. She didn't understand the techniques involved, but layer by layer, the painting evolved. Slowly the mountains began to emerge. Then the loch. Then Sandpiper in the foreground.

When he sat back to examine his work, she stepped forward and slipped her arms around his neck and kissed him.

"Hi, there, handsome."

"I didn't hear you drive in." Luke put down his palette and brush.

"No. You were engrossed." She nodded at the painting. "It's very good."

"It's not bad. I can do better. I just don't seem to be able to capture the reflection of the mountains on the loch. How was work?"

"Tiring. It's too hot. We'll have a storm before the night is out. The hotel is full for the Ceilidh tonight. It seems that Alistair Grant has invited most of the village, including, I might add, Ms Anna MacDonald and her guest. This was waiting for me in the hotel reception." Anna waved her gilt-edged invitation under his nose.

"I thought you said the Ceilidh was just for tenants. Are you going?" Luke rested his hand intimately on her hip.

"Usually it is. I wasn't going to go, except Lachlan is still away and Morag was so looking forward to it that I didn't have it in my heart to say no. Apparently he telephoned her last night to apologise. He's been asked to stay on the rig for another week while his opposite number is on holiday. Besides, this will be your opportunity to experience a traditional Scottish Ceilidh first-hand, and nobody throws a party like the Scots."

Luke groaned. "What if I said I had nothing to wear?"

"I wouldn't believe you. And what's more, even if you didn't, Morag would insist on lending you one of Lachlan's kilts."

"Me? Wear a skirt? No way!"

"But Luke, darling, you have all the right attributes, especially those required to wear it the traditional way..."

"What traditional way?"

"Nothing underneath."

"Nothing? Are you shitting me? So you expect me not to dress for the party?"

"Of course," she said laughing, then ran towards the croft. Luke caught up with her in seven strides.

"Right attributes, huh?" He pulled her to the ground and kissed her until she was breathless.

"Mm," she replied, as her body squirmed beneath his.

Luke's brown eyes smouldered with fire. "And what might those attributes be?" He planted a kiss in the hollow of her neck.

"You've broad shoulders for one thing, great legs, and..." her fingers slid between them to his zipper.

Luke's hand caught hers and halted its progress. "The thought of being seduced by you is delicious, my love, but I have no desire to get my butt bitten off out here by the local wildlife."

"Local wildlife—? Oh, you mean the midges—the mosquitoes. Now that you mention it, they are a bit fierce today."

"Besides," he said, kissing the top of her nose. "My days of making love in the open are long over." He helped her to her feet. "Let's be sensible."

She stood on tip toe and wrapped her arms around his neck. "Perhaps I should call you Mr *Sense and Sensibility...*"

Luke laughed and squeezed her.

"I'm going to make some iced tea," she said. "Would you like a glass?"

"No thanks. I should finish my painting before I lose the light."

"Fine. I'll put my feet up for half an hour and then work on my manuscript for a while. The Ceilidh starts at eight, and there's a buffet too. I said we'd pick Morag up on our way."

Once in the kitchen, Anna switched on her laptop, opened the file containing her manuscript and started typing.

The town, I learnt, was Ullapool, a small busy fishing port on Loch Broom, many miles from my native Knoydart. Here, my husband secured passage for us on a ship known as 'Hector', bound for the Americas.

We sold our ponies and purchased supplies for the journey—salt beef, ale, tea, coffee, flour, and biscuits, which were to be delivered to the quayside, along with our few possessions, in time for our departure. I had new clothes too—a travelling dress of heavy cotton, as well as two others and a heavy coat. Stockings, under garments and shoes filled my trunk, along with linen and a bolt of tartan cloth.

Three days later, we stood on the quayside waiting to board. As a three-mast, wooden sailing ship, 'Hector' had seen better days. Even I could tell her timbers were rotten and see her sails were tattered.

The Captain himself showed us to our cabin. It was tiny, but afforded us privacy, unlike many of my clansmen who I'd seen herded into the hold like cattle. An oil lamp hung from the ceiling on a hook, and there were two beds, one atop another.

I stood on the deck that evening, my plaid wrapped tightly round my shoulders, as we waited for the tide to turn

"One day, m'eudail—my darling, we will return." I smiled at my husband's use of my tongue. He wrapped his arms around me and held me tight. I knew he spoke the

*truth, for the 'Sight' had shown me that it would be our sons
and daughters who returned, not us.*

*Two hundred souls bade farewell to our native land
that day in July 1773. A lone piper stood on deck and played
a lament as we sailed out of the loch. When the coast of
Scotland disappeared from view we retired to our cabin.*

*That first night I lay in my husband's arms and wept.
I cried for our families, for their future and ours. He kissed
away my tears and I became his wife in every way.*

After a hot shower, Anna took her time getting ready.
First, she pinned her long tresses into a neat chignon, being
careful to leave some loose tendrils around her face. Her face
was tanned and only needed the lightest touch of blusher. She
accentuated her bright green eyes with bronze shadow and
then applied a light coating of mascara. A little lip gloss
and...yes, she would do.

She took the plain white, crêpe de Chine dress from its
hanger and stepped into it. The sleeveless, scooped-necked
bodice fitted her figure to perfection. The full skirt fell almost
to her ankles, and she couldn't resist standing on tip-toe and
twirling round.

A parcel of tissue paper lay on the dressing table.
Inside was her grandmother's sash, in the MacDonald clan
colours—soft black, white, green, red and blue, which
shouldn't have blended well into a heathery plaid, but did.
She opened it and touched the soft fabric to her cheek. Her
grandmother's favourite perfume still lingered on the fine
tweed.

"I miss you, nana," she whispered.

Suddenly a fine breeze shook the curtains.

"Nana?" she said, almost unconsciously. The breeze
stopped. Could it be? Could Nana be giving her some sort of
sign, perhaps a blessing? She blew a kiss toward the window,
just in case. Nana had always blown them to her.

The curtain moved once again.

I'm getting like Morag, she thought. She shrugged off
the silly idea and carefully folded the tartan in two. She

pinned the top of the fold to the right shoulder of her dress with the large Cairngorm and silver brooch that had been in her family for generations. Anna had inherited it on her eighteenth birthday.

With one final look in the mirror, and her dancing pumps in her hand, she pranced her way down the stairs.

Luke stepped into the hallway as she reached the bottom tread. The warmth she saw in his dark eyes made her heart skip a beat.

"You look—stunning." He pulled her into his arms.

"Why, thank you, kind sir. You don't scrub up so badly yourself." She kissed his cheek. The scent of his dark, musky cologne intoxicated her instantly. She shook her head to bring herself back to reality, and resting a hand on his arm, bent to put on her shoes.

"I hope this is okay. When I packed for my trip, I didn't think I'd need a tux or a suit."

Anna admired his smart dark slacks, and crisp white shirt. "Trust me. Once the whisky and wine start flowing, no one will pay attention to what anyone else is wearing. If you're ready, we should be making a move. Morag will be wondering where we are."

It was a little after eight when Luke steered the Land Rover through the rusting iron gates of Killilan House. The Georgian mansion looked sad and forlorn. Once an architectural jewel, Anna knew it was now a testament to years of neglect. Grass sprouted from the gutters. Masonry crumbled. Paintwork peeled. But the darkness was kind—in the night, it was still majestic, still proud of its heritage and the family that had inhabited its land for six generations.

"My, my, Mr Alistair has pushed the boat out," Morag declared as her gaze took in the floodlit façade. "Judging by the number of cars, I'd say the whole village and half of Scotland is here to see what he's up to, but then it's not often the Ceilidh is held in the big house."

"Mm, I see what you mean. Look, isn't that old Dougal?" Anna pointed to a gentleman almost bent double with age.

"Aye, it is. And there's Mrs McCloud and the Fraser twins."

A lone piper, in full Highland dress, stood on the steps of the west wing playing a lively reel to welcome the guests.

"Ah, the pipes. Don't you just love them?" Morag wiped a tear from her eye. "My Lachlan is such a bonny player; what a pity he can't be here." She spied Luke cringing. "Do you no like the bagpipes, then?"

Anna squeezed his arm in warning.

He cleared his throat. "They're sorta like classical music and opera—an acquired taste."

"Aye, well maybe you're right. You have to be a native of Scotland to truly appreciate them. You'll hear a lot of pipe music tonight, and I daresay some *puirt-a-beul*, too."

"You've totally lost me, Morag. Poor-a-beel...?"

"'Poorsht-a-beel'," Anna enunciated. "Highland mouth music."

The large drawing room, which ran the entire length of the west wing, had been transformed into a ballroom. Two wide bay windows, draped with faded gold silk curtains, lay on either side of the centre full height glass doors, overlooked the sweeping front lawn. The hardwood floor once a deep red, had faded to a soft pink. Damp patches showed on the ornate stuccoed ceiling, and chandeliers appeared to be missing some of their crystals. Tapestries, threadbare and faded like the curtains, hung on the walls. Tables had been placed at one end, leaving the rest of the room free for dancing.

The room was two-thirds full when they entered. Raucous laughter filled the air.

"Wow!" Luke glanced around the room and gestured at the portraits. "Get a load of all those ugly mugs. Must be his ancestors."

"Yes, well, you're not here to admire the antiques," Anna said as the band, specially hired from Glasgow, started tuning up at the far end of the room. She took Luke's hand, and pulled him along behind her as the first chords of an eightsome reel filled the room.

"Come on," she said, taking her place among the dancers already forming a circle on the floor.

"Hey, wait a minute! I said nothing about dancing..."

"Oh, don't be such a bore. A reel is easy. Any idiot can do it."

"Not *this* idiot. Anna!" But his refusal fell on deaf ears. Anna tugged him to the left, then to the right in time to the music. With her shouts of 'right,' 'left,' 'give me your hand,' and general words of encouragement, she ensured he fumbled his way through to the end.

As the last notes died away, a breathless and flushed Anna slipped her arm in his.

"There, that wasn't too bad, was it?"

"It depends on your definition of bad. I think I'm going to have a heart attack. I need a drink. A great big one."

Anna laughed as he snagged two glasses of wine from a passing waiter, and handed one to her.

"*Slainte!*"

"*Slainte mhath,*" she said, taking a sip. "A couple more of these and you'll soon get the hang of things. Want to sit this one out?"

"Yes, and the next, and the next...."

Anna laughed. "Sorry, but I didn't go to all this trouble to be a wallflower. If it makes you feel happier, we can wait until the band plays something more sedate for the older generation."

Luke's left eyebrow arched a fraction. "I may be a little older than you, but I've got loads of stamina."

"Yes, I know, darling," giving his ear a playful nip. "You can keep it up all night."

"Anna, behave!" he warned, turning round to make sure no one was within earshot.

"Listen, that's the opening bars of the Gay Gordons. It's easy."

"None of this shit is easy."

"This one is." Anna took his glass from his hand and led him back to the dance floor. "Even you could do this fully anaesthetised."

"In that case," he sighed. "Bring on the ether..."

Chapter Twenty-Three

From the edge of the dance floor Laird Alistair Grant, resplendent in full Highland dress, watched Anna thread in and out of the couples in her set. Her white dress swirled about her ankles. He knew the sound of her laughter—even though he couldn't hear it, he felt it. It singed him. He didn't normally go for redheads; blondes were more his taste, but even in her youth, she'd possessed a certain something. Under different circumstances, he might have found her appealing.

"I see you invited the MacDonald woman," Mac said, with a nod.

"That's my business. And what are you doing in here? I specifically asked you to supervise the parking arrangements."

"I don't see why I can't join in the party. I put on me suit, see?" He tugged on the oversized lapels. The outfit was light brown polyester double knit, probably stolen from some thrift shop. It wouldn't have been fashionable in the mid-seventies. Alistair winced.

"You're quite dapper," Alistair said. "Better than the orange Day Glo thing you wore while parking cars."

Mac sniffed. "All the other employees of the estate are here. Folk would think it odd if your trusted factor was excluded. Besides, you gave me a shit job to do. I'll get you for that."

"I'm sure you will. Go easy on the whisky, MacKinnon. I don't want you getting drunk tonight, of all nights."

"Don't look down your nose at me, your Lairdship. I'm just as good as this lot, if not better. You're planning something; I can see it in your face."

"Nothing that concerns you. Just a charm offensive, that's all. Now if you'll excuse me," Alistair said, fingering his lace jabot. "I think it's time I asked the lovely lady to dance."

Anna spotted the proud figure of Alistair Grant walking purposely toward her. She scanned the crowded room for Luke and Morag, but they were nowhere in sight.

"Oh bother," she mumbled, and pasted on what she hoped was a welcoming smile.

"Anna, my dear," he said, and kissed her on the cheek. "You look especially lovely tonight."

"Thank you. And thank you for the invitation."

"You're welcome." A smile tipped the corner of his mouth. He leaned closer and whispered in her ear. "I'll let you into a secret. I had an ulterior motive in asking you to come this evening."

An unwelcome blush crept into her cheeks. "Oh? And what might that be?"

"I wanted to spend the whole evening dancing with you."

"That's rather unfair to the other ladies present."

"Perhaps, but as most of them are middle-aged married women, I daresay they won't mind. Besides, none are as pretty as you. Ah, a waltz. I think this dance is mine." He put his arm around her waist and led her on to the dance floor. "Now tell me, how are you settling back into village life?"

"I'm getting used to the slower pace. There are certain things I miss, such as the big grocery stores. Mrs McCloud does her best, but it's not like shopping at Safeway."

"I wouldn't know about that. I leave such tedious details to my housekeeper. But you must miss the theatre.

Oh, and restaurants. My favourite is still that little Italian on Leith Walk, Villa Rugiada, although I'm also rather fond of Etienne's, the new French Bistro at the side of the Caledonian Hotel."

"I've never been to either," Anna replied, remembering how little her lecturer's salary afforded her after she paid rent.

"No matter. A beautiful young woman like you should be treated to such luxuries. You never know—I may be the one to take you."

"I'm perfectly happy with what the hotel serves, Alistair."

He snorted. "I wouldn't exactly call it haute cuisine. Dog food, perhaps..."

"Alistair, you are such a snob."

"No, my dear, I'm not. However, I like do like to be able to wine and dine a beautiful woman in style, rather than in the public bar of a two star hotel."

"Which happens to be *your* two-star hotel, Alistair, or have you forgotten?"

"No, I haven't."

"Then why don't you upgrade the restaurant to Michelin Star standard?"

"You know, I'd never thought about that. What a good idea. I knew I'd made a wise decision in renewing our friendship. Have you thought any more about having dinner with me?"

Anna thought about his offer for a stanza. "Oh, dear, how can I say this without offending you? It's very kind of you to ask me again, but no."

"I see. Are you sure I can't change your mind?" He bent and kissed the soft skin between her neck and shoulders.

Anna pulled back. She forced a superficial smile. "Alistair, please don't do that. It's not...it's not appropriate."

Aware that Malcolm Fraser and his wife were beginning to take an interest in them, Alistair steered her into the rhythm of the waltz once more.

"Anna, darling, think carefully before you turn me down. I'm offering you a life of luxury—this house, and a villa for the season on the Riviera. That's much more than average man in the street could give you."

"Now you're being conceited, Alistair, and that's a trait I dislike in any man. Besides, you're forgetting the two most important things in any relationship."

"I assume you're talking about love and trust."

"Yes. I am. Don't you want that?"

"Perhaps. But men in my position often have other things to consider when choosing a wife."

Wife? The word shook her. "You don't know me. I'm not the girl I was twelve years ago."

"I realise that, my dear. But you're sufficiently intelligent to see that a relationship such as I'm proposing could work."

"Look, Alistair, you're a good catch for the right woman. But I'm not her. You need someone of your own social standing, someone who moves in the same circles as you. Not a lowly unemployed university lecturer."

"I think that's for me to determine. And I happen to have determined that I want you."

Perspiration collected on her forehead. "Alistair, I've said all I'm going to on the subject. No matter how hard you try to persuade me, the answer is still no. Listen, the music has stopped. The orchestra is taking a break. I think it's a good time for you too, don't you agree? Thanks for the dance. It was nice seeing you again." She swirled away and left the dance floor.

Alistair caught her by the elbow.

"Now, now, Anna. Please hear me. I have real feelings for you. Deep feelings. Love and trust. I've waited years to see you again. Don't push me aside so easily."

"I'm not pushing you aside, Alistair. I'd like to stay friends. Just friends."

"I can't be just friends, Anna. Look, let's talk it over away from all this. I have a bottle of champagne chilling in my study. No one will notice if we slip away for an hour. I only want to talk."

"Ouch! You're hurting my arm. For the last time, Let. Me. Go!" She pushed him away from her. "If you don't let go of my arm this instant, I'll...I'll stamp on your foot!"

Anna stormed off. He followed.

McKenzie MacKinnon leaned against the corner of the bar nursing a large whisky, his second of the evening, and watched the interplay between his employer and the redhead. He could tell from her body language that whatever the Laird had said hadn't gone done well. He swigged down the contents of his glass and signalled the barmaid for a refill.

While he waited for his drink, he scanned the room for the American. It took him a moment or two, but eventually he spotted him on the far side of the dance floor talking to some old biddy with a feather in her hair.

There was something about the American that set his teeth on edge. He couldn't say what it was, but instinct told him the guy was trouble. But for the moment at least, he was safely occupied.

He pulled out his cigarettes and felt in his jacket pocket for his matches.

"I'm sorry, sir, but you can't smoke in here. You'll have to go outside." The barmaid placed a glass of whisky in front of him.

Mac nodded and put down his glass, then slipped out onto the terrace. He'd only taken a few drags when Grant and the redhead appeared in the doorway. He hastily stubbed the cigarette out lest the tell-tale glow from its tip gave his presence away, and quickly took cover behind a large statue. As he listened to their muted conversation, it didn't take him long to realise that prissy Ms MacDonald was none too happy with the Laird's seduction technique. Hah! Bloody hah! It served the stuck up tosser right for thinking she'd be interested in the likes of him.

He backed away from the statue, being careful not to make any noise, and walked quickly across the lawn to the front of the house, re-entering the grand drawing room a few moments later.

At least he could handle things his way from now on. And now was the perfect time to show the Laird just who was boss.

He went straight to the bar.

"A double malt. And don't forget the ice."

"I'm sorry, but you've already had your quota," said the barman.

"What are you talking about man? Give me that drink."

"I can't. The Laird told all the staff you were to have no more than two glasses."

"Well, the Laird's not here, is he? Now fill my damn glass before I come round there and ring your scrawny neck!"

"Yes—yes, sir." The barman paled, and quickly re-filled the glass.

Mac leaned against the bar and scanned the dance floor. Morag McInnes was dancing with Angus Murray. He caught her eye and she turned away quickly, but not before she'd looked at him as if he'd slithered out from under a stone. He laughed, and tossed down his drink.

He slammed his glass down on the bar. "Fill it again, laddie."

"But, sir, I'll lose my job."

"No you won't. I'm the factor here and I give the orders. Now, pass me the damn bottle and the ice."

The barman did as he was told and pushed the ice bucket toward him, the ice pick still inside. Mac stared at it, a plan forming in his mind. He swirled his glass. It might just work. He tossed back his drink, poured another, and drank it. He weaved his way across the floor towards the exit, pushing the dancers out of his way as he went.

Chapter Twenty-Four

Luke's dark and brooding eyes followed Anna round the room as she danced with the tall man in Highland dress. While his expression was unreadable, his emotions were beating the hell out of each other. Deep inside his chest, the little green warrior was hard at work. His fists clenched and unclenched as his temper flared. He was about to cut in on Anna and her Highlander when he was blockaded by an elderly woman with an enormous feather pinned in her hair.

"Now there's a bonny couple," she nodded in Anna's direction. "I met my husband at the village Ceilidh, you know. We were married exactly one year later. I was eighteen and he was twenty-five, and we've never spent a night apart since. It's our fortieth anniversary next month."

"Congratulations," Luke said, and left her still talking about who-knew-what. He skirted the edge of the ballroom until he found a better vantage point. He stood with his hands in his pockets, observing the interchange between Anna and her partner. She was smiling and laughing, and obviously enjoying herself. His temper went from simmering to red hot. Suddenly he saw her expression and body language change. When she abruptly stopped dancing, he decided that was his cue to intervene. He strode purposely across the room and reached them just as they were about to step though the French windows and out onto the terrace.

"Anna, honey, are you all right?" Luke gave her companion an icy stare.

"Yes," she said, with a grateful smile. "I was just saying to Alistair that I needed to sit down and cool off, as it's rather hot in the ballroom."

"In that case, allow me to escort you outside."

Annoyed at the untimely intrusion, Alistair released his hold on Anna's elbow and nodded at the other man.

"Are you going to introduce me to your friend, Anna?"

"Yes, of course. Alistair, this is Luke Tallantyre from Cape Cod. Luke is staying with me for a while."

"How do you do? Grant, Alistair Grant of Killilan." His distinguished features settled into an expression of contempt.

"Nice to meet you. Wonderful place you have, although the upkeep must be hell on your wallet."

"Not if the well is deep. What brings you to Scotland, Mr Tallantyre? Business or pleasure? Or something else?"

"Pleasure, Mr Grant, pleasure. Now, if you'll excuse us, I'll take Anna for some fresh air."

"Of course, don't let me detain you. It's about time I resumed my duties as host. I don't want my tenants complaining. This is, after all, for their benefit." He strode away stiffly.

Anna felt Alistair's sharp eyes boring into her as she and Luke walked through the wide-open French doors, and out on to the brightly lit terrace.

"What a phony! *I say, I say, old chap!*" Luke mocked. "Who does he think he is, the King of Scotland?"

"Unfortunately, Scotland doesn't have a monarch, although many of us wish it did," Anna replied coldly. "Alistair happens to have the benefit of a very good education."

"So do you, but you don't talk like a jerk. Anyway, what was that all about?" He pulled her round to face him. "Do you two have a history or something?"

Anna closed her eyes, and wished with all her soul to be at home with the dogs. "No, not in the way you mean. We're old friends, that's all."

"Friends, eh? You two look at lot closer than that."

She let the comment go and rested her hand on his chest. "Luke, what's got into you? I've told you. Alistair is an old friend, nothing more, nothing less. We've known each other since we were teenagers. Besides, he invited us here. Did you expect me to be rude to him?"

"No. But I want to know why the pompous ass was hassling you."

She glared at him. His tone infuriated her. "Were you watching me?"

"Kind of unavoidable. You two made a real spectacle of yourselves on the dance floor, and afterwards."

"It was just a dance, something men and women do occasionally. You're a stranger in the village. You don't understand the small community mentality. You can't just stroll in here and expect to tell us how to behave."

"Perhaps not. But I'm the guy who makes love to you every night. Does that count for anything? Ever think you might be stomping on my feelings?"

"I wasn't stomping on your feelings. I was being polite to our host. And if you must know, Alistair asked me out to dinner for old time's sake."

"Well, I hope you said no."

Anna regarded him from under her eyelashes. Why was he being so possessive? Could he possibly be envious of her old friendship with Alistair? Was there a chance, a slender chance, that he saw their relationship as something more than a causal fling? When she finally spoke her voice was soft, almost a whisper. "Of course I said no. But would it really matter to you, if I'd said yes?"

Luke pulled her into the shadows, crushing her to him. His eyes never left hers for an instant, as his mouth took hers with a savage intensity. "Does that answer your question?"

"No!" she wailed, bursting into tears. She pushed him away, and turning on her heel, sprinted back towards the house.

Anna breathlessly re-entered the ballroom, but the sound of singing floating over the crowded, hushed room brought her to an abrupt halt. Morag's pure, hauntingly beautiful soprano melted her frail composure. She closed her eyes and tried to shut out the pain, but the poignancy of the *Eriskay Love Lilt* sliced open her heart. She fought back her tears as Morag sang the verse.

When I'm lonely dear white heart,
Black the night or wild the sea,
By love's light my foot finds
The old pathway to thee.

Desperate to be on her own, Anna made her way out of the ballroom into a long dark corridor. Old portraits of long-dead Grants stared down at her, accusing her of abandoning their descendent so abruptly. She tried not to look at the rows of eyes. They almost seemed fixed on her. A trick of the light? The intent of the artist?

Artist. Luke.

She didn't want to think about him now. She had to get out.

After a couple of wrong turns, she eventually arrived in the main hallway, and was faced with a choice of four doors. The first opened into a formal morning room, complete with lumpy-looking sofas and tired floral chintz curtains. The second door she opened contained a chain-pull lavatory and small washbasin that looked as if they had been installed when the house was built.

She pushed open the third door and was relieved to find a small cosy sitting room where a welcoming fire burned in the grate. Settling back against the deep blue velvet sofa cushions, she forced herself to relax, breathing deeply until she was sure no more tears would fall. She looked at her watch; it was barely ten o'clock and the Ceilidh, she knew, wouldn't finish until well after midnight. Somehow she had to find the strength to get through the rest of the evening.

The door creaked open.

Luke.

"Anna, we need to talk."

"I'm not sure I have anything to say to you right now."

He squatted down in front of her and took her hand in his. "I owe you an apology. I was way out of line. These are your friends and I shouldn't have reacted the way I did."

She gave a choked, desperate laugh. "And you think that flimsy apology makes it all right?"

"No. I don't. I hurt you, and I never intended that to happen. Anna, look at me."

She swallowed hard, lifted her chin, and boldly met his gaze.

"I saw Grant's hands on you and I got pissed. He looked like he was going to drag you off the dance floor...and with everything else that's been happening to you, I was worried for your safety. How could I know he was just an old friend?"

"You couldn't, but this conversation isn't just about your behaviour..."

He stood up and pushed his hands deep into his pockets. "No? Then what is it about?"

"It's about... how we feel—"

"Why, here you are!" Morag said breathlessly, entering the room. She flopped down into a chair, and fanned her flushed face. "I've been looking all over for the two of you. You have to admit, Mr Alistair has done us proud this year. Everyone is having a marvellous time. I hope you're going to sing for us, Anna." She turned to Luke and smiled. "She has such a wonderful voice you know. An alto. Far better than mine. And what's more, she sings in Gaelic."

"Morag, I don't think Luke is interested in my singing abilities. Now, I don't know about you two, but all this dancing has made me hungry. Shall we go through to the buffet?" She rose fluidly from the chair and started walking toward the door, stopping only briefly to look over her shoulder at Luke, "Are you coming?"

While her friends enjoyed the delights of their host's table, Anna pushed the food around on her plate. She'd lost her appetite, and for her, the evening was officially a disaster. After supper, she steadfastly refused to sing, despite Morag's entreaties. She didn't have it in her heart to perform to an audience, preferring instead to let her friend take centre stage.

Luke's behaviour had not only upset her, but had given her a headache too. Every time she looked at him, she wanted to hurt him...yet she also wanted to make him want her. He doggedly remained by her side throughout the rest of the evening, even accompanying her on the dance floor for some of the less energetic dances.

Outwardly, Anna was smiling and happy, but inside she was a mass of conflicting emotions. By the time the clock struck one, her headache had reached mammoth proportions, and she could take no more. When the band finally struck up the opening chords of *Auld Lang Syne* she breathed a sigh of relief. She joined the circle, linking hands with Luke and Morag, and sang along with everyone else, but all she really wanted to do was go home and crawl into bed—alone.

Anna climbed into the passenger seat of the Land Rover, closed her eyes and pretended to sleep. Still annoyed with Luke for his behaviour toward Alistair, she had nothing to say to him as he drove back to the croft.

A soft sigh escaped her lips as the elderly vehicle rattled over the last cattle grid. Without waiting for Luke to open the door, she climbed out, marched up to the front door, and inserted her key into the lock. Ensay and Rhona, tired of being shut in, greeted her like a long-lost friend before rushing outside into the twilight.

It was humid, and out over the ocean storm clouds gathered. Anna followed the dogs down to the beach, and looked out across the dark, mysterious waters of the loch. Luke's yacht rode silently on its mooring and the tall mast appeared to touch the stars.

Despite the warning voice in her head, she'd walked into their relationship with her heart wide open, knowing that once the part Luke needed arrived, there'd be no reason for him to stay. And yet part of her hoped that he would.

Luke took off his jacket, and placed it round her shoulders. When his hand brushed the back of her neck, she turned to face him. His arms wrapped around her waist, pulling her into the warmth of his body. He rested his forehead against hers.

"Am I forgiven for being an idiot?"

The touch of his hand on her cheek was unbearably tender, and she felt a familiar rush of desire. Half-heartedly she tried to push him away, but the need grew and grew until all her resistance dissipated. When his mouth claimed hers in a slow, thoughtful kiss, she was lost.

"No...Yes," she whispered against his lips, her voice husky with passion.

The first rumble of thunder echoed round the hills as Luke scooped her up into his arms and carried her into the house. The dogs followed at his heels. In the hallway, he paused just long enough to lock the door and turn out the lights, then he carried her upstairs to their bedroom.

Once inside, his lips recaptured hers in a demanding kiss that left her breathless and wanting more. When he reached round and lowered the zipper on her dress, she was powerless to stop him. It fell to the floor as his hands began a slow sensuous dance over her body. She couldn't breathe, couldn't think. All she wanted was him loving her—forever.

His lips seared a path down her neck to her breasts; a delicious shudder spread through her body that left her gasping for breath. She watched him intently as he outlined her hardening nipples through the lace of her bra with his fingertips. Heat surged through her as he continued to stroke and tease until she was hot and breathless. She felt his fingers snap open the clasp. Gently his hands caressed her breasts, his thumbs rubbing the taut nubs.

Anna arched her back, inviting him to touch and taste. When his hot, hungry mouth replaced his hands, she cried out his name. In her haste to feel his body against hers she tore at his shirt, sending buttons flying across the carpet. Even though her heart fought a battle with her mind, her body ached for his.

He lifted her onto the bed, then quickly undressed before lowering his body over hers. With long, lazy strokes, he explored the creamy expanse of her flat stomach and thighs. Her body quivered in response. She inhaled sharply as pleasure radiated through her. When Luke pulled aside the silk of her panties, seeking the core of her desire, she moaned.

"Luke, I need you to..."

"Yes..."

"I want you inside of me...now."

"Anna, look at me," he demanded.

Their eyes locked. She felt his hot silky length enter her. Her hands raked his back, sending them both over the edge. The first shudders of her orgasm surged through her.

Chapter Twenty-Five

The following morning, Anna lay in the drowsy warmth of their bed and listened to the sound of raindrops falling on the window. She stretched languidly, enjoying the luxury of a lie-in. The sound of the radio, accompanied by Luke's tuneless whistle, drifted up from the kitchen below, along with the smell of bacon cooking. She rolled over to look at the clock on the bedside table and was surprised to see it was nine-thirty. Stifling a yawn, she threw back the quilt, climbed out of bed, and padded to the window to draw back the curtains.

The storm that had swept in overnight from the Atlantic had passed, leaving the mountains shrouded in mist. With any luck, Anna thought, it would burn off before lunch. She smiled to herself. It was a typical Scottish summer, fine one day, raining the next.

After a quick shower she dressed and followed the scent of coffee downstairs. She paused to pat the heads of the two dogs lying on the mat at the bottom of the stairs, and then entered the kitchen. Luke sat at the kitchen table, eating breakfast.

"Aren't you going to work today?"

Anna poured herself a cup of coffee and carried it to the table. "Not until later. Ewan hired some extra help so that the staff could attend the Ceilidh. They'll deal with breakfast and cleaning the rooms. I agreed to go in this afternoon to help serve high tea and dinner."

"Judging by what I saw last night, there'll be a whole lot of folk with hangovers this morning. What a fun bunch they'll be."

"Aye, no doubt. Even Morag was a more than a little bit tipsy." Anna buttered a slice of toast and put it on his plate. Then she rethought the gesture and reached to take it back.

"Hey, that's mine!" He smacked her hand gently. "It's pretty miserable out, Anna. Too wet for a long walk. What are you going to do with your morning off?"

She chewed thoughtfully on another bite of toast. "Unfortunately, the dogs need exercising regardless of the weather, unless of course you've already taken them out."

Luke shrugged. "Whoops."

"In that case, I'll take them for a run. I really ought to work on my manuscript too. I'm way behind schedule. Are you going to eat that?" she asked, indicating a piece of bacon on his plate.

"Yes, I am. Why?"

Anna smiled sweetly. "It would go nicely with my toast."

Luke laughed. "I'm sure it would." He stabbed the rasher with his fork and took a bite, making a show of his enjoyment. "If you want more, feel free to make some."

"You're very ill-mannered, Mr Tallantyre, even though you're a handsome devil."

"Anna, about last night—"

"There's really no need to explain."

"I disagree. After my temper tantrum, I thought you might be so pissed off at me that you might want me to leave."

"That's just silly," she said, pleased at how nonchalant her voice sounded. "We're both grownups. Anyway, you weren't the only one acting like the playground bully. Alistair's behaviour wasn't exactly exemplary either. I think what happened is best forgotten, don't you?"

Luke's face split into a wide grin. "In that case, I thought I'd row over and check on the yacht, if you'll be all right on your own for an hour or two." He cut a piece of sausage and offered it to her.

She shook her head and swallowed the last of her coffee. She walked into the hall and pulled on her boots and waxed jacket.

"Hang on. I'll come with you." Luke put his empty plate in the sink, and then followed out of the kitchen into the hall. He pulled on his coat and followed her outside.

They stood on the beach. The pebbles were grey. So was the sky. And the water. And the fine mist-like rain.

Anna squinted at Sandpiper. "You worry too much about me. You'd think I was six. I was right about the other night; it was just a disorientated hillwalker. I've told you a dozen times, the girls and I are used to our own company."

"I don't think you're six. I know you're a strong independent woman, but you have to admit these are unusual times. Stray hillwalker or not, I don't want you wandering too far from the croft on your own until we get everything figured out."

"I'm not going far, just up to the bothy and back. I won't be long—perhaps three-quarters of an hour—an hour at most, that's all."

"A bothy? What's that?"

"It's a kind of shelter," Anna replied fastening the hood of her jacket. "There are a few on the estate. Most of them are tumbledown ruins inhabited by sheep."

"Mm...I still don't like it. I'll go with you."

She rested a hand on his arm. "No, you won't. I'll be back before you know it."

"Well, if you're not here when I finish checking the yacht, you know I'll come looking for you."

"Luke, that isn't a good idea, not in this mist. I don't want you getting lost."

"Be careful. Promise?" He kissed her cheek.

"I will." Anna untied the dinghy and handed him the line. She called the dogs to heel and walked off in the direction of the waterfall, her mind full of the events of the previous evening.

No matter how hard she tried, she couldn't understand why Alistair continued to show interest in her, especially after Morag's revelations about his playboy lifestyle in France. She certainly wasn't his social calibre. Her wardrobe consisted of jeans, sweatshirts, and chain store clothes. She didn't know the names of current designers, let alone own any of their creations. Yet, there was a certain attraction to his half-said offer.

He'd behaved oddly. She'd hoped he might have forgotten about the invitation to dinner, but she wasn't surprised when he brought the subject up again. But what was it about his manner that warned her against accepting? And why did he keep on saying that the estate and his lifestyle could be hers. It was as if he was proposing marriage without saying the actual words.

Marriage. Something she'd never allowed herself to dream about. No one had ever asked her. Not even Mark.

She wondered if Luke had thought about it. He'd been engaged before. He wasn't opposed to the idea. Or he hadn't been with this...Nicole. Did he ever think of it with her?

Was she just a summer distraction, or did he love her? While she longed to hear his answer, she lacked the courage to ask him. Besides, no matter what the duration of their relationship, she couldn't betray him by having dinner with Alistair, at least not right now. All of which left her no option but to let things take their natural course.

Oblivious to the fine rain soaking her hair, she trudged on through the bracken and heather towards the old shephards' bothy high up on the hill.

At last she approached the bothy. Stone built and with a corrugated-iron roof, it was originally constructed to provide shelter for the estate's deer watcher. Rarely used now, except by hillwalkers as a place to camp out in overnight, it was devoid of furniture and although never locked, the door stood ajar.

Curious, she signalled the dogs to wait in the porch, and cautiously stepped inside. She gasped in fright at the sight of a strange man standing by the fireplace. Middle-aged, with a deeply creased face; he dangled a half-smoked cigarette from the corner of his mouth. His unshaven face looked as if it had been carved—badly—from granite. A tattered wax jacket was thrown on the floor, and the tweeds he wore, Anna noted, were well-worn and splattered with mud. His eyes were the colour of flint. As grey as the sky and the sea. And they were hiding something.

She cleared her throat, and tried to sound much braver than she felt. "Good morning. I haven't seen you around before."

He doffed his cap, revealing a round bald head. He stubbed out his cigarette on the floor.

"Sorry if I started you miss. Name's MacKinnon. I'm the new factor on the Glen Killilan estate. I've been tracking an injured stag. I got caught out by the weather and thought I'd shelter in here until the worst passes. That's not a problem, is it?"

"No. The bothy is on estate land. I can hardly object. Did you put the poor beast out of its misery?"

"Aye, miss, that I did. A bullet straight through the heart. It's the only way to kill 'em," he replied, deliberately stroking the barrel of his gun where it rested against the wall.

"I...didn't see a stag outside."

"It's down the hill a way. I'm just waiting for the lad with the garron—the Highland pony. Once he arrives, we'll load up the carcass and carry it back to the estate."

Anna shivered and nervously bit her lip. MacKinnon's emotionless voice made her flesh creep. He suddenly took a step toward her.

"Have no fear of old Mac. I'd never lie to you."

She stepped back. "I see. Well, you have everything under control. I'll leave you to it."

"Wait! You're soaked to the skin. Why don't you stay here until the worst of the downpour is over? The last group of walkers left some kindling and logs in the porch, so I could light a fire. I've even got a drop of the hard stuff to help keep out the chill." He pulled a small silver flask from his pocket, and gave her a twisted smile.

"That's...er very kind of you, Mr...Mr MacKinnon...but I really should be going. Friends...my friend back at the house will be wondering where I am. And the dogs...they'll be getting restless and bored, so if you'll excuse me, I'll be getting on my way." As calmly as she could, Anna turned and walked away, her pace matching her increasing heartbeat.

She kept walking until she judged she was out of sight of the bothy and then broke into a run. The dogs ran beside her. She didn't stop until they reached the top of the waterfall. She bent over, hands on knees, winded, but feeling safer. She sat down on a boulder and patted the dogs' heads.

"I know you love running, girls. I just wish I did too."

She glanced back toward the bothy, now far from her line of sight and wondered why Alistair was employing such a dangerous looking man.

Chapter Twenty-Six

Anna drove into work later that afternoon, and met Morag walking along the tree-lined drive. Pulling the old Land Rover to a halt at the kerb, she pushed open the passenger door and called to her friend.

"What on earth are you doing walking in this weather? Hop in, and I'll give you a lift."

"Thanks, Anna," Morag said as she shook the rain from her umbrella and climbed into the passenger seat. "I was hoping to bump into you or one of the other girls before I got soaked to the skin."

"What made you choose today, of all days, to walk to work?"

Morag frowned. "Well, I didn't wake up and decide it was a nice day for a stroll, that's for sure! The truth is I forgot to put petrol in the pickup. Do you know that's the third time this month I've done it?"

"It's easily done. That's why I keep a spare can of diesel at the croft. It was a good Ceilidh," Anna said, setting the vehicle in motion.

A smile creased Morag's face. "Yes, lass, it certainly was a grand occasion. The food was wonderful, and the band Mr. Alistair hired from Glasgow was very good. Although I must say, I didn't expect him to invite so many of the gentry, especially as the Ceilidh was supposed to be for the tenants. Someone told me the Chief of Clan Grant was there, although I didn't see the man myself."

"Really? I did spot that racing driver...the one who won the last Monaco Grand Prix. Alistair has certainly moved up in the world to be hob-nobbing with the likes of them."

"That may be, but he should be spending less time with his fancy friends and more on the affairs of the estate. Do you know old Mrs Ferguson reported her roof was leaking six months ago, and it still hasn't been repaired despite the fact her rent has increased?"

Anna drew the Land Rover to a halt outside the kitchen door of the hotel and turned to her friend. "I guess the old Laird let things slip a little. But now Alistair is in control I'm sure things will improve, unless the rumours are true and the estate has financial difficulties. It would certainly explain why he felt the need to increase the rents. But why hold a hugely expensive party if it is? It doesn't make sense."

"No, it doesn't, unless you're trying to impress someone, such as a prospective buyer. Or trying to keep up appearances," Morag said

"Did I mention he asked me to dinner?"

Morag glanced at Anna, then stared out of the window. "What, the Laird? And what did you say?"

"Why, Morag, I said no of course."

"Even though Luke will be returning home soon?"

"Yes, even though Luke will be *leaving*," Anna said. "I can't go behind his back and have dinner with another man, no matter how innocent the invitation may be. Besides, he's not my type."

"Who's not your type? Who are you talking about—Luke or Alistair?"

"Are you being deliberately obtuse, or are you just trying to annoy me? Why Alistair, of course. He's too...smarmy. Too false, if you know what I mean."

Morag's brown eyes sparkled. "Mm. Does this mean romance is in the air? That you like Luke?"

Anna ignored the bait. She got out of the Land Rover and made a dash for the front door of the hotel, leaving her friend to follow. "Come on, it's time for work."

"You didn't answer my question," Morag said, as she hung up her coat and put on her apron.

"Do you want a coffee before we start, or should we get on with setting the tables for dinner," Anna asked as she filled the kettle.

Morag rested her hands on her hips.

"Anna! Now who's being difficult?"

The young woman in question couldn't help but laugh.

"Oh, Morag. You should see your face. You look just like my third-year school teacher when she admonished a recalcitrant pupil."

"Hmph! I'm glad you think it's funny."

"I'm only teasing you. Of course I like Luke. If I didn't, I'd have made him leave after the first night." She handed Morag a mug of coffee.

"Is that so?" Morag studied Anna over the rim of her mug. "Well, judging by the way the man was watching you last night, I'd say he's more than a little in love with you. What do you think about that?"

"I think you're crazy."

"Why do you say that?" Morag asked.

"Because we've both acknowledged the fact his presence here is only temporary."

"What's that got to do with it? I tell you, that man is in love with you, and if I'm not mistaken, you love him too. The question is, what are you going to do about it?"

Anna sat down at the kitchen table and rested her chin on her hands. "Even if you're right, what I can I do? I can't ask or tell him to stay. That has to be his decision. And besides, he's a foreigner. This isn't his country."

Morag pulled out the chair next to her friend, and took her hands in hers.

"Being in love shouldn't make you so sad. You must tell him how you feel."

Anna started to speak, but Morag held up her hand to silence her.

"I know you want to be swept off your feet, but the world isn't like that anymore. You have to fight for what you want. And trust me; if you want Luke, then you're going to have to tell him before he climbs aboard that yacht of his and sails into the sunset!"

"I can't, Morag. Besides, he has a successful career on the other side of the Atlantic, not to mention his yacht and, by all accounts, a wonderful home. All I have is a run-down croft, two dogs, and a decidedly unhealthy bank balance. He's going to want someone of equal social standing. Not me." Her eyes began to overflow.

Morag pressed a tissue into Anna's hands. "You're mistaken, and before much longer, Luke will prove he loves you. You mark my words."

Anna laughed through her tears. "Another premonition, Morag?"

"Aye, lass. Each one is a little more distinct than the last, but more worrying is the danger I see around you."

"Oh really? And are you going to tell me what this threat is?"

"I would if I could see it clearly, but I can't. I can only describe it as a dark shadow surrounding you. Just be careful, that's all I ask. Now, if we don't get a move on lass, we'll have folk wanting to eat and the tables not even set." She rose, picked up the pile of freshly laundered tablecloths, and went into the dining room.

Anna's stomach clenched. The fear in her friend's eyes was real. As usual, she was about to say the premonition was due to too much late-night TV, but something about Morag's demeanour made her stop this time.

Suddenly, there was a crash from the dining room. Anna ran to find Morag on the floor, gasping, pale, and staring in terror at nothing.

"Morag! Are you all right? Speak to me! Morag? Morag! Answer me, for God's sake!"

Anna wrapped her arms around her trembling friend. Morag screamed and began to cry. "Oh, no, Anna. No, no, no!"

Anna rocked Morag, shushing her as if trying to reassure a child. "Quiet now, Morag. It's okay. Everything's all right. I'm right here with you. Can you talk to me? What happened?"

"It was...it was..." Morag looked far away. Her mouth opened and closed rapidly, trying to find the words, but none came.

A small blonde woman ran into the room. "What happened? Is she all right? Should I go and get the doctor?"

Anna shook her head. "Give us a moment, Katrina. I've seen her do this before...a long time ago when we were young. She should be all right in a minute. You go back to the front desk. If we need a doctor I'll come and let you know."

Katrina gave her a sidelong look in disbelief, and left. Anna held her breath and waited.

Suddenly, Morag coughed and rubbed her forehead. She blinked. "Anna, did I pass out? I'm so sorry. I'm embarrassed."

"Embarrassed? I thought you'd gone and died on me!"

Morag managed a wan smile. "No, far from it...I can tell you why. I had such a headache this morning, I didn't bother with breakfast. I only had a cup of tea."

"Morag McInnes, whatever I am going to do with you?"

Morag grabbed the edge of the table and pulled herself unsteadily to her feet. "You'll put up with me as you always have."

"You can't go around fainting. What will Lachlan do with you dead of starvation? What will I do? You're the only real friend I have in this whole world. I couldn't bear it if anything happened to you."

Morag smiled, crow lines crinkling around her eyes. "I won't die on you, I promise."

"I intend to hold you to that promise, you know. And you're all right now?"

"Of course I am, lass. It was nothing really. But if it's all the same to you I'll just sit here for a few minutes." Morag slumped onto a chair, and rested her head in her hands.

"You're telling me the truth?"

"Have I ever lied to you, Anna?"

"You're not—are you?"

Morag looked away. "No, of course not."

Anna instantly regretted the pain the partial question had caused. "I'm sorry—I'm so sorry. I didn't mean... At least let me get you a glass of water."

"Don't worry. Really."

"You can't tell me not to worry. What was it?"

"Stop pestering me!" Morag rubbed her temples.

"I won't—not until you tell me!"

"You won't believe me."

"I will—I swear it."

"Morag sighed. "It was the Sight."

"Not again, Morag..."

"You asked me, lass, so I'm telling you. It was dreadful. This time it came in the form of fire. The room vibrated with a low hum until I could no longer see...until I saw it."

"Saw what?"

"Fire. Searing fire. The vision had me in its hold. It tossed me in all directions, like some unstrung marionette. The fire licked at my legs and arms. I can't describe the pain."

"A seizure, that's what it was. You need to see the doctor. It's a seizure!"

"No, it wasn't, lass, and if you'll listen to me, I'll finish. As quickly as the vision appeared, it vanished. I wasn't burned. It wasn't true fire, you see, not at all. It represents something far more dangerous."

"What could be more dangerous than fire?"

"Having your entire life burned away. That's the message, lass. You've had your past destroyed for you, and if you're not careful, very careful, your future will be taken from you as well."

"So now you're being cryptic," Anna said. "You're right, this was no seizure. I've seen dementia patients. They're not this lucid. You've had some sort of waking dream."

"Call it that if you like," Morag said, "but be careful. Please." Unsteadily, she picked up the linen she'd dropped. Anna bent down to help, and they spread a crisp white cloth on the nearest table.

Anna didn't want to admit it, but she was shaken by Morag's fantasy. She wasn't convinced that her friend didn't have some sort of physical ailment that triggered 'the Sight', but she knew that continuing to discuss what Morag had 'seen' wouldn't be helpful to either of them.

"By the way," she said, deftly folding a starched napkin into the shape of a fan. "I crossed paths with the new factor while I was walking the dogs this morning."

Morag started. "You what?"

"He was sheltering in Ardtoe bothy. He said he'd been tracking an injured stag."

"Did you believe him?"

"No. There was no injured stag. Apart from the fact the deer are way up in the hills at this time of year, he would have needed a high powered rifle with a telescopic sight to bring one down. You don't shoot deer with a shotgun."

Morag paused between tables. "What did you think of the man?"

"To be honest, he gave me the shivers. He looked at me as if I was dinner on his plate. And you're right; I wouldn't trust the man either. He has the appearance of a thug. I can't imagine why Alistair would want to employ him."

"You're not the only one wondering that, lass. It's some months since he took over Sandy's job, and from what I've heard, he's no very good at being the head ghillie."

"I'm not surprised, although he obviously knows how to shoot."

"Well, any damned fool knows that. All you have to do is load a gun and pull the trigger," Morag replied caustically.

Ewan poked his head through the swing door. "Ah, Morag. Here you are. There's a call for you. You can take it on the phone in reception."

"Thanks. Hmm, I wonder who it can be." She hurried through to the front of the hotel.

A few moments later, Morag re-entered the dining room a few moments later carrying a tray of wine glasses.

"Oh, Anna. Lachlan's just phoned. He's on his way home. Can you believe it?" She put the tray down on the nearest table.

"But I thought he was staying on the rig."

"He was. But they've found someone else to cover for the laddie who's on holiday. Lachlan's in Fort William waiting for me to fetch him. Do you think you can manage to finish up here on your own?"

Anna smiled. "Of course I can. Don't keep that man of yours waiting any longer than necessary. Now off you go."

Morag stopped. "Wait! I can't go! The petrol tank is empty. I've no transport."

"Here," Anna said, pulling her keys from her pocket and placing them in into her friend's hand, "take the Land Rover. The tank is almost full. I'll get Ewan or Katrina to give me a lift to the garage. I'll get a can of petrol, and then take your pickup home. We can swap back in the morning. How does that sound?"

"Oh, lass. You're wonderful!" Morag hugged her enthusiastically.

"Give over, I'm just doing what any friend would do. You're still rather pale. Are you sure you're well enough to drive that far? Because I can easily—"

"I've told you, I'm fine, more so now that my man is on his way home. Please stop fussing." She kissed Anna on the cheek and rushed out of the room.

Morag climbed into the Land Rover, adjusted the seat and mirrors, and turned on the ignition. The old engine coughed once, twice, then rumbled into life. She fastened her seat belt, eased off the handbrake, and put the vehicle into reverse, carefully backing out of the parking space. Straightening the wheel, she selected first gear and headed down the driveway.

As the Land Rover picked up speed, she hummed along to the radio, the windscreen wipers keeping time with the rhythm. It would take an hour, perhaps less, if she didn't meet any tractors on the twisting, single-track glen road, to get to Fort William. She smiled to herself; Lachlan had been away for five long weeks and was finally coming home. She missed him so much and wished he'd reconsider buying a farm. She hoped he could find work closer to home.

As she approached the crossroads, she put her foot on the brakes and was surprised at the amount of effort it took to bring the Land Rover to a halt. The road was slick because of the rain, she reminded herself, so she reduced her speed. Perhaps she could get Lachlan to persuade Anna to pension off this old heap and trade it in for something more modern. She drummed her fingers on the steering wheel as she waited for a car coming in the other to turn left.

On her way once more, Morag turned up the volume and sang along, her clear, delicate voice echoing in the small space. After seven miles, she reached the first of a series of tight bends. She tapped the brakes, and steered into it. Suddenly, the wheel had a mind of its own. She tried to turn right. The Land Rover veered left. Her heart pulsed. She yanked the wheel harder.

The back of the Land Rover swung out.

She screamed, and depressed the clutch, but the gear didn't engage. Panicking, she tried again, and this time the lever shot home. Morag let out the breath she didn't know she'd been holding.

Her heart thumping, she stretched out her hand to turn off the radio. She'd been too busy singing when she should have been concentrating on the road. Fortunately, she regained control, and the Land Rover rounded the bend without a scrape. Not that Anna would have noticed; there were already numerous dents on the bodywork.

The road straightened out, and Morag shifted into back into fourth, keeping a wary eye out for any sheep that may have strayed on to the highway. As she passed the entrance to Home Farm at the top of the hill, she downshifted into third in readiness for the sharp right-hand bend at the bottom. She pressed the brake.

This time the pedal went all the way to the floor.

Shrieking, she frantically pumped it. She grabbed the handbrake.

The Land Rover sped up.

She downshifted again. The engine screamed in protest, but still it didn't slow. The nearside wheels mounted the grass verge.

The bodywork skidded against a dry-stone wall, chipping stones away as the Land Rover went faster.

Morag jerked on the steering wheel. The vehicle skidded back on to the road, but it was too late to make the turn. The Land Rover smashed through the wall, and took flight.

It spun over a field. Morag screamed. She prayed. She called for Lachlan. Then a large Scots pine loomed out of the bushes.

A massive thud. Her head hit something. There was no pain. Only darkness. Something wet covered her face. She tried to catch it with her hands. They were numb. She thought of Anna. Then she thought of Lachlan. Then she thought no more.

Chapter Twenty-Seven

Anna closed the gate, climbed back into Morag's pickup, and wondered if her friend had collected her husband from the station in Fort William. She hoped for Morag's sake that they'd soon be able to buy the farm they wanted, and Lachlan could stay at home.

As she carefully negotiated the pot-holed track to Tigh na Cladach, all she could think about was an early supper and a long soak in the bath. It had been strange day with her run-in with the new ghillie, and doing Morag's job as well as her own. She was tired and, if luck was on her side, Luke would have at least prepared dinner.

Silence greeted her as she opened the door to the croft. Luke must have taken the dogs for a walk, she thought, as she hung her coat on the stand in the hallway, and made her way into the kitchen.

She stopped. She wasn't alone.

Mark, her former lover, leaned against the Aga, his hands folded across his chest.

"What the hell are you doing in my house?"

"Anna, I knocked, but the door wasn't locked." He took a few slow steps towards her.

Her green eyes narrowed. "You've got some nerve walking into my home uninvited. I'm going to call the police."

"If I remember correctly, you don't have a phone."

Out witted, she slammed her bag on the table. "Get. Out. Now."

"I wrote to you, but you didn't reply. Did you get the letter?"

"Yes, I received it. It burned very nicely in the Aga."

"Please give me time to say my piece. Then I'll leave if you still want me to."

"Oh, I'll insist. That's guaranteed. Speak if you must, but make it quick. And then go."

Mark offered her a nervous smile. "Anna, darling. Our time apart has changed me. I was hoping it might have changed you too."

She set her chin in a stubborn line. "Oh, I've had time to think." She pulled a kitchen chair away from the table and plunked into it. "You have five minutes, which is more than you deserve. Then I want you to leave."

Mark thrust his hands into his pockets and looked out of the window.

"I'm waiting, Mark."

He turned to face her again. He leaned back against the draining board, and spread his hands in front of him. "I'll admit it—I was wrong to give your promotion to Stella, but she is...was better..."

"You drove all the way out here to tell me *that*?"

"No—of course not. That didn't come out right. Let me try again. I was under a lot of pressure at the time, and I made a serious mistake."

Yes, about eight stone of it. "Please, Mark, don't insult my intelligence by offering another excuse. We both know why you gave her the job, and it wasn't because she was better qualified. You made a fool of me, and that's something I can't forgive."

"Can't or won't?"

"Both. Time's up. Now go."

"Anna, please. I was shocked when you handed in your notice."

"You were shocked?" She jumped to her feet, and glared at him with reproachful eyes. "My God, Mark! What did you expect me to do, shake Stella's hand and offer her a welcoming smile?"

"Well, no. But I thought you'd realise it was for the best. I was naïve. I was a fool. I thought you wanted hands-on experience rather than mountains of paperwork. Besides, we'd been together for nearly two years. I was hoping—"

"Hoping what? That we'd enjoy a threesome? You slept with her, for God's sake! How do you think that made me feel?"

"It was only once—" he replied, not meeting her gaze.

"Liar!"

"Okay, so it was more than once, but I swear it meant nothing. It's you I care about. She's out of my life now. She went back to London to marry her Australian boyfriend. So it's over."

"So, that's really why you're here. You're pathetic."

"You have every right to be upset. I don't know how many times you want me to say I'm sorry. But you didn't have to resign. And when you left Edinburgh so quickly, I—"

"You what? Felt sorry for me?" she shouted, finally giving in to her anger.

"I felt guilty. You didn't give me a chance to explain. Not properly."

"You had ample opportunity. In fact, I distinctly recall us having a similar conversation. Nothing has changed. Time's up. Go. I don't need you."

"But Anna, I wanted to make things right between us. Is that wrong of me?"

"Absolutely. And I don't want you in my life."

"Really?" He held up a stack of pages. "Well if this manuscript is anything to go by I suggest you go back to teaching. No publisher will touch it."

"You had no right to read my work. You son-of-a-bitch! You break in and go through my personal papers. Out!"

"Look, I'm sorry I said that. I'm just angry. I'm sorry. I didn't come here to argue."

"No? If you didn't come here to argue and you didn't come here because your girlfriend went back to someone better than you, what did you come for, Mark?"

"I've told you, to apologise for being stupid. I thought...that once you knew how sorry I was, you'd take me back. I miss you." He grabbed her. His fingers dug into the soft flesh of her arms, making her wince, as he tried to kiss her.

Anna twisted her face away, and screamed. "Let-me-go!" she shouted, pushing him away, but he tightened his hold on her waist. She beat her hands on his chest, but he refused to release her. Finally she stamped on his foot.

"Ow! What did you do that for?"

"Because I don't want to be mauled by you!"

"Anna, please take me back. I'll make it up to you, I promise. We were so good together."

She tore free from his grasp and slapped him with a force she didn't know she possessed. He put a hand over his red cheek and stared at her.

"Anna...I didn't mean...I didn't intend...I love you."

"There is no us, Mark. Not anymore. The only person you love is *yourself*. Now get out."

Before she could say anything more the dogs burst into the kitchen followed closely by Luke.

"Hi, sweetheart," Luke said, bending down and kissing her hungrily. "Who's our visitor, and why does he look like you slapped the shit out of him?"

Anna gritted her teeth. "Luke, this is Professor Mark Jackson. Mark, this is Luke Tallantyre, a—"

"A very close friend," Luke interrupted, studying Mark with the eyes of a man who was used to meeting his adversaries face on. For the second time in as many days, he felt a stab of jealousy. He draped an arm around Anna's shoulders, and pulled her close. "Honey, you got any more friends I should know about?"

Anna turned pink. "Mark is head of the English Department at the University where I worked. He was passing and decided to drop in to say 'hello'. Isn't that right, Mark?"

Mark nodded and offered his hand. Luke ignored it.

"Just passing through?" Luke replied. "Weird. The road doesn't even come this far. I hope the trip was worth it. Anna doesn't make the best coffee in the world. And what happened to your face, dude? Run into a tree? Or a hand?"

Mark bristled. "I came here to discuss something with Anna—in private. Not that it's any of your business."

"Anything that concerns Anna, concerns me."

"Anna and I are...were good friends as well as work colleagues."

"Good friends, huh? Your definition of the term is just a little bit different than mine. Where I come from loyalty means something."

"Stay out of this, Mr Tallantyre."

"Not a chance, jackass."

"Now, look here," Mark eyes narrowed in response to Luke's icy stare. "I don't have to take insults from you."

"I agree. So do as the lady said and get out."

"Luke," Anna said, squeezing his arm. "Perhaps you'll feed the dogs."

Luke turned his face to hers, his expression softening. "No, honey, you feed the dogs. I'll escort Jackson back to his car."

"Actually," Mark interrupted. "I was hoping to talk to Anna over dinner. I've reserved a table at the Monymusk Arms."

Luke crossed his arms. His biceps bulged. "Not gonna happen, schoolboy."

"No, I suppose not," Mark hesitated. "Anna, I don't suppose you'd consider coming back to work, would you? You'll get the promotion and a raise in salary. I'll even confirm it in writing. The new term starts on the eighth of September. What do you say?"

Anna was stunned. It was what she wanted, or had wanted. But then pride took over. She answered in a rush of words. "That's very kind of you, but no. I couldn't work with you again. It's a question of trust, you see. And I don't think I could trust you under any circumstances."

"Okay," Luke said, taking the other man by the elbow. "Time to go, old buddy."

"I've had enough of your interference. Get-your-hands-off-me!" Mark's fist shot out and hit Luke squarely on the jaw. Luke staggered back. Blood trickled from the side of his mouth, and his head hit the frame of the kitchen door, adding to the pain.

Mark stared at Anna, his eyes full of contempt. "I suggest you keep your tame ape under control and in his—" before he had chance to finish the sentence, Luke's fist connected with Jackson's nose in a bone-shattering crunch.

Anna watched aghast. "Stop it! Both of you. Stop it now!"

The two men ignored her. Mark aimed a kick at Luke's groin, which Luke deftly avoided. The kitchen table toppled, sending Anna's manuscript fluttering in all directions. Luke landed another punch, this time on Mark's cheek. The professor stumbled, but regained his balance in time to return the blow, but it lacked force. He grabbed a saucepan off the draining board, held it in front of him, and waited for the opportunity to strike Luke.

Luke's left foot shot out, and the heavy pan flew from the other man's hand.

"You'll have to do better than that, Jackson!"

Anna screamed. Tears streamed down her face. She tried to get between the two men to intervene, but Luke pushed her safely out of the way. She stood in the doorway and watched in silence, as the two men circled each other in the confined space. Luke dodged another blow and she gasped in relief. Never taking his eyes off his opponent, Luke feinted left and whacked Mark in the gut. Mark bent in half, cradling his crushed midsection. The air whooshed out of his lungs as he slowly sank to his knees.

Anna rushed to Luke's side and smacked him on the arm. "Did you have to do that?"

"Hey! Hey! He started it. Besides, I wasn't the one who called him a bastard. Although that's something we agree on."

"You were listening?"

"Yes. And I'm not going to apologise for doing so. And I am not gonna apologise for hitting him. If it walks like a duck and talks like a duck, it's a duck. In other words, he's a jerk, not only for putting you in such an untenable position that you resigned, but also for cheating on you. I'm glad you turned the son-of-a-bitch down—on both counts."

Anna glanced down at the man on the floor, groaning and clutching his stomach.

"Don't worry," Luke told her, "once he gets his breath back, he'll be fine. Come here." He opened his arms to her. Despite his aching jaw, he kissed her passionately.

Mark coughed and winced. Luke released his hold on Anna and bent down to help Jackson to his feet.

"Get out, and don't come back." Luke pushed him into the hallway.

"Don't think you've heard the last of this, Tallantyre," Mark cautioned, as he stumbled to the door, blood dripping from his nose. "I'm going to see you're charged with assault!"

"You started it, asshole."

"Mark, go." Anna said softly.

Mark turned and looked at her, his hand on the knob of the door. He stopped. "I can't believe you prefer this—"

"Don't go there, Mark," Anna interrupted. "You and I are finished. Accept it. There's nothing more to say."

Mark slunk away, handkerchief held to his bloody nose. Anna closed the door and turned back to face Luke. His right eye was beginning to swell. Blood congealed at the corner of his mouth.

"Come into the kitchen, and let me get some ice for your face."

"I'm sorry about the mess," Luke said, righting the kitchen table and stooping down to gather her manuscript.

She opened the refrigerator door. "Don't worry about that now. You're going to have a black eye come the morning." She held an ice pack to his cheek. He winced. "And just look at your hands—you'll not be able to paint for a few days."

"I've had worse," he said pulling her body hard against his. He brushed her hair back from her face. "You're shaking. Want me to light the fire?"

Anna shook her head. "No. I'm not cold. I'm shocked by Mark's behaviour." she said, giving him a smile that made the heat pool in his groin.

"Yeah, well, adrenaline will do that every time."

"I'm also tired and hungry."

"Is that so?" Luke replied, taking the ice pack from her hand and dropping it into the sink. "There's a casserole in the slow oven. It won't be ready for another couple of hours. In the meantime, why don't you tell me why Morag's pickup is outside?" He kissed the soft spot just below her right earlobe.

"Mm. Do you want the short or the long version?" she asked, wrapping her arms around him. No matter how many times Anna told herself that all she and Luke were destined to share was a few weeks of hot sex, she couldn't stop herself responding to him.

He gave her a smile as intimate as a kiss. "The short version. While the casserole can wait, I can't." The fingers of his left hand skimmed her cheek before settling in her thick hair. His right hand slipped under her T-shirt and slowly caressed her back.

"But your face..." Anna said as she felt the now familiar tingling in the pit of her stomach. Her nipples hardened at Luke's soft caress. The smouldering passion she saw in his eyes echoed her own.

"It's only a few bruises. Nothing to stop me from making love with you."

Chapter Twenty-Eight

There was no sign of Morag when Anna entered the hotel kitchen on Sunday morning. She hung up her coat and made her way through to the bar, pushing open the swing door only to stop and stare at the pale-faced man sitting next to Ewan. She gasped.

"Lachlan, this is a surprise," she smiled. "Is Morag with you? Only I didn't see the Land Rover in the car park."

"Anna, you'd better come and sit down." Ewan said gently. He rose from his chair and crossed the room to take her arm.

Her smile faded when she saw the sombre expression on Lachlan's face. "What's the matter? Morag's all right, isn't she?"

"Sit down, Anna," Ewan repeated, giving her a gentle push towards a vacant chair. Returning to the bar he poured a measure of brandy into three glasses, and carried them to the table.

Lachlan took a deep breath. "There's no easy way for me to say this. She was supposed to meet me at the railway station, but she never arrived."

Morag is missing? Anna grew light headed. "But I don't understand. She left immediately after you telephoned. I saw her drive off."

"I don't understand, either. I waited till nine o'clock, but there was no sign of her. I telephoned the house. There was no answer, so I hired a car and drove home. I thought perhaps she'd broken down on the way, and that I'd find her and the pickup on the side of the road. But I never saw another vehicle during the whole of the journey."

"She took my Land Rover," Anna said, lowering her gaze so Lachlan wouldn't see the tears in her eyes. "She'd run out of petrol on the way to work, so I gave her my keys. We were going to swap vehicles this morning."

Lachlan leant forward in his seat, his face visibly tense. "I see. Anna, you know Morag as well as anyone. What sort of mood was she in? I know she doesn't like me being away, but was she depressed?"

She took his hands in hers. "No, quite the opposite, she was delighted at the prospect of having you home. But she felt unwell for a while before she left. In fact, I offered to drive her, but she refused, saying she felt fine. Have you...have you notified the police?"

"Yes. No one's reported an accident. And no one fitting Morag's description has been admitted to hospital in either Fort William or Inverness. But they need to know what she was wearing. Perhaps you could help me with that."

"Of course." Anna dug in her bag for a piece of paper and a pen.

"I must tell them she was driving your Land Rover, and not the pickup." A powerful and well-built man, with ginger hair, Lachlan stood. "You'd better write down the registration for me, as well."

Anna nodded and scribbled it down.

"You can use the phone in my office," Ewan offered. "While you're doing that, I'll get one of the girls to make us some coffee. I think we're going to need it."

When Lachlan left the room, Anna sat quietly, her body stiff with shock. She took no notice of Ewan, until he thrust a glass of brandy into her trembling hands.

"Here, lass, drink this. You're as white as my great-grandmother's ghost. I don't want you fainting on me, do you hear me? Coffee is on its way."

Inclining her head in a gesture of thanks, Anna took a sip. The amber liquid burned her throat. "It rained all afternoon, and the glen road can be treacherous in those conditions. Morag isn't used to driving the Land Rover. I knew I should have gone with her. I'll never forgive myself if anything has happened to her."

"Now, now, lass. Don't go blaming yourself. Morag can be stubborn at times. There's bound to be a simple explanation."

"Do you really think so?"

They both watched Lachlan re-enter the room, his face tight with anxiety.

"Any news?" Ewan asked.

"No," Lachlan said, bowing his head in despair. "The police won't do anything for forty-eight hours and have suggested I go home and wait. But I can't sit here and do nothing."

Ewan nodded. "In that case, we'll organise our own search party. We've all helped out on training exercises for the mountain rescue team, so we know the drill. We're fortunate in that they store some of their equipment here, although I'm not sure if there are any radios."

"Ewan, I know the glen as well as anyone. If you can spare me, I'd like to help," Anna volunteered.

"Aye, I daresay the hotel can manage without you, lass. We'll make this our base," he said, resting a hand on the younger man's shoulder. "Lachlan, you go home and leave a note for Morag in case she turns up, telling her to contact you here. In the meantime, I'll organise maps and check what equipment we've got. I'll round up the villagers and ensure there's plenty of hot coffee and sandwiches for everyone. I suggest we meet back here in an hour."

"Lachlan? Is that all right?" Anna gave his hand a reassuring squeeze.

"Yes, yes, of course," he sighed.

"In that case, if I can take the pickup, I'll go home and collect my hiking gear. I'll be back as soon as I can," Anna kissed him on the cheek and hurried out the door.

Luke was checking the croft's generator when he heard the sound of a vehicle approaching. He wiped his hands on an oily rag and strode round to the front of the croft in time to see Anna climbing out of Morag's pickup. She rushed headlong towards him. Instinctively, he wrapped his arms around her.

"I thought you and Morag were trading cars this morning."

"We were supposed to," Anna cried against his shoulder, "but oh, Luke, Morag's missing. We're organising a search party. I've come home to change and collect the dogs. I thought they might be useful."

"Hey, back up." He held her at arms' length. "What do you mean, Morag's missing? I thought you said she went to pick her husband up from the train station."

Anna took a deep steadying breath. "She was supposed to. I thought she did. But no one's seen her since she left the hotel yesterday afternoon to fetch him."

"I see. What about the Land Rover? Anybody seen it?"

"No. That's the strange thing. If it had broken down, Morag would have left it at the side of the road and walked to the nearest house, assuming there was one. If there wasn't, she would have stayed with the vehicle, no matter what."

"Did Lachlan call the police?"

"Yes. But they won't do anything for forty-eight hours. Ewan's called in the local mountain rescue team, but it will take them awhile to assemble and get here. Rather than wait, we've decided to organise our own search."

The fingers of his left hand curled under her chin and tilted her head to his. "Well, I'm glad someone's thinking on their feet. Sitting around waiting doesn't help anyone, especially Morag. I know her friendship means a lot to you." He gently brushed away her tears with his thumb. "Tell me what we need. If she's out there, we're going to find her."

"Oh, Luke, I hope so. If she was out all night in the storm God knows what state she'll be in." Anna shuddered as she thought about the possibility of her friend lying hurt. "It's not going to be easy. It's more than fifty miles to Fort William by road. That's a huge area to cover, and if Morag abandoned the Land Rover and took to the fields, it could be even further. Are you sure you want to help?"

"I'll do whatever it takes. Now what do we need?"

"Proper clothing and footwear to start with," Anna said, glancing at his T-shirt and jeans. "Water and a first aid kit—there's one in the bathroom. There's a spare rucksack in the bottom drawer of the chest in your room. I've got two space blankets, so we can each carry one. And you'll need a walking stick to search the undergrowth with. There's a couple in the hall."

They hurried into the croft. While Luke changed, Anna made sandwiches and filled two flasks with hot, sweet tea. Then, taking the stairs two at a time, she hastily swapped her own clothes for a pair of thick denim jeans, a lightweight sweater, and walking boots.

Luke threw the first aid kit into his rucksack along with an extra sweater and his oilskin. He sat down on the edge of the bed, laced up his boots, and tried to piece things together, but came up with a big fat zero. He didn't like the situation one bit, and the fact that Morag had been driving Anna's Land Rover was all the more disturbing.

The life he'd tried so hard to forget suddenly came flooding back. There had been that kidnap case he and his partner had been involved in just after he'd joined the agency. They'd searched for the missing teenager for best part of three weeks, before finally locating her body hidden in a disused well on property owned by her uncle. He'd interviewed the uncle twice, and although he couldn't find any evidence linking him to the girl's disappearance, his gut had told him the man was involved. Luke blamed himself for not following his instincts and finding her sooner.

The sound of Anna's voice calling him brought his thoughts back to the present.

He checked the safety catch on his gun, slipped it into the specially designed holster in the back of his jeans, and pulled on his light-weight jacket.

The bar of the hotel was crowded when Luke and Anna walked in fifty minutes later. Anna recognised some of the faces. There was Mr MacIver and the Fraser boys, and two of the farm hands from the estate. The Reverend Cameron had put aside his church duties to join the searchers. Even a couple of guests had offered to help.

A pale-faced Lachlan stood shoulder-to-shoulder with Ewan in front of everyone. Ewan banged his heavy fist on a table and the room fell silent.

"Now, if I can have your attention, everyone. I want you to work in pairs," he told them. "No searching on your own. We don't want anyone else getting lost. Katrina, would you hand the maps round, please? Thank you. Morag was driving Anna MacDonald's old Land Rover. You all know what it looks like."

"Aye, more rust than Land Rover!" Mr MacIver said. His comment gathered a few nervous laughs.

"Well, just in case you've forgotten, let me remind you. It's pale green in colour and has a red bonnet." Ewan pointed to areas on his map. "If you'll follow along, you'll notice that each area I've marked covers two miles. For those of you searching the village, make sure you knock on every door, check every byre. The rest of you will use the road as your reference and search it, and the fields and moorland either side, up to a distance of half a mile. Unfortunately Morag could be anywhere between here and Fort William."

Anna put up her hand. "Morag's been out all night. She'll be cold and wet, and probably very scared." she said, trying, but failing, to hold back her tears. "Make sure you're carrying extra clothing or a blanket, as well as water and a hot drink."

"Okay, folks. Time isn't on our side," Ewan said, pinning his map to the wall. "There are short wave radios on the table. Please take one on your way out. I'll stay here with Lachlan and act as co-ordinator. It's now eleven thirty; I suggest we meet back here in five hours. Agreed?"

Everyone in the room nodded and said yes. Anna glanced at the map in her hand and then turned to Luke. "We've got a section of the road from the hotel to the crossroads," she said, shouldering her rucksack and turning to leave.

"Anna, if you have a moment," Ewan called. "I think it best you and your friend, Luke, search the estate rather than the road."

"But...I—"

Gently, he took the map from her hand, and replaced it with one of the estate. He looked at Luke for support.

"Anna, I know what you're thinking. But you and Morag are good friends. It's bad enough that she's missing. I don't want you to be the one to find her, not if she's..."

"She won't be!" Anna cried.

Luke took Anna by the shoulders and turned her to face him. "Ewan's right, sweetheart," he said, wiping a tear from her cheek. "Trust me; you couldn't live with that kind of pain."

"But—"

"Come on," Luke took her hand, and led her out of the hotel. "You know the estate pretty well—where's the best place to start?"

"The stables and outbuildings, they're closest to the road. And there are numerous cottages and bothies."

"All right, we'll start with the cottages. Tell me, was there a special place you used to meet, a place that only you and Morag knew about?"

"You mean when we were teenagers?"

"Yes."

"We always met in the village, at the croft, or at her parents' home. Why?"

"Sometimes when people are scared," Luke replied, climbed behind the wheel, "they go to a place where they felt happy and secure."

"But Morag had no reason to feel unhappy or insecure. She was happy and eager to see Lachlan."

"I know. I just wanted you to think where she might go, if she were, that's all."

Apart from giving him directions, Anna didn't say another word until the vehicle pulled up outside an abandoned croft. She climbed out of the Land Rover, and held the door open for the dogs.

"Ensay, Rhona, seek—find Morag!"

The two dogs eagerly circled the cottage, sniffing every bush, every rock, before returning to Anna, and sitting at her feet. Luke walked up to the door of the cottage and tried the handle. The door was firmly locked.

"Stay here," he said, before disappearing round the side of the squat building.

A few moments later, the front door opened.

"Before you ask, I climbed in through the kitchen window." Luke stepped aside to let her in. "It doesn't look like anyone's lived here for quite a while."

"It used to be Sandy's croft. He was the ghillie, but he left earlier in the year." The front door opened directly in to the sitting room. It was empty apart from an old sofa and an armchair. The room smelled of damp, and mice had taken over, removing the stuffing from one of the chairs for a nest.

"I'll check upstairs just in case, but I think you can cross this one off the map."

"Would you mind if we left the Land Rover here and continued on foot?"

"Good idea. We can cover all the ground in between as well as the buildings."

By two-thirty the rain clouds had pushed away to the east, and although the sun was yet to put in an appearance, the temperature had risen considerably. After searching four abandoned crofts, Luke suggested they take a break. They sat down in the shelter of a dry-stone wall, and the dogs lay on the grass nearby. Luke opened his rucksack, and offered Anna a sandwich from his lunchbox. She shook her head.

"You need to eat, Anna."

"I can't. I'm too concerned about Morag."

"At least have a drink." He popped the tab on a can of soda and handed it to her.

"Luke, what if we don't find her?"

He grasped her hand firmly. "We will. It might not be today, or tomorrow, but I promise you, we will find her."

Anna's face said she wished she could believe him, but deep down he knew she didn't.

Throughout the afternoon, they continued to search, the two-way radio Luke carried remaining silent. Dejected, they returned to the hotel shortly before six.

Anna dropped her rucksack on the floor and slumped into a chair, the dogs at her feet. Ewan raised an eye at the two collies, but said nothing. He didn't have the heart to tell her to take them outside. "Did you find anything—anything at all?"

Luke shook his head. "Nope, not a sign. What about the other searchers?"

"They've not found anything either, although not everyone has reported in yet."

"Did the mountain rescue team get here yet?"

"Unfortunately, they're dealing with a nasty incident in Glencoe. A party of missing school children, I believe. Once that's been resolved, they'll be on their way here. Until then, we'll have to manage on our own. I'll get Katrina to bring you something hot to eat and water for the dogs. Anna looks done-in. You should take her home after you've eaten."

Anna opened her eyes at the sound of her name. "No! I'm not leaving, not until we find Morag."

Luke frowned. "Anna, sweetheart, Ewan's right. You're worn out. You need to rest."

"Luke, please. I won't go home until I hear something positive." She wiped away a tear that had rolled down her cheek.

"Look," he said gently, putting an arm around her shoulder. "Why don't you stay here with Ewan? I'll go out again and have another look round."

Anna leaned against his warm body, and let exhaustion wash over her.

"Perhaps I will rest for a while, but only so I can search again tomorrow."

"Good girl," said Ewan. "Dinner won't be long. Katrina!" He bustled off in the direction of the kitchen.

After dinner, Luke left Anna in the bar. He took the dogs and re-joined the search party. When the light began to fade, they abandoned the search for the night and returned to the hotel.

Chapter Twenty-Nine

The following morning, summer roared back to the Highlands. Thousands of midges took to the air, nibbling at every warm-blooded being in their path. With temperatures in the seventies and smothering humidity to match, the search party met at eight. Despite a sleepless night, and against Luke's wishes, Anna joined the Fraser boys and everyone in the hotel bar for the briefing.

Ewan held up his hands. "Quiet everyone! Quiet please! Thank you. Sadly, yesterday's search found no trace of Morag, or the Land Rover. So, I suggest we continue as before, fanning out from the village for a radius of five miles. Agreed?"

Luke was the first to offer an opinion.

"You'll be wasting time. After two nights, we have to assume Morag's had an accident somewhere between here and Fort William. We should confine our search to the road and surrounding area.

"Bloody foreigner," Angus Murray shouted from the back of the room. "Who do you think you are, telling us what to do?"

The Reverend Cameron joined in the argument. "Aye! It's fifty miles, man! There are only twelve of us. It would take us a month to cover that distance."

Luke's voice was calm and commanding. "I've been involved in searches before, and I'm telling you, we need to concentrate on the road. The Land Rover might be lying in a field or gulley. I suggest those of us with cars drive out to given points and start our search from there. That way we'll cover the ground quicker. Since Morag hasn't been seen since Saturday afternoon," he said glancing at Anna and taking her hand in his, "we have to presume she's hurt, and hope she's with the Land Rover."

"You can't make those assumptions. She could have amnesia...and wandered off," Jamie, the elder of the two Fraser boys suggested.

"It's possible, I guess," Luke responded. "But somehow I don't think so."

"I think Luke's right," Lachlan said, his voice resigned. "Morag's hurt and unable to seek help—we'd have found her otherwise. We should do as he suggests and not waste time arguing."

Suddenly Anna felt weak. On the verge of fainting, she pushed her way past Luke and the other searchers. Once in the hallway made her way to the ladies' room. Barely able to stand, she splashed her face with cold water, and looked into the mirror. The woman who looked back was pale. And guilty. She couldn't forgive herself if anything happened to Morag. She had to summon the strength to find her friend. Morag had always been there when Anna needed her, and now Morag was in need somewhere out there. Anna would not let her down.

Revived, she threw the ladies' room door open and bumped straight into a man.

Alistair Grant.

His face blanched.

"Anna, this—what a surprise," he spluttered. "How...how are you?"

"Not well and in no mood to talk right now, Alistair," she said. "I have to help with the search."

"Search? What search? What on earth are you talking about?"

"The search for Morag McInnes. She's missing."

"Who? Morag McInnes, missing? Since when?"

"Since the day before yesterday. She was supposed to collect her husband from the railway station, but she never arrived."

"But isn't that her vehicle in the car park?" he replied, looking over his shoulder.

"Look, I haven't got time to explain everything now, but Morag borrowed my Land Rover. Heaven knows where she is."

"Well," he stammered, "you should search the estate, of course."

"Thank you, but we've already done that, and found nothing. Are you all right, Alistair? You sound breathless, and your hands are shaking."

"Oh, my, look at the time! I've just remembered...you see...I'm expected...I have to...uh..." And with that he turned and sprinted from the hotel.

Anna stared as the door squeaked back and forth on its hinges. What was all that about? She'd known him for years, but had never seen him act like this.

"Who were you talking to?" Luke asked, cutting into her thoughts.

"Didn't you see? It was the Laird, Alistair Grant. He was acting very strangely—as if he'd seen a ghost."

"Honey, everything about that man is strange. We're ready to go. Are you coming?"

"I'm ready. We must find her. We're going to find her," she said, picking up her rucksack. "Alive!"

"I pray we do, lass," Ewan said, joining them in the hallway. "I pray we do."

With the search now focused on the road and its environs, Luke could no longer protect Anna from what they might find. At Ewan's suggestion, and accompanied by two other members of the search party, they'd driven down the glen, leaving their vehicle in a lay-by four miles west of Home Farm. The plan was for them to make their way towards the farm, with Anna and Luke searching the surrounding moorland and occasional field, while the other pair concentrated on the road.

"We'd cover the ground quicker if we worked either side of the road," Anna suggested.

Luke studied her face before replying. There were dark circles under her eyes and her skin had lost its rosy glow. She moved woodenly, as if each step took all her strength.

"Quicker, maybe. But this way our search will be more thorough." He took her hand, his fingers warm and strong as they grasped hers. He could see her composure was little more than a fragile shell.

"I suppose you're right," Anna said, taking comfort from his touch.

He kissed the top of her head. "That's my girl. Now, call those dogs of yours and let's get started."

Anna held a sweater, previously worn by Morag, while the dogs familiarised themselves with her scent. "Ensay, Rhona. Find Morag!"

The two collies set off at a trot, quartering the rough terrain, their noses pressed hard to the ground. Luke and Anna followed more slowly, searching every rock, crevice and bush.

After two hours, they stopped to rest. Anna took a bowl and bottle of water from her rucksack and gave the dogs a drink. Luke opened his pack and was in the process of pulling out a can of soda when the two-way radio he carried crackled into life.

"Luke? Anna? Can you hear me? Over."

Fearing the worst, Luke's expression sobered. "This is Luke. Anna is here too." He hoped to God the other man took the hint and chose his words carefully. "Go ahead. Over."

"The rescue team from Fort William has arrived. As soon as they've set up I'll send some help your way. Over."

Luke glanced at Anna and exchanged a smile. "Thanks. Over."

"That's a relief," Anna said. "I thought the police would never take Lachlan seriously."

"They can't ignore the situation any longer. Do you know if the mountain rescue team's got access to a helicopter?"

"I think so. Why do you ask?"

"A helicopter with an infrared or thermal imaging camera can pick up a heat signal, no matter how faint it is."

"Even at night?"

"Yes, if the weather conditions are right."

Anna leapt to her feet and whirled round to face Luke, sadness and pain turning into white-hot anger. "Then why haven't they sent one?"

"Hey, don't take your frustrations out on me. It's probably on its way right now. Ewan will be in a better position to pass on information once the mountain rescue team sets up their equipment. In the meantime, try to relax a little."

"Relax? How dare you tell me to relax when my best friend is missing!" She fought back her tears.

Luke clasped her body tightly to his, and gently rocked her back and forth. Her fists beat his chest as she tried to struggle free, but he merely tightened his hold on her waist. She shuddered as one deep, tortured sob, and then another racked her body. "About time," he muttered, waiting for her to cry herself out.

"I'm sorry.   I know...I should be strong.   But I can't...bear to...think of...Morag...lying hurt."

Luke pressed his lips against her forehead. "I know, babe, but with so many people looking for her, we're bound to find her soon."

"Do you really think so?" Anna asked lifting her face to his.

He led her to where they'd left their rucksacks. "Yes. Now sit down. Can you keep going or do you want to go back to the hotel?"

"I'm not giving up, Luke, no matter how tired or upset I am. I won't give up until we find her."

"In that case, rest here awhile and have something to eat." He offered her a sandwich from his pack.

Under his watchful gaze, Anna accepted the sandwich and took a bite. It tasted like sawdust, and was difficult to swallow, but she ate it anyway knowing that Luke would insist she go back to the hotel if she refused.

Chapter Thirty

Back at Killilan House, Alistair Grant paced the floor of his library, his features contorted with a mixture of relief shock, and anger. Anna MacDonald was alive! His hands shook as he poured a measure of whisky into a glass and took a sip. The amber liquid dribbled down his chin and onto his silk tie. Cursing, he yanked off the tie and threw it on the chair. He glared at the huge portrait of his father that dominated the high-ceilinged library.

And to top it all, that morning he'd received another letter from his London bankers. The threat of foreclosure was now a reality. Five days remained in which to sign the contract before the bank took possession of the estate. He snatched up the ornate Louis XV clock off the mantel and hurled it at the painting, causing a six inch tear in the canvas. The clock fell to the floor, an odd discordant clanging coming from its chimes. He laughed at the irony of it all.

"It's your fault, you old fool," he screamed. "I wouldn't be in this mess if you'd done as I'd asked and made the estate over to me. But, no, you wouldn't listen. You waited until the bank threatened to foreclose. Even when I found the way to prevent them, you refused to sign the contract. You wouldn't betray the tenants! Instead, I had to wait until you were nothing more than an empty shell that sits and drools all day long to gain control. Well, it's too late. Your precious family is about to become bankrupt. I hope you rot in hell!"

The decanter now empty, he slumped into the chair behind the desk, put his head in his hands, and wondered what to do next.

Anger and despair fought for control inside him. With shaking hands, he opened the desk drawer and removed the keys to the gun room, turning them over and over in his fingers. It seemed the irony was endless. There was no way out, and here he was considering taking his own life.

Feeling weak and vulnerable, he staggered to his feet, but got no further than the centre of the room when a knock on the library door shattered his self-pity.

"Mr Alistair? Mr Alistair, I'm sorry to disturb you," his housekeeper, Mrs McTavish said, opening the door. "The police are here to see you."

Alistair lurched toward the door. Police? Here? The terrifying thought that he could be about to be served with an order for repossession hit like a blow from a sledgehammer. He had to hold his nerve. He had to! His whisky-befuddled mind struggled over what to do.

"Show them into the morning room please, Mrs McTavish. I'll join them in a moment," he replied, trying hard not to slur his words. "Oh, and give them some tea and coffee or whatever they want."

He waited until the housekeeper left, closing the door behind her. Placing his ear against the wood panelling he listened, but couldn't hear anything. He remained behind the door until he was sure his visitors were safely ensconced in the morning room. Opening it a mere three inches, he peered into the hallway. It was empty, but the door to the morning room was ajar.

On tiptoe, he crossed the hall and dashed up the stairs. Once in the safety of his bedroom, he quickly shed his clothes, and took a cold shower, all the while cursing his family's stupidity. He gargled with mouthwash and, as a final precaution, liberally slapped cologne on his cheeks.

If not completely sober, he was certainly more alert. He lurched back downstairs into the morning room. Two uniformed policemen sat on the sofa opposite the fireplace. He straightened his shoulders and cleared his throat.

"I'm sorry to keep you waiting, gentlemen," he said, stepping forward, vigorously shaking hands with the officers. "How can I help you?"

"As you're probably aware, there's a woman missing from the village," the older officer stated.

Alistair looked away hastily before replying, lest the policeman smell the alcohol on his breath. "So I understand. I believe her name is Morag McInnes."

"That's right, sir."

"Dreadful business. But I don't see what it has to do with me. I've only met the woman a couple of times."

"Well, sir, it's like this. The mountain rescue team is on its way from Fort William. The hotel is a bit too public, not to mention cramped, so we were hoping you'd agree to let them make their base here."

Panic rose in Alistair's chest. Play it cool. Play it cool, he told himself. "I see. And that would entail...what?"

"They'd need somewhere to set up the communications centre. They'd also need access to a phone line and the like, not to mention somewhere to house their dogs. Mr Abercrombie, Ewan, at the hotel, has offered the use of the bunkhouse, should they not find her today, so there should be sufficient accommodation for everyone."

Alistair leant back in his chair and drummed his fingers on the leather armchair pretending to consider their request. Things were growing infinitely more complicated by the moment. If he said no, it could arouse their suspicion. And if he said yes, the police and the mountain rescue team under his feet day and night would be problematic.

The officer cleared his throat. "Sir?"

"Oh, sorry, I was thinking. Of course you can. In fact, I have the very place. There's a small cottage on the back drive. My former ghillie lived there. It's been empty for a while now, but there's a phone, and a small byre which would be suitable for the dogs. I'll arrange for you to collect the key from the estate office. Now if that is all..."

"That's very much appreciated, sir." The men stood to leave. "There's just one more thing. If we need to bring in the helicopter, I assume you've no objection to it landing here?"

"No, I haven't, but I'd rather it didn't land on the front lawn."

"I'll make a note of that, sir."

Alistair chewed on his lip as he stood by the window watching the police car drive away. His legs felt rubbery, and he almost fainted with relief. He fell into an overstuffed armchair, and closed his eyes. As close calls go, that was one of the closer kind. But for the time being at least, he was in the clear.

He was still congratulating himself for handling the matter well, when MacKinnon burst into the room. "Why have the police been here? What's going on?"

"Keep your voice down, man, and close the damned door." Alistair hissed. "I don't want Mrs McTavish getting suspicious."

"I don't give a toss about your housekeeper."

Alistair ran a hand through his hair. He couldn't, wouldn't allow MacKinnon the upper hand. "That's as may be. However, this is not the right time to discuss our...our business transaction. I'll meet you at Ardtoe bothy in two hours."

Mac's fists bunched at his sides. "Don't you tell—"

"Get out. If you want your money, you'll leave now!"

The two men stared at each other in silence, both reluctant to back down. Finally, Mac lowered his gaze and turned to leave.

"If you're one minute late, just one minute, I'll come looking for you." He slammed the door behind him.

Alistair let out a ragged breath and withdrew his shaking hands from his pockets. He needed time to think; if possible, to formulate a plan before they met again. Most of all he had to ensure that no blame for this fiasco could be laid at his door.

An hour and a half later, making sure his housekeeper was out of the way, Alistair slipped out Killilan House and made his way up the hill towards the bothy.

It was a steep climb to the tumbledown cottage tucked away on the far edge of the estate. The higher he climbed up the heather-clad hillside, the hotter he became. He pulled his handkerchief from his pocket and mopped his face. A red grouse catapulted out of heather, its tell-tale 'go-back, go-back' calls startling him and other birds in the vicinity.

His father's ghillie...what was his name? Sandy, that was it, used to bring him here as a boy for the annual deer cull. They'd spend days camping out in the sparsely furnished croft. He'd hated it even then. And nothing had changed now, twenty years later. The isolated cottage still gave him the creeps.

He climbed the last few yards to the bothy, pausing now and then to catch his breath. He'd made sure he was early so as to have an advantage over MacKinnon. There was no telling how the thug would behave, seeing as he resented authority of any description.

Alistair took out his handkerchief, wrapped it around his hand, and opened the door of the bothy. It was empty. Back outside, he squinted against the sun, and scanned the hillside, but there was no sign of the man. He leaned against the door frame and waited.

Thirty minutes passed. MacKinnon slunk in the bothy without explanation or expression.

"You're late!" Alistair barked.

Mac shrugged. "It was difficult to get away. One of the shepherds had a problem with a tractor and asked me to give him a hand to get the engine started."

"You still took too long."

"And I don't care. What did the police want? If it was about those antiques that went missing from the Manse, I had nothing to do with it."

"For God's sake! Isn't the money I'm paying you enough?"

"I told you, it wasn't me."

"Then how... oh, never mind! The police didn't come about missing antiques. They came to ask if the mountain rescue team could use the estate as a base for their search."

"Search? What search?" Mac took a drag on his cigarette.

Alistair folded his arms across his chest, ignoring the question. A long brittle silence ensued.

"I asked you a—"

"I heard you," Alistair snapped. "Members of the mountain rescue team are combing the village and surrounding area as we speak."

Mac chuckled. "That's a relief. I thought the police had the eye on us. Instead, it's some stupid hillwalker who's taken a wrong turn while halfway up the bloody mountain."

"This has nothing to do with a hillwalker. It seems as though a woman in a Land Rover is missing."

Mac laughed. "Yeah, well, they're lying at the bottom of the hill on the glen road. I saw the accident myself. Horrific it was—the Land Rover came down the hill so fast it failed to make the turn. It took to the air and landed in a field."

Alistair suddenly felt violently ill. Sweat beaded on his forehead. He gulped in air in a desperate attempt to calm his stomach.

"Really? What if I were to tell you our intended target wasn't driving the Land Rover?"

"Impossible!"

"I assure you it's true. I saw Anna MacDonald in the hotel this morning. I even talked to her."

Mac grabbed Grant by the front of his shirt. "If this is some sort of sick game to avoid paying me, you'd better think again, your Lairdship. I've already got blood on my hands. Adding yours won't make any difference."

He knocked MacKinnon's arms away, and pulled his handkerchief from his pocket to wipe MacKinnon's spittle off his cheek. "Check it out for yourself. Although I should warn you, the police are setting up road blocks."

"But I saw the vehicle leave the road."

"That may be so. But incompetent fool that you are, you didn't check to see who was driving, did you?"

MacKinnon's fist slammed into the wall. "Well, no. I didn't think there was any need seeing how it was her Land Rover!"

"God damn it!" Grant's eyes narrowed in rage. "It's a fucking disaster. I'm ruined. Completely ruined! Well, don't expect a penny more from me."

"Shut up! I'm trying to think. There has to be a way to sort this."

"How? I—"

Mac's face was vicious. "I said *shut up!*"

Alistair swallowed. He'd been a fool to confront MacKinnon. To hell with the estate and the family name; perhaps he should just cut his losses and run. But then what would he do? Find a job? Doing what? The knot of hatred for his father tightened round his heart. He watched MacKinnon pull a flask from his hip pocket and take a swig.

"I don't think getting drunk is the answer to our problem," he said, breaking the silence.

Mac gulped down more from the flask and wiped his mouth on his sleeve. "Right, your Lairdship. 'I've had a drink and a think, and I have an idea. This is what we'll do..."

Chapter Thirty-One

The unrelenting sun beat down on Anna's back as she searched the undergrowth beneath the old birch, pine and spruce trees along the granite strewn riverbank. Luke and the dogs were somewhere off to her right, out of sight, searching nearer to the road. Hot, tired, but determined to carry on, she lifted the bottle of water and drank heartily. It slipped from her fingers when someone called her name.

Squinting into the sun, she stared at the person standing on the bank a short distance away, but couldn't see who it was. Ignoring the weight of her rucksack, she scrambled over boulders and pushed aside clumps of nettles in her frantic efforts to reach them. Twice she fell, but managed to struggle to her feet. She clawed her way up the bank and stopped on the edge of the field to catch her breath.

It was then she recognised the figure.

"Hello, Alistair. Have you come to help with the search?"

"Actually, I've brought you a message from Ewan."

She wiped the sweat from her eyes. "Why didn't he call on the radio?"

"He tried, but the battery must be flat. He said you and that American fellow were searching this area, so I volunteered to come and give you the message."

"I see. Here, help me take this off for a minute," she replied, turning so he could pull the rucksack from her shoulders. "Oh, God, that's better." She rotated her shoulders to ease the pain that had settled there. "So, what's the message?"

"Oh, yes! You're to search the other side of the river. Apparently, a hillwalker reported seeing a woman meeting Mrs McInnes' description crossing the old footbridge over the gorge. He said she was acting very strange, as if she was disorientated."

"Are you sure?" She gazed at the mountains that towered above the far bank of the river. "That's awfully rough terrain. I think the walker must be mistaken; Morag would never take to the hills. She was going to Fort William."

"I know, my dear, it does seem strange. But there could be any number of explanations as to why she might have headed that way. I'm only relaying the message."

"I appreciate that Alistair. Even so..."

"Even so, every lead has to be followed. You know that."

"Okay. I'll sit here for a moment while I get my breath." She examined a deep scratch on her arm and wondered whether to put an elastoplast on it. "Would you mind passing me my pack? Thanks." She rinsed the dried blood off her arm, smeared on some antiseptic cream, and took a bite of a high energy cereal bar. "Are you coming with me, Alistair?"

"I have to get back to the house. But I am doing my bit. The mountain rescue service is due to arrive any moment. I've said they can use Sandy's old cottage as their base. It will be a while until they get their comms—communications sorted out, so I'm acting as go-between. I'll join the search tomorrow, if it continues."

"Well, I'm glad they've finally arrived, we need all the help we can get. This heat is unbearable. I just wish it was a little cooler. Well, I guess I better make a move." She took a long drink, picked up her pack, and tucked her hair into her baseball cap. "Be sure to tell Luke I'm searching the other bank if you see him."

"I will. I will."

Aware that Anna was probably still watching, he resisted the temptation to wave. He continued walking, his steps measured and unhurried. Safely back in his car, he pulled the two-way radio out of the glove box, and changed the frequency.

"I've passed on the message. Over. Anna's heading up the gorge."

He started the engine and returned to Killilan House.

ৠৠৠ

Under normal circumstances, Anna would have enjoyed the walk along the tumbling, foaming river, thundering through the deep gorge, but today she gained no pleasure from her surroundings. At nearly two hundred feet deep and a mile and a half long, the gorge was a dangerous place even in summer. Signs warned walkers to take great care on the narrow path. The moss and fern strewn walls rose sheer for seventy feet, the floor a mass of smooth granite boulders. Close under the banks, small pools of brown water formed, topped with peaty froth. The air was heavy with the pungent scent of bog-myrtle.

Pausing now and then to catch her breath and scan the steep sides, she studied every projecting ledge and every visible nook and cranny. But there was no sign of Morag. She followed the rough track, worn into the bank by generations of walkers, sheep and deer. The further she went, the steeper it became. She glanced over her shoulder and was surprised how far she'd come.

Once or twice she thought she heard the uncanny double echo of boots on rocks, and the occasional snap of branches, but when she turned round to see if someone was following her, she was alone.

An old, narrow wooden-decked suspension bridge lay half a mile upstream, and spanned the river at its narrowest point. On summer days it was a popular photo stop for those tourists with a good head for heights. But Anna found it deserted, except for the famous Scottish "midge," which swarmed over the roaring curtain of water that flowed beneath.

She walked across the wooden-planked bridge, and it creaked and swayed slightly under her weight. She paused halfway and leant over the rail and peered down at the river below. Once on the other side, Anna followed the twisting, arduous path through the trees, swatting ineffectively at the tiny buzzing insects that nibbled at her unprotected flesh. Finally, no longer able to tolerate their itching bites, she sat on a boulder and slipped off her pack, only to remember that Luke had put the insect repellent in his rucksack.

She pulled out her map, checked her position and tried to understand why Morag might have come this way. The more she thought about the reported sighting, the more perplexed she became. The gorge was a good three miles from the road; even if disorientated Morag would have followed the road, rather than head into the mountains.

A branch snapped.

A blackbird screeched in protest. Anna spun round.

"Hello? Morag? Morag is that—"

A hand clamped over her mouth. An iron-hard arm crushed round her waist, and dragged her off the boulder. She clawed at the unseen hands, her feet kicking wildly at whoever stood behind her. She sank her teeth into her captor's palm, and drew blood. There was a muffled curse.

Suddenly, something slammed into the back of her head.

Her world exploded into a million stars and went black.

Chapter Thirty-Two

"Anna! Anna!" Luke called, squatting down to examine the parallel markings in the grass. Lines of concentration deepened along his brow. These were vehicle tracks. No doubt about it. The flattened grass was still relatively green. He stood, shifted the weight of his pack, and cupped his hands to his mouth.

"Anna! Anna!"

No answer. The air was still and heavy; perhaps his voice hadn't carried to the riverbank. He followed the tracks back to the bend in the road. Shading his eyes against the sun, he looked back down the incline. From up here, it was easy to see where they crossed the field before disappearing into a stand of birch and pine trees.

He picked up his two-way radio. "Luke to base. Over."

"Go ahead."

"Ewan, it looks like a car crashed through the dry-stone wall at the bottom of the hill, about a mile east of Home Farm. I'm going to check it out. Over."

"Checking the map. Hold on. Okay, Luke. I see where you are. I'll radio the mountain rescue team leader and pass on your location. Over."

Luke clipped the radio back on his belt. With the dogs at his heel he re-traced his steps. The tracks cut a swath through the rough pasture, flattening everything in their path.

Clumps of heather and cotton grass gradually gave way to silver birch and rowan, interspersed here and there with tall Scots pine. As he neared the trees, the ground became a steep incline, and Luke saw the raw wounds where branches had snapped off bushes and trees. A young birch lay on its side, its willowy trunk clearly no obstacle to whatever had passed this way.

Treading carefully, and ducking under low boughs, he picked his way through the trees. He stopped and listened. Water?

Suddenly, a combination of wet grass and loose stone sent him plummeting down a steep bank. He reached out wildly—he grabbed a branch. It gave way with an explosive crack. Desperate, he seized a tree root with his left hand. Thankfully, it held. His shoulder muscle screaming with pain, he thudded to a stop right at the edge of a high-sided ravine.

Breathing heavily, he thanked God he didn't roll another six inches.

Then he saw it: Anna's Land Rover.

It lay in a heap. Rear wheels in the air, the bonnet curled around the trunk of a huge Scots pine, the only thing between it and the boulder-strewn floor of the narrow gorge fifty feet below.

His heart pounding, Luke dragged himself backwards to firmer ground and got shakily to his knees. As scratched as he was, somewhere down in the gorge lay Morag.

Ensay and Rhona barked in the distance. He didn't hold out much hope for the radio, but unclipping it from his belt, he hit the send button.

"This is Luke. Can you hear me? Someone answer!"

A burst of static, then, "Search control. Over."

He offered up a silent prayer of thanks. "I've located the Land Rover. Repeat. I have found the Land Rover. Over."

"You're breaking up. Confirm. You have found the vehicle."

"Affirmative. It's halfway down the gorge. I can't tell if anyone's inside."

"Understood. Emergency personnel are on their way. Stand by."

Fearful of dislodging boulders lest they upset the vehicle's precarious balance, he removed his pack and inched his way towards the mass of twisted metal.

"Morag! Morag, are you there?"

Silence.

He hoped she'd walked away. But he feared the other possibility, which now seemed much more likely.

He called her name again. There was nothing but the sound of a few birds twittering in the branches of the trees above him. He crawled back to his rucksack and opened a bottle of water, pouring it over the top of his head. The cold stream felt good, but it did nothing to diminish his growing fear. This was Anna's best friend. How could he not find her?

His muscles and joints heavy with fatigue, he rose, and using first one tree, then another for support, wove his way back up the incline to the waiting dogs. He kneeled down, and gave them a reassuring pat.

"Where's your mistress? Where's Anna?"

The dogs panted and gave no other reaction. Strange. Luke walked to the edge of the trees and called her name once more, hoping she'd respond. But as before, there was silence. Surely she'd heard the dogs barking, so why hadn't she come to investigate? He wanted to tell her he'd found the Land Rover, but knew he should stay with the vehicle, at least until the emergency services arrived. He thought for another moment, turned, and with an impatient shrug of his shoulders, walked back to the dogs and sat down to wait.

Luke leaned back against the trunk of the tree and closed his eyes. Perhaps he was the target all along. God knows, he'd put enough people behind bars during his time with the agency.

Could this be payback time?

It was no secret he lived on Cape Cod, and that he kept Sandpiper in the local marina. And anyone could have climbed aboard and installed a tracking device without his knowledge. If they'd wanted to kill him, they could have done so while his yacht was in open water, where it would have sunk to the seabed without a trace. A small incendiary device, hidden in the engine compartment or fastened to the hull, would have blown him to hell and back. Everyone would have assumed it was an accident. He could even see the headlines— 'Cape Cod artist perishes at sea.'

He shuddered.

Before he had a chance to consider the possibilities further, a siren wailed in the distance. Would Anna hear it, and realise its significance? Luke braced himself—this was the moment he'd been dreading. While he hoped his fears for the outcome were premature, he was also realistic. Morag's injuries, no matter how superficial or serious, would only have been compounded by the delay in finding her.

A short time later a vehicle arrived, the words 'Mountain Rescue Team' emblazed on its side. A tall, burly, bearded man climbed out of the Land Rover and strode towards him.

"Andy Munro, Team Leader," he said in a broad Scots accent. "Are you Tallantyre, the guy who found the missing vehicle?"

"Yes. It's hanging over the gorge. It's very unstable. I couldn't see whether the driver, is still inside."

A hand the size of a ham descended on Luke's shoulder. "Well, we'd best find out."

"Wait a minute. Is this the whole team?" Luke looked over his shoulder at the two men accompanying Munro.

"No. We're the first to arrive. The rest will be here soon, along with the police. There's an ambulance on its way from Fort William."

"An ambulance? What about a doctor?"

"Mike, our doctor, is travelling in the second vehicle. Don't worry, laddie, we've all been trained for this. Your friend, assuming she's still inside and alive, will be in good hands. Besides, if things are as bad as you say, it's going to take some time to secure the vehicle and get her out."

"Sure, but won't you need a helicopter?"

Munro rested his other hand on Luke's shoulder. "Look, I know you're concerned, but to be frank, the longer you keep me here talking, the more critical the situation becomes. I'll decide whether we need to call in a helicopter nearer the time. Now suppose you show me where the vehicle is. Robbie will wait here until the rest of the team arrives."

"It's this way. So what happens now?" Luke asked, as he, Munro and another man walked briskly towards the gorge.

"Jamie, my deputy, will help me do a recce—that's what we call a reconnaissance of the scene. Once we've decided on the best way to approach the vehicle, I'll go down and assess the situation."

The three men crawled towards the edge of the ravine, and peered over, visually measuring its depth.

"You can reach it, can't you?" Luke asked.

"I think so," Munro replied. "But search and rescue is an imprecise affair, more art than science. And oftentimes our success depends on prayer. If you haven't already started praying, I suggest you do so now."

Luke stood off to one side as Munro, already geared up in safety helmet and harness, abseiled down to the Land Rover. With great care, he manoeuvred around the vehicle, and examined it from every angle. Occasionally, his foot dislodged a small rock, sending it plummeting down the hillside into the gorge below. By the time he climbed back to the top, the rest of the team had assembled and were waiting to be briefed.

"Right, lads. This is a tricky one. We need to stabilise the vehicle before we attempt to extract the driver," explained Munro. "We'll do that with a combination of pulleys and winches. And I want a five point anchor belay for the stretcher. It's too dangerous to lower the stretcher to the bottom of the gorge for a carry-out."

Luke's eyes widened in surprise. "Morag's inside? Alive?"

"Aye. Incredulous as it sounds, the driver is still inside the vehicle. And yes, she is alive, but she appears to be in a bad way."

As he turned to walk away Luke caught him by the arm. "There must be something I can do to help."

Munro was about to say 'no', but thought better of it. "Sure. You can give us a hand unloading the equipment."

Luke dragged a rucksack out of the Land Rover and heaved it on to his shoulder. It had to weigh all of thirty pounds. By the time he reached the top of the gorge he was breathless and sweating. After three trips he was exhausted.

The rescuers gathered on the top of the bank, a vast amount of equipment at their feet. Luke watched in awe as two team members set up a complicated system of winches and pulleys, while two others hammered wedge-shaped metal blocks into cracks in huge granite boulders for the rope belay anchors.

Carefully avoiding tree roots and ropes, Luke made his way to where the medical team were assembling their gear.

"Here, let me help you with that," he said, taking hold of one half of the stretcher and holding it steady while a young woman inserted a bolt.

"Thanks," she smiled. "This thing can eat fingers. I'm Irene, by the way."

"Luke. I can't begin to tell you how impressed I am by all of this. You guys are truly amazing. They must pay you very well."

"I wish. We're all volunteers. Didn't you know?"

"No. I thought you were like the police—on call twenty-four/seven."

"We are. But every team relies on donations."

"And yet you risk your lives trying to save others? I don't know what to say. 'Thank you' seems so inadequate."

Irene grinned. "Care to help me get the vacuum mattress out of this bag?"

"The what?"

"Vacuum mattress. We use it to immobilise anyone who's been injured. Once the air is pumped out, it forms a rock hard shell around the patient and helps reduce the risk of further injury."

"That's amazing."

"Well, things have changed quite a bit over the years. Oh, look. They're getting ready to go down and stabilise the vehicle."

Luke watched from the safety of a rocky outcrop and wondered where Anna had got to. He became increasingly uneasy. No longer able to sit and watch, he got up and started pacing about. She must have returned to the hotel, he reasoned, rather than see her friend pulled twisted and broken from what remained of the Land Rover. Part of him wanted to go and find her, comfort her, but he knew he had to see Morag safely on her way to hospital.

The minutes became hours. Somewhere in the distance, he heard the thud-thud-thud of a helicopter approaching, the pilot circling, looking for somewhere suitable to land. Finally, Morag, safely ensconced in a casualty bag and vacuum mattress and strapped to the stretcher, was brought to the top of the gorge by eight members of the team. Luke listened intently as the doctor relayed a list of her injuries by mobile phone to the hospital, fifty miles away.

"One female casualty. Approximately forty years of age. Weak pulse. Tachycardic..." The list ran on and on. He was too stunned to take it all in.

"Casualty? You said she was alive!" Luke said, as the doctor stood back to allow the stretcher to meet the waiting helicopter.

"You're an American. You may call injured folk something else, but that's what we say here. Yes, she's still alive, but badly injured. We've managed to stabilise her."

"How bad?"

"Quite extensive I'm afraid. Fortunately, she was wearing a seatbelt, but she has chest injuries, a broken collar bone, broken left and right tibia, and, as you would expect, she's badly dehydrated. She's also in considerable pain, but I've given her something to help with that."

Luke hung his head. "Be honest, doctor. Is she going to make it?"

"Her age and the fact that she appears to be relatively fit are factors in her favour. However," he paused and looked away. "I'll not lie. The next twenty-four hours are critical."

"Can she speak? Can I talk to her?"

"She's been drifting in and out of consciousness. You can try, but no longer than a minute or two, mind you."

Luke reached the stretcher party just as it reached the top of the gorge.

"Morag, can you hear me? It's Luke," he said softly, taking hold of her hand.

Her pain-filled eyes fluttered open. "Anna—danger," she whispered hoarsely.

"What about Anna? Morag!"

The doctor brushed him away. "I'm sorry, she's lost consciousness."

"But..."

"Let us get on with our work, man. We can't delay getting her to hospital any longer."

Nodding, Luke backed off, allowing the stretcher party to make their way to the waiting helicopter. The door closed. The rotors sped up, the downdraft pushing him into the ground as it lifted off into the haze. He turned and walked back to where Munro and members of his team were resting.

"Is there any chance you could lower me down so I can have a look at the Land Rover?"

Munro's blue eyes stared at Luke. "Are you mad? You've seen for yourself how unstable it is."

"Let's just say I have a suspicious nature."

"After examining the marks on the road, the police are of the opinion it was an accident caused by steering failure. What makes you think any different?"

"Anna took good care of that old piece of junk. I know. I drove it a couple of times."

Munro scratched his beard. "You think it may have been tampered with?"

"Call me crazy."

"All right, laddie, you're crazy. Even so you should be having this conversation with the police, not me."

"If I'm right, I will.. Now, do I get to go down, or not?"

Munro glanced at his deputy for signs of objection. "What do you think, Jamie? Should we let him have a look?"

"I don't see how it can do any harm, not if he's careful. I'll get him a harness."

Equipped with safety helmet and gloves, Luke took a deep breath and stepped backwards over the edge of the gorge. Only the skill of six men and a couple of ropes stood between him and certain death. One rope controlled his rate of descent— the other was a back up or safety rope.

Exercising extreme caution, he inched his way down under the mangled Land Rover. Unsure of what he was looking for, he examined each wheel in turn. The tyres appeared undamaged, except...he pulled off his glove and ran his fingers over the brake pipe. They came away wet.

It took several minutes for him to reach the safety of the trees and free himself from the harness. Munro looked at him questioningly.

"Thanks, Andy. I saw what I needed to see," he said, stepping out of the harness.

Without another word, he turned and walked towards the waiting dogs.

He'd kept his promise. He'd found Morag, all right. Alive. She might not make it, though. He knew he had to tell Anna.

But where was she?

Chapter Thirty-Three

Alistair Grant squatted on the filthy cellar floor in the disused farmhouse, three miles from Killilan House. He knelt next to Anna's battered body and felt her wrist for a pulse.

"You've hit her too hard," he spat at the other man.

Mac's eyes narrowed. "Stop fretting. I only tapped her on the head."

"Then why is there so much blood?" Alistair dabbed ineffectively at the back of Anna's head with his handkerchief.

"I don't know. I'm not a bloody doctor."

"And did you have to bind and gag her?"

Mac grabbed Grant's shoulder and spun him round. "Stop whining, for God's sake! I got her out of the way, didn't I? It wasn't easy you know. Not with the glen crawling with police and searchers. Besides, you don't want her waking up and screaming her head off, do you?"

"No, but I didn't expect you to hurt her so badly."

"Hurt her? I should have killed her."

Alistair flinched. "Good God, man! Isn't one death enough?"

"If she wakes up and recognises you, the game is up. Then what? Think of that while you feel pity for her," Mac said.

"I...I don't know."

"Trust me. I know what I'm doing. She's out of the picture for now." Mac nudged Anna's leg. "See? No reaction."

Alistair flinched.

"Well, well," Mac sneered. "Look who's found his heart. Disgusting."

"I never wanted her dead, you damned fool, only out of the croft. What happens when she comes round?"

"She won't. At least not yet. Come on, your Lairdship. Best get back to the house before anyone misses you. After all, you need to sign those papers and get my money. And don't do anything stupid like contact the police. You'll regret it."

The door slammed behind them.

The key turned in the lock.

Anna's eyes flickered open. Was this a nightmare? She struggled uselessly. Her hands and feet were bound. Her mouth was full of something—cloth?

She lifted her head, and agony seized her brain, sending her spiralling into the void. Occasionally, she thought she heard voices and footsteps. And somewhere in the distance, a door slammed—then silence, as the blackness descended once more.

She woke once again. More alert, but she had no sense of time. Where was she? Anna pulled against the ropes, and tried to spit out the rag in her mouth. With the room spinning around her, she dragged herself across the floor until she felt a wall and thrashed into a sitting position. Closing her eyes, she swallowed hard, pushing the acid back into her stomach, determined not to vomit. Everything hurt. The ropes were too tight. The pulsating headache bled her dry of strength.

Breathe in. Breathe Out. Repeat, she told herself. Fight the panic. You'll get out of this. Little by little, her eyes grew used to the dimness. Her heart rate slowed.

The dank room was tiny, no more than six feet square. Weak strands of light filtered in through a tiny frosted window high above her head. No furniture, no carpet. Bare concrete. A cellar? A pantry perhaps? A faint scratching sound. Mice?

Rats? She shivered. She didn't know. She didn't care. She had to stay alive.

ঝঝঝ

With Morag safely on her way to hospital, Luke hurried back to the hotel. He pulled open the swing door and ran headlong into a departing guest, carrying a holdall.

"Gee, I'm sorry. Are you okay, buddy?" He asked, and picked up the bag.

"Thank you. How do you say... it is nothing." Outside, a car horn sounded. The man snatched it out of Luke's hand and left the hotel.

Luke stared at the man's back. Something about the way he carried himself made the hairs on Luke's neck stand on end. He continued to watch as the guy opened the trunk of the Jeep and slung his bag inside. Lying next to it was a leather rifle case. Luke was just about to chase after the guy when the door of the bar opened.

He heard a cheer. Ewan stepped forward out of the crowd and slapped him heartily on the back.

"Well done, laddie. Well done. Here," he thrust a pint glass into Luke's hand. "Drink this. You deserve it. You're quite the hero."

The ice cold beer tasted like nectar. "Thanks, Ewan. I was lucky, that's all. Save your thanks for the guys from the mountain rescue team. They're the ones who deserve it."

"Aye. You're right, but all the same, if you hadn't spotted those tracks—say, where's Anna? Is she not with you?"

The glass paused in mid-air. "You mean she's not here?"

"I haven't seen her."

Luke held his breath for a moment. Something was very wrong. "I thought she'd come back with some of the other guys."

"Malcolm! Charlie!" Ewan shouted over the noise of the crowd. "Did you see Anna MacDonald down by the river?"

Malcolm Fraser pushed his way through the mob to where Luke and Ewan stood. "No. And we didn't pass her on the road either."

"Now I'm really worried," Luke said.

"You don't think she met up with some of the mountain rescue guys and hitched a lift back to Killilan House, or even Tigh na Cladach, with one of them?" Charlie suggested.

Luke played with his watch. "I doubt it. She wouldn't leave the dogs behind. You know how she feels about them."

"Aye. I do," replied Ewan. "I wouldn't worry. There's probably a perfectly reasonable explanation. In the meantime, finish your pint. There's food too, if you're feeling hungry."

Luke pushed away his glass. "No thanks. I'm going back to the croft. God, I hope she's there."

"All right. If she shows up here in the meantime, I'll tell her where you are."

"Thanks, Ewan. I appreciate it."

Luke drove like a mad man. Scarcely fifteen minutes later, he unlocked the door to Tigh na Cladach and stepped into the hallway. The small cottage was eerily silent. He entered the kitchen, and dropped his keys on the table. The breakfast dishes were still in the sink waiting to be washed. Anna's manuscript lay on the table next to her laptop.

He climbed the stairs two at a time, and pushed open the door of Anna's bedroom. It was empty—the bed unmade, the sheets in a tangled heap from their lovemaking earlier that morning. He closed the door and hurried back downstairs.

He gave the dogs a bowl of water and some food, and grabbed a can of soda from the fridge, then sat down at the table and started scribbling on a page from Anna's manuscript.

If he wasn't the target, who was?

There was something bad happening in the Glen. That much was obvious.

Morag's disappearance, the attempted break-in at the croft, and the shooting incident all had to be connected.

But how?

The hairs on the back of his neck tingled. Rage seared through his veins. He hadn't felt like this in years. Not since...not since Nicole had died. Then he'd wanted to go out and murder the bastard who had run her down and deprived him of the one person who mattered the most. He closed his mind. Now wasn't the time to re-visit old wounds.

Anna had said the land was worthless, so why would anyone want it? As far as he knew there were no vast deposits of gold or precious metals or minerals in Scotland, so that ruled out someone wanting it for mining. But it still didn't explain why it was so important. And who or what was behind all these so called accidents?

No matter which way he looked at it, his mind returned to one man—Alistair Grant. What was it Anna had said about him that morning? That he'd been surprised to hear about the search. But there was something more. Something disturbing. If only he could remember. He picked up the can of soda and gulped down half the contents.

Then it came to him. Anna had said Grant was surprised to see her. *Surprised* to see her? What an odd thing to say. He drew a ring round Grant's name on the paper and put a question mark next to it. What could possibly link him to Anna, the croft, and Morag?

The harder he tried to ignore the truth, the more it persisted.

There was only one way to find out if he was right.

Dusk descended as Luke pulled the pickup to a halt in front of Killilan House. Unlike the night of the Ceilidh, there was no welcoming piper. He climbed the half dozen steps to the front door and rang the bell. No one answered. He leaned over the ornate balustrade and peered through the window into what appeared to be the drawing room. It was empty.

He beat his fist against the door. "Grant, open the goddamned door!"

Silence.

He re-traced his steps and climbed behind the wheel of the pickup, inserting the key into the ignition. But instead of driving away, he rested his chin on the steering wheel and stared at the house.

What the hell?

He turned off the ignition. He climbed out and removed a tyre iron from the toolbox. After a quick look over his shoulder to make sure no one was in sight, he made his way round the side of the building, keeping as close to the wall as possible. The gravel pathway crunched under his feet. He cursed, and wondered why Grant couldn't lay real sidewalks like everyone else. Every window and door he checked was bolted or nailed down tight.

With time running out, he inserted the tyre iron between the door and the frame and lent on it with all his weight. The frame splintered and the door opened, but no alarm sounded. With a lightning-fast motion, Luke stepped inside. His heart hammering, he waited for a count of five before creeping down the dimly lit corridor.

Three rooms opened off the passage. He approached the first, but rather than enter it, he placed an ear to the wooden door and listened. When he heard nothing, he moved on to the next.

The final door opened to reveal a narrow staircase. Was he in the servants' quarters? He neither knew nor cared. The door at the top was closed. Slowly, he turned the knob and pulled. The door hinges screamed as like a woman in labour. Undeterred, he climbed the last three steps and entered the main hallway. He stood motionless, frantically trying to recall the layout of the house. Was the library on the left or the right of the grand staircase?

The door on the left was ajar, and the light cast a shadow on the floor. He crept toward it, ignoring the creaking floorboards under his feet.

Eureka!

A huge mahogany pedestal desk stood in the centre of the bay window. He crossed the room in four quick strides. There were six drawers. Unsure of what he was looking for, Luke systematically searched the first two, but found nothing.

The third drawer held a number of brown folders. He pulled them out, and tossed them on the blotter. The topmost file was full of letters from Grant's bankers, each one more threatening than its predecessor.

Luke let out a long low whistle. Grant wasn't just overdrawn; he was in hock to the point that he was lucky to own the clothes on his back. The estate, the London house, everything he 'owned' was really owned by someone else.

Luke stared out of the window and played with the strap of his Rolex. Grant was broke. So what? Most people would cut their losses, by selling their assets, so why hadn't Grant? What was so important to him that he'd consider anything, anything at all, including murder?

One simple word crept into his mind—pride.

That's what this was all about. Grant was too proud to sell the family home. So how did you set about protecting that when your bank threatened to foreclose?

Luke rifled through the second file, shuffling the papers impatiently. Among them was an article from the local newspaper. A single paragraph at the bottom of the page was circled in bright red ink. He glanced at the date—it was six months old. On the top of the page Grant had scrawled a telephone number.

Luke picked up the phone and dialled the number, waiting for it to connect.

"You have reached the offices of Proteus Surveys. I'm sorry no-one is available to take your call. Please leave a message after the tone."

He slammed down the receiver.

He'd found the link he'd been looking for. He stuffed the papers back in the drawer as Alistair Grant appeared in the doorway.

Chapter Thirty-Four

Anna heard footsteps approaching. They grew closer and closer, until finally they stopped outside the door. She swallowed her scream. Huddled in the corner, her body trembling uncontrollably, she stared wide-eyed at the door.

There was a long brittle silence. A key grated in the lock. The handle slowly turned.

A bald headed man stepped inside.

Anna recognised him instantly. She couldn't breathe. She could barely think.

MacKinnon squatted down next to her and stroked her cheek. "Well, well, my pretty, we're not so feisty now, are we?"

Anna flinched and kicked out with her feet, but he dodged the blow. She shuffled backwards, trying to stay out of reach. He grabbed her arm and held her steady, then backhanded her into the wall. The blood roared in her ears. She was on the verge of passing out again when he grabbed her shoulders and shook her violently.

"Ah, you want a fight! Good. 'Cos I don't like passive women." He slapped her face, splitting her lip. His calloused hand closed around her throat, cutting off her breath, all but squeezing the life out of her. Just as suddenly, he released her, tossing her against the wall again. He looked at her quizzically. His wild, manic laughter echoed round the room.

"Don't worry, I'm not ready to kill you yet."

He sat back on his haunches.

Anna was beginning to hope her ordeal was over, when he leant forward and ripped open her shirt. He licked his lips and clawed at her breasts.

Please God, please don't let him rape me. She bit down hard on the gag, pushing the vomit and blood back into her stomach, knowing that otherwise she'd choke. She lashed out once more with her feet, this time aiming for MacKinnon's groin, but there was no weight behind the kick.

Then she realised the more she fought him, the more aroused and crazy he became. Terrified, and with tears welling in her eyes, she stopped thrashing about and willed herself to be still no matter what he did to her.

"Be a good girl," he said, continuing to paw her breasts until tears ran down her cheeks, "give me what I want, and I'll make sure it doesn't hurt too much when I kill you. But if you don't, well, I'll let you think about that."

Anna focused her mind on Luke. Once he realised she was missing, he'd come for her. He wouldn't leave her here to die at the hands of this lunatic.

As suddenly as it started, MacKinnon's abuse stopped. "As much as I want to continue our little tête à tête, it's time to move. Come on."

He dragged Anna to her feet. Her legs buckled. He scooped her up, and slung her over his shoulder as if she were a sack of oats. His arm clamped tight round her thighs. Already dizzy from his earlier blows, her reality slipped away.

ঙঙঙ

"What the Hell do you think you're doing breaking into my house and going through my desk, Tallantyre?"

"Well, well, well. If it isn't the Laird himself. The game's up, Grant. I know all about your little scheme. It's all here in your files." Luke tapped the folder in front of him.

"I have no idea what you're talking about."

"Sure, you do. You're bankrupt, Grant. The ancient family seat is mortgaged to the top of its chimneys. Your only hope rested on Anna's grandmother selling you the croft. But she died and left it to Anna. But you weren't going to let a mere woman stand in your way, were you?"

"I...I was desperate!"

"I'll bet you were. You saw the article in the paper about that company looking for a deep water loch. They planned to fabricate drilling platforms for the oil industry. The loch's perfect. It's deep and wide and remote."

"It's my land, damn it!"

"Not really. It's Anna's, and you can't sign the contract until you make it your land. So you got your lawyers to make her a huge offer for the croft. But you didn't count on sentimentality. So you hired someone to scare her off. Or did you change your mind and out and out plan to kill her?"

Grant sank to his knees and buried his face in his hands. "It was MacKinnon. But he was only supposed to scare her, I swear!"

Luke grabbed Grant by the collar of his jacket and hauled him to his feet.

"Oh, yeah? He did more than that. He tried to shoot her. Fortunately for Anna, I saw the sun reflect off his gun when he took aim. I pushed her out the way."

"You're lying."

Luke shook his head. "No. I have the cartridges to prove it. How did you hook up with him?"

"A friend... a friend in the South of France recommended him."

"Some friend! What is he? Ex-army? That would explain his choice of shell. Lynx Game King. Made solely for the African market. Africa is just a short hop across the Mediterranean Sea from France."

"I...he's...I thought he was just your typical thug, into petty crime. I had no idea..."

"Obviously beneath your social station. You're as guilty as he is. Where's he holding Anna?"

"I... in the cellar of one of the ruined farmhouses... but he was talking about moving her."

"Where to?" When Grant didn't answer, Luke belted him across the face. A piece of tooth went flying, along with a spurt of blood. "Need me to ask you again?"

"I don't know—"

Luke pushed Grant away in disgust. "The police are on their way; in fact I think I hear their sirens now. There's nowhere for you to run. You'd better pray I find her alive—"

He ran out of the house just as two police officers raced up the steps.

"You'll find Grant in the library!"

"But, sir! Sir! We need—"

The police officer's words were lost in a hail of gravel and dirt as Luke climbed behind the wheel of the pickup, and sped off down the drive.

As he reached the gates, a middle-aged, unshaven man dressed in camouflage jacket and trousers stepped out of the bushes. Luke slammed on the brakes and skidded to a halt.

"You old fool! I nearly ran you down!" When the man didn't move, Luke shouted, "Who are you? What do you want?"

"I'm Alexander Gordon, although most folk know me as 'Sandy.' I'm ghillie to the Laird."

"The Laird? I don't want to talk to anyone who works for that weasel. Get out of my way! Can't you see I'm in a hurry?"

"No, I'm ghillie to Mr Alistair's *father*. I think you should listen to what I have to say. It concerns the lass, Anna."

Luke froze. "What do you know about Anna?"

"That she's not been seen since this afternoon. She's missing, isn't she?"

"Yes. But anyone in the Monymusk Arms could have told you that."

"Maybe. But I know who's scaring her. And I know why."

"Get in!" Luke thrust open the passenger door, and offered his hand to the old man.

Deceptively strong for his age, Sandy pushed Luke's hand away and climbed into the passenger seat.

"Calm down, laddie. You concentrate on driving while I tell you what I know."

"Tell me about Anna!"

"Things have not been the same on the estate since Mr Alistair's father became ill and moved to London. I lost my job when the son took over and appointed a new ghillie."

Luke rubbed his chin. "Yeah, yeah. Get to the point, man."

Sandy smiled benevolently. "I've followed MacKinnon's every move since he arrived on the estate. Of course the man's too stupid to notice he's being stalked like a stag. But I've seen the way he watches Anna. I can tell you, the man is pure evil."

"Grant said Anna was in the cellar of a ruined farmhouse. But he was talking of moving her. Any idea where?"

Sandy thought for a moment. "There are umpteen empty farmhouses and ruined cottages, not to mention bothies on the estate. He could be holding her in any one of them. It would take hours to search them all."

"Then what are we waiting for? Tell me where to go."

"Don't be so hasty, laddie. MacKinnon's a devious bastard. He'll want to be sure he won't be disturbed. You said he was about to move her?"

"For all we know, he could be dumping her body in the loch."

"He won't do that. He'd have to drive through the village, and run the risk of being seen."

"Come on, Sandy, time's running out. Think man! Think!"

Sandy rubbed his whiskery chin. "There's an old ice house near the walled garden. It's about a half mile from Killilan House. I reckon that's where he'll take her."

"Tell me how to get there, and you'd better do it now!"

"I'll do better than that laddie. I'll come with you. It's the least I can do for Alisha's granddaughter."

Luke was about to argue, but the grim determination in the older man's face told him he'd be wasting his time.

"Which way?"

"Turn right by the stable block. We'll leave the pickup there and go the rest of the way on foot."

A short time later, Luke crouched behind the crumbling masonry of the walled garden and waited for Sandy. Somewhere in the trees above his head an owl hooted. He'd always hated stake-outs, waiting for the bad guys to show up. The silence and the familiar rush of adrenaline, accompanied by a slight feeling of tension, and uneasiness, always made his palms itch. Too many things could go wrong, and tonight was no exception. If Sandy's description of MacKinnon was right, things could turn to from sugar to shit at any moment.

Always prepare for the worst; that was his motto. He pulled his gun out of its specially-designed holster. It was loaded. The safety catch was on. The scene was set. All he needed were the players.

Leaves rustling alerted him to the older man's presence. Sandy knelt down beside him and whispered in his ear.

"MacKinnon's vehicle has just turned into the back drive. He should be here in a minute."

"Is he alone?"

"I couldn't tell, but we'll know soon enough."

Luke nodded. Show time.

He felt the familiar rush of adrenaline. Staying low, he and Sandy pushed their way through overgrown bushes and bracken toward the ice house. No more than a tunnel carved into the hillside, it stood as a reminder of days long past. With only one way in and out, it was a tactical nightmare.

Overhanging ferns partly concealed the small metal door. Luke and Sandy positioned themselves to one side of the doorway and sat down. They didn't have long to wait.

A twig snapped. The owl hooted once more. Someone cursed.

Finally, a shadowy figure carrying something large across its shoulders emerged from the tree-lined pathway. Luke's eyes narrowed as he tried to distinguish the man in the moonlight. At that moment he would have given anything for a pair of high-tech night vision goggles. He couldn't be sure it was MacKinnon.

His gut told him it was.

And that Anna was with him.

ༀༀༀ

Anna didn't know what was worse; MacKinnon's sour body odour or the constant pounding in her head. Both made her want to vomit.

He carried her over his shoulder as if she weighed no more than a child. She tried to hold her head up to see where MacKinnon was taking her, but the strain on her neck muscles made her nausea worse. Hysteria bubbled in her throat and she wondered how she'd ended up in such a predicament.

Her hipbone banged against a wall. Pain ripped through her body and added to the nausea. Something sticky clung to her skin. A spider's web? Something crawled through her hair. She shivered.

Then the air changed. It was no longer musty and damp. She breathed in. The scent of pine filled her nostrils. She was in the forest.

All at once the world was full of noise. Birds. Wind. MacKinnon's heavy breathing, and the crunch of his footsteps on the gravel path. The thud of her own frightened heart.

She tasted blood. Her lips throbbed where MacKinnon had struck her, but the pain checked her panic.

Somewhere to her right, a tawny owl hooted, and she listened for an answering call. When it came, it sounded unlike any owl she'd ever heard before. Then something clicked in her brain.

Sandy!

Sandy had taught her how to put two leaves together to make that sound. She felt a vague glimmer of hope and renewed strength. She shifted her weight, trying to unbalance her captor, but he merely tightened his grip and shortened his stride.

"D'you think Anna heard you?" Luke whispered.

"Aye. If the lass is conscious, she'll know it's me all right."

"Okay. Now you're sure you know what to do?"

"Don't you worry about me and yon lassie. Just make sure you get the bastard!"

Luke briefly rested his hand on the old man's shoulder, before disappearing into the undergrowth. It took him several minutes to get into position above the ice house.

Seconds ticked by.

With care, he parted the heavy growth of ferns and peered out. MacKinnon climbed the hill and was close enough for Luke to hear his laboured breathing. He had just one chance to get it right. Then, as he'd predicted, MacKinnon dumped Anna on the concrete floor.

Luke waited until MacKinnon stepped forward to unlock the door. He jumped; landing on MacKinnon's back and knocked him to the ground. The Factor groaned and struggled.

Right on cue, Sandy leapt forward and dragged Anna to safety.

MacKinnon fought dirty. He rolled to one side, and pushed Luke off, kneeing him in the groin in the process. The air whooshed out of Luke's lungs. MacKinnon landed a heavy blow to Luke's jaw, before sprinting down the path towards the stable yard.

Dragging air in between his teeth, Luke followed as best he could. He reached the courtyard in time to see Sandy step out of the bushes and level his shotgun at MacKinnon's chest.

MacKinnon skidded to a halt. Icy contempt swept into his eyes. "Get out of my way, old man. We both know you won't shoot me." He walked slowly toward Sandy.

"He won't, but I will," Luke took aim.

MacKinnon spun round towards the sound of the voice behind him. The way Luke held his gun, MacKinnon could see he wasn't dealing with an amateur. He weighed up his chances of making it to the bushes, but didn't like the odds.

"I'm just a simple hired hand. It was the Laird's idea," he shouted.

"I know! He was babbling like a jackass when I left him half an hour ago." Luke said, walking slowly towards him.

His finger tightened on the trigger. "How much is he paying you?"

"A pittance."

"I said how much?"

"Fifty grand!"

Luke snorted. "That's peanuts compared to what he'd have if his plan worked. But I guess you were okay with that. Right, asshole?"

Anger flashed in MacKinnon's eyes. His muscles tensed. Suddenly, his foot shot out and kicked the gun out of Luke's hand. It skidded along the path. A shot rang out. MacKinnon sank to the ground. Clasping his right knee, he screamed in agony.

"Go on, laddie, go see to your lassie. I'll watch this piece of vermin till the police arrive." Sandy said with a nod of his head.

Luke found Anna propped up against a tree. He gently removed the gag from her mouth, then pulled a knife from his pocket and set about cutting the twine binding her wrists and feet.

"Oh, Luke," she sobbed. "I heard a shot."

"MacKinnon. Don't worry, he won't be going anywhere. Sandy's with him." He knelt down and pulled her into his arms. He did a swift assessment of her condition. She had a nasty cut on the back of her head, which would require several stitches. Her beautiful face was battered and bruised, and covered in grime. There were rope burns on her wrists and ankles. He cursed silently. For the second time in his life, he wished a man dead.

"Shush," he said wiping away her tears with his thumb. "You're safe now. But we can't stay here. If I help you, could you walk as far as the drive?"

"I think so."

He helped her to her feet, and, wrapping his arm around her shoulder, led her back to where he and Sandy had left their vehicle.

Chapter Thirty-Five

"I still think you should have done what the doctor suggested and gone to the hospital," Luke frowned.

"I'm fine," Anna said. "I prefer the comfort of my own bed."

"You're not fine. You've got a concussion, and a bunch of contusions. He really did a number of your lower lip, too, the bastard!"

"There's no need to remind me." Anna replied, gently touching her mouth.

"You're darned lucky to be alive."

"Luke, stop fussing."

Anna was silent for a moment. "If only Morag had remembered to put petrol in her pickup, she wouldn't have borrowed the Land Rover and none of this would have happened."

"Come on. You know you didn't create this mess."

"Perhaps. But I can't help thinking I'm partly to blame for her accident."

"Hey, don't cry, love." Luke sat on the edge of the bed and wrapped his arm around her shoulders. "She's strong. She'll pull through. We should know more from the hospital later today. The police are downstairs. Do you feel up to answering their questions?"

"Only if you'll stay with me."

"I'll be right by your side, honey." He kissed her forehead and went downstairs, returning a few moments later with two police officers.

"I'm Inspector Drury, and this is Constable MacFarlane. How are you feeling miss?"

Luke sat beside Anna and wrapped his arm around her shoulder. She rubbed her forehead.

"Tired. A bit bruised and battered," she answered softly.

"I'll try not to take too long, then. Why don't you start by telling me how you came to be with MacKinnon?"

"Alistair—Alistair Grant found me. He said he had a message from Ewan and that I was to search the far side of the river."

"That would be Ewan Abercrombie, the manager of the Monymusk Arms?"

"Yes, that's right. I asked him why Ewan hadn't called on the radio. He said he'd tried, but the batteries on the set must be dead."

Anna hesitated and dabbed at her bottom lip.

"Go on."

"I made my way up to the suspension bridge, as he'd suggested..."

"My God, that was barely a mile from where I found Morag," Luke said.

"I sat down on a rock to have a drink and the next thing I remember is waking up in some sort of cellar. I kept drifting in and out of consciousness. MacKinnon came. He hit me. I knew he was planning to rape me... Oh, Luke, I was so scared—I just wanted him to get it over with!"

Luke swore. Anger blazed in his eyes. He pulled Anna into his arms, rocking her back and forth, stroking her hair. "Hey. Hey. It's all over," he assured her. When he felt her body relax he eased her back on the pillows and wiped away her tears.

"Can you go on, Miss MacDonald, or should we come back later?"

"No. I want to get this over with. MacKinnon is a monster."

The Inspector nodded. "He is that. He's got a lengthy list of offences and he's no stranger to the prison system. He's a mercenary who hires himself out to the highest bidder. We're pretty sure he was responsible for Mrs McInnes' accident."

Anna's head snapped up. "I don't understand. I thought the steering had failed."

"Something had failed—but not in the way you think," Inspector Drury said. "Someone tampered with the brakes."

Anna gasped.

"I'm glad I checked for leaking brake fluid," Luke said. "If I hadn't, everyone would've believed it was just an accident."

Anna turned to him. "But I drove the Land Rover to work, and the brakes were fine. Surely, I would have noticed if something was wrong with them?"

The Inspector shook his head. "Not necessarily. The mechanic who inspected the vehicle afterwards said the hole in the brake pipes was tiny—probably made by a needle or sharp implement of some sort. The brake fluid would have drained away little by little, each time the pedal was depressed. We found an ice pick in MacKinnon's cottage. His prints are all over it and on the Land Rover too."

Luke squeezed her shoulder. "The Land Rover is totalled. Sorry, honey—"

"So what? I can replace it. I can't replace my best friend."

"No. You can't. And thank God, you won't have to."

Suddenly, Anna realised what it all meant. "It wasn't Morag he meant to kill. It was me."

"Yes, babe, but MacKinnon didn't act alone. Grant was paying him."

Anna's eyes opened wide. "Alistair? Are you sure?"

Luke nodded. "I'm afraid so."

"But I don't understand."

"Alistair wanted your land, so he hired MacKinnon to scare you away."

"Mr Tallantyre is correct," the Inspector said.

"He was the prowler?"

Luke nodded. "Among other things. Do you remember that day on the hill, when we were shot at? I went back later and found the spent cartridges he'd used. They matched those the police discovered in his cottage."

"Lynx Game King?" Anna asked.

The Inspector's eyebrows shot up in surprise. "How did you know?"

"I found two bullets in the firebox of the Aga. I thought they must have fallen off the shelf in the cow-shed into the box of kindling or been tossed in there by a passing sportsman. Then I wondered about the guy staying at the hotel—the one with the rifle."

"Mr Abercrombie told us about him," replied Inspector Drury. "We caught up with him at Glasgow airport. Seems he was just a tourist hoping for some sport. He didn't realise the deer stalking season didn't start until July."

"Then I don't understand. Why would Alistair want Tigh na Cladach? He has more than enough land of his own."

"The Grants are bankrupt," Inspector told her. "Grant thought that if he could sell your land to an oil company to develop a deep water harbour, he could save the estate."

A soft gasp escaped her lips. "Do you think he was behind the solicitor's letter offering to buy the croft?"

"Almost certainly, although we're still waiting for confirmation from our Glasgow colleagues."

"And when I didn't accept he decided to renew our friendship," Anna said. "That explains why he came to see me and asked me out to dinner. The night of the ceilidh, in particular, he kept talking of marriage. I thought he was crazy." She turned to Luke. "The same night I was so angry with you for acting like a pompous idiot."

"I was jealous. I'll admit it. The sight of you in Grant's arms made me nuts."

"But he means—meant nothing to me."

"I know that, my love. After you turned Grant down, he gave MacKinnon the go-ahead to get you out of the way. I suspect MacKinnon tampered with the brakes that night."

Anna turned to the Inspector. "What happens now?"

"MacKinnon has been charged with attempted murder. I'm betting when we look more closely at his background, we'll find he's wanted for other crimes—the robbery at the Manse for one thing. Grant's got prison in his future too."

"Poor Alistair. He should have swallowed his pride and sold the estate."

"Maybe. But with his Father still alive, he had no right to. Thank you for your time, Miss MacDonald. I'll need you to make a formal statement when you're feeling better. Perhaps you'd drop by the station in a day or two?"

"Of course, Inspector, anything to help."

"Right then. I'd best be getting back to Fort William." He turned to leave. "Oh, one more thing, before I forget. I hope you've got a licence for that gun, Mr Tallantyre?"

"What gun?"

He shot Luke a knowing glance. "Hmph. Just as I thought! Don't get up. We'll see ourselves out."

When the Inspector and his constable had left, Anna snuggled up to Luke.

"I still can't believe Alistair could be so..."

"Greedy? Stupid? That's funny—I can."

"For an artist, you seem to know a great deal about law-breaking."

Luke smiled. "Ah. Well, I haven't always painted watercolours."

"Oh?"

"No. I worked for the FBI for twelve years as a member of the art theft recovery team. When this first started, I thought I was the target, that someone I'd put away was seeking revenge. It took me a while to work out that it was really you they were after. If I'd realised that sooner, I might have been able to stop things before they got out of control."

"You said worked for the FBI—past tense."

"Yeah. I thought about quitting when a colleague got shot on a case. We were trying to recover a stolen Rembrandt, and he'd been working undercover for months, getting closer and closer to the group responsible. Unfortunately, his cover was blown. But it was Nicole's death that finally made me get out. I'll never know whether she was the intended target, or I was. So after she died, I got out. I realised that I couldn't put my family's safety at risk, so I've been painting full-time now for five years."

"You protected me."

"No, I didn't. I should never have let you out of my sight after Morag disappeared."

"You weren't to know Alistair had hired MacKinnon or what he had planned."

"Maybe. But my gut told me something was wrong. And like an idiot, I didn't listen to it."

He kissed the top of her head. "Now, you get some rest. The doctor said to take two of these." In his palm were two white tablets. He handed her a glass of water. "I'll bring you something to eat later."

Chapter Thirty-Six

The following morning Anna had another visitor. A small, lean, sinewy grey-haired man popped his head round the bedroom door.

"How are you, lass?"

Anna shuffled up the bed. "Oh, Sandy. I can't tell you how relieved I was to see you last night or was it this morning? I lost all track of time in that cellar."

"Last night, but we'll not argue over a few hours."

"We all thought you'd left the glen."

The old man grinned and took Anna's hands in his. "What, let that upstart Mr Alistair drive me away? You know me better, lass. The dogs and I have been here all the time."

"Where did you sleep? What did you do for food?"

"On the estate—there are plenty of disused cottages and places for a man to hide if he knows where. I planned everything before I left; stockpiled tins here and there and lived off the land as my forefathers did. I trapped rabbits, ate berries. I didn't go hungry."

"You amaze me."

"Besides, I sensed there was something iffy about MacKinnon. It didn't take me long to suss out that he didn't know one end of a sheep from the other. I think the only time he saw lamb was on his plate, complete with mint sauce and all the trimmings! He certainly knew nothing about driving a tractor. So I hung around to see what he was up to and to watch over my best friend's granddaughter."

"I never saw you."

The grey eyebrows arched. "No? The dogs knew I was here. In fact, you nearly saw me that first night he tried to scare you."

"So I did see a man! I thought I was dreaming!"

"No, lass, you weren't. That bastard was creeping around and if it hadn't been for me, Ensay and Rhona would have alerted you to his presence. As it was, they only sensed an old friend."

"Ensay and Rhona did their job."

"Aye, lass, they're grand dogs, even if I say so myself. But I couldn't watch MacKinnon all the time and I blame myself for him finally succeeding."

She patted Sandy's hand. "Don't reproach yourself for that."

"And you have a good man here in Luke. Which reminds me; I have a message for him from Ewan. The part for his boat has arrived."

Anna sank back into the pillows. She felt the stab of another pain far worse than her physical injuries. When she said nothing, Sandy interpreted her silence as tiredness.

"Ewan's putting me up at the hotel until the bank decides what to do with the estate," he continued. "In the meantime, I've got my old job back, until a new owner is found. Now, lass, I'll leave you in the capable hands of your man." He kissed her on the cheek and quietly left the room.

When she heard Luke knock on the door of her bedroom a few minutes later, she feigned sleep. Morag's injuries, Luke's imminent departure; it was too much to take in. She needed time to think. Sooner or later she would have to tell him that the part for his boat had arrived.

But not just yet.

He'd never lied to her; he'd made it clear that he would leave once the part for his yacht arrived. But would the events of the last twenty-four hours be enough to make him change his mind?

She doubted it.

She turned on her side and thumped the pillow. Luke was a successful artist with a wonderful home and lifestyle. Why would he want to live in a tumbledown croft in the middle of nowhere? The answer was he wouldn't. And besides, there was the woman he dated back home in Cape Cod.

Anna knew she couldn't leave the croft. Not yet. She couldn't leave the glen while her friend was so ill. There was her book to finish, if only to prove that she had what it took to be a successful author. And then there were the dogs, Ensay and Rhona. Whatever happened, she couldn't leave them behind.

Of one thing she was certain. She loved Luke. She loved him completely.

Life was so complicated, she thought as she drifted off to sleep.

Three days later, her bruises had faded to a rainbow of colours. Anna ran a comb through her hair and went downstairs. Luke sat at the table nursing a mug of coffee.

"Do you feel up to a walk after breakfast? Some fresh air will do you good."

Anna helped herself to cereal and coffee. "Okay, but nothing too energetic. I'd like to go into the village later to post my claim to the insurance company for the Land Rover. Once Morag's out of hospital, Lachlan will need his pickup back. I'll need to replace it before then. By the way, I forgot to mention it, but Sandy told me the part for Sandpiper has arrived. Ewan's keeping it for you at the hotel."

"Would you like to go see Morag this afternoon? If so, we can drop your letter into the mail box, and pick up the part at the same time."

"Yes, if you don't have any other plans. I don't feel up to driving yet."

Later that afternoon Luke drove a frail and subdued Anna into Fort William to see her friend.

They left the pickup in the car park in front of the main hospital building and walked the short distance to the intensive care unit.

Surrounded by machines, her legs in splints and a drip in her arm, Morag lay still and pale. Her eyes were closed. At first Anna thought she was asleep. Then she realised it was more than that.

She sat down at the side of the bed and took Morag's slender hand in her own.

"Oh, Morag!" She wiped away a tear, and glanced at Lachlan who sat on the other side of the bed.

"How is she?"

"They took her to theatre again this morning. He wasn't happy with the way her left leg was set. She's not regained consciousness since she came out of the operating room, but the doctors seem satisfied with her progress."

Anna offered up a silent prayer.

"I'm so sorry, Lachlan. If I'd known any of this was going to happen, I would never have let her borrow the Land Rover."

"It's not your fault, Anna. She's out of danger, thanks be to God. The doctors say she'll make a full recovery in time, although she may be left with a slight limp." He stroked his wife's cheek. "I've told the rig I'm not going back. I don't want to leave her on her own again."

Anna looked at him in surprise. "I'm sure Morag will appreciate that, but what about your dreams for a farm?"

"I don't care about that any more. Morag is more important. Once she's recovered, I'll look for work closer to home. What about you? Will you stay on at the croft now this is all over?"

Anna tilted her head to gaze at Luke. "I have a lot to consider. I'm not sure...it depends..."

"I understand. It can't be easy, not after what Grant and MacKinnon did to you."

"No. And, it will take a while for folk in the village to come to terms with their antics. I wonder what will happen to the estate now."

"Ewan says the Bank has taken control for now. He heard it from Mrs McTavish. I expect they'll put it up for sale."

Morag stirred. She moaned and her eyes fluttered open. "Lachlan? Anna?" Her voice was dry.

Lachlan leaned forward and tenderly kissed his wife's forehead.

"*Ho mo leannan.* Oh, my sweetheart...I'm here. Everything will be all right."

"Anna. She's... she's safe."

Anna lifted her friend's hand to her bruised cheek. "I'm here too. Don't worry about me. I'm fine, thanks to Luke and Sandy. I'm so sorry you got hurt, Morag."

"Don't cry, lass."

Anna wiped away her tears. "Don't talk. Save your strength and put all your effort into getting better."

A nurse appeared at the bedside. "I'll let doctor know you're awake, Mrs McInnes. But I'm afraid your visitors will have to leave. Not you Mr McInnes; just the lady and the other gentleman."

Anna leant forward and kissed Morag on the forehead. "I'll come again in a few days, when you're feeling stronger."

Morag smiled at Anna, then closed her eyes again. And slept.

The nearer Anna and Luke got to home, the quieter and more withdrawn she became. For most of the journey she stared out of the window, alone with her thoughts.

There was no denying they'd reached the point where their relationship had to be resolved. But she needed another few days to come to terms with the fact that he would soon be leaving.

She turned to look at him. There was an inherent strength in his face. He'd obviously loved his fiancée very much. But could he love that deeply again?

And would he stay if she asked him to?

Anna turned back to the window, lest he see her tears. Her heart was torn in jagged pieces. She bit her lips, ignoring the pain.

It was dark by the time they reached the croft. Luke helped her down out of the pickup and into the croft.

"You sure are quiet," he said.

"Sorry." She rubbed her aching temples. "I was thinking about Morag. May I have a couple of those painkillers the doctor left?"

"Sure. You should have waited another day before you visited Morag. You need more rest. Why don't you go lie down?"

"Would you mind?"

"Of course not. Go. I'll call you when dinner's ready."

After they eaten their meal, Luke carried the coffee tray into the sitting room, then bent down and put a match to the logs in the grate. He sat down on the sofa next to Anna.

"Thanks for cooking dinner again. I don't seem to have much energy at the moment."

He gathered into his arms. "MacKinnon gave you quite a beating. It will take time for you to recover, both physically and mentally."

She settled back, enjoying the feel of his chest against her back. "But at least I won't have any physical scars like Morag."

"No. Sadly, she'll be left with a permanent reminder of MacKinnon's handiwork. It will be a good six months before she'll be fully recovered. But she has a good man in Lachlan. He'll take care of her."

"It's strange the way things worked out, with Lachlan giving up his job on the rig and his idea of buying a farm. Morag never wanted to move. And then there's Alistair losing the estate after fighting so hard to save it."

"Yes, but you're forgetting one thing."

"What's that?"

"Without your land, the construction company can't go ahead with their plans to build a deepwater harbour for the oil industry. The glen will remain as it is—an unspoilt wilderness. And there's plenty of folk in the village who are pleased about that."

"I guess you're right."

"What will you do now? Will you stay here after everything that happened?"

Anna twisted in his arms and looked up at his face. "I don't know," she told him. "It depends on a number of things."

"Such as?"

"Morag, for one. I can't walk out on her when she needs me most. And to be honest, unless I apply for another teaching job, I've no option but to stay here."

"You know... you could always come back to Boston with me."

This was it—the moment she'd been dreading. Her face clouded with uneasiness. She looked hastily away.

"But what about your girlfriend back home in Cape Cod?"

"I told you. Kate's not my girlfriend. She's just someone I see sometimes—I mean someone I *saw* sometimes. That's all over now. For obvious reasons," he smiled.

She pushed herself free of his grasp. "You say that. But how do I know it's true?"

"Kate is a free spirit. She pretty well does whatever she wants. I saw her whenever she happened to be in town, which didn't happen to be all that often. Trust me."

Trust me... how many times had Mark said that to her? And each time he'd let her down. Her parents had said it too. Each September they'd take her back to school *'We'll send for you at the end of term, promise.'* But they never did. With the exception of her grandparents and Morag, everybody she'd ever loved had let her down. What reason did she have to believe Luke was any different?

"It's kind of you to ask, but..."

Luke pulled her to her feet and wrapped his arms around her.

"*Kind of me*? Haven't you figured out that I'm in with love you?"

Anna's lungs felt like they stopped working. "You love me?"

"Of course I do. And I got the impression you loved me too." He gave her a heart-melting smile.

"I do love you. But our lives are so different."

"And that's a problem...why?"

"Don't you see? You're a successful artist. Until now I've always taught others how to write. This is my chance to find out if I can make it as an author."

"That's a seriously weak excuse, Anna. What we have is something rare, and you know it. It sprang full-grown the first time we looked at each other. Do you really want to throw it away?"

"Of course not." She turned away from him and stood by the window, ramming her hands into her pocket. "I knew you wouldn't understand."

"Damned right I don't," he said, turning her round to face him. "You know I'd never prevent you from doing something you love."

"I know that. But I'm sorry, Luke. I can't come with you. Not right now. Perhaps..." She left the sentence go unfinished. She didn't have the right to ask him to wait.

"I see." He let her go. The silence lengthened between them. "I'll stay for as long as it takes for you get a replacement for the Land Rover and a phone installed. I'll move my gear back into the spare room. In the meantime, I'll go check on the yacht. I'll be back in an hour or so."

Anna watched him leave the croft, fists bunched. Tears streamed down her face. What had she just done?

Chapter Thirty-Seven

Five o'clock in the morning. Out on the loch, the mist rose off the water. A shiny green Land Rover stood on the lawn in front of Tigh na Cladach. Morag would be out of hospital in a few weeks' time.

Down on the shore, an otter called to its cubs, its high, piercing whistle carrying over the still water. Anna closed the door of the croft and locked it. She stuffed her hands into the pockets of her wax jacket, and followed the dogs along the track through the trees, past the ruins until she reached the stalkers' path. She climbed steadily up hill, through swirling mist, her pace never slowing until she reached view point.

It was drastically different to the last time she'd climbed *Buidhe Bheinn*.

On that occasion Luke had been with her.

Now, as then, he was her reason for coming here.

Heather covered the hill like a purple carpet, and the berries on the bog myrtle were beginning to turn orange, a sure sign that autumn was on its way. Halfway up, she came across a group of five hinds and their calves, who, unperturbed by her presence, continued grazing.

Breathless, she reached the viewpoint. She sat down with her back against a granite boulder and waited. Ensay and Rhona, sensing her mood, lay down beside her. As suddenly as it had arrived, the mist lifted, bathing her in vivid sunshine. In the distance the mountains of Skye rose, dark and brooding.

Anna glanced at her watch—five forty-five. The tide would be on the turn by now.

She didn't have long to wait before a yacht sailed into view, its blue spinnaker catching the breeze as it rounded the headland and headed north. She could just make out the shape of a figure behind the helm.

Tears blinded her eyes. She dashed them away. If she lived to be eighty, she would never forget a single detail of his handsome face. Her thoughts filtered back to the day she'd met him, the firm set of his jaw, his intense brown eyes, and his tall, lean body. But most of all, she remembered the warm touch of his body next to hers, and the smouldering passion they'd shared. The dull ache of desire filled her senses.

Head bowed, her body slumped in despair, her heart aching with pain, she remained well after the yacht had disappeared from her view.

Luke was right. Too late she'd realised that he would never prevent her from doing something she loved. And besides, what difference did it make where she wrote? Cape Cod, Scotland, anywhere. If only she'd been less proud and told him so, she'd be with him on the yacht.

But she hadn't. And she wasn't.

Cold and stiff, and her eyes nearly swollen shut from her tears; she edged her way back down the hill, the dogs following faithfully at her heels.

Back at the croft she immersed herself in her manuscript. She lost all track of time. Hours became days and days became weeks, until she reached the final chapter.

Six weeks we remained at sea. Conditions onboard were wretched. The steerage passengers suffered most. Confined to narrow berths, they were expected to work despite having paid for their passage. The stench from below decks was vile and pervaded every inch of the ship.

We endured violent storms and rough seas, small-pox and dysentery. Eighteen children died many adults also. Yet Niall and I survived. Out of the two hundred who joined the ship at Ullapool, one hundred and twenty ragged souls stepped ashore in Newfoundland.

As my husband was of gentle birth we were fortunate. Unlike many of the Highlanders who left Scotland that July, we did not sail into a life of servitude. We had coin and within a few weeks had purchased a small plot of land. With the aid of our clansmen we built a log cabin, making it our home. And whilst I longed for the Sight to come to me so that I might see our future, it never did.

This new land is not Scotland, nor never shall be. But we shall stay here until we walk the earth no more. Then and only then, shall we return to the hills and glens of our homeland.

Anna leaned back in her chair and read the words on the page. A lump formed in her throat. While she couldn't comprehend how the victims of the Clearances had felt at leaving their homeland, she knew how it felt to be parted from someone you truly loved.

She stared out of the window. The wind had wiped the loch into a frenzy of white capped waves. Autumn was nearly over and she had to decide whether to stay in the croft over winter or move back to Edinburgh.

With her manuscript complete and ready to submit to a literary agent, there was only one other thing she felt she must do.

And that was to write to Luke.

She got up from the kitchen table, threw another log into the firebox of the Aga. She filled the kettle, placed it on the hot plate, and waited for it to boil. There were so many things she ought to tell him; Morag's continued recovery and the fact that she'd finished her manuscript, but she knew they weren't what he would want to hear. The shrill whistle of the kettle interrupted her thoughts. She made a mug of tea, and carried it back to the table. Rhona, sensing the sadness of her mood, came and sat by her feet. Anna reached down and absently patted the silky black head.

She lost track of time. It was only when the sun started to slip below the horizon and the kitchen filled with shadows, that she felt able to put pen to paper.

Her first draft waffled on for pages, never really saying what it should. As the mound of screwed up paper balls grew in number, Anna despaired of ever finding the right words to explain her feelings. There was only one way to do this, she decided, that was to keep the letter short, and write from the heart.

Darling Luke,

Thank you for giving me the best summer of my life. At the time I thought I was doing the right thing in letting you go, but I was wrong. I miss you more and more each day. If you can find it in your heart to forgive me, please write back.

Love, Anna.

She read over it a second time, and then added her signature to the bottom of the page. Sealing the envelope, she placed it on top of the box containing her manuscript. If she hurried, she could get it in the mail before the post office closed.

ৡৡৡ

Morag returned the last sheet of paper to the box and wiped her eye. "It's a grand story, lass. You have a fine way with words. Thank you for letting me read it."

"I hope the agent agrees with you. I sent a copy off to London this afternoon."

"You'll find a publisher, I know you will."

"Is that the Sight talking or you, Morag?"

"Me. It's a strange thing—I've not had another vision since the accident."

Anna smiled. "I would have thought that was a good thing, not a bad one."

"Maybe. Pass me that knitting needle will you. This cast is driving me nuts. I'll be glad when the darn thing comes off."

"When do you see the specialist again?"

Morag slipped the needle down the side of the cast, and ferociously scratched her healing skin. "Next week. I'm fed up with visiting the hospital. Three operations are enough for anybody. But it was such a complicated fracture, I'm lucky to be walking again, even if I do have to use a crutch."

"Well, hopefully you'll be able to throw it away soon."

"I hope so. All this sitting around doing nothing is making me fat!"

"I'll admit your face has filled out, but you're certainly not fat. Have you heard if the estate has been sold yet?"

"No, lass. Sandy told me a few folk have shown interest, but with an asking price of over a million pounds, I don't think it will be sold anytime soon. He also mentioned that a date has been set for that man MacKinnon's trial."

"Yes. I had a letter from the court. I've been called as a witness. I'm not looking forward to seeing him or Alistair again, even if it is from the opposite side of the courtroom."

"What about Luke? Won't they need his testimony, too?"

"I asked Inspector Drury about that. Apparently they've arranged for Luke to give evidence by a video link. He won't be attending the hearing." Anna felt an odd twinge of disappointment. She'd hoped Luke would attend the trial. It would have been her one and only chance to ask for his forgiveness and tell him she'd changed her mind.

"What a pity. I would have liked to have seen him again. He left in such a hurry I didn't get chance to say goodbye or thank him for rescuing me."

Anna looked away. The misery of her last night with Luke still haunted her.

"He was anxious to get home."

Morag stared at her friend, but said nothing.

"Besides, it's a long way to come," Anna continued, "I thought I told you—he said something about having to get ready for an exhibition"

"Hmph. Well I still think he should attend in person, rather than by this video link. I'd hate to think of MacKinnon getting off on a technicality."

"He won't. Neither will Alistair. Inspector Drury assures me there's more than enough evidence to put them both away for a very long time."

"Good! It's nothing less than either of them deserve."

Chapter Thirty-Eight

Eight Months later.

Morag stared at the painting in her hand. "I don't see why you couldn't wrap it up and just post it back to him."

"I wouldn't entrust it to the postal service," Anna replied. "It's far too valuable. It's the painting that inspired Luke to visit Scotland." Even now after all these months, it still hurt when someone mentioned his name. It hurt even worse when she said it herself. "I think he said he found it in a gallery in a place called Bar Harbor." She wrapped a suit in tissue paper and placed it in her suitcase.

"Mm. It's an awful long way to go just to return a painting. But seeing as you're going to New York , I suppose it makes sense to deliver it in person. Have you noticed something? There's no signature. I wonder who painted it."

"I wondered if it was a Jamieson. It looks very similar to his work."

"Jamie who?"

"F. E. Jamieson. Although he's known to have painted under other names too. He's famous for painting Highland landscapes and coastal scenes. There's quite a collection of his work in the National Galleries in Edinburgh. Do you think I should take this?" Anna held up a chocolate silk cocktail dress.

Morag nodded enthusiastically. "Yes. You never know what events your agent will expect you to attend. Are you excited? You must be. After all, not every first-time author is lucky enough to snag a New York literary agent. Tell me again, why do they want to see you?"

Anna let out a sigh. She'd lost count of the number of times she explained the reason behind her trip. "They want to discuss the proposal for my next book, and it's easier to do it face to face than over the telephone."

Morag continued to stare at the painting. "Morag, are you listening?"

Morag snapped back to the present. "What did you say, dear?"

"Never mind. You were somewhere else far, far away!"

"The picture..."

"What about it?" Anna tried not to sound too impatient. At this rate she'd never get her packing done. She began folding a cream coloured blouse.

"Don't you recognise the scenery, Anna?"

"Should I?"

"It's Tigh na Cladach. Or rather it's the bay. It must have been painted before Tigh na Cladach was built."

Anna dropped the blouse and yanked the painting out of Morag's hands. She examined it more closely. "Why, you're right. I never noticed that before."

"Didn't I tell you that man had come looking for a past he didn't know he had? I read a book about the glen while in hospital. It was about the Clearances. It mentioned something about folk from Loch Hourn sailing to America in 1773. Do you ever hear from him by the way?"

"Luke? No. Not even a phone call or a postcard to say he'd arrived home safely." When she lifted her eyes, the pain still flickered there.

"I expect it takes a while to sail across the Atlantic. And I daresay he's been busy with his painting."

Anna bent her head to hide the hurt. "Well, unless Luke sailed home via Australia, he should have arrived back in Cape Cod months ago."

"I'm sorry, lass. I should have known better than to mention his name. I've got some news that I hope will cheer you up. It certainly cheered Lachlan and me." Morag beamed. "I'm pregnant!"

Anna dropped the painting on her bed and gathered her friend into her arms. "Oh, Morag. That's wonderful news. Is Lachlan pleased? That's a silly question! He must be delighted."

"Aye, lass. That he is. Why, he's already turned the spare room into a nursery. By the time you get back from your wee trip, I'll be as round as a house. I know at forty-two I'm a bit old to be a first time mother, but the doctor says I'm fit and healthy."

"But shouldn't you be taking it easy, especially for the first few months?"

Morag blushed. "I'm fourteen weeks pregnant. I didn't want to mention it before in case...well you know—"

"I'm so happy for you both."

"And it goes without saying that we want you to be godmother."

Anna hugged her friend tighter. "I'd love to. But are you sure you're fit enough to take me to the airport?"

"Apart from an occasional bout of morning sickness, I'm fine. Lachlan has it all arranged. We'll see you off at Glasgow airport and then he's treating me to a night in a posh hotel. We're driving back the following day. Sandy's looking after Ensay and Rhona, so you needn't worry on that score. Now, you'll never be ready in time unless we get on with this packing!"

ॐॐॐ

During the seven hour flight to New York Anna tried to read the Dan Brown paperback she'd picked up in the airport shop, but found she couldn't concentrate. She put it to one side and stared out of the window at the vast expanse of the Atlantic Ocean. Her mind reeled with memories and dreams.

As the hours ticked by, the huge plane got closer and closer to its destination. Anna became more and more uneasy. Her fingers tensed in her lap and she moved restlessly in her seat. By trying to contact Luke, was she about to make the second biggest mistake of her life? Would he even agree to see her?

Immigration and customs provided minimal distraction as did the taxi ride from Newark airport to the hotel, which seemed to take forever. Anna was tired, hungry, and longing for a shower. Fortunately, the meeting with her agent was scheduled for midday the following day, which gave her a chance to get over her jetlag.

Finally, the taxi pulled up in front of the Ritz-Carlton Hotel in Manhattan. She paid the driver, collected her luggage, and made her way into the lobby. Check-in was a mere formality; her agent had taken care of all the details. She was about to leave the desk when the concierge handed her an envelope. Hopeful that Luke had somehow heard of her success, she ripped it open and glanced inside. It contained an invitation to dinner from her editor. She sighed and slipped it into her handbag.

Her suite was twentieth floor overlooking Central Park. It was pale pink and lovely, with stunning views of the city, but with a separate living room, two white tiled bathrooms and two bedrooms, she felt dwarfed by the space. She sat on the king-sized bed and rubbed the pulsating knot in her temple. Damn it, Luke. Couldn't you pick up a pen and reply to my letter if only to ask me how I am? How Morag is? Would it have been so hard? Do you hate me that much for turning you down? Her eyes filled with tears of frustration and exhaustion. She hastily wiped them away.

All she wanted to do was crawl into bed and sleep. But she knew she'd never get over her jetlag if she did. Instead, she threw open her case, she pulled out her bathrobe, shampoo and conditioner, and headed for the shower. Too tired to eat in the hotel's restaurant, she ordered room service and watched a little TV before crawling into bed.

The following morning she met with Wanda, her agent, in her Madison Avenue offices. Wanda's blonde hair was an impossibly high beehive. With her black horn-rimmed glasses, sleek black designer suit, and tall spike heels, she was even taller than Anna. Wanda gave her the slightest whisper of a hug and air-kissed both of her cheeks.

"Darling, didn't I tell you, we Americans would simply adore your novel? If your standard of writing is this good in your next book I can see you topping the *New York Times* best seller list!"

"Yes, Wanda, you did."

"You Brits. So strait-laced. And your accent...Just love it, darling. I've pitched your proposal to all the big houses. Two might be interested in a three book deal. That good with you?"

"It's fantastic."

"Of course it is. Now, honey, don't be so modest. I've set up meetings with them later this week so you can meet the editors and decide who you want to work with. Then, once we've got the deal, you can scoot back to Scotland and start working."

Scoot? Anna never imagined scooting to Scotland, or anywhere else, for that matter. But a three-book deal sounded like the best thing that had ever happened to her.

Almost.

The rest of the week passed in a whirlwind of meetings. On Friday, Anna signed a contract, agreeing to deliver three novels in three years. She didn't believe for a moment she could do it. But Wanda insisted. And Anna knew she had to try.

With the meetings safely out of the way, she was free to do as she pleased. On Saturday she hired a car—a Mercury something or other—just a regular family saloon, but even that was huge by European standards. She took a moment to familiarise herself with the controls, which thankfully included an automatic gearbox, before heading out of the city onto Interstate 95. Nervous at first, she soon got the hang of driving on the wrong side of the road. She followed the wide, three lane highway north towards Boston.

And Cape Cod.

Once out of the city limits, the roads were quiet. Six hours later, she pulled to a halt at the side of the kerb on Chatham's picturesque and historic Main Street. A mixture of upscale boutiques and clapboard houses, it attracted tourists all year round.

Armed with only the briefest descriptions of Luke's house, she headed for the nearest coffee shop. Painted in pale blue and decorated with a variety of seafaring artefacts, including lobster pots and fishing nets, the small coffee house was busy.

"Excuse me," she said to the dark-haired woman behind the counter. "I wonder if you can help."

"Sure, honey. You don't sound like you're from around here."

"I'm from Scotland, actually."

"Scotland," the woman repeated mystified. "We don't get many Scottish people here. In fact, I don't think we've ever had one before. Herb," she yelled into the kitchen. "We ever had Scottish people here before?"

"Dunno," came the reply.

"Well, there you are. What can I do for you?"

"I'm looking for a friend. He's an artist. You may have heard of him. His name's Luke Tallantyre."

"Yeah. I know Luke. Tall guy, salt and pepper hair, drives one of those big SUVs. He drops by sometimes. Haven't seen him in a while, though."

"I was wondering if you can give me directions to his house."

"Sure. You drive on up Main Street and take a right at the end of the road. Follow it around to the beach. His is the last house—a big clapboard affair with a tower. You can't miss it."

"Thanks. I appreciate your help."

"But you won't find him at home on a nice day like this. He'll be off painting some place."

Anna closed her eyes feeling utterly miserable.

"Are you okay, honey? You look pale. Why don't you take a load off and have a coffee? It's not that great, but it's on the house."

"That's very kind of you."

"Cream? Sugar."

"Just cream, thank you."

Anna quickly slipped a $5 bill in the tip jar on the counter before the waitress returned with the coffee.

Half an hour later, and after more than one wrong turn and an occasional drift into the left lane, she slipped out from behind the wheel of the rental car and climbed the weathered steps to the old Coast Guard Station. The clapboard house was stunning. Painted in delicate shades of cream and white, with sea-green shutters framing every window, it stood tall and proud on top of the dunes.

She looked around. There wasn't another house in sight. It was a perfect place for an artist to live and work. Suddenly, she understood Luke's refusal to part with the house after the death of his fiancée.

She wiped the palms of her hands down the side of her jeans and lifted the door knocker. She felt a momentary panic. It gnawed away at her confidence. What if she'd come all this way and Luke refused to see her? What if his sometimes girlfriend had become more permanent? She'd feel like a fool. Swallowing the last of her pride, she knocked at the door.

The house was still. Deserted?

Her spirits sank even lower.

Not knowing what else to do, she walked along the veranda that wrapped around the side of the house, and looked out over the beach to the ocean, to where the Atlantic rollers thundered ashore in a froth of white water. Soft white clouds drifted over head and the beach-grass swayed in the light onshore breeze.

The beach was empty save for a solitary figure throwing sticks for a pair of Labradors to chase. She thought of Ensay and Rhona back home in Scotland, and realised how much she missed them. They would have loved it here.

Lonely and homesick, she slipped off her shoes and stepped down on to the beach. She couldn't face driving back to the city just yet.

ঔঔঔ

Luke threw his paintbrush down in frustration. No matter what technique he tried, he couldn't quite capture the old lighthouse at Long Point. He looked at his Rolex. Another half hour and the light would be gone. He packed up his paints and carefully removed the canvas from the easel, loading it, along with the rest of his gear, into the back of the SUV.

During the forty minutes drive from Provincetown back home to Chatham, he thought about his inability to paint. Ever since returning from Scotland, he'd struggled to put oil to canvas. It wasn't as if he was short of ideas—he had plenty. Not to mention sketches and photographs from which to work. He just wasn't satisfied with the work he produced. It lacked the fire, the passion that his paintings were known for.

Luke turned into his driveway. Yet another car was parked in front of his garage. New York plates. Despite the 'private' signs, another city slicker had evidently decided to use his driveway as a parking lot. He really should have ordered those gates before the tourist season kicked off.

He unpacked his gear and carried it into the house, his footsteps echoing on the wooden floor. The house was way too big for just one person. It was meant to be a family home. But he didn't have the heart to sell it, after spending so much time, and money restoring it to its former glory. Pausing only to drop his coat over a chair, he climbed the staircase to his studio in the watchtower and gazed down on the beach. Apart from his neighbour throwing sticks for his dogs and a woman with hair the colour of copper, the beach was deserted. Tumbling copper-coloured curls... Luke swung the telescope round and focused on the figure...it couldn't be...could it?

Anna shivered in the breeze. In her nervousness, she'd left her coat in the car. She rubbed her arms and carried on walking until she ran out of beach. So much for her hopes of finding Luke at home. There was nothing for her here. The sooner she returned home to Scotland, the sooner she could try and forget about Luke. He obviously couldn't forgive her for turning his proposal down and had decided to get on with his life.

If only she could do the same.

Head bowed, her face pale and pinched, she turned and walked briskly back along the sand.

The scream of a seagull pierced the air.

Lifting her head, she squinted into the late afternoon sun. Without warning, memories of Luke, as she'd seen him that first day, came pouring back. His easy stride. His tall, athletic body. His smile. His laugh.

A lone figure walked towards her. With the sun behind him, he was no more than a tall silhouette, but something about him seemed familiar.

"Luke!"

She ran then, her feet scarcely leaving footprints in the sand. When she reached him, she was breathless. All she could do was stand and stare, her emerald eyes full of love, longing, and hope.

"You're here," she finally said. "I thought...I knocked and there was no answer."

His smile was glorious. "I was out painting. What are you doing here?"

"I came to return your painting—the one you bought in Bar Harbor."

"Oh that. There was no need to go to all that trouble."

"I disagree. I've..." Anna's breath caught in her throat.

"You've what?"

She couldn't bring herself to say it, instead she told him. "I finished the book. It's going to be published later this year. I'm here to sign a contract for a three book deal."

"So you've realised your ambition."

"Yes."

"Was it worth all the effort and pain?"

"Pain?"

"Yes. You gave up your home, your job, and your boyfriend. Remember? What was his name?"

"Mark. You mean, Mark?"

"Yeah. That guy. Seen him lately?"

"No. Not since I told him to leave that day at the croft. Why do you ask?"

"No reason. You must be tired if you drove down from New York today. Especially on the wrong side of the road."

"I figured it out as I went along."

"You look really good, Anna"

She winced. "So do you. This place suits you."

His hair was longer than she remembered, and slightly greyer. The wind tossed it around. He brushed it out of his eyes. "Where are you staying?"

"I don't know. I hadn't thought about it..."

"You don't have a lot of choices round here. There's the Wayside Inn or The Captain's House. Both are okay. Would you like to come up to house? I'll make coffee."

"Well, if it's no trouble."

"How's Morag? Is she better?"

"Yes. She walks with a slight limp, but doesn't need crutches. Oh! And what's more, she's pregnant! I'm going to be a Godmother."

They turned and walked side by side back down the beach towards the house. He nodded heartily. "That's great. I'm happy for her and Lachlan. And how are the dogs?"

"They're fine. They're staying with Morag and Lachlan. They bought Home Farm from the bank with the compensation they received for Morag's accident."

"They'd love it here."

Tears welled in her eyes. "Yes, I imagine they would."

Luke held open the porch door. "Come on in. I think you'll like the place. Well, I like the place, but I'm biased."

The interior of the house was decorated in the same pastel shades of cream, white and sea-green. Two leather sofas stood at right angles to the huge stone fireplace. Anna followed him through to the brightly lit modern kitchen.

"You have a beautiful home, Luke." She took at seat at the breakfast bar.

"Thanks. You still take your coffee with cream, no sugar?"

"Yes, thank you. So how's Kate?"

He stopped stirring her coffee. "Kate? Man. I hadn't thought about her in ages. She's long gone. She ran off with a surfer from California while I was away. Got fed up of calling and finding no one here. No patience at all, that girl."

"I see."

"So the painting only reason you dropped by?"

Anna blushed. "No. Yes. I mean—"

"It doesn't matter." He came round to her side of the counter and took her hands in his. "You're all I care about. I can't begin to tell you how much I've missed you. Climbing aboard Sandpiper and sailing out of Loch Hourn was the hardest thing I've ever done. But I knew if I'd forced you to come with me, you'd have hated me for it. I couldn't have that on my conscience."

"Oh, Luke, I've missed you too." Shocked by her own driving need, she clung to him.

"You don't know how many times I tried writing you, but I wasn't sure where to send the letters, or if you where still living at the croft."

"I am."

"Later, when I got your letter—well, just let's say my pride got in the way."

"I was wrong to send you away, Luke. But don't you see? The book wasn't my only reason for turning you down."

"I know, but you finished it, all the same. And you're happy about it?"

"I am."

"I have to tell you, for a while I wondered whether our age difference had something to do with why you found it so easy to let me go."

"It wasn't easy, Luke. I just told you that."

"I'm forty-three, Anna. Ten years older than you. Is that too much?"

"No. Age had nothing to do with it."

"But you had more concerns than the book, didn't you?"

"I...I had to be sure Kate meant nothing to you. That you weren't like Mark—that I could trust you. Can you ever forgive me?"

He pulled into his arms.

"I never stopped loving you, Anna." His kiss was slow, thoughtful, and full of passion.

"I love you too, Luke. I have since the first day you knocked at my door."

"I can't live without you. Tell me you're here to stay."

"If you want me to."

Luke pulled her against him, his strong arms encircling her waist. "Anna, will you marry me?"

The woman in his arms smiled radiantly. "Yes!"

"In that case, love, I have an idea."

"Which is?"

"What do you think about spending your honeymoon sailing back to Scotland on Sandpiper to collect those dogs of yours?"

"Good idea," she said. "But first you need to give me a proper tour of this wonderful house. It's going to be my home too, after all."

"Makes sense. Where would you like to start?"

She laughed and kissed the base of his throat. "Why, the master bedroom, of course."

"I think that can be arranged. Just bear in mind, if we start our tour there, you might not see much of the house for a while."

"Quite a while, I should hope."

"Quite a while," he smiled.

Historical Note

In 1975 Howard Doris opened the Kishorn Yard—a fabrication yard for the construction of oil platforms—on the north shore of Loch Kishorn, in Wester Ross on the west coast of Scotland. Loch Kishorn is very deep, and technically a fjord, as is Loch Hourn. It was therefore, well suited for the fabrication of deep sea oil platforms.

A condition of the planning approval was that the site had to be treated as an island, and all deliveries would arrive by sea, rather than by road. By 1977 over 3,000 people were employed at the site, housed in temporary accommodation, and in two retired liners moored in the loch, the Rangatira and the Odysseus. The Ninian Central Platform, at that time the largest object created by man, was built in the Kishorn Yard in 1978.

By the early 1980s a downturn in oil exploration and production reduced the number of employees to 2,000. In 1986 Howard Doris fell into bankruptcy and the yard closed in 1987.

SPECIAL BONUS PREVIEW

THREE WEEKS LAST SPRING

by

Victoria Howard

Skye Dunbar needs to get away from London to put a disastrous affair behind her. When she rents a small cabin in Washington State's San Juan Islands, the last thing she expects is to be accused of computer hacking.

Marine biologist Jedediah Walker is called in to investigate the large number of dead marine life being washed up on the islands beaches. And he has another problem – an unexpected, beautiful and suspicious new tenant renting his cabin. When Walker discovers that the fish contain a high concentration of toxic chemicals, he suspects that the chemicals are being deliberately dumped in Puget Sound. And later, when someone hacks into his computer, he realises it is no coincidence and sets out to find out more about his mysterious new tenant.

However, Skye doesn't like Walker from the moment she lays eyes on him. He feels the same. But, that is about to change...

Chapter One

England April 1999

Skye Dunbar stood by the window, and looked out across the meadow as she waited for the transatlantic phone call to connect. It had been a miserable weekend—dull, wet and cold—cold as the heart that beat inside her breast. She glanced at her watch, and calculated the time difference; early morning in San Francisco—Debbie should be up by now.

After a few rings, a sleepy American voice answered.

"Hello?"

"Debbie? It's Skye. Did I wake you?"

"Not really, I was lying here thinking about getting up. Talk to me, you sound anxious."

Skye took a deep breath. "I've decided to take a month's sabbatical. I've contacted the airline and have an option on a flight leaving in just over a week's time. They're holding it for the next twenty-four hours."

"Why, that's great. You need to get away and you know San Francisco loves you."

"Actually, Debbie, that's why I'm calling, I'm not coming to San Francisco. I'm going to Seattle and—"

"Skye, you can't possibly want to spend a month there, not after all that happened last year."

"I can't explain why, but I need to go back." Skye twisted a strand of her hair between her fingers as she listened to Debbie's response.

"I don't understand, and if you want my advice, you'll come here and stay with me. After all that lying bastard put you through, I'm amazed that you can even contemplate being within a thousand miles of Washington State. Please, come here and stay with me. We can visit all our old haunts—Fisherman's Wharf, Chinatown. We can go for a drink in the John Barleycorn and listen to that folk singer you liked so much. And if that doesn't appeal, then we could hire a car and drive along the coast. You haven't seen the Marin Headlands or Monterey yet. And if you wait until I get to the office on Monday and I'll see if I can beg for some vacation time. Or we could meet somewhere else. How about Vermont?"

"That's a lovely thought, Debbie, and I do want to see Vermont, but in the Fall. Please, save your holiday time. This is just something I have to do on my own. I go to bed at night and in my dreams I see this figure on a beach. I know it's me. It sounds crazy, I know, and I really don't expect you to understand. Just give me your blessing and tell me that if I need you, you'll be there for me, okay?"

"I guess you know what's in your heart, although I really do worry about you, Skye. You have to put what happened behind you and move on. So tell me, just where are you staying?"

"I've rented a cabin in the San Juans."

"You've done what? No one goes to the San Juan Islands in the middle of April. It's too cold for one thing and Friday Harbor will be deserted. What will you do there for a whole month on your own?"

"I thought I would catch up on some reading, go walking and generally enjoy the scenery."

"Hmm, I don't know. If you ask me, the last thing you need is to be by yourself. However, now that you've made your mind up I don't suppose there's much I can say to dissuade you. But promise me, if you become too upset or lonely up there, you'll get on the first available plane to me, here in San Francisco. Deal?"

"Deal. And Debbie," Skye hesitated before continuing, "thanks for understanding. You're the best friend anyone could ask for. As soon as my plans are finalised, I'll let you know."

Skye replaced the receiver and turned once more to look out of the window. Was she being stupid wanting to go back to the Pacific Northwest? What would it achieve? Would it even put her mind at rest? They were questions she couldn't answer, yet in her heart she knew she was doing the right thing.

She'd met Michael while on a visit to Debbie the year before. He knocked her to the ground while roller skating in Golden Gate Park. He'd helped her up, apologised, and insisted on buying her a coffee. Coffee had somehow turned into lunch, and before they knew it, they'd spent the whole day together. Skye was due to fly home the following day and Michael had insisted she give him her address. She'd agreed, but hadn't really expected to hear from him again. Six weeks later, returning home after a particularly fractious day at work, she'd found his letter waiting on her doormat.

That initial letter, like those that followed, had been read and re-read time and time again, the words feeling as if they were almost engraved on her heart. Finally, six months later, Michael had written asking her to visit.

Skye quickly pushed the thought of him out of her mind. She had so much to accomplish in the coming days that daydreaming wasn't a luxury she could afford. Her flight confirmed, and the cabin booked, she needed to concentrate on clearing her diary. Then all she had to do was pack her suitcase and talk herself into getting on that plane.

The following week passed in a blur. Each day she arrived at the office early and brought all her files up to date for John, her business partner, to takeover in her absence.

They'd had met at university shortly after Skye's mother's death, and had been good friends ever since. At thirty-nine, he was five years Skye's senior. Six feet tall, and of muscular build, with brown eyes, unruly curly hair, he had a smile that could melt the iciest of hearts. John had been a Graduate Teaching Assistant when Skye had started her degree course.

When Skye graduated, they set up business together. Years of long hours and neglected holidays had finally paid off and their services were in demand by major corporations all over the world. But despite the success they experienced, their relationship had never passed beyond friendship.

None of Skye's closest friends knew what she did for a living, apart from the fact that she was a high-level executive, and whatever it was, she didn't like to talk about it. In another few months, she and John would be making a presentation to Government officials in the hope of securing an exclusive contract—top secret, and the most demanding of their respective careers.

The day before Skye was due to leave she scheduled a meeting with him.

"Skye, what are you going to do with an entire month's leave? You'll be bored by the end of the second week, and you know how busy things can get here. There is still a lot of testing to do."

"I realise that, but you did say you could handle it. The code is complete, so you really don't need me."

"This has to do with what happened between you and that navy guy last year, hasn't it? I wish you'd tell me what brought you scuttling back to the office two weeks earlier than planned. I told you not to trust a guy in uniform and in particular a sailor, but you didn't listen. What you need is a real man, not one of these military types who still play with the action man they got as a child."

"And just who did you have in mind—yourself?"

John ignored her comment. "You've been like a scared rabbit ever since you got home. You never go out; you're slowly becoming a recluse. You spend every waking hour here at the office. Just what did the bastard do to you?"

"I don't wish to discuss my love life, or lack of one with you. And what if I do spend all my time here—that's my choice. At least the work gets done and we are ahead of schedule on one or two projects."

"Look, love, I know something happened and whatever it was, it must have been something major to have affected you this way. But you have to pick up your social life. You can't continue to bury yourself in your work or it will make you ill. You'll meet someone else and I promise you if he really loves you he won't hurt you. Besides if you're frightened of being left on the shelf you could always marry me."

"I appreciate your concern, John. But you and I both know that while our business relationship works, a more personal one wouldn't. You're not the type to settle down, so just leave it there before one of us says something we'll regret. Now about the Jones account—"

"Before we get back to business hear me out. Professionally you're one of the most logical people I know. You've an eidetic memory and know instinctively when a project is about to go pear-shaped. You're a shrewd and ruthless businesswoman when necessary. You've even got a temper to go with the colour of your hair, but then nobody's perfect. But having said all that, you're just a big softie at heart." John reached across the table, took Skye's hand, and gave it a reassuring squeeze. "What I can't understand is why you couldn't see that this guy was trouble." Skye's expression told him he'd over-stepped the mark. "If you must go on this idiotic trip, will you at least let me take you to the airport on Sunday?"

Skye smiled. Only her voice betrayed mild annoyance. "Thank you for that character analysis. Remind me to return the favour one day. I am quite capable of organising a taxi.

But if you feel you must take me, then I'll accept your offer. Check-in is at noon."

"In that case, I'll pick you up at nine-thirty."

Sunday dawned warm and sunny, and although early April the daffodils were already in bloom. As she showered and dressed, Skye couldn't help wondering if this was the new beginning she was seeking or whether she was just being plain stupid.

She'd chosen her clothes with care—a pair of well cut navy blue trousers and midnight blue shirt, colours that not only gave her confidence but which also matched her sparkling eyes. Her medium length auburn hair had been cut the day before, and it now framed her pale, delicate, feminine face. Her suitcase stood ready in the hallway as she sat at the kitchen table drinking a final cup of coffee waiting for John to arrive.

A short time later, John's BMW pulled into the drive. Skye took one last look around the house, picked up her purse and opened the door.

"Ready, Sweet Pea?" John asked. "Have you got your tickets, passport and packed everything you need?"

"I think so."

"It's not too late to change your mind you know. Even Debbie thinks you're slightly crazy for wanting to do this," John said, making one last attempt to get her to stay.

Skye stopped in her tracks. "You've been talking to Debbie, behind my back?"

"Actually, she called me. Now, Sweet Pea, don't be annoyed with her, she's just concerned about you. Besides, Seattle wasn't exactly the happiest of places for you, now was it?"

"I wish you two would accept that this is something I need to do, instead of hounding me to change my mind. You're both good friends and I know you have my interest at heart, but please allow me to do this and don't tell me I told you so, if I come home in tears."

John put his arms round her diminutive frame and gave her a hug. "I just don't want to see you hurt again, that's all."

"I know. Now, are we going to stand here all day or are you going to put that suitcase in the car?"

They hardly spoke during the journey to the airport, John sensing that Skye needed to be alone with her thoughts. He repeatedly glanced across at her. She seemed so small, so vulnerable and yet beneath that very feminine exterior he knew there was a strength and stamina that defied her appearance. But she had taken such an emotional beating over the last year that he couldn't help the feeling of wanting to protect her from more hurt.

Forty minutes later he pulled the BMW to a halt in front of Terminal four at Heathrow Airport. He collected Skye's luggage from the boot, then walked round to the passenger side of the car and opened the door.

Once inside the terminal building, he waited patiently while Skye completed the checking-in formalities for her flight, then accompanied her as far as the security check-point.

He gave her a hug, and kissed the top of her head. "Have a good flight, Sweet Pea. Get some rest and lay that ghost. Then come home and be prepared to do some work."

Skye wiped away a stray tear at his use of her nickname, and tried hard to smile. "I'll do my best." Without a backward glance, she turned and walked quickly through security into the departure lounge.

She found a seat close to the gate, and took out her book. But she couldn't concentrate on the words. Instead she amused herself by watching the people in the terminal, wondering where they were all going to and the reasons for their journey.

Time passed quickly, and soon her flight was called. She settled into her seat in business class, and fervently hoped that the seat beside her would remain unoccupied. The last thing she wanted was to spend twelve hours next to someone who wished to talk all the way to Seattle. Luckily, her wish was granted, for within fifteen minutes of boarding, the flight attendant closed the doors and the aircraft pushed back from the ramp.

As the plane taxied towards the runway, Skye suffered one last moment of self-doubt, but knew it was too late to turn back. Seconds later, she felt the increased tempo of the Boeing 747's engines as it thundered down the runway. After what seemed like an eternity the huge plane lifted gracefully into the air.

During the flight Skye read a little, then slept. Her mind reeled from all her thoughts and dreams. She was startled awake when the landing gear hit the runway, and shook her head to regain her focus and get her bearings. She looked out of the window—the terminal buildings looked as grey and uninspiring as they had a year ago.

Once inside the terminal, the Immigration formalities were completed with a minimum of fuss, and the delay at Customs was only mildly annoying. The usual questions and then 'have a nice day.'

Skye then made her way to the rental car desk where she collected the keys to the car she had organised. Within minutes, she was manoeuvring the vehicle out of the parking lot and down the ramp on to Interstate 5. Fortunately, she did not have far to travel to her hotel and soon found herself being shown to her room on the third floor.

After breakfast the following morning, Skye took out her road map and traced her route north. The hotel receptionist told her that it would take about two hours, depending on traffic, to drive the seventy or so miles to Anacortes.

As she wasn't due to check into the hotel in Anacortes until early evening, she decided to do a little sight-seeing. She found a place to park on Alaskan Way, locked the car, then climbed the Harbor steps, to admire the fountain, before continuing along First Avenue to Pike Place Market.

At the Westlake Centre she caught the monorail to the Space Needle. The panoramas from the observation deck were stunning—well worth the white-knuckle ride in the express elevator. For once the weather was kind to her, unlike her previous visit, when the sky had clouded over. Today there was hardly a cloud visible, although it was a little on the cool side. Far below she could see a State ferry sailing to one of the islands in Puget Sound. A few small sailing boats were out in Elliot Bay, no doubt, like her, taking advantage of the fine weather.

Skye leant against the safety rail and looked out across the bay, and remembered the postcard she'd received from Michael. Lost in her thoughts, it was only when she glanced at her watch that she realised she'd been standing daydreaming for nearly an hour. Annoyed for having allowed Michael into her thoughts yet again, she rode the elevator back down to ground level. She quickened her pace as she walked down Broad Street and on to Alaskan Way, past the Aquarium and Omnidome until she reached *Ivar's* restaurant. There she found a table overlooking the bay, and ordered a bowl of clam chowder and a pot of coffee. After her meal she returned to her car, and headed north towards Anacortes.

According to her guidebook the bustling port of Anacortes was founded in 1877. Shipyards, seafood processing facilities, and tourism all contributed to the local economy. Spectacular panoramas, combined with exclusive real estate, yacht charters and marina facilities brought residents and visitors alike to the area.

The ferry to Friday Harbor left at eight the following morning, and the travel agent had recommended that Skye stay at the inn close to the terminal. Tired from her drive, she ate a solitary dinner in the hotel restaurant before retiring for the night.

A short time later, she slipped between the cool white sheets of the double bed and settled against the comforters. Sighing deeply, she wiped a surreptitious tear from her eye. Where did we go wrong, Michael? Why couldn't you talk to me? Why did you have to hurt me the way you did?

Victoria Howard was born in Liverpool, England, at a time when the Beatles (Twist and Shout!) were becoming popular. Her family moved to the Wirral on the "posh" side of the river Mersey when she was eleven. She attended the local girls' grammar school, going on to college where she graduated with a Medical Secretarial Diploma.

She worked as a medical secretary to an ophthalmic surgeon before going on to work as a legal secretary. In 1980 she moved to Scotland with her husband. She spent the next twenty years living in a croft on the outskirts of a village in the Highlands, and while there, managed a company involved in the offshore oil industry. She feels Scotland is her spiritual home, which is probably the reason why she used it for the setting of her second novel.

In October 2000, Victoria moved to South Yorkshire to be with her new partner, Stephen, and until recently, she worked for Britain's National Health Service.

An avid reader, Victoria has always enjoyed writing and recounting stories– mainly in the form of letters to friends. She recently completed an Open University course in writing fiction, and has attended a number of writers' conferences.

Victoria is a member of the Romantic Novelists Association and Romance Writers of America. A frequent traveller to the United States and Europe, Victoria also enjoys walking her border collie, Lucy, gardening, listening to music, and designing knitwear.

The House on the Shore is her second novel. She is currently working on a third manuscript, *Ring of Lies*.

Lightning Source UK Ltd.
Milton Keynes UK

171605UK00002B/5/P